COME ON YOU BLUES!

CHEERS,

Adam

ADAM
FLETCHER
GRIFFITHS

YOU'LL NEVER AMOUNT TO ANYTHING ROY!

outskirts press

You'll Never Amount to Anything Roy!
All Rights Reserved.
Copyright © 2021 Adam Fletcher Griffiths
v5.0

This is a work of fiction. Names, characters, businesses, places, events, locales, and incidents are either the products of the author's imagination or used in a fictitious manner. Any resemblance to actual persons, living or dead, or actual events is purely coincidental.

The opinions expressed in this manuscript are solely the opinions of the author and do not represent the opinions or thoughts of the publisher. The author has represented and warranted full ownership and/or legal right to publish all the materials in this book.

This book may not be reproduced, transmitted, or stored in whole or in part by any means, including graphic, electronic, or mechanical without the express written consent of the publisher except in the case of brief quotations embodied in critical articles and reviews.

Outskirts Press, Inc.
http://www.outskirtspress.com

Paperback ISBN: 978-1-9772-3359-2
Hardback ISBN: 978-1-9772-3363-9

Library of Congress Control Number: 2020920543

Cover Photo © 2021 www.gettyimages.com. All rights reserved - used with permission.

Outskirts Press and the "OP" logo are trademarks belonging to Outskirts Press, Inc.

PRINTED IN THE UNITED STATES OF AMERICA

ACKNOWLEDGEMENTS

I would like to thank:

My Aunt Annette who told me when I was 13 that everyone has at least one book in them!

Dr. Jill Patterson for her kindness and encouragement after reading my very first draft.

My Daughter Emma and son Billy for their continuous belief in me.

My sisters Lisa and Juliet for their humorous recollections.

Cristy Nordstrom's unending support.

Michelle Dombro for her early praise.

Ali for a lifelong friendship

Dr. John Farrell's coaching.

And lastly to my dad Roy, the most loving father and inspiration for this book

PROLOGUE

"So, what are you doing, Ad? You're up early!"

"Putting the finishing touches to me new book."

"Well done – I could never do that!"

"Not sure I could 'ave until now – always started many novels – never actually finished one!"

"What's it about?"

"Chesterfield Football Club."

"Really?"

"And Dad!"

There was a long pause before she spoke."When it's done, what are you gonna do with it?

"Publish it, then make it into a movie! Then with the proceeds, I'm gonna buy The club and do what we do in the book!"

"Sounds brilly'ant, Ad – I'll definitely buy a copy! What's that you're listening to?"

" 'Brilliant Mind' by Furniture! My favorite song of the moment."

"But its years old, Ad!"

"I know – I love all that new music from the '80's!"

"Well, you're definitely out of yours!" said Julia.

CHAPTER 1

"Good, you are sitting down," Doctor Doran said.

The rest of his scientific diatribe was lost on me and my dad. Our doctor's calm demeanor belied the premise of a chemistry teacher's "don't spill this" and "handle with extreme caution." The sincerity of Dr. D's head bobs created the surreal illusion that his toupee was giving my father his last rites, his hair being best described as a Frank Oz creation. The Toupee leaned in toward us both. We were seated in the doctor's love seat, a place too tight for grown men, though we did love each other very much. The Toupee described how chemicals burn and course through our bodies. Images of flaming chemistry lab benches peppered with holes from the careless student stumbled around our brains. We sat like students in detention, pinned by our size, forced by high-sided Chesterfield sofa arms to be closer than was comfortable for a father and son. But the sofa served its purpose, and its lack of size affixed us to his conversation—the headmaster, Toupee, giving both educational guidance and professorial expectation. Our being wedged was somewhat comforting. Our arms bled into the couch of puffiness as it wrapped its leathery grip on our shoulders, two detainees harnessed against the fall.

The Toupee and Tweed Suit sank to its haunches before my dad and me, uttering words of "Radiation," "Follow Up," "Recommended Reading." The Toupee leaned forward as if to catch a falling baby from a tricycle. "Radiation" resonated like that first test-bomb in my ears. I didn't know if Dad could hear it, as he seemed unmoved. For now, he surely could only fall forward from our restricted position, and the Toupee in his olive tweed suit would surely catch him. The saggy, worn Tweed Suit, I imagined, would have had to catch many a faller, given that his elbows had patches on them.

The Tweed Suit was meant for comfort; it bent down easier than it stood up, owing to its mileage on such courses.

My father and I were too close to look at one another comfortably on that Chesterfield love seat. The Tweed Suit smoothly backed away from the time-bomb he had planted, took shelter behind the enormously oversized, unnecessarily large headmaster's desk – the Toupee kept on talking through the blast, "appointment," "check-up," "counseling" were some of what could be heard. The Toupee was sincere, dour, and assuredly composed through its words. After a while of sitting, the Tweed Suit stood up before its loyal subjects reached out a hand, and again the Toupee mumbled into our PTSD deafness: "See you in a month."

From the mustiness of the doctor's office, we were once again amongst the general population – nothing had changed. The clamor, the inappropriate cell phones, the sickeningly bright effervescent lights, and Mrs. Jenkins. She came to the waiting room right after us – I pitied her as she stood up before the gates of hell. She, in contrast, walked excitedly to the door we held open for her. It was her turn and a moment of social delight.

I tried to remove the helmet of confusion from my head—remember those days when you would wear Mom's largest saucepan as a knight's helmet? Maybe that was just me. The echoes in my head were as if someone were pounding that saucepan, with my head still in it. I can't imagine what my father must have been feeling, imagining.

Leaving the oppressive ergonomic sunlight of the doctor's office, my helmet would surely protect me from the bitter dampness of late-November icy drizzle. My father said not one word the whole time. I was curious if he had heard what I had. He could hear, but was he listening? The words "stage four" are best heard at a Glastonbury festival. From your physician, these are words of Damocles' punctuation. The bus conductor punched dad's OAP bus pass and looked at me with frustration as I fumbled for the right change amidst a soggy palm of copper-colored coins and Ibuprofen. Dad proudly took his place in the space right next to those reserved for seniors and handicapped. Forever youthful, he stoically smiled at the elders younger than him who jumped at a chance to take the "reserved" seat as paid for by their taxes. They would take those seats like a birthright. Despite leaning on his walking stick for balance as the alligator bus snaked around tight curves of neighborhoods, Dad would not be old like others. He used a stick the way a recuperating skier would. The physical therapist commended it to him on his hip recovery – my father's injury was of a sporting type to him, following years of football and rugby. This badge of honor should not be confused with aging; it was mileage. He would be playing five-a-side football by the spring. At sixty-eight years young, he still had the defensive moves of a wildebeest.

"I have to see the physio in the morning," dad said. Apparently, he had removed his saucepan helmet. My saucepan had turned into a deep-sea diver's helmet with little round porthole windows. I could see Dad's mouth moving. What was he saying? I fumbled around the front of the diver's helmet for the little catch to open the window – to let in air – to let in his voice. Visibility was challenged – haziness and mistiness.

The rain-drenched mist pummeled the bus, enshrouded it so only the driver knew the way.

"Sorry?" When I was a child, Mum had filled my ears with cotton wool for an earache; so many days I wondered if she had ever removed it. Today was such a day.

"Physio, tomorrow. If I'm to play in the spring, I have to continue to get this hip better."

"Sorry— yes of course, Dad."

"I don't want to lose me place on the team."

"Yes, right of course, physio tomorrow." Helmets of cotton wool....

Like parent teacher night where parent and student knew there was an F in there, but neither would address it. The rest of the report card was excellent.

We were not going to talk about this new issue, in the same way we would not talk to the strangers getting on the bus. We would avert our eyes from their attention. Each passenger, more soggy than the last, the filmy mist of the day, moving glacier-like down the crags of their faces. Droplets hung aboard eyelashes waiting to be flipped away in the blink of an eye. Traces of the day's weather carved more life into the crinkled faces of the elderly. The Ashgate Road stop had delivered several pensioners, all women, all sporting a clear cellophane babushka with string ties beneath their chins. This headwear was the hallmark of the pensioners' club – its distinctive uniform as worn by my nana, forever a mainstay in her handbag.

The rain-pocked cellophane permitted one to see the delicately prepared mane of the pensioners' club, those silvery locks adorned with a hint of blue coiffed carefully into place, their heads wrapped in plastic for preservation as a lettuce might be, the wrapping likely adding to its shelf-life.

Brockwell Lane added grandparents and their granddaughter. A sunnier trio, equally soaked in "droplets of sunshine," the granddaughter's bright red anorak adorned with Sesame Street characters in yellows, blues, and greens of primary school colors. Primary school where the whole world is brightly colored, inviting, playful, innocent, and naïve. The granddaughter's bounce brought the Sesame

Street characters to life and they all danced down the aisle dragging the anchor-line with them. She soared down the bus's aisle the way a kite tugs at its tail to push against the wind to reach higher. Big Bird, Cookie Monster, Elmo, and The Grouch pranced toward my dad and me, practically begging us dance along. Just don't ask me to sing. But the granddaughter did sing; her tiny voice pranced along with her bouncy striding Telletubby wellies. Po and Tinky-Winky caked in puddle-mud skipped to her inner song and outer chime. Granny slipped her grip, somewhat reluctantly, somewhat relieved, for her granddaughter couldn't escape from the bus and now at least she could let go of the May Pole. The dizzying spin of kindergartners' wonderment at the world either forces you in or forces you out. At this particular minute, the grandma needed out. At least until they reached Spar. Her granddaughter wore the weather of the day the way we enjoy an Amazon showerhead -- 119.99 quid at your local home improvement store. Grandma's greyness sloughed between the shiny handrails, leaving Granddad to flash their passes to the conductor. The passes, being laminated, were protected from the weather but their sharp edge nicked Granddad, who started to bleed from the paper cut. Impatiently the rest of the queue waited behind him as he licked the wound and put the passes back in his wallet. Surprising is the increasing time we need to manage the smallest of tasks as we age.

"Here, Granny, let's sit here!" No more than five, the granddaughter led her family straight to the seats reserved for the handicapped or elderly. Being available, she dragged them there next to my father. My father's face lit up, energized once more by the child's exuberance. How fascinating a bus ride is to a child! How mystical! Each adult going through the motions of the day, bussing from A to B via Ai, Aii, Aiii, Aiv, Av, Avi, Avii, Aviii, Aix, before ever arriving at B. In a child's mind, this is a roller-coaster of excitement—someone else is driving and there is mystery around each corner: a new landmark, fresh houses being built, a park with swing-sets and paint-chipped slides all brightly painted. The chipped handlebars revealed the smooth iron until it was painted over, leaving pock marks for little fingers to grip. A child sees the sky, birds atop the trees, entire flocks crossing the midday sun. With her face pressed against the lowest edge of the windowpane, a granddaughter can see vertically, capturing the entire world above as if she were lying down. She peered excitedly through the break in the misty, clingy fog. They must be moving away from the river and up the embankment.

"Look, grandpa—a robin!"

"Where, love? I don't see anything."

"High in the tree, right there near the top. Can you see it? Can you see it?" She pointed as far as her pinky fingers would allow, marking the window's condensation with an inadvertent arrow to the sky.

"Sorry, love. I can't see anything."

"It was there, I promise you." Excitedly the granddaughter searched the world appearing before her, for her world held yet more spectacles.

Dad was glad of the break in the dour bus ride – she was the sunshine peeking around the cloud, reminding us all that indeed the sun was forever directly behind the rain.

Another stop. The bus rested its haunches in the brief breath of sunshine. A cheerier mix of elderly embarked. Again, it was mostly women bathed in scarves, moistened headwear, one dragging her wheelie cart. Either she was shopping, or she carried her back-up outfit with her. A four-pronged cane of aluminum and rubber scuffled behind, pushing its prongs through the grey-brown slurry formed by the residue of the day. The cart's wheels carved parallel lines for the latex tips to stay between. The cane bore the strain of its stooped owner. Strangely, the pensioner gripped his cane with both hands; the kettle-bell grip afforded him the stability. Ageing, peeling, sensible shoes cautiously waded behind the cart and stick, wearing a dry patch on the aisle floor for those who followed as a snow plough clears the road. A couple more stops, and the bus would be full. As the new passengers gingerly took their seats, the windows steamed up on the inside. The little girl cleared a circle with her hand. Then another to form binoculars to her outside world. She enjoyed her world with the curiosity of a glass-bottomed boat while those around her coughed, hacked, wheezed and sniffled their time away. The hanky generation blew, dabbed, wiped at their snouts and mouths repeatedly. These rose-ordained lace delicacies captured much of the mucus expurgated; some, however, slipped by the tardy catcher's mitt. The diesel-capsule to the people grew more unhealthy.

An ambulance siren approached; the bus lurched to the side. The bus filled the narrow lane, deferentially sliding to the curb, a mere matter of inches. The little girl stood excited, tip-toe reaching above her seated guardians, eyes alert for the sirens and flashing lights. The capsule began to light up like a disco, shadows of light strobing across the prefab ceiling panels. The little girl jumped and jumped, honey curls bouncing like Slinkys with excitement. Her granny's heart jumped as the strobing ambulance lights blanked their retinas, showing her granddaughter for the first time the blood vessels of sight like random snakes across her vision. Grandma cupped the child's delicate ears against the screaming siren—Grandma lovingly protecting her granddaughter, relieved that the sirens and lights were rushing by and were not for her, a day she dreaded. The pensioners collectively sighing with sadness and relief, praying that it would pass by their neighbors' street. The macs, raincoats, plastic babushkas slipped back into the fiberglass seating, the melancholy resumed, pausing, no one broke the silence as the muffled sirens departed. No coughs, no sneezes, no heavy breathing; everyone sat in pew-like reverence. The steamy cotton-wool air choked its congregation. The granddaughter's binoculars once more closed.

Saltergate emerged from the swampy weather – the rusted, blue and white paint peeling Kop remembering its former majesty. The Pantheon of Chesterfield nearly demolished. The Stand Road end now recycled concrete, the away fan's barriers now melted down for rebar – the two would re-connect in the future home-site foundations.

"I would have given anything to play there as a child, Ad," were Dad's first words after a long silence.

"Me too, Dad – can't believe they are tearing it down."

"Chokes me up." Dad swallowed hard. He'd been quiet for the bus ride so far. The familiar route of no interest until now.

"So many brilliant memories—eh, Ad?"

"Yep, we've had a lot of Saturday afternoons there."

"And nights too! Remember that Anglo-Scottish Cup night?"

"Yeh, second leg of the final, the place was throbbing! Thought it might actually burst with the pounding bass of 'Come on You Blues'! thought we might have a Jericho night! Thought it would look like it does today after that match!"

"One of the best days of me life, Ad. Remember, Phil Bonnyman nearly brained you with that missed free-kick?"

"Never will forget that flying at me head—good job you were there to catch me!"

"Yeh, so much for sitting on the barrier for a better view!"

"You nearly got too much of a view of that ball! It was a rocket! I think it was the only thing Bonnyman missed that night."

"So many good times. A lot of games blend into the annals for me now; not that game, though. Remember it was pouring down?" Dad was always better at remembering.

"We were sopping wet and mashed in by the capacity crowd. I don't remember being cold, though. The crowd was so tightly packed in we had all that body warmth. It were a lot like being on this bus, clammy, clingy damp."

"Yeh, but no bagpipes on this bus!"

"Still quite a racket with these deaf grannies yelling at each other and the constant grating of gears shifting up these hills! I might even take the bagpipes over this row!"

"The echo of 'Come on You Blues' rang in me ears all night! It were totally brilliant. Remember big Ernie, he had to be in his thirties then – scored the third goal. Everyone went mental for him! chanting Ernie, Ernie, Ernie! Ernie, Ernie, Ernie!"

"I remember being hugged by scruffy soggy strangers, tears in their eyes when that third goal went in! Realizing it was Ernie, we all exhaled with delight and pride. A just reward for sticking with this bloody team for years. He was the butt and the pride of the Town. It was the icing on the cake!"

"He wasn't the butt of any jokes that year – cart-horse to show-horse, he was!"

"Has he still got that shop with Geoff Miller?"

The wheels of the bus ground round and round, lurching in to stop after stop, the windscreen wipers conducting its many noises.

"Yes, it's still open. He and Geoff still work it from time to time."

"I'd love to go see him. Thank him personally for that great memory alone. I wonder how many goals he scored in his career?"

"A lot less than he missed!"

Dad had seen a lot more of Ernie's career than I had. He was there when it was Moss and Randall lifting the title as Division Four champions 1969/70. It's better known as Division Two these days. Town it seemed were lifelong members until a young Ernie partnered with Kevin Randall.

And that was Ernie. Ernie Moss, the great goal-scorer for Town, more legendary because of the ones he missed! Beloved and bemoaned by all. The sort of bloke you could go up to who would thank you for just recognizing him. Which wasn't hard to do in our town – he was a giant at six foot two!

Nostalgia was getting the better of me. 1981 was a memorable year. I had taken my O levels later that year and it was also the year the greatest band ever came to be. Talk Talk. Chesterfield beating the mighty Rangers on the way to winning the Anglo-Scottish Cup and Talk Talk all in one year – it was the sweet spot of being sixteen. Yep, you remember right, me dad had lifted me off the barriers like a baby at that game, and I was sixteen! The shot nearly brained him as the white orb flew by us from Bonnyman's lethal boot. You never stop protecting your kids. Bonnyman would have had three had the nets been four inches to his left when he shot! The greasy pitch a lot like this bus ride. Sloppy days in Chesterfield.

Something to talk about was the weather. Unusual, really, because I remember it being the same every day. Like living in a snow globe of rain. I could feel the sweat breaking through my deodorant, arms pinned to my side between the bus and Dad. Dad and I weren't large on the bus, but our coats made us so. The driver had the heat cranked to clear his windshield so the wipers could see the orchestra. Like Mum's pressure cooker, we were all starting to cook in our plastic wear. Boil-in-a-bag passengers!

"Bonnyman, Birch, Wilson and Moss – best year, best team we ever had; at least the one I saw."

"That's cos you were in the States – you should have been here in '97 at Old Trafford against Middlesborough!"

"I was just a little distracted – remember Emma was born that January!"

"I know, Ad – just giving you grief – they were the best of times. You can't write stuff like that FA Cup run – no one would believe ya."

"Were they that much better than 1981?"

"Probably not, but the atmosphere was at a different level – this was major league, not diluted by any Scottish clubs!"

"Ha, funny! I can't believe that they were faster than Danny Wilson running like a mini-train through the heart of the midfield? He was the fastest player I'd ever seen, and he had Velcro on his boots!"

"He did that alright – he was magic, wasn't he? He danced around player after player mekking 'em look like proper 'nanas'!" Weird he should say that—it was me granddad's phrase when he was alive.

"And Alan Birch—come on, Dad, really, the '97 team was better than the wizard Birch on the left side? There's no way – he scored goals from 45 yards out week after week. And I don't mean like Beckham from the free kick—I'm talking about on the full-speed run, head up and in top gear. He. Was. A. Magician!"

"Don't get me started on Beckham – why did you have to mention that poser?

We're talking real quality here! You didn't have to foul the conversation with that twit."

Beckham was Dad's nuclear button.

Not a fan of Beckham, me dad. I was and still am. When he hit the England team in tandem with Michael Owen – they were for the first time in my memory a truly mesmerizing team to watch. Dad, of course, remembered 1966 like it was yesterday.

"Whatever happened to Birchy?" I was trying to distract him back before we got off on that the Beckham tangent, so I hit him with another question he'd likely know. "Who was the other bloke who played alongside him?"

"Not sure where he went, but the other lad was Alan Crawford, and I think Geoff Salmons was on that team too. Came over from Sheffield United. He was at the end of his career but right good with his head."

"Who was the keeper back then?"

"John Turner, I reckon."

"I just remember him having a blinder in goal. We always produced great keepers back then."

"Except for Phil Tingay!"

Phil and Ernie notched years with Town and they always generated this same level of ambivalence. "Nice blokes, the pair of them," people would respond when you were asking about their talent! Like the signature answer in a dating game – nice personalities. And they were genuinely nice blokes.

"Ah, come on, Dad, he wa'nt that bad."

After a morning with me dad in the clinic and on the bus, I could feel my Chezy accent coming back full throttle. I'd only landed back yesterday, but already the Town and the town were back in my blood. Me and dad going back in time. It was like visiting Dr. Who. We stepped inside the Tardis of Highlow Close and the History of the World, my world, strangely preserved—only the bus drivers changed. The din of the bus cocooned us – it was like that night on the Kop, face forward, chant to the field of childhood dreams, played on by the chosen few, lauded by the faithful.

"We are the faithful" went up the chant. "They are the shit!" Can't tell you it was great poetry, but the visceral chorus had its disciples. Me and Dad, articulate and educated, called out in full voice with our Kop. Not proud but accepted tribal members. Followed by the "We are the mighty Blues" – then came the slow crescendo of Saturday afternoon male baritones, fueled by John Smiths' Bitter, Bovril, meat pies…the lasting call of "COME ON YOU BLUES!" "Blues" became a three-syllable word to us all! Imagine all the "o's" in place of "ue" and you get the picture. These were the sacred colours of our Saturday joust.

"Do you 'member the Millwall match, Ad?"

"Can't say I do, Dad."

"Birch danced through that defense – ball on his right foot, then left foot, right foot again slicing between three players through the edge of the box, then blasted it bottom corner with his left. He skinned 'em. Millwall were frozen. Players jumping in to get the ball and Birchy pulling it away last minute like Lucy in Charlie Brown; boy, did he make 'em look shtupid."

I didn't remember this at all, to be fair, but Dad did. He wasn't college educated or nothing, but his memory was photographic-like. I went on YouTube sometime after this bus ride and confirmed that Birchy, as Dad remembered, "skinned" the defense. Dad had a gift for remembering detail, where for me so much just blended into the fog of my life's history.

"Shit, Dad, we're here! Better ring the bell!"

"We're alright, Ad – Joan's on the bus. She's on it." Joan lived a few doors down, and except for today, usually made a fuss of Dad, often sitting with him. He wasn't alone today; I was there.

Don't know why I sort of panicked! It wasn't like missing a connecting flight, the next stop was only a hundred yards down the street. Which I suppose is why it took us 45 minutes to go two and a half miles!

Dad had a car, but older now, he wasn't as sure of himself so preferred the bus – it was his only consent to aging.

"Alright Roy?" Joan announced, getting up from the third row.

"Yes, Joan," Dad answered in his telephone voice. Weird, why would he do that – was he attracted to Joan? That would be ridiculous.

"Hi, Mrs. Millward. How are you today?" In my deference to living in the States, I had addressed her accordingly. Somewhat casually. And even though I was a grown man, she would always be Mrs. Millward, never Joan. Not even if she and Dad got married. I'm getting ahead of myself.

"Still viewing the daisies from the right side!" Ever the quick wit she was. Dad moved like he didn't need the cane – the placebo effect of an attractive woman's presence, I believe. Childlike, I was left in his wake. Literally, the floor had nowhere to drain and we sloshed around. I'm not quick, but just maybe here was the reason for taking the bus and not driving.

He couldn't drive yet anyway—he hadn't got clearance from the physio—but something in her radiance as he chivalrously let her off the bus first indicated that it might be a long time before he would be back behind the wheel.

"How do you like America, Adam?" Mrs. Millward inquired. Not "the US," but the formal-sounding "Americer."

"I like it a lot, but always enjoy coming back as a tourist!"

"That's nice to hear. I know your dad misses you when you're gone—don't you Roy?" addressing him now. She was done with me. Small talk over.

"Would you like to come in for tea, Roy?" relaxed and friendly Joan offered, and my dad accepted by handing me his house keys.

I was the interloper in their world. As easily as I popped in, they popped me out.

The next day was much the same – another dreary bus ride. A fine homecoming!

"Does this bus go all the way to the physio, Dad.?" Hoping that we could break this monotonous daily loop of going into town and back.

"No Ad. We will have to change at Chester Street. Dad said with the excitement of a Captain Cook cartographer.

"Rate." said I. This then would be something to look forward to. Why is it when we are on the bus each stop is reached in a timely fashion, and yet when you are waiting at the bus stop, it seems forever before one arrives?"

"It's part of public bus lore, Dad! There are rules of the universe that the great physicists of the world have yet to conquer! It follows the chapter of lost socks in the washing machine! there is a migration pattern that is invisible to the naked eye! Like the Antarctic penguins – there's just no explaining it!"

"T'car should be fixed next week, and I should have the all-clear to drive again. We will be back in isolation, comfort, and self-reliance. Although, I have to say it's been an experience to take the bus again. Humbling, familiar, common – a poor man's chauffeur! We live so much in isolation in our connected world – taking in life at the end of a keyboard or smart phone. Even the misery of waiting for a bus seems delightfully nostalgic in our instantaneous world where all we ever seem to wait for is the wifi to work and a tablet to boot up!"

Dad would likely keep taking the bus, I thought. I mean, someone had to help Joan down the bus's treacherous steps. Chivalry lived in Dad the way rationing does in his generation, the way kids today hit "like" on Facebook but prefer Snapchat.

These passengers are remnants of eras gone by. They are the unconnected, the relics and the infants.

"See—look around you, the elderly and the young, the children of life's bookends. Minds of the capable becoming the minds of their grandchildren, reverting to dependency. What we have is a bus full of children." Dad was channeling his inner Willy Wonka.

"What about us then, Dad?"

"We are misfits, son, in their world—barnacles on their boat, invaders in their parallel history. We are time travelers stopping by to observe and will next week be mobile, free, independent, and alone behind the wheel. Being with people makes you want to take the bus more. The members seem content in this form of livery. Time given for thought to other things or nothing at all. Not many days we can think of nothing at all anymore. We are so informed all the time there is no room for boredom and mindlessness. So many pings, dings, vibrations, alerts, lights to stimulate the addict's cravings."

"Really? Isn't privacy what we all want? Not this shoulder-to-shoulder crush of strangers?"

"Perhaps yes, but aren't things less private now than ever? We see people through a four-inch window or on a 50-inch flat screen. Often, we see more than we wanted without ever being really with them. A book of faces in our phones, tablets, and laptops—many familiar, famous, and fleeting. Virtual friends, strangers, and family all. We peek through tiny windows at each other but not together. We don't look upon the world together any longer. Then in an Instagram moment, they and we are gone. This is my stop."

"Want me to come in?" As if I were addressing an eighteen-year-old. You're now mature but still you're the kid. And I'd been with Dad endlessly since I'd landed.

"Actually, I'm feeling fatigued. Let's meet tomorrow – same bus, same bus station." I guess he needed privacy.

"I'll stay on then through to Julia's – see you tomorrow!"

CHAPTER 2

"Car park's fillin' up fast, Ad – must be a big game tonight!"

"It's the Anglo-Scottish Cup Quarter-final against Rangers – me and me dad are going after this. Worrabout you? You no' goin?"

"Nah, prob'ly not – lorra 'istry 'omework from Stevie!"

"He's a bugger, that one – I hope I don't get him for me A levels."

"Loves to give homework he does – a right bloody pain – but we learned a lot!"

"So, you're not going for sure then? Biggest game in Town history! Now there's an 'istry lesson you can take to Stevie tomorrer!"

"Bit humorless – I'm not sure he'd understand. Best to just crack on – besides, it's just Town!"

"Just Town! – come on – I'd give me left foot to play on that pitch!"

"Well, you're an idiot!"

"Eh, watch it! I can still take thee, ya know, as small as I am!"

"No, you pillock – what are you gonna kick with if you only have one foot!"

There's a reason Ali was always the smartest guy in the room. Well, first, he did his homework instead of going to see Town on a school night! His mastery of semantics would take him on to law school while my love of Town – well, we shouldn't go there right now, should we? Suffice to say Ali was always the smartest guy in the room. And that night? Well, that Tuesday night, that might have been one time when sitting on the gate at The club car park when I just for once won out. The one time I was the smartest guy on the gate.

"Besides, it's pissing down. I don't want to stand out in this more than I have to." A car pulled up. "That'll be 50p," he said to a man in an orange Ford Fiesta, wipers going full whack, flipping its watery excrement on me and Ali as we took the cash.

"Used to be free in here, mate! Right bloody rip off!" His face hidden by a parka's fur edge gave the punter an alien edge of surliness. It wasn't a lot of cash, but the Tennis Club used to let people park for free. That is until the smartest guy in the room, Ali, decided there was an opportunity to raise funds for the Junior

Tennis team. At a general meeting, he presented his idea, and my dad, as head of the juniors, had agreed to monitor the volunteers and half the cash would go to The club the other half to the Junior Tennis account for balls, soft drinks, and cookies to be enjoyed on Sunday Match Day.

A deal was struck. We wouldn't look back. We practically lived at The club, so it was easy for me and Ali to volunteer on Chesterfield Town's match day. We would perch like friendly, adolescent vultures atop the iron gate. That gate must have been 8 feet long – rounded bars of iron stretched the whole way – it looked like something out of Southfork Ranch!

It was a short walk from the tennis club to Saltergate, the hallowed ground—I would have sacrificed a limb in order to play on it! And since Town was on this record-breaking run of wins, it was harder and harder to park close. The regulars grew angry as these new fans jumped on the bandwagon and into what was unofficially their part of the street to park on.

"I used to park on street for free, then I parked here for free, now I have to pay to see me own team! It's like all them folks that show up at Christmas and Easter to fill the pews while t' regulars have to stand." The Town fans would grumble at us – well, the team was pretty good, so really there was less for them to grumble at! There was genuine talent on the pitch and we were exciting, so the "miserable Town fans" had no reason to gripe – the lack of parking gave them an outlet!

"It's still 50p, mate!" I reminded the "windger." Ali was the lawyer in waiting – I on the other hand was the blunt one, the future fiduciary, and so I was in charge of taking the cash.

"Got change?"

"Yep."

He gave me a quid and I gave him ten 5p pieces. I carried a lot of change, and this way they would know to have the right money next time!

The grumblers would try to get out of paying – well, we were just kids, so we really didn't count, apparently. They would treat us as though we stole their parking space! For years these folks had parked on private grounds unfettered by conscience or The Club's Board! Ali and I would take their indignant stares and reflect back disbelief at these temporary squatters. Illegal possession and trespass is still that, even if it went unprosecuted. Some people have a weird sense of entitlement. "The car park was empty, so it must be mine"—you could almost hear them think it. Like the empty house welcoming a commune – no, that's not right.

We have the Magna Carta – it tells us just so. That each has a right to his or her own property. This right of humanity came amidst the Dark Ages – we can't go back. There's a socialist revolution – "it's not being used, so I can use it" declared one punter. No, that's not the rule. Suddenly we have returned to the pre-King John era, except this time it's not the nobles and kings taking our property, it's the Bolsheviks! As much as we like to share, there is always a group of folks who want to share more! Some, like the King's men, got angry about it.

"What are you gonna do 'bout it?" one bloke said, getting quite thuggish about it.

"I have the key to the gate. You only leave when you pay up!" Ali was gonna do great in court. I was thinking I would key his car, but whatever. We went with Ali's ploy. Ali had nobility – here was his Runnymede. I, his loyal servant would want to batter the selfish "barstard." Thanks to the TV comedy *The Young Ones*, everyone had become a "barstard" thanks to the character Rick. This show's unique irreverence was now solidly embedded in our teenage vernacular.

We raised tons of cash – supply and demand – we hadn't had our first Economics class with Ces Thompson yet, but we were living it! We now had cash-flow. Biscuits and soft drinks, pah! What we wanted was "child's-play," not child's play.

We were on the Junior social committee – the Wild West of being a teenager. It's a tennis club – you're wondering how much trouble can tennis club juniors get up to even with a bit of a cash flow? Ali and I had ideas of being the next Stringfellows! When you're sixteen and have no girlfriend, there are few ways to meet the opposite sex in an all-boys school. Ali and I would create the honeypot.

"Quarter of an hour – I'm going in – meeting Dad on t' corner – he's coming from Brocky Lane."

"I'll take the cash and put it in the safe behind the bar – we can divvy it up later." Ali would count it anyway – fiscally sound and forthright, too. That was my job usually, but tonight was an exception in what would turn out to be an exceptional night.

"Cheers, Al –thanks for doing that, mate. 'Come on You Blues!' I joined the chant of the crowd walking down Hawksley Avenue. There were hundreds of us spilling onto the street. Cars were backed up – some punters foolishly still looking for a spot to park in – the Iron gates of The club were officially closed. It was nearly game time. I was yelling, chanting, echoing whatever the crowd is preaching. Tidal, we moved to the hallowed ground. I fully expected to find a pyre of left-legs in someone's back yard – having been given up to have one last solitary run around on the altar of Saltergate. It was mad to see this amoeba of dissonant folks – I was shoulder to shoulder with this royal blue and white hatted army over-striding our way to see Town. Last year's relegation survivors who couldn't get hundreds in the ground to watch them had a passionate army of William Wallace proportions marching through the glistening streets with their boot polish shine thanks to the solid rainfall and orange street-lamps. Dad would never find me in this lot, I was sure.

"Hey, Ad!" He was a dad, of course, and he saw me immediately! Cigarette in hand – the tiny beacon of red waving genuinely at me. It must take a lot of rain to put out a cigarette, I thought. Then with a slight pinch of the lit end, the embers fell away, and he slipped the remainder into his coat pocket.

"Can't believe this, can you? What a night!" Dad joined the sponge of supporters now swollen by more showers and hope.

The clothes that we were wearing were sopping wet as we entered the stadium. There was a binding that comes when wool and outer garments are soaking wet; they're somewhat glued together, and we moved as one, like a number of sponges pushed through the turnstile.

"Not seen anything like it since the final games of the 1969/70 season, and even then it wasn't like this!"

"Before my time, Dad!" I smiled at him from below the average height of the crowd. You're still a child at sixteen, still vulnerable, not yet equal—me, I was still small for my age; Dad, though not at all tall, was always a giant in my life. Until of course those regrettable moments you have in college where you think you know something and you're loaded with beer-filled reasoning.

"Bagpipes! – oh my God – can you believe this?" The bagpipe squeal hit our ears like North Sea waves on an Easter holiday. "Amazing Grace" echoed from where we had just walked. Echo might be too kind – like a Stuka bomber, the bagpipes lit up the rainy skies. Rangers' Tartan Army was on the march into Chesterfield. We had no fife and drum response – only "Come on You Blues," which was a sad retort to a team that also played in blue jerseys.

Rangers fans were notorious, notorious for their fierce take-downs of their arch rival Celtic fans. The bagpipes heralded a public menace, and I prayed Dad would stay close and that the rain would drown the "bag." Dad joined the swelling numbers as we sidled up to the gates of Saltergate – there didn't seem any way we could get this lot through the turnstiles. Like a woolly jumper, the crowd was squeezed through the mangle. The chanting and the rain veiled the amoebic garment, its collective crunching down on the crushed stone of the causeway. Small chips of pebbles, grinding against one another, sank beneath the puddles left by Dr. Marten and his steel-toe-capped band. You could feel the importance of tonight's match in the weight of the elements. The crowd tightened as we neared the spinning mangle of the turnstile. Dad gripped my hand like I was three years old again, safe. Now older, I still looked up at him, short as I was as a teenager. We could both feel the enervating compression of hundreds of bodies like globules of mercury being pushed into the thermometer—a thermometer, by the way, that unnecessarily went up to 100 degrees Fahrenheit – clearly this wasn't branded for the British Isles.

Instinctively I wanted to pull away from Dad's hand as an adolescent, but he reaffirmed his grip with a knowing, glassy blue-eyed knot. The wind and the rain shone in Dad's eyes, barely imperceptible tears at the corners. This seemed to be the natural reaction of a man who worked outside, whose tear ducts had endured much of Britain's gale force winds. The warmth of his hand reached mine; no gloves and sitting on the iron gate for an hour, I was practically numb. The grip was discreet, and as we shuffled through the gravel, no one would see, but Dad's assuredness meant we were distinct in the baying mob. We were going over the top of the trenches into the Saltergate Colosseum. The cigarette hand had the tickets and it reached over my shoulder to the attendant behind the barred window. The squeeze of the bagpipes grew louder, amplified by the stadium roof of the Stand Road end. Blood pressure rose within us – the Tartan Army was coming for us. Who could say how this was going to go down once the first kick had been thrust?"Tickets please!" Frustrated, the attendant yelled over our shoulders – his foot pedal released the cylindrical gate and propelled me, then Dad, through to the inner sanctum. We were in. This was where the modern-day gladiators preyed. There was for us ten feet of breathing room before joining the crowd again, up and into the Saltergate Kop end. Hordes of youths, royal blue and white scarves raised, swaying to the chants of the day –, beating back the call of the bagpipes, raising our spirits to the cause menacingly beckoning the stadium's newcomers to join their ranks. Dad stood behind me, his calloused grip on my shoulders. This was it, this was the night when we represented Chesterfield Football Club. The night, this moment carried with it the gravitas of rival gangs and the poetry of Pele's beautiful game. The Tartan army were at first recognized by their waving scarves a la Bay City Rollers. This dark-ages gang of plaid moved like a swath of checkered fog, their unity of sound and fury equally deafening and fearsome.

I knew Dad was recalling the West Ham versus Leeds United game of four years earlier by the strength of his grip and the pointedness of his fingertips that I could feel pinching vice-like in the top of my shoulder blades. This time, he would be there for me. There would not be the regrets he endured after that match--a match similarly significant, in similarly indignant weather! Leeds, West Ham, and the Scottish Glasgow Rangers—well, their fans were first division hooligans, tribal teenage thugs; we at Town more parochial and smaller in number, except for tonight. Our hooligan element was swelled with—well, people like me dad, his curious pub friends, our neighbors, grandparents having read of the success in the *Derbyshire Times*, Chesterfield historians, football coaches with their proteges, and of course the high school girlfriends of our wayward thugs. If it came down to blows, which inevitably these matches did, I would tap-in the Sharons and Tracys over the Barrys and Micks as their lawless street fighting resembled a savage guerilla karate. Option two would be to send in the historians – dear God; few punches are likely to stun less than an enthusiastic historian's monologue. Worst case, we could all run while the historian chloroformed his enemy with minutiae of Chesterfield's medieval past. Should the chloroform not work, we could be running while the historian was getting the stuffing kicked out of him. If the historian were a "she," the Scottish Pamelas and Angelas would be the ones to stick the boot in or scalp accordingly; no boy on girl fighting allowed in the hooligans' Geneva convention. Girl on boy fighting was permissible—your worst nightmare! Sharpened, razor-like fingernails could pop an eye in one merciless swipe, with the hooligans' convention limiting your retaliation.

I was elevenish—that being the dark ages of a boy's childhood—and on my way to the bathroom at Elland Road when I was jumped by probably thirty youths from my age of 11 to 17; anything over that, and you were no longer an apprentice. Luckily for me, the hooligans' convention was age-banded. The bathroom was in a building distant from the main stand. I Bedecked in my Hammers regalia and old enough to not need Dad to go with me to pee, I made the epic journey across the tarmac.

"Sir, which way to the toilets?" I had found a friendly steward, who like an Auschwitz guard, pointed me in the right direction.

I marched confidently toward the coal-stained brick shed with visible insignia for men and ladies. Thinking about it, it really wasn't that far after all. Dad was right; he had spied it on the way in. The route had been lined with thugs of all ages on the way in, but now it was just the apprentices and those who came to fight, not cheer. Most West Ham fans were corralled from the train station to their pen by police dogs. We were local and had driven to the match. Unfamiliar with the Elland Road etiquette, we joined the pack of fans to find ourselves among the home team supporters. We were an unthreatening father and son, and as such we were treated with polite indifference.

As the youths descended the ramparts of Elland Road toward me, I was optimistic for the same treatment—perhaps some mild footy banter and a reminder of who had the better team. Like the form room of school with your Monday-morning mates jockeying your argument as to why a team in the relegation zone was far better than one likely to win Division One. Not so at Elland Road the baying "yobbos" (I didn't call them that to their face) descended quickly and soon I was circled by youths of my own age and older. All of them yelled like they had rehearsed it:

"Fucking West Ham wanker!" was one I could make out. This had been the chorus of their army's drill sergeant as they charged at my Light Brigade. Circling around me, this pack of wolves screamed and yelled in my face, graveyards of teeth showing, venomous saliva missiles hitting my face. The circle shrank in toward me, more venom, more yelling, the spit of anger tortured me. I no longer needed to pee. I couldn't tell where the first blow came from and how I had become pinned to the ground, face down on the asphalt mattress, arms behind my back, hands and wrists forced police-style to the shoulder blades. Some of the mob sat on my back; others jumped on my calves, stapling me to the tarmac. Punches rained over my head into my face as my head was pulled back by my '70s hair. The puddles of the day seeped into my jumper and jeans. My scarf made a temporary noose and reins for thugs to ride me. My head crashed to the asphalt as I was ridden harder, paralyzed by the yobs' weight. Kicks, blows, punches poured into my legs and ribs. I couldn't breathe and retreated to that quiet space before blacking out to the words:

"Off, ger off him! You bloody animals – off him!"

The steward of this chamber of horrors regretted sending me this way but was too slow, and the youths too fast and too many, to prevent the beating.

"Good God lad – you alright?" He was gently cupping my head like one of his beloved pigeons.

Through a pounding head, I nodded. Like a witness at Nuremburg I remembered his face now. All that remained of the mob was their spit and bruising. That, coupled with my bleeding lip, nose and heightened loathing of Leeds United. From this day on I still think of Leeds United as a rapist. That despicable club stole my football innocence. I could feel the rasping chill of the air on my neck where my scarf had been. Ironically, it was a relief to be cold there after being choked. The claret and pale blue noose was gone along with my hat, badges, and rosettes. I had proven an easy inviting target. The puddle water I was lying in gave disguise to the fact I had wet myself. Tears of blood mingled in the gravel. I lay like a discarded carcass; my arms weren't broken but I was severely tenderized. The steward removed his hanky, and gratefully I let him dab at my bleeding.

"Let me 'elp you t' toilets," begged the steward in his gravelly whisper. Clearly a smoker and someone's dad.

"Awright," I mumbled, licking the blood from inside of my teeth. A quick check and they were all present—sore, tender, and some soft in their foundation, but all there. Gingerly the steward raised this Bambi up from the dirt. I was shaking, and the enemy was gone from the alleyway, blending back with its troops in the Kop.

"We'll ge' yer cleaned up, we'll have you good as new."

"But me stuff? The—the bastards took all me stuff!"

"I shun't worry about that now, lad. Can you lean for'ard in t' sink?" The steward cupped the icy water and let it pour over my neck in to the Adamant bowl. There were no blood streaks. He just wanted to calm me down. As I leaned there, he got a roll of crispy toilet paper, softened it in the running water and gently wiped away blood, gravel, and tears. He took his jacket sleeve and wiped off the muck from my coat and trousers. He checked me over, and looking in the brown mottled mirror, I could see that the bleeding had stopped as I barely recognized the new puffy, swollen version of myself. The pounding in my heart and head started to subside. Unfortunately, the adrenalin started to subside too, and I could begin to feel the bruising in my ribs and shins by the time the caretaker delivered me to my dad. My father was visibly shaken and wanted to leave, after he'd singularly murdered about thirty youths. But this was my team I had come to watch. When you have been violated you always want to get a good look at your enemy, remember their faces, just in case you are unable to forgive and forget.

As my dad wrapped me in his coat, we saw another young fan fall down the steps of the Stand to our right with a knife in his back. "Enough," said Dad, and we left. No happy ending, either. Blocked in by dozens of cars in the carpark, we listened with the heat on full blast to West Ham lose two-nil on Radio Leeds.

I know that day six years ago was top of me dad's mind at the Rangers Game that night; Much older now, still my dad wasn't letting me out of his sight. Safety in the power of a construction worker's hug.

"I'd give anything to play here, Ad." This was something we had always agreed on.

CHAPTER 3

"Over 'ere, Mick—on me head, son," he yelled to his best mate of seven years – they had grown up on the same street, same side of the street even, just three doors apart; now they were teammates in a pick-up game of football at the park. The threat of Hitler's bombs now gone for good. They lay satchels laid down for goal posts at each end of the rugby pitch, a full-size field being too much for young legs. Roy and Mick were always on the same team no matter the occasion. The ball lofted over with an aircraft bomber's precision, finding Roy in the clear for a spectacular diving header – the ball ricocheting off the satchel for dramatic effect as it careened into the imaginary netting.

"And the crowd went wild," yelled a young Roy, waving his arms and shaking his head for added effect – he ran across the goal mouth to meet the delivery boy Mick. What a duo they were – like something out of a *Boys' Own* magazine. They drew up soccer plays and rehearsed them endlessly before practices. Roy ran across to thank his dead-eye marksman, stopping quickly before him as though Mick were football royalty. Roy bowed his head slowly as if crossing the sprinter's tape – but it was measured, rehearsed.

Mick pretended to put the winning medal around his friend's neck; and Roy reciprocated. Together they lifted their arms in triumph - an imaginary trophy held between them declaring:

'FA Cup Champions 1946!"

"You're a bleeding idiot, Roy! Dad is going to kill you! Look at the state of you!" The imaginary playground FA Cup having been hoisted, brother Bill brought Mick and Roy squarely back to earth!

"Look at you, yer big narner! Yer covered in mud, Roy, yer uniform's a right old mess! Ma'll never get that cleaned before Dad gets home. And if he finds out you have been playing footy again, he'll have your guts for garters!" Older brother Bill, ever the worrier, ever the protector – well, to a point. Some kids just bring it on themselves. Roy was that kid – he had a million questions in class, a proper distraction that made him entertaining and annoying. The constant baiting of the teachers ground them down. Repeatedly he would hear Mr. Haskins begin his class - 'Get out your Geography books, rough books and Griffiths!' closely followed by 'You'll never amount to anything Roy!' Perhaps it was the need to debate the blueness of the sky or the verdant grass that he found himself repeatedly in the corridor headed to the headmaster's office. Roy, was annoyingly smart in a lawyerly and pestering way.

"Ma would kill you an' all if you weren't her favourite!" complained Bill, staring his little brother down.

"You've got to admit it was a great header, though! Mick here is ace at lobbing the ball in just right—aren't you, Mick?"

"We're like twins, Roy; we've got instinct! Do you know the difference between in and out? In-stinct! Best joke ever!"

"Grab your gear, Roy. We have to get home. We'll be late for tea."

"Five more minutes, Brock?" The brothers each called each other "Brock." "T' game is tied, next goal wins!"

"Your skin, not mine – I'm off." Bill turned and walked off. He'd seen this act his whole life, and like Roy's teachers, he was frustrated.

"No hold up – five-minutes, honest, Brock!" Roy needed the cover his brother gave – it was so hard for his mum to be blinding mad while his well-behaved brother stood next to him. His father, on the other hand, had no such code.

Bill had already gone out of his way to Cromford Meadow to find Roy; having found him, he wasn't waiting around and began the steep hike back towards home.

Cromford Meadow was sufficiently far from home that these unsanctioned pick-up football games could go on without witness. The Meadow was tucked in the valley of the River Derwent. There were few level playing fields in this part of the world of steep valley walls jutting into rolling meadows of evergreen. This rain-soaked valley, vulnerable to flooding, entertained cricket, rugby, football, sheep and cow pastures. Only last year had the rugby posts been put back up after the originals had been cut down and used as war munitions years before. The markings of the rugby field once again outlined the playing field now that Dobson the groundskeeper was back from Gallipoli. The fields were frequently waterlogged; the football of the day sucked moisture from the pitch like a turkey baster until it was as leaden as a medicine ball. Only a truly hungry goal-scorer would take on a header after twenty minutes or so. The rough-stitched ball with protruding laces left a zipper-mark like a crude 1970s knee operation.

As Roy and Mick chased after Bill, the incline out of the meadow started to catch up to them before they ever gained on Bill. If the sopping mud of Cromford

Meadows in Roy's school jumper didn't give them away, the badge of glory on Roy's forehead surely would. The welt left by the laces was worn like a battle-tested soldier, but real courage would be tested by facing up to his father. Bill senior had been absent most of Roy's early childhood – his memories of his father clouded, except for the joyful wedding day photo on the sideboard. Raised by their mother, Roy and Bill gained her acerbic wit and temperament: it oftened the war-hardened temperament of sarcasm and survival. Bill senior spent most of his sons' formative years in India fighting the good fight. At home Roy proved too much to handle for Liz, who lied to the school about Roy's age so he could be admitted to the nursery school early. Big brother Billy was articulate, well read, and at nine years old had assumed the additional role of father to his precocious little brother. This would be his only sibling, Dad being gone at the height of his reproductive years. The war stunted many families' growth – either husbands were lost to the field of battle or they were gone so long and traumatized by the exile, horror, and insanity that no future children were possible. The war finished off families in both ways: prophylactically and murderously.

Strong mothers ruled the home front aided by elder siblings, cousins, neighbors, and air-raid shelter acquaintances. Advice came from so many villagers, preventing panic as the Malthusian effects of a war-torn world aborted families. Brother Billy, his dad's namesake and shining beacon of goodness, parlayed his father's childhood teachings toward Roy. From Roy's infancy, Billy sat his little brother amongst his teddies and played school. The teddies loved the story of their childhood hero Paddington, and Roy, too young to comment, presumably loved him too. Roy was home-schooled by Billy since the day he could sit up. Billy, an early reader thanks to years on his mother's lap, loved the limitless world of books. But it was his father's workshop where the real magic happened – books on engine parts, manifolds, and carburetors were Billy's true fascination. While Dad fought the war in India, Billy devoured the mechanics' text books. Self-learning became a big part of this fatherless world. Billy's insatiable drive would take him all the way to the engineering studio at Rolls-Royce.

Roy adored his paternal big brother.

"Wait up, Billy, wait up! You're walking too fast!" Roy's school shoes were caked in Cromford mud. He slipped as he ran up the embankment, his satchel of school-books pulling him backward, like he was trapped on a down escalator. Billy didn't slow down. Roy needed to respect him – Billy marched on with a schoolmaster's ardent stride, never looking back, smiling internally—Roy would always be his favorite teddy bear. After the tiring hike back to home, Billy took Roy to the outhouse where a rusted, chipped pail of rainwater nestled by it, a rag of a flannel draped over the pail, originally there for drying one's hands. No one knew how many days the rag had been there. Today, with a boxing trainer's care, Billy grabbed the icy flannel and mopped up the pick-up football star. Billy knew how talented his little brother was; the football aficionados knew how good Roy was. Problem was. he was the standout stand-off-half for the school rugby team as well. Billy nursed the welt on Roy's forehead back into his brow – the rainwater was ice cold and served as a real anesthetic and inflammation reducer. Billy coaxed the scar of the stitching back in to his head and brushed Roy's hair forward to disguise the rest. Billy's protégé wouldn't get the belt today.

Bill senior had gone to war as a machine shop worker: diligent, soft-spoken, broad smile on broad shoulders. On his way back from India he picked up a meat-hook temper, and silence that would cower a bear. We never knew what he had witnessed or done, for the silence took over most of his personality. The bronzed glow of his face from time spent out East had faded, and with it any hope of the effervescence that once charmed the working men's club. This Welshman never once sang again, only ever miming to the National Anthem. Life for Bill senior was lived in his workshop shed cocooned with spanners, hacksaws, oily jars of screws, bolts, washers labelled as such. A gnarled wooden workbench, navel high with a vice bolted to it, was his altar – where his fingers preached to a choir of engine parts lit only by the filter of a murky transom windowpane. Bill senior was safe in here, but no one else was. This was Bill senior's little empire.

Billy's little brother had the silky moves of Sir Stanley Matthews the great England and Stoke City midfielder. Billy had seen Matthews on the newsreel at the cinema and had described the shimmy and body swerves to Roy. Billy drew them up in his rough book – diagraming with dotted lines the track Matthews took around defenders while showing the body position as he did it. Roy the sponge had picked up the talents almost immediately. Roy was a little wizard and the best pupil Bill would ever have. The brothers even took one of their dad's old white shirts and used red ink pens to mark the stripes of Stoke city on it, so that at the Cromford Meadow pick-up games there could be no hiding and no mistaking who Roy was modeled on.

CHAPTER 4

"Morning, Ad."

"Morning, Dad. Nice to see Joan yesterday. She hasn't changed a bit in all the years I've known her!"

"Yes, we tend to cross paths more now that I drive less."

"Not sure she can drive? I remember Eric was always driving her around like Miss Daisy? I think she even sat in the back, so any casual observers would think she was royalty."

"Well, she did grow up in Dronfield, you know!" Dad affected their slightly snobby tone, which was always weird, coming from the north of England as we did. She was as likely a toff from Knightsbridge as anywhere, but to come from seven miles away was quite precious!"Eric doted on her. She was his driving force; kept him on his toes even though he was quite a bit older than her. She's actually more my age." Dad announced this with a hint of affection. He declared it as if rhetorically enquiring whether I would approve of a friendship.

"In my mind, they were like Philip and Queen Elizabeth. Philip always looked more like the butler than a husband. And the same can be said of Eric. Wouldn't have been surprised if he didn't have a chauffeur's hat on the passenger seat where a typical wife would sit. Eric was her accessory a pseudo bodyguard and sperm donor. She had the blood-line of royalty and that's what made it work!"

"Well she's much more real now since Eric passed last year. The cancer that so terrified them initially had returned. He chose to refuse the medication the second time. After all, the first time you take on Mike Tyson the money might be worth it, but a second? Well, the second time you're aware of the abject brutal beating, endless misery, constant fatigue, pain, nausea, and nurses' attentions." Dad gave out a sigh. Not that he and Derek were close. They didn't run in the same social circles. Eric didn't drink for one, or smoke, or have any more than a cursory interest in football. Eric knew the scores and tracked the Town as part of business small talk. Right before he took your company. The mildest man in the chauffeur's seat wielded a cut-throat business acumen. Like a cancer, he was the master of the hostile takeover. He lived long in the way that only the good die young.

"I suppose taking the bus everywhere can be quite humbling after being chauffeured around her adult life?" I had a tone of snippy jealousy about how life had worked out for them and less so for my dad.

"It's also very cheap. She is a Dronfield, girl after all!" Dad smirked and winked at the stereotype. He had put in a lot of streets and driveways in Dronfield and had to haggle for every penny to get paid. Famously, he'd even battled with Fiona, her sister, to get paid for a patio he'd installed off the back of her house. Even Joan was embarrassed by that episode.

"Almost 8:24; time to make our way to the bus stop."

Dad went to the hall closet to grab his coat – from the kitchen window I could see the ant-trail of pensioners leaving their homes to get the same bus. All these parents, many single now, used to be at parent-teacher conferences when I was in school. Their kids were either younger or older than me, so I didn't know them well other than by sight and was never sure if they knew who I was. We lived at the bottom of the hill in the Close, so unless you inadvertently drove past your own home, there was no reason to go to the bottom of the hill and then only to turn around. The bus stop was the other direction and that might be the only time you would bump into your neighbors.

The 8:24 was a popular one – it got you in to town before 10, so was ideal for shopping and "dossing" first, then going on to have a coffee at Littlewood's, Marks and Spencer, or Joplins'. The routine of retirement was to be savoured. Dad, like many of the mums on this run, had a system, a trip was carefully mapped out. "Roy cheese" was the first stop.

"A quarter of Edam, Roy, if you don't mind, Roy." The trip always started out the same way.

"Pleasure, Roy; how are the kids?" It was Roy to Roy; in fact there were three of them. Roy Cheese of course, Roy Cloth, and me dad, Roy Tarmac. Roy Tarmac had put in or patched all of their driveways over the years, Roy Cloth choosing a red asphalt that rolled before you like a red carpet welcoming you to his estate. Lot of money in cloth! Lot of hours on market stalls, too! The sun doesn't often shine on a Chesterfield Market Stall, and you could see the weathering in their faces and their driveways.

Roy Cheese asked of the kids each and every week, and not much would change. He used to ask after Christine, but her passing gave him great sadness, so he never mentioned her again.

"Doing well, Roy, how about you? How's Doreen?" Roy Cheese packaged the Edam. Thin white wax paper enveloped the waxy cheese.

"I'll have a little of that Stilton today if you don't mind too, cheers."

"Coming right up. Stephen's at business college. Thinking he might come work for me one day and take over the shop. But you can't force 'em can you? Doreen's same as ever – she is in Norfolk this week with the broads. Broads in the broads!" neither Roy had grown out of their 1950s heyday!

"Nice to get out of this muck, eh?" Dad would say cheerfully.

"Not for me, Roy; there's enough spice in this pepper-jack to keep me going. I'd rather be here than on that houseboat! Don't like tight spaces. Had enough of that in the 'mob.' Happy to be here in the shop – this is where my friends come."

Roy and Roy had met in the Royal Airforce, aka, the "mob." They weren't real chums in the day, but coming home they had bonded over beer and stories. Their wives, Doreen and Christine, got along easily so their group was comfortable. Business owners and their wives. Talking up strategy and family.

"See you Wednesday, Roy!" said Dad, reaching over the counter to take the cellophane packages totaling a half-pound of the cheeses.

On market day we always walked over to Roy Cloth whether we needed anything or not. You have to check in with friends, like reading the obituaries.

"Alright, ladies?" Dad was in his element back at the bus stop, leaning on his temporary walking stick – he would be done with this in a few weeks. Looking up at the mottled gray comforter of a sky:

"No rain today! I think we are in for a good one!"

"You must be mad, Roy," said Joyce, looking out from her umbrella. "Weatherman says rain on and off all day!"

"Then if that's the case I'm sure to be right, eh?" Chuckles abounded. Seven raincoated ladies huddled inside their macs, laughing simultaneously. Dad always had the measure of his audience. I could see why Mum had been drawn to him. He was quite a bit older, confident, athletic, charmingly funny, never crude. He winked at me like a fisherman – caught another one. He looked older with the stick, but he was still twenty-nine inside his head – single, brimming with charisma. The stick would be gone soon, and these vignettes at the bus stop would be more animated.

"Morning, Roy!" Joan had sidled up behind us. Her kitchen window afforded the best view of the bus stop.

"Morning, Joan!" Dad's cheeks warmed and he echoed the greeting of the Highlow Close ninja.

"Morning Mrs. Millward." I, the interloper, tried to include myself in the bus stop tryst.

"Got your umbrella, I see, Roy – just for show I assume – no rain forecast today." She grinned at him.

"That's why I brought it! No rain forecast usually means heavy showers. You could guarantee that if I didn't bring it there would be rain, so in two ways the umbrella is my insurance policy against getting soaked!" Dad started the laughter, at himself and then communally, as the bus stop line shared and enjoyed his sentiments.

"Roy, you are a card!" declared Mrs. Rainsberry. *Not heard that phrase in a while*, I thought having lived in the States for a while. Not sure anyone under seventy years old still says it. Mrs. Rainsberry was like Joan's "Goose" to her "Maverick" from *Top Gun*. Mrs. Rainsberry's guffaws kept the head-scarf and mac crowd bubbling with giggles. Suddenly, I was the third wheel on a big rig of Dad's courtship. Eileen, that was her name—god that was killing me to try to remember her first name. She taught me in year one, so she will always be Mrs. Rainsberry, but Mum and Dad knew her as Eileen. Like Joan would never be Joan to me. It freaked me out; I remember years back when I heard that Eileen, I mean Mrs. Rainsberry, had moved to our street. It was weird because ours was a small dead-end street at the winding tip of a maze of houses. The invading German army would have been greatly disappointed to find no pot of gold at the end of this maze, just cluster upon cluster of middle-England three- bedroomed, dormered, detached houses with enough lawn to disappoint a power mower in front and only an allotment-sized vegetable patch in back.

Mrs. Rainsberry was at the front of the line—I mean queue; we are in England, after all. I loved her class. Not that I remember much – but I remember a sense of warmth, of being loved and safe with her in the room. To a six-year-old she was actually very attractive, young and tall like a younger mother would be. She never did marry or have kids, I learned, which often struck me as slightly odd. Odd and unfortunate for some young gentleman to have missed out on the charms of Mrs. Rainsberry. She hadn't married but had always called herself Mrs., from our first day in school. I assume because she was so young and young looking she wanted to affect an air of maturity, or what else I don't know. Whatever it was, it stuck. She seemed shorter to me now. I remember her being tall, elegant, lean, moving like a skater between our tiny desks. Mrs. Rainsberry introduced us to nap-time, and who wouldn't love that idea then and now? I remember even falling asleep to whatever hypnosis she put me under. I was the kid who never napped at home. I stayed up late and got up early on the button. The silver cymbals on my West Ham United alarm clock awakening me at 7 sharp every morning. Loved mornings; still do. So, it was peculiar that I would actually fall asleep in her class. Mrs. Rainsberry taught us the magic of reading and writing. The former I love; the latter I'm cursed with being passionate about.

I noticed Dad really didn't speak to Mrs. Rainsberry—not rudely, just not much rapport. Nothing above the polite "how do you do's."

"Come on, Eileen! Step on board!" sang the annoying bus driver. They were familiar and we all would have the Dexy's Midnight Runners song stuck in our head the rest of the day! An upbeat way to start any day, I guess. The missing front tooth of our driver had never been replaced. His overriding grin from weary eyes having stared down the labyrinth of narrow streets greeted all alike. Slightly wan from years of smoking and being holed up behind the oversized wheel of a bus. Stooped from the shoulders, as if the surgeon had removed a little too much chest when he had the open-heart surgery. He was lead singer and conductor to his patrons. Jerry and the Pace-Maker, bus driver and conductor. Jerry gave tickets like passes to his mobile concert.

The bus was filling up nicely, and the head of logistics would be pleased that the route timing maximized customers. Dad and Joan, still talking as they got on the bus, found the two open seats.

"After you, Joan." Dad pointed chivalrously to the open bench for two.

"Thanks, Roy, I always enjoy the window seat!" She laughed as she referenced her preference when flying.

"I prefer the aisle these days!" chuckled Dad, nodding and pointing to let Joan sit first. They both knew he didn't need the leg room.

I looked around for an open space, or I might be standing. I really hadn't been paying any attention as we had got on the bus, just assuming I would sit with Dad. He apparently had other ideas. Would he ever stop flirting? Probably not. I'd heard him say, and it's been echoed by many of his friends: "I'm still twenty-five in my head; it's just my body got old. My brain doesn't know it's sixty-eight years old; it just runs the same. Sometimes a little slower, sometimes remembering its histories a little better, but for the most part it's still me." I look at Dad and know he doesn't move as quickly but he is still really quick-witted. He completes the *Daily Mail* crosswords; the Quick One and the substantial one every day. I can barely complete the Quick One and never with the swiftness with which he tackles it. I know he has the *Mail* delivered every day, but I buy it anyway just for the crossword when I'm over visiting.

I was well educated, I thought, the first in my family to get an Honors Degree. Not pompous but I was a little proud of my accomplishment in the Humanities. Roy had completed his education at the Ernest Bailey Grammar School in Matlock; a pretty good student, by his account. I had nothing else to go on! And no reason to doubt him. He was at school during the war – in my eyes he was lucky to have any teachers at all. I've known some of his "school chums," as he calls them, over the years, but they only ever talk of sports and girls. You wouldn't ever guess they had matriculated in anything but rugby and Maureen Collins! Yet he could still fly through the crosswords before me, despite my majoring in English. Some educators claim the old grade school was better than a degree. I'm not so sure – and certainly today high school is harder than anything I remember undertaking. However much I saw Dad slowing, the old grey matter just kept flowing. He had fifty-five years of flirting under his belt and he had needed no undergraduate degree to enhance that. He graduated from the "charm-school" and the "life-university" of hard knocks in the same year—the year of 1952 when he was called up for national service in the RAF.

It's hard to see a clear space on a bus filled with seasoned patrons all wearing oversized attire. Was there room on the fiberglass seat next to walking canes and shopping bags? I was nearly at the rear of the bus, away from Joan and Dad. Searching, I found Mrs. Rainsberry, identifiable by her brazen red head scarf. She caught my eye too and beckoned me to sit with her. *Okay, this is going to be weird,* I thought, *we haven't sat next to each other since she helped with my ITA reading assignments in class.* Forty years had gone under the bridge and in my mind, she hadn't aged at all. She excitedly patted the seat next to her, the way you would welcome a child or a puppy. My trips home from the States were often greeted this way by old friends wanting to catch up on the new world, though I doubt Mrs. Rainsberry knew that I was an ex-pat now living in the "new country," as it was still referred to in my old neighborhood.

Mrs. Rainsberry removed her wilted, empty shopping bags from the seat, tucking them under her window-side arm for safe keeping. I smiled gently, enjoying her welcome. This was going to be like visiting with a favorite aunt, I thought. Well, an aunt that I had a childhood crush on, that is. Her leather-gloved hand smoothed away any imaginary debris from the seat next to her—smoothed it like they were sheets on the bed, in the open space next to her.

"Adam, come sit here." Her insistence was redundant; I was already on my way, so her saying it was somewhat gratuitous.

"Mrs. Rainsberry, how the devil are you?" I couldn't stop myself from being too casual, ugh! Was it the coquettish red scarf? I don't know. Probably just nerves—yes, that was likely it.

"How's life in Chicago? Your dad tells me bits and pieces." So she did know. Dad had clearly worked the ladies on the bus! I gave her the potted history of my courtship and how I came to be there. My life, wife and kids, the business.

"It must be nice living in America." Whoa, she said it right. She must be self-taught! "What's the weather like?" Politely predictable, the way an American's second question would be "So what do you do?"

"Colder in winter, hotter in summer; sometimes too cold to snow in January, but we are guaranteed a summer!"

"Sounds simply wonderful," and there it was, the twenty-something enthusiasm of a pensioner. Mrs. Rainsberry said it like she was pouring over a chocolate sundae! Suddenly I was back in year one, in love with Mrs. Rainsberry and sundaes! Mrs. Rainsberry had always made it easy to talk to her; I think she may have been the first adult I felt this way about—friendly, gentle.

We carried on our banter, pupil and teacher. I often wondered how hard it would be to be a teacher. You build up so many close relationships with your students – teaching them the basics to the highly complex, but each step is foundational to something new and more challenging. You steer the brain's emotion toward improvement, harnessing what you were given and graduating it through to your next colleague. At least in the junior school, teachers would be around you for many years; if not always teaching, they would have the opportunity to visit in the hallway, assembly or playground, like an extended family all running around the school; then off they would go to high school. I would imagine for some teachers the separation would be hard. I hoped that I was one of those students the teachers truly missed. I hoped the affection I held for Mrs. Rainsberry was reciprocated. The thing is, Mrs. Rainsberry's class was as comfortable as a hand in a fleece-lined glove. Safe and warm and toasty.

Now where was the old man? I had a poor vantage point from here, but I could see Dad sitting perhaps just a little too close to Joan. I say old man, but it felt more like babysitting a wayward little brother after providing lifelong lessons in excellent behavior. He was having all these affairs, vignettes of youthful experimentation, betraying Mum. Which was a crazy thought, since she had been gone for years and he had been selflessly, even ferociously loyal.

His hip was clearly touching Joan's. More than his hip, more like conjoined twins at the lower rib. At least they would be if not separated by the clashing of rain-resistant outerwear. At least Dad didn't have his arm around her. Not that I could see anyone having their arm around Joan, as it would smack of possession or ownership unless both did it. Like in the seventies as couples strode with a hand in each other's back pocket of their Levi's; there's another thought, Joan in Levi's. That I couldn't imagine, Joan in casual jeans, Joan in high-fashion bell bottoms of the era. Wasn't she always frumpy, "mum-like" in her dress sense? I could see their heads bobbing in conversation, but I couldn't tell what they were talking about; now they were laughing, and I could see Joan catching herself with her hand to her mouth. What was he saying? Like spying on teenagers in the basement, I had to know what was going on.

"You were always my favorite, Adam." The fleece-lined glove of Mrs. Rainsberry rested on my knee.

"You were mine too," I replied smiling gently, childishly, a secret shared. *Still are*, I shared with myself – the darkish side.

Her hand stayed on my knee until we reached our final destination; I smiled at it resting there. The Glumangate stop, downtown Chesterfield, the final destination, the dropping off point for patrons and Mrs. Rainsberry's hand. I had lost sight and interest in Dad and Joan for a while. Mrs. Rainsberry put her hands on my shoulders—to steady herself, I think, as she stepped off the bus.

"Maybe I'll see you again, if you are back for a while?" She planted a caring kiss on my lips.

"I'd like that." And she was off on her particular route.

The town was already bustling. It seemed no one had a job to go to, unless their job was to create the effect of a bustling town. Like movie extras all busying around in an Eisenstein motion—old, young, and middle-young alike crossed streets randomly, ignoring the zebra crossings, these random folk littered everywhere, quickly and slowly, in no given direction. Tattooed faces marching into Marks and Spencer. Didn't see many of those in my day! Tattoos on faces, that is. They were reserved for armed forces and worn proudly, stamped on the bicep. Nowadays tattoos are revered, and the more painful the location the greater the accolades. Not even in my punk rock days did tattoos make it to faces – faces were reserved for piercing and dramatic make-up. The only face tattoo I could ever remember was the swastika on Charlie Manson's forehead. A chaotically dressed young lady pushing a stroller carved in front of us as we walked behind the bus, teardrop tattoo on her face. I don't know why? Maybe because the tattoo made her cry? It had to hurt like hell, right under her eyes. Was she a clown or a mime, permanently depressed? What was her statement? If she smiled, was it to declare greater irony? She was pushing twins in the double gauge stroller – were the tears there before or after squeezing the two giggling pumpkins out of her genitals? A constant reminder to her children of her pain and sacrifice? Or were they simply tears of joy?

"So, what did you and Joan talk about?" I asked of Dad as we got on the number 96 to Walton Hospital.

"Nothing really," and that was the beauty of flirting—a lot of connection with nothing said.

"That'll be 80p for you, Son; Dad, you can go." This bus driver was as curt as his military haircut.

Not many going to Walton at this time of morning, I thought. And Dad wasn't answering any Joan-related questions, apparently. It was like retaliation for when I would come home of an evening following a teenage gathering and would not divulge any trade secrets to the man I told everything to! Must have galled him. Okay, it is starting to wind me up, this Joan and Dad thing. If it was even a thing? "It's always sexual," Dad would say. "On some level, a friendly relationship with the opposite sex is always sexual." *Rubbish*, I thought, Nicola Garner had been my best friend in junior school, and there was no way I wanted to kiss her! She always came first in every class project. In truth, we were in the smart class and she was the smartest of the smart ones. Seemed she could do everything but climb the rope in PE. At home, she played the violin. I'd never known anyone to play the violin. My sisters played guitar and piano, but the violin? Nicola was an alien being to me. How could she not climb the rope? Like a rhesus monkey,

I was born climbing—perhaps it was my extraordinarily long arms. "You're not fully evolved into a human yet," Mum argued. Perhaps in a previous Darwinian exercise my side of the family needed to reach higher and swing harder to avoid being prey—or, I like to think, be the hunter-gatherer at the top of the tree; a real social climber.

Nicola carried her violin case around school, tight to her side like Capone. She would try to have it blend in with her uniform skirt, to protect it from unnecessary injury and attention. We didn't have lockers back then, so you carried what you owned in your satchel; in Nicola's case, oh, and the violin. She took lessons after school and played in the school orchestra, which was largely made up of xylophones and recorders with the occasional tinkling of a triangle.

I don't know if it was the fact that she was nimble on the violin, but Nicola always had an edge even when word searching in the dictionary. Girls against boys, never fair; my mitts, like my mates', were for gripping ropes, bats, tree branches, and bike handles. The girls like Nicola and my sisters were adroit at playing keyboards, guitar strings, make-up, and novels.

"Psychology"...I remember the words, even:

"Got it!" she would shout out as team leader of her group; and she rattled off the definition and application with the ease of a University Challenge competitor. Nicola, a croupier, like she was flipping a deck of cards, rifled through the dictionary, finding it instantly while we idiot boys looked in the "S's." Didn't really matter; she would have found it before us even if we had known it began with a "P"! Looking out across the tables, I could see her intensity to be first when it was her turn. I remember report card days – in a couple of subjects back in the day, I was number two in maths and number three in English. A silver or bronze medal in a competition against Nicola was like gold and silver. She assumed the top spot on the podium. At playtime, she was quiet, I remember, but always interesting to talk to – she had no edge or cockiness for someone so smart. Education just came easy to her. She heard something new, learned it, and it stuck. I was mesmerized by this. I had to practically chisel new information into my grey matter for it to have a chance to stick. Her brain consisted of sticky glue while mine was made of Teflon. "How are kids born like that?" Nicola would say of those athletes in PE who could climb to the rafters on a rope. Okay, she wouldn't, but I could dream as I flipped up the rope and stuck to the summit.

I never found myself attracted to Nicola. It wasn't like she turned heads in the hallway. But she was very attractive to talk to; you did want to be with her, because despite her crazy head smarts she was engaged in you. So, maybe to Dad's point, sex was there in the cerebral sense – maybe in a Darwinian way we were matching up. Our kids would be the brightest monkeys in the jungle. But would love last when the memory faded?

The bus trundled up the imaginary rails, or more like it was a cable car filled with patrons being delivered to the hospital clinic, not the Piste. There were no Franz Klammers on this bus, unless Franz had slid into the retention fencing.

"Did you read it in the gazette?" I had a way of asking an unfinished question. And I had asked Dad who had been in his own world since leaving Joan in town.

"No, what?" Softly answered and slightly distant.

"The Chairman of town is putting his 60 percent shares up for grabs. He announced it at the general meeting last night. The Board was completely stunned, by all accounts."

"I didn't see that coming," he said, barely paying attention. I thought this would have woken him up for sure. It was an entirely wrong answer. Clearly, he was distracted because obviously the chairman hadn't had much return on his four million quid in the last six years. A conscious dad would have known that.

"Yeh, he called it a day. They were so close two seasons ago, and now they have a skeleton left of that team. It's really sad to watch them 'spire-aling' down." My pun was lost on the wordsmith – something was up.

"Spiraling! Get it?" I continued rambling into our conversation, hoping he would pick up some slack. If we'd been in the pub, this would have been more than enough to spark the fire.

"I suppose they had it coming." He was curt. I was thinking Joan was a hard act to follow. But we are talking about Town! The hallowed team of misery upon misery, thousands of fans clumped together in hopeless comfort, bonded by the repeated failings of seemingly talented ball players.

"Sorry, Ad, what did you say?"

"The Chairman has put his shares up for sale – which is essentially putting Town up for sale!"

"Wow, which mug is gonna buy that disaster?" He was suddenly distant about the Town, almost vitriolic in his response. Condemning any future suitor.

"I doubt anyone!" I tried to follow in the same coolness that he had started.

This was not our usual refrain. This topic was one of passion, not prostitution. Perhaps Dad's feelings for Joan were more deep-seated than I had thought. Perhaps this on the bus flirtation was more core than casual. Or was it Dr. Doran's words of "stage four" starting to settle in? Was it in the quiet moments of travel, of a world passing us by, that our innermost fears catch up to us, inevitably passing us by, leaving us in the dust?

"We're here, Dad." He had to know that; he was staring out to the horizon where the clinic stood. Today should be a good day – it'd be a workout, and painful, but nearing the end of the treatment gave cause to raise his spirits, I hoped. The hip was nearly fixed.

"Hop up on the treadmill, Roy." Jessica had led the team of Roy's recovery. She had been there in the early days, having laid out the action plan.

"Got to say, Roy, you are one of my favorite students." She beamed, and he beamed back. Clearly, Jessica loved her job.

"I was never afraid of hard work, Jess! In fact, I always kind of enjoyed it!" he laughed.

"I can see you've been doing your homework." She watched him closely as he paced evenly on the treadmill. "You are my record-breaking stair-master."

"As a kid, I never liked homework, but I like this kind!" True enough, no teacher ever said, "Now here's your homework assignment: I want you to be able to do fifty push-ups, eighty burpees, and to run a mile in under seven minutes by the end of the semester." We did PE and that was it; there was no assignment, no homework, no measure of health and strength goal. She had a hard time picturing Roy as a young schoolboy. Her own high school years were not that far behind her, and to her, Roy would have been substantially old for her lifetime.

"I can see you've been eating right too, Roy," Jessica complimented him. It was true; for this three-month session, Roy had taken to heart Jessica's total body regimen of reformation.

"Five a day, love. I've been eating five a day! I cut back on bread and taters, and if you asked me to walk the stairs five times a day, I did ten."

"You are quite the gunner, Roy!" She smiled again at him. The twenty-five-year-old in him lit up. "I bet you were quite the athlete in your day, Roy." Her kindness was genuine and enough to deflate him, the 'in your day' hit home. His current homework assignments would get him back to the healthy mobile pensioner he was before – but nothing could recreate the magic of his youth. No matter how great Jessica's game plan, no matter how well he executed the homework, the mileage on his frame could not be denied, and there were no glory days in the future. Everything but being Jessica's favorite student, best most accomplished student, her most diligent sycophant, was behind him. All the races he would win would be based on his senior status, unlike when he was a high school student and champion of all classes. Roy was simply the best all-around athlete, bar none. For three months, he had been coach Jessica's best athlete/patient bar none.

"Looking good there, Roy." The hint of scouse accent blossomed. "Let's have you on the Stairmaster for ten minutes," she sang.

Student athlete Roy was working up a sweat of commitment to her –

"No worries, Jess, I'm ready!" And he was. Our house had a steep set of stairs rising straight from the front door to what seemed liked the roof – a senior's nightmare in most cases. Me and my sisters worried endlessly about Dad falling, and especially with the new hip. We had put up a makeshift bed in the dining room while he recuperated. Dining room – well, it was the other end of the one room that seamlessly ran into the lounge. But he slept downstairs. The goal was, as Jessica so saucily put it: "The goal, Roy, is to get you back to your bedroom!" The blushes had effused from the face of her Irish heritage.

"You know what I mean!" She laughed at Roy laughing at her. He was going to enjoy this three months, and indeed he had. He'd never had a proper coach as a kid. He was self-taught, even though PE was mandatory. Jessica was the head coach and delegated the fitness plan to her team. But on final send-off day – she was here to monitor the progress herself. Roy had to take the test live in front of his tutor. There could be no cheating, fudging, or skimping.

The stairs at home had proven to be a great training ground for the final test. My eldest sister but younger than me, if you can figure that one out, wanted Dad to have one of those stair chairs put in. But Dad had flatly refused and taken umbrage at the very idea. "Them's for old people," he told her.

So, at home there was no stair chair in the way, just the wickedly vertical staircase. He had conceded to replacing the carpet, as threads were starting to show and those could have been a hazard. Up until this incident, he wasn't that bothered. But he needed new turf on his training ground, so to speak. The fact that it was considered part of a training plan made it a priority; so long as it wasn't just decoration, he was going to be okay with replacing it!

"Go as long as you can, Roy," Jessica asked. He was the Stairmaster marathoner. He wouldn't disappoint his coach; he had spent the entire Jeremy Kyle show going up and down the stairs at home. It was a show he had no interest in – life's losers, and by contrast it energized him to be a winner. These were his Rocky Steps. Jessica had time to check on her other patients around the room. It looked more like a gym with padded benches than any kind of medical facility. The high-tech freezer bags and stim machines were the only indication that this was no ordinary fitness center. Roy's internal *Kyle Show* had clicked off –

"You can stop now, Roy," Jessica announced from halfway across the room. She was well impressed. But he wanted to keep going – impress her further—show off to her.

"Let's have you up on the table and check your flexibility." He lay on his back, breathing heavily and sweating hard into the paper sheet. Jessica grabbed his left leg above the ankle, above the sock line, gripping his dripping shin – the bright, pale-blue latex gloves allowed her purchase to raise Roy's straight leg perpendicular to his body. "Now your right leg, Roy. Looking good!" She was to him, the twenty-five-year-old him that resided in his failing body.

His damp T-shirt plastered to the paper and it wrapped around him like used toilet paper as he rolled onto his stomach. Truly humiliating. Jessica brushed the paper aside like swatting a fly, grabbed the sweaty leg again, and pulled it up behind him like a contortionist.

"It's not supposed to bend that way, Jess!" He grimaced. "I'm not a Cindy Doll!"

"Let me be the judge of that one!" Jessica continued play with him, to stretch the hip. Jessica had the perky, friendly optimism of a cheerleader and the steadfast demands of a matron. She commanded her gym of recovery like a lion tamer, a crack of a demand here and a treat of a compliment there. Jessica herself was lithe, moving fluidly between patients. Her gym tackle wasn't foreign to her, and she freely demonstrated all facets to her new pupils. Consistently Jessica wore her professional polo shirt with the clinic's name emblazoned over her left breast. It came in various colors, but the khaki trousers were standard issue: comfortable, flexible like yoga leggings, with a pocket for her phone. Today her blackish hair was in a high bun, a little more formal than the swinging ponytail of previous meetings.

"Going somewhere today, Jess?" Roy asked between agonies.

"I'm trying on my wedding dress at lunch time, Roy. Why do you ask?'"

"High bun, more formal than your usual look."

"Nicely spotted, Roy. I'm meeting me mum at Joplins, then going to try on the dress for a final fitting."

"When's the big day?"

"June 3rd. Season will be over then. My fiance is Jamie Howe."

"The right winger for Town?"

"One and the same!"

"Is he coming back? He was injured, right?"

"Yep. He tore his ACL over a year ago – he's been on loan to Halifax and making a good impression, by all accounts. We met here on this very same bench you're on, Roy!" Roy felt like an interloper—in his dreams, at any rate. "I'm not supposed to date patients, but Jamie was so sad I felt sorry for him, so I actually asked him out—for coffee, mind, nothing more!"

Jessica had never worn her engagement ring during work; she put it on like a winner's medal on her way to and from work. But here in this hands-on environment, it stayed in its presentation box locked in her drawer until it was time to go home.

"Lovely player, Jamie. Me lad and I loved watching him dance down the touchline – like he's got Velcro on his boot. We didn't see the injury and wondered what had happened. Must have been over a year ago?"

"Yerr, it was late January – at Millwall. A late sliding tackle. Not even a yellow card and Jamie was carried off. It's been a whirlwind of a year. Neither of us are getting any younger and Jamie's wanting to make one last run at making it to the EPL. His knee is doing brilliant and his head is in the right place."

"Sounds like his heart is, too!"

Jessica blushed. Training was hard at first; he din't think his knee would hold up. I sent him to a sports psychologist – well, actually, he's just a psychologist down the hall here but I figured Jamie wouldn't go if you know, well, that Dr. Moss was just a regular psychologist. He's Ernie's son, so I told him that he specialized in footballers!"

"Lying to your husband already, eh Jess!" And she blushed even more.

"Sometimes you gotta do what you gotta do! It's in his best int'rest right?" Knowingly, like a father, Dad nodded.

"Just a few more reps on the stability board and we'll have you out of here!"

"What, no graduation ceremony?" Roy chuckled wryly.

Dad balanced his way to the sounds of the Bee Gees Strut of 'a woman's man'."Thanks for everything, Jess; you've been great. Hope the wedding day goes well, and tell Jamie we hope to see him back at Proact Stadium again soon, or on the telly! Come on, Ad, let's shake a leg if we're gonna catch the 12:53."

Dad practically ran out of the clinic, with me struggling to keep up. My leg had gone numb from sitting on the plastic waiting room chair. Note to self – sitting cross-legged for a really long time is not good for circulation. Dad was already at the door.

"Hold up, Dad; hey, you forgot your cane!" Dad was out the door, moving faster than Sherlock Holmes from a crime scene certain he had the next clue.

"I left it for Jessica – it was my gift to her," he shouted back to me.

"Slow down, we'll make the bus!" But Dad was making up for lost time—or rather, time he was about to lose.

On the bus back, Dad was as impassioned as ever. We were talking again. Clearly Jessica had gotten his blood flowing.

"I'd have given anything to have played for Town," he said with the vim of someone just off the podium in a medal ceremony. Dad still had childhood dreams even looking at the wrong end of the egg-timer.

And that's when it occurred to me. I was going to call the chairman of Town and see what I could do to fulfil my dad's bucket-list wish.

CHAPTER 5

"Hello, Chesterfield Football Club—Angela speaking," answered the receptionist as if straight out of receptionist school, crisp bright with no hint of local accent. I couldn't help wondering how much longer she would have in the job if the performance on the field got worse.

I really didn't know what I was doing, so I asked for the outgoing chairman.

"I'd like to speak to the chairman if I may?"

"The Chairman is no longer with The club, I'm afraid. Is there someone else I can direct you to?" Not having a plan A, and having used Plan B to no avail, I was a little stumped.

"Sir, are you still there?"

"Yes, I'm still here. Could I talk to the coach, then or any member of the Board?" I was reaching – she knew it. Angela must have received a hundred calls a day in recent weeks as the team spiraled to the oblivion of non-league status.

"I'm afraid Dr. Banner is unavailable at the moment, and the manager has been relieved of his duties and currently looking for a new club." Pare riposte! I had been driven back verbally by her simple jousting.

I tried to hide my surprise, but clearly, I was not up to speed on the internal workings of The club – they sacked the manager! When did I miss that news? Or was it in the minutes of the meeting after the resignation of the chairman and subsequently buried as a by-line, seconded and approved by the quorum? They must be in crisis if the sacking of the manager was the addendum to the resignation of the chairman and his subsequent shares being available to Joe Public. From what I could see on YouTube, the rest of the Board was in complete dismay and no one looked to be picking up the reins. Of course, the clip was short and only focused on the chairman himself, which as I understood was the way he liked things. That aside, he had poured millions into The Club, which is more than can be said of the fans this season. But this was the north of England; we don't expect a lot, we ask for less, and sometimes that's just what we get—and then there's the teams from the 1980/81 season and 1996/97 season, where, as fans, we were treated to the heights of football success ... well, almost.

"Sir, are you still there?" She hung up before the last word came out. I just assumed the rest. I was unlikely to be her future employer, so Angela quietly clicked the off button on her panel. I was imagining a panel. Of course, things were bad, so maybe she was at home on a cell phone?

Could this be the same Brian Banner from my tennis club days? I remembered he was a doctor back then. A dentist--he wasn't my dentist, as he worked the other side of town – the posh side. There weren't many buses from our house to his office, so we were patients of Dr. Himmler. Whatever! Few relished going to the dentist, and few dentists relished pulling teeth like Dr. Winkler, not Himmler. He didn't even have an accent, although he did enjoy singing the refrains from *The Sound of Music*, but I digress.

So, Dr. Brian Banner was our new guy in charge, acting chairman without really playing the part, the fall-guy-in-waiting, the next batter up, the unfortunate understudy who had been happy in the wings while the Chairman assumed all the migraines and root canals of club leadership.

Brian and I were somewhat friends when we were younger at the tennis club. And when I say friends, I mean he didn't loathe the Junior team players the way that the older club members usually did. "Children should be seen and not heard; especially around The tennis Club"--which was understandable really as we were quite loud and I was incredibly obnoxious and they of course having never been teenagers would not understand us. I was the rebel without the green hair, nose piercing, black eye shadow, and studded belts; I did, however, wear a yellow polo on club match days!

Brian, or Dr. Brian, or Doc as he was known to his doubles partners, was club champion at various times and carried the title with the same humility as he did the title of "Doctor." I liked that about Brian back then. He drank pints of John Smiths like a regular northerner even though he had grown up in Dronfield and moved to the lesser neighborhood of Chesterfield. Brian always seemed to be at The tennis Club when I was there, so I deduced that he must have the best job ever. I was only in school and had summers off – he had a proper job and was there most summer days. His architect buddy Andy was there too. Like me and Alistair, they were there most of the summer during the day. They were in their late thirties and not yet retired friends of my dad—Dad considered himself their half-peer, as dad consistently lied about his age.

Dr. Brian never used his title, because of his modesty or because Dr. Gooding, the local medical celebrity, the published proctologist was The Tennis club director and the senior over-55 Champion. Even in the upper echelon of the community and medical community, there was a social structure and etiquette. The dentist deferred his social standing to the proctology doctor, which had to be a real pain in the ass for Brian.

Angela was brilliant at deflecting any calls; and even if I did know what I was doing, I decided to change dentists!

"Dr. Banner's office. How may I help you?"

"I'm newly back to the area and would like to set up an appointment for this week." I was crisp now and knew what I was doing. I might not know how to call a chairman, but I was more than capable of booking a dentist appointment.

"Sorry, he's all booked up for the next three weeks. Is it an emergency?"

I didn't miss a beat. "Yes, I fell and loosened a tooth!"

"How does 8:15 tomorrow morning look, sir?"

"Perfect!" I was in. Now all I had to do was injure myself!

Don't kid yourself – injuring yourself is not as easy as it sounds. Accidentally injuring yourself is very easy; consciously doing it is another matter altogether! Unless of course you have some edgy adolescent mental breakdown where carving yourself up becomes your crutch. I was not that kid and feel pity for those children who find solace in cutting themselves open.

Punching oneself is difficult task enough without having to be accurate to one's mouth. The real challenge was that I couldn't decide which tooth to loosen. The molars were impossible, way back in there; not even Joe Bugner could knock them out! My two front teeth were an easy choice, but really did I want that gappy-look even for a day even for a stupid ruse? In the States I could pretend that I did it playing ice hockey – here on the island there was little to no chance of that occurring. Even a soccer ball might give you a fat lip, but loosen a tooth? Hardly.

A cricket ball; that would do the trick! But why would I be playing with a cricket ball in football season? It didn't add up. And I didn't even have a cricket ball handy! Wham! Without thinking – trying to catch myself off guard, I hit myself in the mouth!

"Shit, fuck, fuck!! That hurt!" Damn, that hurt, and I was even holding back. My lip throbbed like hell and started to swell; tears joined my eyelids to see what all the fuss was about. Adam's gone mad, they concluded. Teeth marks were evident just above my knuckles – little reddish quarter-inch indentations. Dr. Brian wasn't gonna have to be Sherlock Holmes to figure out how the teeth got loose when that bruising showed! They weren't even loose, and I wasn't about to hit myself again. The lip swelling would have to be enough to justify the appointment.

"Gooood morrning Adam!" declared Dr. Brian like he was Mufasa in *The Lion King*. This was his professional tone, apparently, and it threw me right off. I was his first appointment, but his day had begun earlier with his usual five-mile run, muesli, and coffee. Quite a bit of coffee, by all appearances.

"It's great to see you, Brian—I mean, Doc. How's your tennis game these days?"

"Senior division these days, if you can believe that? Where does the time go? Still trying to knock off that old buzzard Colin Gooding from his perch of senior men's champion!"

"I thought you would have had his number, Brian? You and Andy always were tops in your day…my day." I respected Brian. He was academic but approachable, easy company in a well-spoken way, as if sitting down with a male version of Dame Diana Rigg.

"Two shoulder surgeries and a knee replacement have put a real crimp in my talents, but I do enjoy the camaraderie of the game, and The Club has come a long way since you were here, Adam." I started to remember my fondness, my addiction to The Club, my love of the shack me and Ali painted one summer between sets. We lived there, brought our own coffee. Learned to drink it black because we forgot to buy milk and sugar. I never thought of it as a place that engendered camaraderie – for me it had the feeling of gladiators milling around until summoned to the colosseum. Our weapons of Donnay, Prince, and Wilson sheathed ready waiting for an open court, or the rain to stop so we could go into battle. It was combat on the courts, personal close quarter combat, mano à mano. Even in doubles-play you were often paired with your personal nemesis. Friendships born of enemies, respect and despise rolled in to one.

"Visiting your dad are you, Adam? How long have you been in the States now?" I always liked the way Brian was always interested in you.

"About twenty years give or take?"

"You like it out there then?" His statement rolled into a question I had often heard. Mystical to them that someone born in the East Midlands of Britain could find themselves at home in America.

"Yes, but I love coming back as a tourist and visiting everyone! Sometimes you have to leave a place to really appreciate it! Nothing like walking around Bakewell and Baslow, eh?" I had been answering this way for years now. Because underneath the question or statement of "you like it there then" is a sense of jealousy or bafflement, and I'm not sure which. So almost apologetically I declare my love of the Peak District. It's true I do, and my ashes should be scattered in Monsal Dale where I escaped to often on my Raleigh ten-speed as a child. Not that there aren't a hundred other landmarks of my life I could choose, but from Monsal Dale my ashes would be swept up in the valley's breeze to start a whole new journey. All of it was true; I did love coming back to see everyone. In a shallow way, I was kind of a celebrity, and coming over we always made a special effort to gather in a grand way either at dinner or in the pub.

"So, what did you do to yourself here, Adam?"

"Doc, thanks for seeing me at such short notice! Over did the forehand at The club yesterday, tried a new swing and smacked myself in the mouth!" There was a story he might swallow. I should have gone with the racket instead of my hand. At least only my mouth would hurt.

"Didn't see you around The Club yesterday?"

"Early, I was very early, hitting against the wall. Not there long on account of hitting myself in the mouth!" My God this is why I hate any kind of fibs, lies, stories if you like. It brings out the worst and the most creative in you at the same time.

"I like to play early too, weather permitting. We should go hack some balls one of these mornings?"

I could feel the blush in my cheeks rising like that of a cheap 1970s hooker as my lie unfolded:

"I would like that, though I'm seriously rusty these days – I should have gotten me shoulder done but went with extended physical therapy instead. Not sure it's done the trick, but I'm a little afraid of the knife, to be honest!" A little afraid of anything medical, to be honest! Honesty in the midst of a lie; how novel! Even here in the dentist's chair, chatting away, I could feel my armpits gushing like the Niagara splash as it hits the rocks and spreads effortlessly throughout my shirt. I was failing the lie detector test! I think we all would if it was taken under the duress of a dentist's chair – seated next to medieval yet shiny drills, pokers, and scrapers!

"Alright, Adam, so let's have a look at what you've done to yourself then." His segue to my mouth was smooth, and also probably recognized that his waiting room would be filling up fast with regular and actual paying customers who gave him the annuity of lifestyle he enjoyed.

This was his busy season. Long ago, he and his partner realized that they could each work half to two thirds of the year. Brian would work the winter months while Nigel would work the summers. Nigel loved to ski, so as soon as the first snowfall hit anywhere in Europe, he was off. He was old school and didn't take up snowboarding – that was far to crass for his respect of the slopes. Brian, on the other hand, would plough on through the damp and cold of Chesterfield winters, ready to enjoy the warmish damp summers to play tennis daily. So many summers in Chesterfield you couldn't tell without looking at the wall calendar's helpful and appropriate photos what month you were in! The rain might be a little warmer, the winds not so biting. But you knew you were in winter, as there hadn't been a fluke warmish day since the calendar's photo of waves crashing hard on to an overcrowded beach in Bude. In summer in Chesterfield you could get a cold snap briskly work its way down from Iceland over the Outer Hebrides through the Yorkshire moors and slap you an icy good morning. The opposite was not true. Once winter slid past the wet grass of summer and autumn, gone was any chance of a continental zephyr to thaw your chilblains. In Chesterfield, we were resigned to rain year round. No wonder the Romans left when they did. I can hear their centurion leaders now – "Straight roads, lads! Straight roads! Over the hills, not around them; we need to get out of this watery hell before Noah arrives and head back to balmy Tuscany!" and thus the legendary Roman Road was created! Roads formerly curved to appreciate the dales, the rivers, the climbing plateaus were now dissected with a surgeon's straightness. I believe the roads were built in "double-quick time" where that expression may have originated from – you can hear the centurions now – "Get me off this godforsaken hell-hole of green; I can't take it anymore!" Those that remained started the first Cambridge Footlights! A form of madness brought on by vitamin D deficiency and trench foot! But I digress.

"You say you hit yourself in the mouth. Open wide and let's take a look. Hmm, well obviously I can see the swelling on your lip and in the gum line." Brian started to poke at my tooth with the standard pick, the one that looks like it was from the children's game of Pick-Up-Sticks. The champion of this game went on to dental school, apparently.

"There's some slight movement with the left incisor."

Whew! I'd at least done enough to warrant a check-up. Brian continued to poke and scrape at my blackboard teeth. It literally went through me like someone scraping at my teeth!

"Quite a strong tongue you've got there, Adam!" I wanted to say all the better to lick you with but that would have been inappropriate; plus, I was about to get a tongue lasso from his assistant.

"Kelly, would you pass me some gauze?" His assistant reached to her serving plate and gave Brian the saliva-absorbing, tongue-scraping gauze. He took it and wrapped my tongue in it so he could hold it back, like a corner man raises the rope for the boxer to enter.

"Perhaps a little more, Kelly, if you don't mind, as we've got quite a gusher with Mr. Griffiths here." My mouth was sweating like my armpits or releasing the weeks of Chesterfield rain my body had absorbed!

"Suction," Brian instructed nonchalantly. "Good." Now foam went in my mouth. Good lord, I was being choked. The foam felt like the size of the mats we used to dry out the clay courts!

"When was the last time you had a checkup, Adam?" He spoke as if we were side by side at the pub. I couldn't speak I had a face full of marshmallow dental debris and carpet-gauze! So, I shook my head pathetically while he had sharp instruments in my mouth. Kind of radical, in the way that you wouldn't wave your hands around a circular saw.

"If you could stay still just a little longer; Kelly, more suction, please. Ok, I think what I'd like to do is get a couple of X-rays. Do you have time for that this morning?"

I nodded – it was safe now both Kelly and Brian had slid back their stools each by their carving stations. Tools down, ready for the autoclave. Brian fished around for the foam after unwrapping my tongue – no surprise there; it was still a tongue. It was a very dry tongue, and I was waiting for the instruction to gargle. I thought rinsing and gargling were a mandatory procedure. I was a pro at gargling and spitting! While I was fitted with a full metal jacket the weight of medieval armor, I tried to scrape off the fibers of gauze from my tongue. Yuk! Like I had just licked the afore mentioned carpet.

"Rinse?" offered Kelly – ah, there it was. The manual hadn't been rewritten after all!

"You can spit into the bowl. Would you like me to suck out the rest?" she winked a smutty smile – clearly part of her flirty way to keep you coming back to the dungeon. She enjoyed spending more time with the patients than Brian. A twisted voyeur of pain, in my rarely humble opinion! He was the pilot, just making sure his passengers were comfortable twice a year or if they needed him during any dental turbulence like today. Kelly was the face, the audience, and the personality of the practice.

Kelly raised the seat to a more normal sitting position. My legs crossed. Now what to do with my arms? The narrow chair crimped you into place like an open coffin.

"Ok – open wide," Kelly grinned, slipping the dental negatives into place.

"You really are a gusher!" she laughed as I started to flood out over my gums to the pink ribbed paper!

I tried reciting the alphabet backwards to see if she really understood what patients say when their face is filled with dental insulation – she nodded agreement as if I had made Nobel Laureate-worthy comments – I knew it! They're full of crap; they can't tell what we're saying!

"Ok; stay still, you won't feel a thing! And neither will I!" She stepped out of the room and the alien periscope she pointed at my cheek, smiled a dot of red light, click, and was done. "I'm gonna do both sides so we have a record of them." Another red wink and click. Kelly came back in took off the lead gown. "We just have to wait for doc to come and take a look, ok?" She sang her way through the formality.

"Ok, I'm back," announced Brian.

"Pass or fail, Doc?"

"I hope you have some time on your hands next week!" he said joyfully, enjoying his winning drop-shot.

"Why? What's going on?" I was out of sweat by now – I just started to percolate in the chair.

"When did you last go to the dentist?"

"Hmm," long pause – I wasn't ready to lie about that one. "Well, it was after Queen Victoria was on the throne, though I believe you're still using the same instruments!"

He cut me off:

"You have two cavities. I can take care of them next Thursday if you are available?" I pondered for a while – I was technically on vacation. Some people go to the beach or explore ancient cities; my time off would appear to be under the influence of Novocain!

"What time were you thinking? The year 2047?" I figured I had to go with my cover story but was really gutted that my enamel had let me down!

"Nine-fifteen; we'll have you out in a jiffy."

"What about the loose tooth?" Clearly, I was under duress to bring up more issues.

"I'll say you caught a break there! There doesn't appear to be any damage to the root system," he said as I pictured swamp-born trees.

"It should settle down of its own accord and by your next appointment should be healed. See you in a week then?" Like it was a new romance! He then moved quickly in his tennis pumps—Stan Smith's, if I'm not mistaken. He reached for the doorknob like he was taking a one-handed backhand. Out the door and gone like a golf ball down a gopher hole.

I hadn't even mentioned Town and executing my Dad's wish to play for Town. This was looking like a very long shot; outside the 18-yard box with defenders all around me – I was going to have to dance my way out of this one to get off a "long-ranger." As of now, I was passing back to my goal-keeper. Brian was too busy to chat – I didn't realize the conveyor belt of dentistry. Multiple chairs in multiple offices, with fleeting visits with the dentist while all the Kellys of the world do much of the routine work. Brian popped in and out of the offices like Santa, too busy to notice anything more than the name on the present drop it off and move on. Patient reviewed, diagnosed, new appointment set, and match. Then the penny dropped, and the copper Two P's, the oddly shaped 20p and finally a flurry of weighty pound coins. The contents of my trouser pockets spilled on to the hygienically mopped floor as I realized my chance to talk to Brian was early tomorrow on the tennis court! Bingo, gotcha! I would still make next Thursday's appointment because God knows I have cavities and don't need those turning in to root canals. Two words, root and canal, by themselves not really outstanding or fear inducing? Put them together, though, and visions of medieval torture and agony manifest themselves. Visions of joyful Baldricks with hot pokers fill your mind. Can't say you've ever wished anyone a "Oh, happy root canal day!" "Oh, I have to have a root canal today; what a relief! Looking forward to getting that over!" No, it's visions of twisted devils with hot pokers, sixteen-inch pincers while being head-clamped in a witch's brace. I don't care how "painless" they claim modern dentistry is – you can't dumb down and fairy-cake the word combo of "root canal." That sweet little hybrid creates all sorts of nightmares! That combo ruins any thoughts of lazy winding vacations through the Norfolk Broads, simple ripples trailing behind, trees lining the river banks, locks ahead, beautiful, sipping Pimms as you float through the deliciously flat British inland waterways – you look at the river bank with trees gripping in to it like an eagle's claws around its prey and think, oh "root canal" haha! Vacation ruined. You can no longer look at the riverbank without thinking dungeons of misery. Root canal, root canal dominates your thoughts. So yes, if you were wondering, I'm getting the fillings. I'm not the masochist I thought I was.

CHAPTER 6

"Nice-looking backhand you've got there, Adam!"

"Thanks, Doc!" *It should be good,* I thought, *I've been hitting against this wall for two hours already!* I wasn't sure how early "early" was to Brian. Apparently, 6 a.m. is too early and 8 a.m. is just about Goldilocks right. Dad had painted a white line on the wall when he first built it – net height, of course. I must have, without exaggeration, hit the wall a million times with balls over the years. Hour upon hour lashing balls at the breeze-block. Hour upon hour of recovering the balls that missed the wall and went flying into the court beyond, or worse, into the adjoining, often annoyed neighbors' gardens. The wall was only as high as the side netting and no more than 12 feet wide, 12 blocks wide. In the day, we had chalked target zones on the wall to tighten our accuracy. This was where my backhand learned its discipline, this was where I relentlessly pounded Slazenger balls in to smaller and tighter chalk zones. We were gun-range serious about accuracy.

"You have a game today?" he asked. Of course he had to ask; it makes sense unless I was training for the senior tour. Unfortunately, I couldn't think of anybody I might remotely be in contact with who could make a match at 8 a.m. in February!

"My sister was supposed to join me. I just got a text from her that she wasn't feeling too well this morning. So, I figured I would just keep hitting." That sounded about right.

"I remember when your dad built this wall, Adam," Brian reminisced as he started to take off his rain gear and pull out a racket from his bag of four. He took out a second racket and pinged the frame off one of the strings of the other to determine which string tension he preferred. He had been in his prime when Dad pieced together the practice-wall on the edge of hard-court number 3.

"It made a difference to everyone's game! Practice makes perfect! Want to hit some balls?" He was changed into his Sergio Tecchini track suit, probably with matching attire beneath. Brian always looked the part. Part one of beating your opponent – look like you are prepared to beat him, be prepared for battle. By contrast, I was a patchwork of Dad's old sweat pants, my brother-in-law's Ralph Lauren Pink Polo from TK Max, and my kagool. The running shoes were mine, the racket was my sister's; the grip was too small, but I liked it that way anyway. My thumb was already starting to plump up into a blister from hours of angry hitting. I had started out gently, but after seven ludicrously bad forehands, I began to thrash in frustration. I had emotionally collapsed at about 6:15. I was reliving Dr. Doran's statement from days before and decided to smack the panther-print off of the Slazenger ball. Clearly Dad's wall was going to outlive him, reminding me that we are not built to last.

I could see Brian relishing the thought of practicing with the bum across the net from him. It was well known that despite my numerous victories in my day, I was always a better practicing partner. As one coach candidly told my dad on this very same court. "Adam just doesn't have the mental scope that his game does. Don't get me wrong, Roy, he has all the shots, speed, and stamina—some shots that are not even coachable, like that inside-out forehand? Wherever did he learn that?"

"That was from me," Dad had responded, and it was true. Dad had never been coached so had little to no backhand; as he was my first coach, I witnessed how you could run around the backhand and drive an inside-out forehand across court from my backhand side to the opponents'! You just had to be quick like a pickpocket to get back in to position. Some coaches have brass balls, and Christine had them. Her candor was also why her son and I played doubles together, especially when he couldn't find someone else.

By the time Brian centered the first ball to me I was warmed up, worn out, and a little blistered. But it felt so good. His feed from mid-court was spotted like a pro and the rally was controlled, hitting about twenty ground shots each before an unforced error. His surgeries didn't show up anywhere in his fluid swing, the oversized Wilson doing so much of the work, given Brian's lovely timing. It was tennis poetry to hit with Brian.

"So how is Roy these days? We don't see him around here much anymore." It was true, Dad's tennis club phase was deep-seated in me and my sisters, belonging to the juniors. There was a lot of sporting wear and tear on Roy. Besides, he was ten years older than he let on.

"Roy stopped playing too soon, in my estimation," added gentleman Brian, smoothing a single-handed backhand across to my waiting backhand. He spoke in the rhythm of his strokes as I did. His measured tone matched him the way my asthmatic wheezing started to mirror some of my wayward shots. My forehand had gone I don't know where, it had just gone. Probably over the wall to a neighbor's yard – I'll fetch it later.

"I think we all think that, Brian. He loved it here; the game, the friendships, the competition, the frustrating adversaries on the Board. He loved the challenge."

"Few were ever as involved or committed as your dad. What he did with that junior program was nothing short of miraculous!"

Brian beamed behind another screamer of a cross-court forehand. Even as we practiced, he could sense my forehand swing and timing was breaking down. He varied the length of his shots to prove his point to himself. "Roy had real passion for you kids. No one wanted to invest the time; we were all too absorbed in our own games. It's a singular sport that way. I remember old Betty was the only one who seconded his motion to start a Junior team. She had given up coaching, didn't have the body to run any team, never mind about getting one started. Your dad was feisty in the meetings – that one particular night, he stood alone. Betty the secretary, Colin club chairman, me and John Robinson. A couple were missing, as was always the case. I'll never forget the anger that no one was stepping up. There had been no leadership. But your dad came to that meeting. He had signed you kids up to the Sheffield and District League unbeknownst to any of us. He had spent the last eight months doing battle over there to get you kids represented. I proposed the motion and your dad frostily stared the board down. Roy and Betty had gone to battle over the last couple of years as these growing numbers of pesky kids trampled the rules of clubhouse, court etiquette, and attire. But what Roy had seen was raw fighting talent. These kids could play, behind their moxie was the adolescence of you can't tell me what to do.

"I proposed the motion, thinking it was dead on arrival, and then old Betty, with only the slightest hint of hesitancy announced:

'I second the motion! Good luck to you, Roy. Clearly you want this more than we don't – teach the kids some manners on the way, would you?' and with that, she stood up reached for your dad's hand and shook it crisply. Old Betty had found her way to corral these troublemakers, and Roy was the go-to sheep dog. And she would stay on him like a farmer's entrusted daughter."

Brian was working up a sweat, too. His playing partner would be here in fifteen minutes or so.

"So how is Roy doing, Adam?" Brian cared. Not enough to randomly call, but that was not a very British thing to do anyway. All that rang in my head were the lyrics to Terry Jacks' "Seasons in the Sun." "Good-bye papa it's hard to die."

"He's doing well, Bri." I took a breath to swing my racket. This morning had been a marathon, and Brian was joining in at the halfway marker. "Thanks for asking; physical therapist gave him the all-clear to carry on normal living." And not needing to, I reached for breath. "Therapist said his hip was good to go."

"Did he have it replaced?" Brian asked, sliding to his backhand to force the ball down the line on to my fading, flailing forehand. I was glad we were just warming up. My game had gone to hell over the years of not playing, and my shoulder had a scrap yard's mileage!

I was sucking in February wind again.

"Yes, that's both of them now! He's used up all of his lifetime quota of Lego!" Brian grinned a gift of happiness to my dad in his absence.

"He's like frigging Action Man now! Catching up on wasted time. Racing around to find a bucket to put his list in. I see you're keeping yourself busy too, Bri." Why did I do that around people I respected? I would do the disrespectful thing and shorten his name. I hadn't seen him in years, and now I was acting like his kid brother and borderline swearing into the bargain.

"I saw you on the YouTube video, Brian; you were with Chesterfield's Chairman when he resigned." So now I was starting to make progress.

"It was a real shocker. The press was called in at the last minute, and we didn't really know what was going on. We knew things at The Football Club weren't going well, injuries, and a manager change made for some painful Saturday afternoons!"

"I thought you were a Sheff United fan anyway Bri—" God, I butchered his name again. No point in me correcting it; might as well just go with it!

"I am, but growing up in Town, I felt an obligation when a spot on the Board opened up. This team has been around for a hundred and fifty years, and I didn't want to see it disappear."

"That's mighty of you, Brian. So, it must have come as a right shocker then the other night?"

"Yes and no, I suppose." We were picking the balls up at the net now, most of which I had hit there. Some hit the tape, but mostly my forehand was driving the balls like spent fireworks arcing to the ground. "Our Chairman had put his money where his mouth is and looked several times to be getting a return on his investment. We threatened the top of the table early both this year and last year. You probably saw the transfers at the end of the year last year, and the money was too good for our board to pass up. Unfortunately, we never gained that respect back on the field; coupled with injuries at center back, we became that team everyone wants to run on."

I smacked my racket on the ground in a poor attempt to pick up the ball with style like I used to. It punctuated Brian's measured commentary. I was over-trying to be smooth with Brian and was horribly awkward as a result.

"What's the next move then, Bri?"

"Someone needs to come in with the 'readies' to buy new players, or the whole Board will have its shares up for grabs! We had some great prospects in mind that just didn't pan out at the professional level. There's a lot of work on a daily basis blending skills, strength, and personalities. Then like in the playground – you have to pick a team. You have to play favorites. It was a lot for some players to stomach. Especially for the new kids. This may be the first time they didn't make the team at any level. Rejection is difficult and for a lot of these talented players; this episode of not being selected can be quite devastating." (As an aside, Chesterfield had rejected me when I was twelve!) "We don't have a large squad, as evidenced by our recent spate of injuries, but we do have two people for most every position on the field. That means half of your team doesn't start, and many don't even dress on game day. It can be rough cheering for your teammates knowing that you want to be there in the worst possible way. Then you get your chance because of a 'worst possible way'--an injury. Stepping in like a substitute teacher with a chance to shine knowing that your teammate might be back next week. This is very intense pressure; as you stand on the grand stage of Proact Stadium, you have an audition, and everything is evaluated in real time and on film the next day. You have to have thick skin. And then you might get injured. Everything you have worked hard for to make it to the Big Dance every Saturday and every other Tuesday gone for now. Then there's the money worries of the players, managers, trainers, and owners."

Brian leaned on the net; he seemed more worn down by his eulogy than by our rallying. "Better players just don't want to come to sides that are struggling. Well, with incentive they might, and we don't have any funds left for that."

"Seems such a shame, Brian. Me and my dad would have given anything to play for Town. We were just saying on the bus the other day how we revered the hallowed ground of Saltergate as kids."

"Well, if we don't get a big cash infusion soon, we might be calling you in." Brian of course was joking. This was serious business and serious money at stake. Sponsors would want contracts renegotiated and not in Town's favor. The advertising money was incentivized like a performance bonus. Greater success gave way to greater ad revenue. The deal struck by the Board, looked like a sure bet after six games. Town had only dropped a point and cemented a five-point lead at the top of the table. Soon folks would be talking about them again, and that meant cash would be dropping in the tray from Three Cherries of ad revenue. "We've only taken four points from matches since. The situation looks dire." The club's future was drying up faster than a desert plum.

"Yep, Dad put his childhood dream on his bucket list."

"What was that, Adam?" Brian, composed and kindly interested, inquired while feeding balls from just over the net for me to volley.

"Brian," I was more formal now – like requesting a visit with the bank manager after losing your largest client.

"He'd like to play for Town." Short and sweet, it was out there.

Brian was completely thrown off. A reliable volleyer on account of all the doubles we play at Chesterfield Lawn Tennis Club (lawn had been long topped with asphalt), he clubbed the volley off the frame of his racket.

I darted forward, stretching to reach Brian's only mishit of the morning so far. The ball spun sideways, a googly in cricket; I was flummoxed by the pitch and caught my running shoes on each other. Like a fencer's lunge, I had flicked the ball back over the net, barely. My momentum and New Balance collision, no irony there, threw me to the ground. I tried to catch myself with my racket, like an icepick hitting the mountain. Not gonna happen. I rolled to my side and the butt of the racket shot back into my mouth! God, there was a lot of blood.

I could feel Noel Harrison's 'windmills' singing in my mind.

A temporary jolt, and I could feel the tooth like a fresh square of Beech Nut chewing gum under my tongue. Dear God, I had actually knocked my tooth out! Brian side-jumped the net.

"Did you catch it? The tooth, that is?"

"Yes." I gurgled through blood and spit. Instinctively (like this happened to me all the time) I worked the tooth to the front of my mouth. Brian had his hand stretched out, and I dropped it into his sweaty palm.

"Let's get you to my office right away. I'll drive you."

I was dizzy and Noel Harrison's 'snowballs' and 'spinning apple' lyrics strangely led me down a tunnel. Too much of my own blood, apparently, a fragmentary concussion. Once I was able to sit up, I caught up with my mind. Brian had my tooth wrapped in a Kleenex. We grabbed our equipment and got into his F-type Jag.

"The boot's barely big enough for your racket bag." What a rubbish comment. "But it sure is finished magnificently," I added, trying to recover myself.

"Put this in the cavity." He handed me more Kleenex. I'm sure he didn't want me bleeding all over the upholstery. Then the cat growled off down the gravel of The club parking lot. "So, Roy wanted to play for Town, eh?"

"Not just wanted—wants to play for Town."

"Bit old now, eh?"

"He still played five a-side up until recently. He's still got moves!"

"So, you're actually saying he wants to play for Town now? This season?"

"Yes, now; it's top of his bucket list. In fact, when it went to press, the only thing on his list was to play for Town." We were in very close quarters in the cockpit of his F-Type. Cocooned like this you can almost hear a man's thought processes, so it didn't matter that I was chatting through a wad of Kleenex; he got my drift.

"Hmm." A desperate sigh came from Brian. He swayed his head from shoulder to shoulder as if weighing his options; it was weirdly theatrical.

You should never interrupt someone's deliberations when you have asked them for a big answer to your problem.

"Yes, he'd like to play for Town now. It wouldn't have to be long, it could be the last 30 seconds of a game." So of course, like an idiot, I hadn't waited; I had tried to further my request.

"It's interesting, Adam; I mean, as you know, I think a lot of Roy, and God knows I feel like I owe him one. It's just we have got so much going on at The club at the minute I can't see putting this on the agenda."

"I know I'm asking you to be Mister Fixer!"

"It would be interesting PR if we did address it."

"Now you're thinking, Bri." Did I really just do it again? I clearly wasn't.

"Unintended consequences; what would the unintended consequences be?"

Brian was taking the idea deeper – this was a good sign. But then we were at his clinic, pulling into his reserved spot – "Dr. Brian Banner Reserved" – "Got your tooth?"

"Yes, I've got all of them!" We slipped out of the Jag. My backside was practically on the pavement, the seat was so low to the ground. I was thinking of a yoga class to help me with the flexibility to get in and out of a sports car. Or I'd just keep driving my Toyota RAV!

I followed him into the clinic. No one was here today – late start, late finish.

"Hand me the tooth, Adam." I unfurled my hand and duly did as he asked. The dentist's chair set me in the reclined position – Brian pulled on his gloves and slid the light over to illuminate my face. And the Oscar goes to…

Brian donned a mask and safety goggles, fired up the spit vacuum, and went to work resetting the tooth.

"It's a long shot."

"I know, but Dad really has only one wish."

"No, I meant your tooth. We'll take a look at her next week when we do the fillings, but I have a feeling we may need to give you an implant. As for Roy playing for Town, I'll try to bring it up to the Board. The problem is, as I think about it – if we do it for Roy, we'd be inundated with requests from all over. I don't want Town to become a gimmick."

The chair was shuddering to the upright position; there was no pink bib this time, given the rush. Brian sat back on his stool removing his goggles, his gloves, and my hope as gently as he could.

"Did I happen to mention Dad has stage-four lung cancer?" I'm so crass; Dad surely would not have wanted me to tell anyone yet. But it's out, like the bomb from *Enola Gay*'s fuselage; no way to drag it back.

"I'll see what I can do, Adam." Brian's sigh was too much for me to hear. I had put him in a terrible place and Dad was going to kill me when he found out. And parents always do find out, don't they?

CHAPTER 7

There was a quiet knock at the door, the way the milkman used to knock when he needed his bill settled. Dad was in the kitchen, sportily dressed as usual, ready to break out into a jog around the neighborhood at any given moment—a fleeting moment like settling snow in Phoenix. He even wore his no-name, no-comfort, brand of tennis shoes. They cost less than a fiver on the market not far from Roy Cloth's stall. The sneakers, or "trainers" as me dad would call them, were a "great bargain." He and his brother Brock, since they took their first jobs, always played the game of who could find and wear the least-expensive shoes. They had to be new, of course, and as time went on they could be for "best" or for just "dossing around" in. Growing up, they had each had only one pair of shoes, so a second pair, or trainers, was considered gratuitous; so, the boys lived the game of one-upmanship where the second pair was concerned. Whoever could find the cheapest, finest-looking shoes had to buy the first round of drinks. This game was now in its fourth decade. Brock was the current champion with a pair of black "slip-ons" for three quid 99p from Timpsons' going out of business sale. Brock also had the advantage of being slightly taller, with larger feet; this meant his size 11 and a half were apt to be on sale more than Roy's standard size 9. Or at least for Brock there was typically more choice in the sale.

The gentle knock tapped again at the blurred-out glass of the side door.

Dad had been sitting at the kitchen table, a small square table, as much as could fit in an "eat-in-kitchen" in this cookie-cutter street. The kitchen looked north up the hill of the Close, a halfway decent vantage point if you wanted to keep tabs on the comings and goings of your neighbors. This morning the sunlight shone through the side door, giving it an extra warmth. Dad's hands cupped his 'greatest dad' mug like he was back in the RAF around the campfire, fingers huddled around the porcelain for warmth and to savor the taste.

The milk float hadn't gone by yet and he didn't see anyone walk by the garage to the side door so he was a little less enthused to open it fearing it might be local yobbos. Fear of confrontation, of being mugged, and many things had manifested in him as he got older. Even now with his bionic hip, he was not going to be able to outrun his assailant. In his ageing, the choice of fight or flight had been reduced to the former. He thought about owning a gun. So, he bought a pellet rifle, as a shotgun was just too intimidating.

The venetian blinds afforded a sniper's lookout—easy to see oncoming prey whilst sitting freely unobserved. The frosty white venetian blinds were an upgrade from the roller blinds we had when I was younger. They were bright orange with large flowery imprints on them in colors that were not always complementary. Mum had decided years back that venetians were the way to go and Dad had agreed to go with the frosty white ones, as they go with every décor. I remember the epic battle of Mum trying to get Dad to spend money on anything! The fact that frosty white went with everything is hilarious because I could only imagine the epic discussions they would have had to have had to approve the orange, ochre, and brown flowered roller-blind.

The slanty-eyed sun peaked over and glistened off the blind. The slats had glistened less as kitchen life had taken off some of its luster. But on this rare occasion in February the morning sun rose up through the blinds. Brilliant lasers of white light shone in off the reflection from the windscreens of the cars parked out front. Bluish skies with fading stripes of pinkish clouds filled the top half of the blind; he was glad that his son's rummaging around for jogging bottoms had woken him up. These were days worth living for; late-winter days that you would bottle up if you could so that this was all you would see. Eliminated would be those great British drizzle days, greyed with fog, mist and "eight eighths cloud cover." Must be an air-traffic control term, we kids thought, never really bothering to find out.

Routinely, after waking, he would make his bed military style. There was no coin could bounce on these old mattresses and duvets, but there was a pride given to the straightened bed with a defined crease where the pillows lay underneath. He had grumbled at being woken, but the sunshine bursts fired him up to test the newly released hip, and he was even mildly thankful. He woke easily to strange noises in the house these days, and his son's visits were a constant joy and nightly upheaval as he came in at all hours from visiting friends and siblings.

He spun his bum around on the stool, pretending that it was a swivel chair, and headed to the shadow behind the glass-side door. A pink and purple Monet painting awaited him; how much harm could someone dressed like that be? He left the latch chain on just in case and peaked through the two-inch gap.

"Roy it's, it's me Joan!" declared the surprisingly sportily dressed Joan.

"I didn't see you come down the drive?"

"I've been for a walk – I came up the back way – can I come in?"

"Of course."

"Got the latch on, I see; can't be too careful these days."

"That's right, even in your pink and purple action wear you could be ready to pounce on an unsuspecting homeowner." He felt a little foolish, but safe, and wouldn't change his habit. "Joan, are you safe walking about this hour of the day?"

"Yes, fine, we stay on the paths. I was walking with Margaret from over the road. We are armed and dangerous! We are the Thelma and Louise of the Close! Look, I have my paring knife wrapped in tissue and pepper spray in me other pocket."

"Impressive, Joan." Then there was a pause, off syntax, or out of rhythm you might say.

"You should see Margaret's knife. It's her dad's bowie knife from when he fought in Burma; leather case and all! Cut your head off in one Federer-like backhand!"

"Jeez, that's crazy! How does she hide it?"

"She doesn't! That's the best part! She hangs the sheath at the side of her water bottle. She took knife throwing lessons and all!"

"You're kidding, right?"

"No, at the senior center in town they were offering self-defense lessons!'

"Seriously?"

"No, not really, but at the senior center one of the biddies told Margaret of this farm outside Darley Dale where an old circus performer used to throw knives for a living!" Another pause, as Joan's mind caught up. "She got home and looked him up on the internet—actually it was her! And she was accurate to within five-eighths!"

"No way! I grew up in those parts – don't remember any knife-wielding circus performers!"

"Well, this woman traveled a lot – the farm was her folks'. They died and she came home – never did bury the hatchet! Couldn't resist. But I guess she joined the circus after teenage troubles. Knife-throwing can be learned, unlike being funny!"

"You are hilarious."

"Thank you, thank you very much I'll be here all day, remember to tip your waitress!" Joan's adrenaline was kicking like a returning comedian on the Johnny Carson show. "Now buy this girl a drink would ya?" she said, suddenly affecting an American accent. "What does a girl have to do around here to not die of thirst?"

"Tea or coffee?" was Dad's simple offering.

"Nothing a little stronger?"

"It's not 8 o'clock, Joan!" Dad was pleasantly shocked for a man much closer to midnight than 8 whose life was being lived in minutes, not days, months, or years. This seemed like a good way to enjoy some of his precious minutes.

"I know, but time of day matters less to me now; it's about time, full stop. Doesn't matter morning, day, or night; it's all just a cluster of hours and minutes! And I feel like a bloody Mary!" she was beaming like it was 7:15 p.m. on date night! She had a glow of the morning, the dew still on her cheeky cheeks.

"Since you put it like that – give me a second! Want ice and lemon, madame?" Roy affected the voice of a continental waiter.

"Of course! I might be drinking at 8 in the morning, but I'm still a lady!"

"I don't recognize this Joan! But I think I like her." He was tending bar at the sideboard in the dining room, which was just the other end of the room from the lounge! Roy was beaming back at her. He brought the vodka tomato juice drink back.

"Excuse me, madame; I need to reach into the cabinet to make things a little spicy," he said, winking as he slid behind her.

"Mr. Griffiths, whatever has come over you?" whispered Joan over her shoulder.

"Paprika and Worcester sauce!"

"Oh, I like a bit of sauce!" she flirted back.

"No, genuinely, I'm covered in Worcestershire – the bloody cap wasn't put back properly! Coming through again!" She slid in again, only a little less this time, brushing his hip as he edged by to the sink and then to the fridge. The little freezer section had enough cubes for one drink. "I'll slice up a lemon in one sec."

"You can borrow my knife if you like!" She full-face smirked, looked him up and down. He wasn't long out of bed, more crumpled next to sporty Joan, baseball hat with a big C on it of the Chicago Cubs, and his traditional denim shirt with chest pockets for his smokes.

Roy presented the breakfast cocktail. "Here you go, me lady, compliments of the house!"

"All the breakfast I need! Packed with vitamins and enough alcohol to keep me from clotting! You not joining me?"

"What? And let the lady drink alone! Not a chance – I'm out of ice, so I'm gonna throw some of Ad's pulp-free orange juice over this here vodka!" He pulled the highball from behind his back. "He's always saying I need to drink more juice! Kids, always telling you what to do, eh?"

"Like it's gonna make a difference at our age, eh Roy?" They clinked their breakfast juices.

"To long life and bigger cocktails!"' They clinked again. "Have a seat," he said, pointing with his highball tumbler.

"Let's get comfy in the lounge, shall we? Got any crisps, Roy?"

"What? Do you think this is the Highfield or something?"

"Just asking!"

"I can do better than just crisps! I can whip up some eggs and bacon, if you like. I'm not a half bad cook, if I do blow my own trumpet!'

"That stuff will kill you!"

"What, blowing a trumpet?" With no pause, he went on. "I'll drink to that," he said, and again glasses were clinking and raised to their lips. Joan sat opposite him – she chose the oversized leather chair. Not really worn in, it was still a little stiff, so she slid around in its shell like an uncooked yolk. She grabbed a pillow as if she were exiting a plane after a water landing. She pulled the pillow to her chest, holding her cocktail with her other hand, resting it on her knee as she sat in a yoga pose. Dad sat on the end of the couch, similarly oversized, too oversized for the room, really. Pillows of various plum colors floated on its shiny surface. He leaned on the armrest for stability, anchoring himself with his left elbow; his sleeves rolled up, his forearm skin stuck and rubbed on the newish couch.

"Yummy—this is very good, Roy! You should give up your day job! I hate to drink alone; and when Eric was alive, I didn't like to drink at all. He never touched the stuff, except a sherry at Christmas. He never was a drinker like a lot of the other boys I dated. He was ambitious and driven, and drinking just wasn't part of his makeup." Joan cupped the cocktail glass like a chalice with both hands, reminiscing, holding out a certain reverence for her husband. "I liked drinking as a child, mostly because my parents were Methodists, you know?" Still sitting in her yoga position, hands cupped around the Bloody Mary Chalice, she could have passed for alcohol's new effigy, poised and balanced. Roy sat awkwardly on the end of the couch, the new hip still a little tight. Joan had arrived before he'd had time to stretch; luckily he had been able to go to the bathroom! It was that need that woke him most days.

"I never saw you as this rebel!" He said, thinking of himself in this former light.

"Eric never asked me not to drink; I just sort of grew out of it. Now, I grew back into it!" The coquettish grin, super-confident Joan, shuffled her pert bum deeper into the couch. "Cheers, me dear!"

"It never left me! I never grew out of it, so I'll cheers to that! I forgot celery. I should get you some to stir it with."

"You don't have to bother, Roy; it's fine the way it is--besides, I'm almost finished."

"You sure? It's no bother." He really needed to get up and stretch – the older and newer hip were starting to lock up. "I'll get it anyway." He tootled off to the kitchen, ran the cold tap, rinsed the stalk, sliced off the white fatter end and presented it to Joan on a napkin.

"Roy! you shouldn't have." She took the stalk and dipped it in the red sauce, swirling it so very gently, slowly, then slower still. She looked deeper into her glass with each swirl; the Worcester Sauce like a gyroscope disappearing beneath the bloody-red, pepper and paprika following not far behind like last jumpers from the *Titanic*. Joan's eyes followed the pepper spots around the glass, until the last one was gone. "Delicious! This is a good one, Roy; you have quite the talent!"

"Had a good mentor as a kid, working as the glass collector. Jan showed me a few cocktails, told me this would come in handy one day – she was right, eventually!"

"I'm suddenly starving – that offer of breakfast still on?"

"It's gonna be a fry-up! No muesli and grapefruit in this house!"

"I'm sure I can skip one time!" And she winked her same right eye.

"I'll say," Roy said, sounding like a teenager. "You look great, Joan; this working out and walking, you look well-toned." And she did; as she sat there, there was barely a tummy bulge. *Who can sit and have no tummy bulge?* he thought. Was she breathing in for the last ten minutes?

"Yoga teaches good posture, like your mother used to!" and she raised her glass to deceased mothers across the world.

"One great British fry-up coming your way!" He was thrilled to be able to do something for her, for anyone actually. Living alone you never got to do anything for anyone else. The simple joy of making a sandwich or a cup of tea for someone goes away. And few things are nicer than having a sandwich or cup of tea made and brought to you. Knowing that it's the simple gifts we receive that count the most, when you have no one to give them to, a part of you, a part of your goodness goes along with it. "Stay right there, the chef is in the house!"

"Not likely. I want to see this maestro in action!" She graciously unfolded her origami self from the chair, sliding effortlessly to a standing position, like royalty, smooth. Roy marveled as he crookedly, like an arthritic scarecrow, pushed up from his end of the couch.

"Few things trump the smell of bacon in the morning, eh Joan?" A single pan was all he needed. He laid out the packages in order: bacon, onion (if needed) black pudding, white pudding (nectar of the gods, Irish Ambrosia) mushrooms (the button kind), eggs, and Granary Bread. Roy fired up the front burner to "high," popped in a knob of butter and laid the bacon into its sizzle. He placed his screwdriver by the stove, added more bacon, rinsed the mushrooms through his hands; he rolled them like dice back and forth to make sure he washed all sides. The water on them fizzed when they hit the foaming butter. "A couple of rashers do you, Joan?" Roy asked.

"Whatever you cook, Roy, I will eat! I have had my exercise for the day."

"Not everyone is a fan of the black pudding – I'll put some in, but don't feel obliged to eat it!"

"Love it, Roy – just keep doing your thing. Nothing more sexy than a man who cooks!" He hadn't been referred to as sexy in a couple of decades – okay, so his name was mentioned with "sexy" in the same sentence – close enough. He wasn't feeling sexy because the minutes, days, months, and years added up to a long time of not feeling sexy.

She leaned in closer to smell the heaven Roy was cooking up. To her surprise, there was artwork in the pan. A breakfast smiley face was grinning at her, the way he used to lay it out for the kids—Roy had laid the rashers out as a big smile at the bottom of the pan, the top was graced with the button mushrooms like a fresh perm hair style, the black pudding hung like earrings, and then Roy cracked in the eggs for eyes. Lastly, he set a button mushroom for a button nose.

"Quite the Picasso, aren't you?"

"Well, I did captain the art team at the county trials!" he smirked. "I just hope you are hungry."

"Don't worry about that – I'll eat and do hot yoga if I have to!"

"Hot yoga? Whatever next?"

"Hot sexy yoga!"

"Alrighty then," he said, not knowing what to do with that statement. "This won't be much longer; be a love and grab a couple of plates from the cabinet behind you." He wasn't really comfortable giving direction, but with the square kitchen table taking up most of the space and Joan the rest of it, he needed her assistance.

"Fork, Roy?" she whispered with innuendo.

"Sorry?" he grinned.

"Aren't you the sauce pot? Looking good."

"And nearly ready. The HP sauce is in the fridge!"

"How posh of you. Most of us just leave it in the pantry."

"It's my son and his American ways. I was at breakfast weeks back and couldn't find it and I learned that's where he hid it. Or rather, where it belonged!" Laughing Roy caught the snort before she heard it.

"Want a dollop, Roy?" Joan patted the bottom of the bottle, encouraging it onto her plate in readiness. Both plates had a brown spot of sauce, no ketchup.

"Alright, Joan pass me your plate." In handing her plate, she made sure to touch his hand. His hand was warm, she noticed. Roy placed one of everything on her plate, excepting the mushrooms; he gave her four, his lucky number and exactly half of the pan's contents.

"Looks smashing, Roy; mind if we eat in the lounge?"

"Go right ahead. Serviettes are on the dining table—and grab me one, would you?" They sat in front of the telly like naughty children. Joan returned to her yoga position with her plate on her lap; he had a smaller table that slid up and over the armrest of the couch like you would find in a hospital. It would be months before he could assume that yoga position, and it was initially frowned upon as it exposed the hip.

Holly Willoughby and Phillip Schofield were chatting brightly on the BBC studio sofa.

"Sex after sixty is today's topic," Phillip announced to Roy's living room.

"Well this ought to be good," said Joan and Holly simultaneously.

Roy's blush could have overcooked his bacon, if you know what I mean!

"We have our resident sex-pert Katie joining us on the couch in a moment," said Phillip.

"Well, I sure hope I'm getting it at sixty!" beamed Holly. "Life without it would be terribly sad!"

"Katie will be here to talk about it right after the weather – which is brought to you by Carol Kirkwood."

"Thank you, Phillip, well a bright breezy day ahead for most of Britain. Scotland will be dry until late as a cold front slips down from the North Sea. Wales and England will see mostly clear skies and a warming trend as the Mediterranean sends a blast of warm air our way. This will lead to storms later in the week, but for now a warmer pleasant way to start the day for most of our viewers." Carol might have been describing Roy's lounge.

Katie the Sexpert breezed on to the set in a carefree way and sat cross-legged like a much younger Joan.

"Research shows that granny and granddad are having more and more sex these days!" blurted the bubbly Katie.

"So, why do you think that is?" bounced Holly, very much intrigued. Roy and Joan were silent, wondering the same thing, thinking that neither of them had been interviewed.

"Kids are gone, empty nesters, more time for each other, more time for exotic vacations, seems to be the main reasons."

"This is at the same time as divorce amongst this age group has doubled over the last ten years?" cooled Phillip.

"Shut up, Phillip, you big downer," interjected Joan through her breakfast, belying her usual poise. "Let Katie speak." Egg started to dribble from the corner of Joan's mouth – never in a million years did Roy envision Joan Millward dribbling runny yolk, sitting on his chair, yelling at his telly – it was a surreal day. Why had she just appeared at his door? He couldn't have been more delighted, but he could never have pictured himself just out for a jog and then casually or deliberately, stopping by any neighbor's house, let alone Joan's.

"It seems," Katie went on "it seems that a lot of couples make an effort to rekindle the old flame. It's challenging at first because for many that side of them has taken a back seat to work and career, raising the kids and their kids' activities.

There was less time and spontaneity just became a when-never."

"Seems that people should always focus on a date night to maintain that connection, no?" Phillip was drawing on Katie's previous episodes and blogs.

"That's right – our bodies can enjoy sex until we die!"

"Well, that's reassuring!" and Holly took another seductive sip from her bowl-like coffee mug.

"Intimacy can go off the boil without constantly reheating. But even those who have put the best of them to the back of the cabinet can enjoy getting to know one another again. We may not look the same or feel the same to each other, but the hormones of simple physical touch, small daily touches can grow into a loving connection.

"Joan, you have a little egg on your chin," said Roy, rising to get it for her. If Joan were four, she would get it herself, but Roy's chivalry put her independence on a back burner. She raised her chin and gazed at him as he stood above her.

"Right about here." He gently caressed her chin. Why he leaned in to kiss her, he couldn't think. Like a close-up in a daytime soap. He gently, with forefinger and thumb, held her chin, kissed her so carefully. Then he was struck with a jolt of static electricity, and they both startled back from each other.

"That's real electricity!" laughed Joan, who then reached up to pull him back closer to her. She caught him by both wrists, manacling him to her. Roy looked down to see her grip on him. These were paraffin soft, manicured hands, delightfully trimmed with French polish. Hands reveal our age, he knew, so there was no denying they were peers. But like in all things Joan, her fingernails were beautifully presented. She hadn't rolled out of bed as he had; her LuLulemon outfit had been carefully chosen the night before. Her nails and hair were coiffed weekly. Her caress slid from his wrists to his hands; she took the napkin, placing it next to her. Her fingers slipped into his palms, and he was aroused by their subtle scratching – with the dexterity of a Vietnam helicopter pilot, she maneuvered him closer. She pulled him in with both hands. She could feel his warmth of no resistance. She softened her look to him as he did to her.

"Joan," he said softly, but she put one finger to his lips. This was no time for talking. At that moment, he could have been back in year five when Christine Davis had cornered him by the drainpipe of the school hall for his first kiss.

"Climb up the pipe, Roy, until we are the same height," Christine had asked. And he had done so – he was used to being teased for his absence of height.

"Now what?" whispered Joan, echoing Roy's schoolyard sentiment.

And just as Christine had done decades ago, she pressed her forefinger to his lips, not wanting a word, and hovering slightly, her lips touched his. Butterfly kisses.

"It starts with small touching," Katie went on, "perhaps over dinner, lunch, even breakfast. You have to begin to sit near each other again; you have to recover the comfort of being in each other's space,"

Roy looked softly back at Joan's eyes. She had a steady hand for her makeup still.

"Sit next to each other in restaurants, not opposite; cuddle in," Katie explained.

"Shall we cuddle in, Roy?" came the echo from Joan to the "Telly Katie."

"I think that would be a good start, don't you?" he agreed softly.

"It doesn't always have to lead to intercourse at first," Katie insisted.

"I think we should stop listening to her about now, Roy, don't you?" Roy pulled her easily to her feet, like at a dance in the village hall he had picked his partner, except this time he had been the chosen one.

"And of course, don't forget protection!" Katie gesticulated. Holly and Phil both splurted their coffee back into their BBC mugs.

"I don't think we'll be needing to worry about that Roy!" She now stood toe to toe with him. Like Christine Davis, Joan was taller. She looked slightly down towards Roy and leaned down to connect with him again. Receptive, Roy relaxed; his usual slightly military stoic-self let him be taken by the moments, the moments in Joan's "hours." She was right, of course; only 178 hours in a week, but weeks no longer mattered. Weeks matter as a way to measure time to the weekend. Every day was a weekend now. Every hour was a weekend. At fifty the egg-timer had been flipped over in his life. That flipping was over a decade ago, many hours ago.

"I bet you have a clear view of the village from your bedroom window, Roy?" She wrangled his attention back. She was right; his home was at the bottom of the close but only halfway down the hill. You could see clear across to the Matlock Road a place he had traversed forty-one years ago. He could still see the road back.

"The village and beyond," he added.

"Come with me, Buzz Lightyear." Joan led him to his own stairs, his gym; had this been what he was training for?

Invitingly, she let him go by. Like children skipping through the field, he took her hand and led her upstairs effortlessly.

"You haven't lost your speed there Roy," she quipped. He nodded.

His bedroom with brightly lit with the unobstructed sunlight. The morning brilliance gave a healthy glow to them, as if they were backlit lovers on *General Hospital.*

He was glad he had made his bed and that the sheets were only one night old.

"Lovely," she said as Joan moved to the window. She threw the curtains back even further past the window frame. The room lit up like a magnesium experiment.

"You can see the Matlock road from there, Joan."

"I want the road to be able to see in here, Roy." She pushed the curtains tight, as far as they could go. Closing her eyes, she breathed the deep sunshine in, like a pagan goddess on an altar. "Do you mind if I open the small window? I do love the morning air rimmed with dew. Come here, Roy; stand with me." He looked out of his window as if he had never seen the view before. Fixed like Hallmark lovers, they stared over the village rooftops, passed the rising fields of Holymoorside farmers, beyond where the mist settles, to the infinity of earth's horizon. The window's magnified warmth rose above the settling zephyr of God's winter breath sliding down from the transom window.

"I feel a bit of a chill, Roy; shall we climb under the covers?"

"I think we'd better." His whisper was barely audible.

They each removed the other's top. But before Roy could go any further, Joan slipped away and under the duvet, pulling it to her nose.

"Come quick now, Roy; it's chilly,"

He couldn't stand the irony. He went around the bed, saw his watch on the nightstand—so that's where he had left it.

"Slide up close to me Roy." She rolled to face him. "Be a love and undo my bra; my shoulders are worn from too much squash."

"Why certainly, madame; glad to be of service!" He shuffled amongst the sheets to get close to her. They were nose to nose on the same pillow.

"Your hand's a little chilly there, Roy. How about I warm it up for you?" She cupped it and breathed warmth all over him. "That should do it, try now." The twin hooks of her snap parted easily. Roy was pleased to see they hadn't reinvented a new clasp. In turn, she rolled down his sweatpants and underwear together; obligingly he lifted his repaired hip to allow the garments to be removed easily. He was naked to her touch, except for his white crew socks.

"Now my turn, Roy." She took his hands to her Lululemon yoga pants. "I may have to give you a hand here; these are pretty snug these days." She laughed. He smiled with her. Was she really only wearing a thong?

"I know, I'm not officially a granny yet, so I'm going to keep wearing my thong." It was like she was reading his mind. The yoga pants and thong unraveled like a pre-baked crescent roll. She used her toes to help push them off her feet. She kept her tennis socks on. Once again she took his hand to warm it up. but the location was different this time. Her other hand went on safari to find his didgeridoo.

"Now Roy, promise me you won't take hours about this, okay?"

He was off the hook.

"I'm not a young girl anymore and I'm not wanting any Olympic champion for a lover. I just want you to be gentle." They both softened into the pillow. "have you taken your Viagra?" and she giggled. "Oh, I can feel that you have!" Their bodies were in each other's imagination of touch. Both were beyond bikini and speedo photo ops. Their hands explored with appreciation; their kisses with gentleness kept them warm. Their breathing was synchronized as they lay patiently side by side.

"I'm ready, Roy. You can come on top of me now," and duly he slid aboard her tiny frame. Not long after—the hour hand hadn't moved on his watch—they were cuddling again. The sun had moved only slightly and filled the room with its southerly exposure.

"Got any cigarettes?" she said stereotypically.

"Not since the heart attack!"

Joan giggled, not knowing where the truth lay in that statement. Supine they both lay there' staring at the ceiling. It still needed painting, as his wife had remarked many years earlier; he was still getting to it. Joan leaned into him.

"So, this in here," she stroked her fingers across his chest, the French polish tips like tiny snow ploughs pushing the hair above his nipples to one side. "This in here had a panic attack? This in here fell out of love with itself? So hard to believe," and she twisted his left nipple. He winced like it was caught in his ice tongs. "Naughty heart, very naughty heart." She smiled across to him. He looked down at her left hand as it cracked the whip of pleasure and pain across his chest. Aback from the white tips of polish he could see her ring finger; there was an indentation where the modest diamond ring had once lived. Joan had removed her ring symbolically and found a chain to hang it upon. She wanted the world of suitors to know she was available, and by wearing it as a necklace, suitors would know that this hadn't always been the case. Roy thought of Eric; his marriage to Joan had left quite an impression on her ring finger. Like the bone inside the skin was weathered away. The sculpting was much less obvious on his own hand, he thought. In large part because of work safety and sports, plus the occasional grudge removal. So many times as a husband he removed the band, only wanting to be friends.

Joan's hand revealed her true age that her face denied. Openly she bragged about having "a little work done" and as close as Roy was now, he couldn't tell.

"Let me know when you are ready to go again, Roy; my hips are all relaxed now." She brushed her hand up through his chest around his carotid artery turning him by his cheek to face her more closely. She leaned into kiss him and started to work her way towards his midriff.

"I think you won't have to wait long,"

"Good," she replied and disappeared beneath the covers. He was beginning to feel light-headed, the way he felt when his blood-pressure medication kicks in. The moment of slight dizziness before you fall asleep as your brain winds out of itself.

It had been a terrible morning. My mouth was still throbbing and I had decided to walk back from Dr. Brian's clinic. I thought the walk would clear my head of the disappointment in my tennis game and the news from Brian not to expect too much from the Board. It was a few miles or so from Brian's to Dad's and the speed of my walk had kept me warm but also exacerbated the pain in my mouth. As I reached Dad's house with its perfectly manicured bushes and matching lawn I wondered how I was going to deliver the news to Dad.

That's weird, I thought, *the side door is ajar. Oh well; at least I don't have to wake Dad up, since I left home earlier without my house key.*

"Dad, you home?" I called out, but not too loud, as sometimes Dad would wake too early and I would find him napping again after breakfast. And I could see he'd eaten—the wrappers and cartons were still everywhere. The gas burner was on low, I turned it off. *Shit, he would never do this,* I thought, so I called a little louder. Still no answer, nothing. I could hear Phillip Schofield and presumably Holly Willoughby rabbiting away on the telly, but there was no sign of Dad. I went to the foot of the stairs and in my speaking voice called up. No answer;

of course I'm thinking the worst, like a parent worries over their child, for life. Crap, there's an intruder? Or worse? But just in case, I ran the eight or nine strides grabbed the nearest kitchen utensil as a weapon. The pain in my mouth was at an 8 and so was the worry for Dad. Back at the foot of the stairs I could still hear nothing out of the norm. You read a lot these days in the papers how pensioners are mugged or even attacked in their homes. Was Dad being held against his wishes—or worse? This wasn't normal – since the heart attack we siblings had been on fire station readiness for anything untoward.

"Damn these stairs are steep," like the walkway to a Cathedral Spire. Halfway up, after avoiding the "squeaky stair," I could see the bathroom door open. The light was on—strange. A vacant toilet, where Dad would have been, came into full view. Relieved, I could see it wasn't an Elvis moment, but worse, now Dad could be in real danger. The pain in my mouth became pain in my chest. Crap, this was bad. I hurtled into his room with the egg-whisk held high, ready to drive it into Dad's assailant. The cold draft of Matlock air knocked me back first. Then Dad was just lying there in bed, duvet cover up to his chin, like a Muppet looking over a wall. I panicked, thinking the worst, like that split-second moment where you lose sight of your child in the supermarket. So I blurted out:

"Dad, Dad—you okay?" His eyes were in the back of his head; the room was icy cold. I repeated myself and a whole mess of blankets and covers piled up like a gopher mound out of nowhere.

"Bugger!" came a female voice from somewhere.

Startled back from his personal oblivion, Dad recovered. "Ad get out, sorry, get out, everything is fine!" he said, irritated. "What's that in your hand?" he said, shocked by the sight of my aggressive pose.

"It's an egg whisk. I thought you were being attacked!" And truth be told, he was being.

"Well, what were you gonna do with that? 'Beat' them to death? Get it?" Looking even more closely at his deranged son, he said: "What happened to your tooth?' The impatient duvet rustled some more. This must be the origin of the female voice.

"Everything is fine. I'll explain later," I said backing out of the room, stepping on my previous footsteps, egg whisk now in non-combat position.

The last thing I expected was this, and if I hadn't been on fire station alert, I would have checked more closely. I slid down the stairs, using the handrails like a gymnast to propel me faster to the ground. I ran into the back yard for air and stared out at the Matlock Road, head between my knees, realizing I had just crashed my Dad's romantic tête-à-tête, feeling sicker than when I had crashed his car! I could hear voices emanating from the small open window behind me; a woman giggled, then Dad giggled. There were teenage children in there, it sounded like!

I went back in the house. Phillip and Holly were still prattling on about something and had I not been terrified that Dad had had a second heart attack or worse, I would have noticed a second breakfast plate smeared with egg yolk at the side of the oversized couch next to a pair of pink Nike trainers too small for Dad, even if he did like the color! I returned the *Psycho* whisk to its cradle, thinking to myself, *Crap – could the day get worse?* I heard more mumblings, giggles and head-boards moving against drywall plaster from upstairs. *I suppose it could!* I lamented. I should have left but I had walked miles, scaled the stairs, and really needed a cup of tea. I'd make a pot; maybe they were thirsty too. "What the… vodka first thing?" I said to Phillip and Holly – that way it was not a clinical condition and I was technically talking to someone else! Who were these people upstairs? The knocking above continued to echo down this "half- a-house," as Dad called it. I filled the Russell Hobbs express kettle that boiled water like a paramedic on constant standby. Always ready to provide relief in an emergency. A cuppa always makes things better. It's our great British therapy, life's panacea.

"Come on..." I whispered frustratingly to myself and not to Phillip and Holly this time, "you have to be kidding me! We are out of tea bags!" Only Russell the kettle could hear me. I toe-poked the floor cabinets out of frustration. A voice came from above – not that voice – my dad, with similar God-like qualities when I was younger:

"Ad, we are out of tea; if you still have your shoes on, could you go down to Spar and pick some up?" Dad yelled down. He must have heard me kick the cabinet, I realized.

Turning to Joan, Dad said, "That should give us about forty minutes."

"But Roy, it's only ten minutes away?" Joan answered, having walked that way earlier.

"Yes – but it doesn't open for another half hour!" And they grinned massively as they slid back under the sheets hearing the side-door closing downstairs.

Remembering Joan's earlier request:

"I'm ready if you are, Joan?" Dad said, winking at her like a schoolboy.

CHAPTER 8

The sign read "Closed." I toe-poked the Spar door and spun around. *Come on!* I yelled in my throbbing head; it had moved back from its temporary station in my chest, thankfully. Funny how a pain like toothache is magnified a hundred times because it's in your head! I wondered, *Is it really that painful? Or is it just in your head? If it's in your ankle you just walk it off, but in your head it's harder to ignore and really hard to walk off!* No wonder Granny always recommended getting the tooth drunk on whiskey. It was noon somewhere, right? The Spar idea was a good one. I needed ibuprofen anyway, and it was probably bad form to be reeking of Walkers Red Label at this early hour. Since I hadn't taken my coat off, I was thrilled for a reason to leave the house. The rhythmic pounding upstairs was starting to make me jealous, and I had no desire to turn the volume up on Holly and Phillip to drown them out. A trip to Spar was a much saner alternative.

"Shit, by the time I walk home, it will be time to walk back again, and then I would have wasted a trip," I said to myself and the animated brussels sprouts on the window advertisement; I being the only person within earshot. The Spar was part of an early '70s town planning strip mall – a conglomeration of essential businesses. The grocery store, which was next door, competed with the mini-supermarket. A laundromat was open 7 to 7, conveniently, with dispensers for powder and fabric softener. The two oversized ladies who ran it would do your wash for you or you could do it yourself—sit and watch your smalls go for a spin! For me it was awkward, to sit there watching and waiting while they worked around you. I felt like I was taking food off their table, but presumably it was okay to not have them do it. It seemed normal to have them starve rather than handle my soiled underwear? An off-license like a therapist's chair beckoned; opened even later than the Spar but stayed open until thirty minutes after the pubs closed to catch the depressed punters who thought they needed a nightcap and realized they had drunk their drinks cabinet dry the night before—or imbibe just one more so there was no chance to remember why they had started drinking in the first place. The off-license was a non-judgmental safe zone, a necessary back-up. It was the extra bullet in the firing squad's rifle.

I stood under the overhang as the dew of the mist continued to rise out of the ground, warmed by the sleepy sunshine. I stared into the off-license like a child in front of Hamleys. "I could murder a bag of cheese and onion right about now," I whispered to my coat. It's hard to find crisps like those in the USA, and when you do, they can be mighty expensive. The over-hang protected from the rain and snow when it didn't rain. Today, however, the weather seemed to have its own microcosm by the shops, there was a heavy mist unable to escape. I was wearing the weather like shaving foam, the brilliant sunshine caused the great cook-off of mist from the sopping ground around. The strip of shops was originally fronted by designed green space – sloping lawns like welcome mats when you looked at the blueprints. Today, forty-seven years on the green of the blueprints was etched in brown puddles filled with debris of crushed cans, cigarette butts, unrecognizable wrappers and used wooden forks from the chip shop. The "lawns" with paths around had been worn down by shortcuts taken from the local estate that looked like alien landings in the New Mexico desert. Paths carved directly to the Spar on one end and the chip shop on the other. These were the anchors of the shopping. Mrs. Wong ran the chip shop – she had taken over from Trevor and June years back. Mrs. Wong's daughter was in Julia's class – Amanda, yes that was her name. Amanda was really bright, and a sunshine personality. Like almost top in her new school bright! A future academic prefect first-rounder.

Mrs. Wong and her husband had brought the family over from China to escape the 1970s purges. Mr. Wong rarely spoke, a diminutive man just worked the fryers. Mrs. Wong was the spokeswoman, on account of being able to speak English. The "chippy" wouldn't be open for hours—around lunch time, although I could go a portion of chips dripping in curry sauce about now. There wasn't a moment in the day when I couldn't go for that renowned delicacy. It wasn't anything you had heard of as a real young person, a whippersnapper growing up, but the Wongs and subsequent chip shop owners offered this delicacy on the menu. At first people freaked out, balked at the idea of curry sauce, not gravy or vinegar going on their traditional thumb-sized, chubby chips, in the same way that they backed off going to the chippy once they realized the new owners were Chinese and not English! Oh, the backlash in the pubs and school gateways:

"Can you ever believe it? Chinky Chinaman running t' chippy on t' green?"

"It's not rate, that. It's not British, it's not what we fought t' war for!"

"At least t' Germans only tried to bomb our chippies not tek 'em o'er completely!"

"What do the effing Chinese know about chips? Their food is all rice and bamboo shoots – they should go back to where they come from."

"Yerr, those are British jobs, not jobs for t' foreigners. I'm not gewing, that's for damned shuher! I'd rather walk t' moor for me chips an' gravy."

"It'll be cold by t' time you get back!"

"What, you a fucking Chinky lover, are yer?"

"Just saying you might want to drive." Things got ugly when you came between a man, his country, his chips, and his lack of transport.

The Wongs had moved into the flat above, so they benefited twice by taking the smell home on their clothes and living with the rising scent through their two-bedroom flat. I know the Wongs lived above the chippy, and we suspected that another family lived there too, or visited on a daily basis.

All the shops had a layer of apartments above them. "Multi-use," it was considered. You didn't have to own the business below, but if you were the owner of the chippy, it was as well you lived above it. The smell and the late nights could be draining. Mrs. Wong had done right – she and her husband changed nothing from the previous owners. No announcement of new ownership or anything like that. One day, Trevor and June were there; next Monday it was business as usual with David and Julie. The Chinese were clever at blending in, keeping traditional and simple British names that they gave their children, or the children picked for themselves what they would be called. I would have been called Johan, given the children's choice, after the famous Dutch and Ajax football star of the early 1970s. He adorned my closet-like bedroom walls with posters and newspaper cutouts. I'll explain what a newspaper is later in the footnote.

So, the Wongs took over one Monday morning around 11:00. Customers must have thought they'd died and gone to Beijing.

"What the...bloody hell! Who're you? Where's June? What have you done with our Trevor?" it went on like that for days. The rumor-mill spread like mumps in a junior school. Suddenly everyone's throat was too swollen with British pride to ever eat "Chinky chips." The chips even changed their name. They were now "Chinky chips" from the "Chinky chippy." This was not meant in a good way – not like saying oh I fancy a Chinese meal tonight, darling, let's go to the Rising Sun Restaurant.

Our neighborhood had a watch, like for security, but in this case it was to report who went to the "Chinky chippy." You would have been black-balled, sent to Coventry in church if you had gone to the "Chinky chippy"; of course that would have meant that people were actually going to church. The one on the village green, such as it was a village, had a huge half acre parking lot filled with white lines and debris from the chippy.

Luckily, since no one went to the church, you could at least go to the chippy without being talked about in the pews. The other church, the pub, could see you not get your regular beverage put on the bar seconds after walking over its threshold if the neighborhood watch had let Tony the barman know of your transgressions.

So, the Wongs took over and no one noticed the difference. The pipeline for that information had been the children. We took our bikes and hung out there every other day in summer. Summer – winter – didn't matter; the seasons, they were all pretty much the same. One season marginally colder than the last; leaves on or off was the primary indicator of the season. The Wongs' chippy was on the corner of the shopping precinct, which meant at the corner there was a right-angle of awning on the building to accommodate more of our gang along both the east and north sides. The dare was on and Rob Johns lost – he was the first one sent in to buy chips from the Wongs. There was no queue, so he went straight to the front. There was no government-imposed age restriction like the "offy" and the pub, so even he could walk to the counter with his "fifty-P" and get chips and peas. We made him get mushy peas, because that to a Chesterfield kid was a modern-day delicacy. Rob nervously looked over both of his shoulders. There was me and about three others that day; I think it was Steve, Tim, Simon—or it could have been Andy. Whatever; not important. But it was a momentous day.

You could see through the floor to ceiling glass windows on both sides, like a square fishbowl. We stared in, still on our bikes, hands around our eyes to shield them from the cloud glare. We four could see Rob asking. Probably slowly, on account of them being foreign and all. It sounded like he was shouting, but I could be making that up.

"He's doing it! He's doing it!" said Andy or Simon, I can't remember which. And we all stared deeper into the windows, noses touching them. Mrs. Wong must have thought she was a panda in a zoo or something. The glass was cold to your nose, but the smell was just the same. Like an opiate from the Orient. Rob was quick; like a panda express he was in and out of there. Goodies wrapped in newspaper. The *Times*, I remember. The *Times* was used a lot because around here no one read it and you could get the unsold for free from yesterday at the newsagent's four doors down. Plus, it was twice the size of a tabloid, so you got could mileage out of the *Times*, like a larger roll of Christmas wrapping paper—the one for the big toys. Unless you came from a poor family like mine, where you needed two rolls of mismatched paper to cover your new Subbuteo box.

The other reason to use the *Times* was that you could be sure that you wouldn't have Sam Fox's tits touching your chips. Chips and Tits might have been a good marketing idea for a gentlemen's club. I can't believe me and Ali didn't think of that one! That would have been wrong, for your mum to be all excited to be eating her fish and chips only to find Sam Fox's perky 36 D cup staring her down. It was hard enough to get the kids to eat their dinner without that distraction.

"Would you like fi' and chi'; that's what she asked me," said Rob.

"Nah, yer meking it up!" we all said in unison.

"Straight up – would you like fi' and chi'?" Rob repeated, slanting his eyes up with one hand. Mrs. Wong I'm sure could see from her fishbowl that Rob was mocking her twice. It wasn't nice, but hey, we were just kids, and kids do evil shitty things, amongst which can be telling the truth.

"Come on then, open 'em up," Simon or Andy said. Probably "Simon said," because Rob did it right away.

He peeled back the financial report to see the familiar chips dripping in the familiar green mush.

"I wanna try first," said Tim, all eager like he wanted to take that dare. That from the kid who wouldn't light a bush fire in the drought of '76 because he was too nesh. We all did it. Story for another day. Maybe he was trying to make up for that show of weakness.

"Gerroff – it were my 50p. I'm goowing fost." Rob was more confident, having come back from the Orient unscathed, he had come back from the frontline where he had conversed with the enemy, though God knows if they could understand each other. Rob had a "reet" strong "Chezzy" accent—even I was lost on occasion. I was the posh kid, remember.

"At least she got yer order reet, mate!" said Nigel. That's right; I forgot – Nige was there too.

"Taste it then," said Simon.

So, Rob had to. He looked down on it like it was a plate of swollen maggots too fat to move. He used the little wooden fork; it looked like a short chubby lolly-stick with minor prongs on the end … probably what they later modeled the Pac-Man shape on.

"Fuckin' lovely, mate!" Rob swore with delight. He was the oldest in our year, so apparently that gave him the right to swear, and a lot, like his degree rested on it. Who were we to argue? We were younger, he had a prized September birthday.

"Let me 'ave one," asked Simon. So, Rob had to give him one; that's how the game is played, remember?

"Them's brill, just t' same as before!" agreed Simon.

The chips were gone in minutes, just like old times – like last week. Well, of course they were good; Mr. Wong ran a successful Chinese restaurant in his hometown before coming here. This, he could see, was tradition and a Friday formality for dinner and the last stop at night on a weekend. The decision to buy a chip shop was a no-brainer based on its simplicity. Of course, he hadn't banked on the accent—I mean ours, not his—and the fear of foreigners. Foreigners who looked like foreigners. Xenophobia can be rife in a town that doesn't understand its meaning.

But the kids, who were the lunchtime regulars, told their mums and dads and the word spread quicker than a grease fire that the chippy "were alreet." And that's how the good word of the "Chinky chippy," not used in the pejorative sense, you understand, survived the xenophobia (whatever that means) of Chesterfield. If we gave it a patronizing name, we could accept it as our own, with a nickname the "Chinky chippy" was ours and being so was the "best in t' fuckin' town, mate!" We were a damned strange bunch. Must have been all the lead paint in primary school; they'd had a surplus, so the art department used it for kindergarten finger paints! Well, after all, it was free, and the kids—well, their art was just rubbishy, sloppy scribbles that only a parent could love "deniably"!

Since Spar was closed for a half hour or more and there was nowhere to just hang out, just chill and relax, I wrapped my arms around myself and headed to my sister's house amongst the orangish Bundt cake houses with a sieving of powdered-sugar snow on their shady roofs.

It was too early for the pubs and there were no Starbucks in Chesterfield yet. They would likely set up downtown anyway, not at a housing estate precinct. *I could use a venti latte right about now*, I thought. If that Howard Schultz guy could just drop one of his coffee shops right next to the Chinky chippy, he'd be guaranteed a customer of one, although I'd be drinking tea, not coffee, like so many of the Brits. Then of course around here they would be too cheap to go out and pay for tea when they could drink it for nothing at home, where Nescafé instant blend was considered bourgeois. We were cheap—not parsimonious or frugal; we were cheap, very cheap in Chezzy. Oh God, why is it songs, annoying ones pop into your head when triggered by certain words. Maybe it was the confluence of walking to Julia's house and the word cheap, but I was now tattooed with the chorus of the Chirpy Cheap Cheap song stuck in me head. Ironically, sung by Middle of the Road – I should probaby step back on the pavement. A café would have been nice, like in France or Joplins in town. A bloody vending machine would work too – any hot drink service would be a step up—with a lid on it, of course.

"Bloody parky outside," I said to myself. All these colloquialisms ran back into my head once I returned to Chesterfield – not once in my now native Chicago do I think and certainly don't say "bloody parky outside"--people would think I'm nuts. But everyone here knew that crispness, a crispness that bit into my aching mouth, still a little numb from my procedure earlier – probably would have spilled that coffee and burned my chin. Safer for me that this backwater didn't have the bitter American coffee shop.

Should have brought my gloves; that way I would have looked less like a mental patient now that I had my hands tucked into my armpits for warmth. The front gardens of the housing estate were originally designed with patches of grass. They seemed huge when were kids playing footy on them. I took the scenic route to Julia's, as the streets and houses were identical, except for the Peugeots and Citroëns parked on our old lawns. I cut down the gennel between the houses – a small path between the houses that cut through to the park. If you wanted a "nebby" you could see right into the lounge of these neighbors, who probably bought it because it meant their neighbor to the one side was further away while the other neighbor was attached to their house. Semi-detached, a notch up from an end-terrace and two notches up from a middle terrace. My hands like planes in hangars tucked under my armpits. This was so much more socially acceptable than the Al Bundy hands in trousers options. Even Chesterfield folk had standards, you know.

I crossed the Pennine Way, accompanied by old chip wrappers and plastic shopping bags caught in the shipping forecast's light onshore breeze. Our Pennine Way, not the original from which it was named, skirted the fields, playground, and footy pitches like an artery around your heart. Its flow of traffic, neighborhood kids, families, dog walkers and perverts all found their way to this village center. "Am gewing t' park," was all any of us said to our parents for them to know where we were. The park was central to the housing development, a token green space boarded by the swooping Pennine Way on the north side and the equally swooping brook on the south. The pitches, park, and playground were trapped in by the vestiges of its origins, the brook lightly lined with oak and willow trees with fields behind that led like a bride's veil to the housing estate above them. That was where I lived. At the bottom end of the upper estate. The fields were like an extension of Dad's vegetable garden—land we enjoyed without owning. An expanse of fields large enough for my dad and our neighbors to teach me how to hit a nine-iron without actually landing on the Pennine Way.

Most of my friends lived down here by the park, and we were considered snobby because we lived in the detached house on the hill. But like in medieval times, as I said, we were at the lower end of the hill, so socially, we were below those above us. Their shit ran down into our garden or sewer line or some such modern-day analogy. The dog-walkers strolled everywhere so no one was immune to their droppings. "Two dogs for every person," me dad would moan. He was right, of course – this was a rainy, needy village, largely unemployed in need of low-cost distractions and love. It took more than one dog to satiate the emptiness of career joblessness and empty calendars. Mastiffs and collies matched in houses not much bigger than kennels. Irish setters and poodles, the "his and hers" dogs, like matching bath towels, were our BMW's, both pooches wrapped in rain jackets to match their owners'. These therapy dogs gave the village someone to vent to about the weather, the closing of the mines, and the early closing time of the pubs. Then there was Norm. Norm raised greyhounds; his therapy was going to the dogs, along with his family's finances. Sheila had a husky team of Chihuahuas – Quarto, Trieze, Duez, and Uno! Seriously, those were their names! One trip to an all-inclusive holiday in Copacabana and she needed an exotic souvenir. Not satisfied with a snow globe, Sheila had to adopt, as was the snobby protocol, the abandoned pets of South America! The prestige gave her jolly holly a nobility and one-up on her store-bought neighbors' hounds.

Closest to the park were row upon row and layer upon layer of semi-detached houses, like folds of pasta each one rolled into the next. Now that my hands were toasty, I decided to walk through the park, taking the even longer way to Julia's. The worn soft and smooth iron strings of the 1970s swings with its layer upon layer of chipped paint invited me to sit, take the weight off, and hang for a while. I scraped the mud off my shoes by dragging them along the rubberized landing pad. In my day, when you took a fall, you took home asphalt etchings like Indian tattoos. Today you were unlikely to get more than a rug burn. As I was taught to, I pushed my slightly less muddy shoes back and forth beneath me to encourage the swing to move. I was beyond the age when I needed a push, and apparently beyond the age when this was supposed to be fun! At what age do we go from wishing the swing would go all the way over to wanting nothing more than a gentle rock in Grandpa's chair?

I collected my breakfast in my mouth again. The centrifugal blood flow pounded the rocks in my mouth where the tooth stood like a battered surfboard. I had reached the peak where I could see over the footy goal posts, and normally I would have jumped like Eddie the Eagle from the zenith of the swing, but I was a long way from being fourteen and fearless. Instead, my heels caught the rubber landing pad on my descent, and unlike the graphite smoothness of gravel engine-braking in the past, they gripped like hands reaching out of a swamp. And wham! I was face down in the rubberized mattress like a high hurdler catching the first hurdle at full tilt. The pulverized rubber grabbed my ankles like playground zombies reaching out from the swamp of re-graded tires. For the second time in a few hours, my maxiofacial protrusion was taking a beating. The impact wasn't as severe, but it was hard to shake the impact of a Michelin Man kiss. Smells like radials with a mere hint of Pennine Way and dog shit.

The swing maintained its momentum and trajectory sufficient to return and crack the back of my head like a dull knife hitting a soft-boiled egg.

"Fuck!"

"Eyup – I though' tha' were you, Griff! Y'all reet mate?"

Oh my God, Rob Johns couldn't have timed it better: my humiliation blooming in the frosty chill, black rubber shavings hanging like charred candy corn from my chin.

"You went d'arn 'arder than a pig in t' X-Games." I think that was a subtle slam on America, but maybe it was even too subtle for Rob. Of all the people I didn't want to see right now, at the top of the list was fucking Rob Johns. Damn, my head hurt front and back. Like a smashed walnut. The local cricket star, returning to the park where it all started for him and never got off the mark for me. Once again, I was face down in pain at the park with Rob Johns standing over me, like the time I mistimed his beamer and the cricket ball caught me square on the jaw.

"I'm fine, Rob; honestly," I lied. Rob was a great bowler as a kid, and as such had put me on the ground numerous times when we played cricket on this park. I was never very good, but I was enthusiastic and had all the gear. So, in summer I would traipse down the hill to the park, stumps, bat, ball, and gloves, hoping someone would see me and join me. I had all the gear, so by rights I had to get better at this game, right? Rob couldn't see directly from his house, so he would hop over Mrs. Gascoigne's yard half a dozen times a night to see if anyone was at the park. For all the hours my dad and uncle doted on my cricket game, I should have played for England. It must be how a dyslexic kid feels in year one. Rob didn't have any gear and his dad hated him playing "that Nancy sport."

We played on a small strip by the brook, not on the hallowed and roped-off cricket pitch itself. It was flat and dry enough. Rob's dad had taught him how to skim stones down our little stream. "It's a fourer," he would yell as his sliver of river rock skipped, bounced, and sailed down the runway of the stream like a Cessna in high winds. Rob had a great arm, and no one threw harder or more accurately than he did. His marksman's precision broke my spirit, and on one occasion, my stumps. Just eighty yards from here was where he splintered my "off-stump." I heard it whistle as it went by like a taunting ghost. I never saw the red wine of a ball leave his hand. The ball whistled the tune from the movie *The Good, the Bad, and the Ugly* and my wicket went down in a hail of Rob's gunfire, scattering the pegs like pins in a bowling alley. Over there, by the line of petticoat willows and majestic oaks on that strip no wider than our Pennine Way was where my dad, not his, taught Rob the in-swinger. Like Rob needed more ammunition!

"Your Ju sed tha' were comin o'er." He caught the flailing swing with his backside and yanked me up like Christopher Robin carried Pooh Bear.

"Why dint you stop by t' 'ouse?" he furthered.

"I dunnno," I answered pathetically – caught out in a lie.

"It's great to see yer, mate!" Rob's enthusiasm from a child to today came like the daily sunshine. Really fucking annoying on some occasions, this being one of them. Today felt like the final interview for your dream job after a bender celebrating a Thursday night. Unplanned head pounding of migraine proportions, yet, having to present your best.

It was true that my sister had bumped into Rob in town, of course. She had taken his number in order to give it to me, in the "likely" event I would call Rob. But what on earth would we talk about? There's a reason we don't do reunions in Britain – they are just for bragging rights or to check out old girlfriends. See how they look today? Hope they have aged horribly since dumping you in year eleven. Or hope that the golden boy has fallen on hard times. Preferably bald or with hopelessly bad hair plugs. For me, the hair game was one I could win easily, so I thought. Then "cricket-star" Rob came up behind me at the swing set with his long blond hair and swooped me on to my feet—*Bastard*, I thought. He looked lean, like a smoker, I thought.

"What are you up to these days, Rob?" I asked through the mask of pain in front and back of my head, bruised the way a failed attempt to crack a Brazilian nut might feel.

"Nags Head, mostly."

And that was the difference – at home, in the States, you get a career-based answer; here it's rude to enquire of your job, so life was your social life, and Rob's was the crappy pub where his dad goes.

"Dominoes 'n' darts. Dominoes on Mundee 'n' Wennsdee, darts on Chewsdee an' Fursdee." Rob sounded like he was living his dad's life. "Yer shud come up, mate; it'd be brill'yant to see yer. Lads'd ger a real kick out of seein' t' famous American." The irony was lost on Rob; he was one of the few local celebrities whose sporting prowess gave him real credibility. While all I had done was leave the country—not yet a recognized Olympic sport.

"Tah, Rob, I'd like that," I lied with smooth ease of a chocolate commercial. What? did he say "famous American"? What was that all about? "How's your mum?" I added, trying to pick up the vernacular again, the famous American trying to blend in the way I was supposed to have blended as a child but never did. I was a "famous American" before I even knew where America was. I fit in like the kid who had all the cricket gear and couldn't throw a ball with a straight arm!

"Mum's not bin t' same since Dah died t'other year." *Fuck*, I thought, *Ju hadn't mentioned that Mr. Johns had passed.*

"God, I'm so sorry to hear that, Rob," I said, thinking, like a child scoring points, that at least my very sick father was still alive.

"I've been coming 'round to see her like most days. She's reet sad. Finds it 'ard to do ennyfing for 'ersen. So I bring 'er dinner on domino nights, then stay o'er after darts. She likes 'aving a man about t' house, she says."

"God I'm sorry, Rob." I was never very good at these conversations.

"You should stop by. You was always one of Mum's favrites." There was a gravitas and sincerity about Rob as he brushed more rubber shavings off my coat, the way Turner might have brushed up a quick horizon.

"I will, mate," I said with more hollowness than Robin Hood's tree. Fortunately for me, Rob hadn't picked up on it. He sat in the swing that had clocked me, and I felt obliged to sit a while longer. Agitated, I sat with nowhere in particular to go to, Rob in his white Johnny Zuko T-shirt and me in my "Eugene" coat, we meandered back and forth on the swings, with syncopated rhythms like a reluctant orchestra pit. A cold, awkward library silence sat in the park air.

"I allos liked yer mum too," I said, reaching back in time for my old accent. His mum was like a real mum. She never worked. Mr. Johns made enough as a coal miner for her to stay home and raise Rob and his sister. Rob's sister was great looking but a little older in an unreachable, un-datable way. Mrs. Johns was always home in a way that Mr. Johns wasn't. He worked long shifts through daylight and slept through the darkness, as if in permanent hibernation.

Mrs. Johns was British summertime. She always wore the ingredients of her baking. And she always had something fresh baked from the oven like a TV mom would. There was a summer break when Rob and I were tight mates for a few weeks; the way that volleyball players rotate in and out, so did me and a bunch of mates. We stepped onto the courts of their family life and after six weeks of summer hols, we stepped right off again. We rotated out when we nearly got busted for lifting Milky Bars from the petrol station (more to that story later—if it stays relevant).

"Your mum still wear t' Swiss watch 'er dad gave 'er?' I was devolving back into my best Cestrefeldian accent. I was pretty proud of myself the way I could erase seventeen years of being in America in just a few short sentences.

"Ship shape and Bristol fashun! Tha's Mum's words t' live by!" said Rob sounding, almost poetic through a hacking cough. "Grandad 'ad sum brill'yant stories from t' war an' gerring tha' watch off' er Jerry made Mum rate proud of her dah. 'E wor lucky t' mek it 'ome after bein' sho' down we' out a gun on 'im or nuffin!"

"A real hero, mate, that's what he was." Shit, I'd dropped back into my other voice. I needed re-programming or a new CD-rom. Try again: "Me grandad ne'er spoke o' t' war, just shewed us 'is knives – bayonet an' a Gurkha knife." Through my humpty-dumpty skull, I was trying to put history back together again. Damn, my head hurt, and Rob is leading two great stories to my one.

"One o' best days o' me life were ov'er thee'er wi' yer dad," Rob said fondly. Strange what people remember of us. Strange what we remember of others – even stranger what others remember of those that are close to us that we should know and remember better.

I was about to live my dad's life vicariously through Rob Johns, of all people—Rob Johns.

"Remember – yer dad worr abou' t' start 'is cricket match right 'ere on t' park while we woz jus' warmin' up.' E come o'er all excited abou' sumfink. 'E 'ad me chuck a couple a balls at yer, then 'e stopped meh. 'Robert,' 'e sed all official like, 'show me that run-up again,' so a did as 'e askt. 'Great speed, Robert. Fastest in the school, I bet?'" Rob affected some private school accent for me dad's voice – thinking he was posh or something because he knew Dad grew up in Matlock.

"He then, yer dah, went on: 'Show me your grip on the ball,' so I 'eld ou' me 'and far 'im. 'Try adjusting your fingers just so around the seam and release from this angle on your run up.' Yer dad wahr a brill'yant teacher. I' wahr tha' tha' go' me t' trial wit' county; brill'yant bloke your dah!" Now Dad was "dah"? But that's the familiarity that me mates enjoyed with my dad.

"'Ow's 'e doowin'?"

"Slowing down a bit, you know." Oh my God, I sounded like Margot Leadbetter off *The Good Life*. I was lucky I hadn't been beaten up more by Rob and his gang, my gang. "Recovering from hip surgery," I added, which to Rob probably sounded like just had tea with the queen, given his recent misery. I certainly couldn't tell him about the lung cancer, as I assume Rob's dad, Bob, had died of black lung like most miners intown. But I wanted to hug Rob like I was Laura Ingalls in the last scene of *Little House on the Prairie.*

"Brill'yant bloke, yer dah!" He shouted it to the cricket pitch like a grateful prayer. Even louder he added, "Tha' bloke is a bloody 'ero! 'E gid me a chance t' play for t' county an' Inn-gland!"

The stray tabby and the confused seagull both took off from the dormant pitch like he'd just winged an in-swinger at them. I was starting to hate Rob or my dad or both. I wanted so bad to play cricket for the county and Dad made his dream come true, not mine. A dream Rob didn't even know he had until Dad shuffled Rob's fingers on the cricket ball and his release point. The ball flew along an invisible slalom zip-line to the wicket.

"Yer dah sed, jus' like this 'e sed t' meh, 'There's no easy outs in cricket."

"Or life," I added finishing Dad's sentence for him.

"'Ow dja know?"

"He was me dad—is me dad, rather."

"Righ'. Any road, tha' sayin' go' me frew many a game--'t reminded me t' stay focused an' never gi' yup! Brill'yant bloke, your dah!"

A pause developed and the seagull flew through the gulf between us. My jealousy cauterized my generosity. As we both looked out from the park to the pitches, it was clear that a lot of mowing had happened since we last connected. I wondered how long this catching-up was going to take before I could be alone again, until I chose to be social. As I walked by the gennel I thought how interesting it would be to catch up. Like a school reunion of sorts. Where people show up to brag about how well they are doing or how well they look compared to so and so. Or to find out if your old school crush is still good looking, or in most cases these days, if they will now go out with you. Because we are all so much more attractive following a divorce, a dead-end career or spousal passing. The expectation to get off with an old fling – the excitement. I for one would win the "after" in a Hair Club for Men commercial! It's still long, not receding too quickly and genuinely needs a cut, not a trim, every four weeks. But I'm a lot softer, rounder-faced, redder-faced, for the obvious reasons – I might still go if only to. Oh, that's right I went to an all-boys school, no reason for me to go back. Marnie Bailey went to a different high school, and it would be plain wrong to go to her school's reunion! It would be more fun, though, as those were the girls we hung out with.

What we needed was a reunion of me and Ali's tennis club discos – yep, that would do the trick. All the people either of us ever wanted to shag had an invitation to those!

I thought how interesting it would be to catch up with Rob – but like on my terms, when I wanted him to come into my world. Not now – I was busy reminiscing – yes, about him and a lot of others, so like the wrong spirit at a séance, Rob had come to the conversation too early. He was way down the list of people who had passed through my life that I wanted to speak to. I had career bragging rights, interesting life in bragging rights, I think we were a tie for hair unless he'd had hair plugs, which I seriously doubt he could afford, although I secretly bet he thought that I could and had. But he had me beat in an area that stung like a jellyfish. He had played cricket for Chesterfield Cricket Club, and worse—I didn't tell you this at the time—he actually played for Derbyshire and was a bowler for England. I could never compete with that; his sporting prowess trumped everything in my world. He held the royal flush of life in my mind to my Jacks…t.

But it's not interesting catching up, and it's not his fault. It's just this park has been mown so many times since we kicked around on it. I mean, I'm sad for him and his mum, but I'm sad for me dad, and now he's reminding me how great my dad is, was, and it's hard to hear. Sometimes I just wish he had been an arsehole of a dad and we would all be able to move on more easily when he, should he, pass.

"Oh bollocks! Me mum 'll be waitin,' loads'll need switchin'. Come by la'er, Ad; Mum'd love t' see yah." Whether it was a real reason or an imaginary one, Rob jumped off the swing like a second-grader.

"All reet then, later," and like a rubbish friend, I knew I wouldn't be. Rob would always think better of me. Better than I deserved. My head was killing me. Rob sprinted off, the purple goosebumps on his arms like Easter egg dye. My mind reeked like the hum of a week-old Easter egg unfound behind the settee. Full of good intentions gone to rot. Maybe I'd feel better if I sat on top of the slide; stiffer breeze might cleanse my thoughts like opening the crisper draw in the refrigerator airs out the moldy gherkin.

"Damn, it's cold up here," I whispered to the seagull, who was still confused by the excess standing water here inland. Rob was gone in an instant, once more skipping over Mrs. Gascoine's fence, pushing down on it like he would a pygmy's head to escape the tribal ring of death.

The slide offered no joint seating, unlike the swings or the roundabout. Anyone just sitting at the top of the slide meant to be there was and left alone—an alpine skier at the starting gate, or a coward facing a lame suicide jump. The starter's gun went off, and a cascade of memories tumbled down the slide.

This was Andy Lunn's park – why couldn't the medium have channeled him? He made it as a professional footballer, Notts County, I know because I bumped into him in a beer-garden years back. It was a surreal scene – we were in a not-so-local pub, a small village pub that used to graze sheep in what was now its beer garden. A beer garden that was then developed, I'm sure not willingly, by the village commission into a child's play land with Wendy houses, climbing frames, and swings. Swings for the kids to yell "Push me higher, Mummy" and for them later to regret eating the salt and vinegar crisps immediately prior. The

Wheatsheaf was its name.

I was over with the whole family. It was early June around the Whitsun break. I tried to time our trips to coincide with my niece and nephew's break from school so we could have the cousins spend all day together. I remember it was dusk, so it was probably around 9:15-ish. Warm too, just a lightweight summer jumper was needed – all the kids were entertained, and we just sat outside in the sheep's field of dreams, enjoying them enjoying themselves, enjoying not having to entertain them. Reminiscing and catching up the way families torn by one who emigrated do. You know—full of love, mild anger, love, some regret, laughter with hint of anger – all the usual stuff.

A little boy not any older than my own daughter came up to our table and specifically targeted my dad. Dad was loved by all me mates when I was a kid, so it wasn't strange that kids were attracted to him, well ok it was a little weird. Like the kids coming up to Tim Allen in *The Santa Clause*. Dad was still dyeing his hair then, so there was no way to claim he was a clean-shaven Santa. The little boy spoke a few words—confidently, I might add. Dad nodded to him, and the little boy ran off.

"What was that all about?" I asked Dad.

"He wanted to know if I was Adam Griffiths' dad."

"Strange, don't you think?"

"So, it is you then, Ad?" commented Andy Lunn from the darkness of the play zone.

"Andy? Andy Lunn?" He sounded the exact same as I remembered him. Sounded like a man before we even got our second molars.

"I sent our Sammy to check if it were you. I recognized yer dad!"

I suppose the older we get, the less we change. I hadn't seen Andy since going around Town for beers twenty odd years ago. Even then, it was in passing. I was much greyer now.

"Y'alright Roy?" He turned to me dad.

"I am, Andy. How've you been?"

"Can't complain." He raised his largely empty pint for emphasis.

I stood up and clinked my glass to his. We were kids last time we played out together. So, shaking hands would have been weird, and we weren't likely to hug either.

"It's great to see you. Let me get you a drink? What you having?" It was the best I could do. I wanted to be there but at the same time escape the strangely familiar.

"Half a Carling, mate." Politeness always came in halves.

"Not a pint?"

"Nah, I'm driving. I've got to get littlen' to get back to his mum later; can't go reeking of beer!"

"Coming up!" I left Andy and Sammy to visit with me dad. When I returned, it seemed they got on easier than my own family did with Dad.

"You are still the best footy player I ever played with, Andy!" I was such a brown nose. But he was, and Andy was likable, especially now as he had remembered Dad. Best way to a son's heart is to remember his mum, then his dad. But in my case, most people I'd grown up with knew me dad as both.

"Did you make it to the pros?" It was a hollow question – I set him up to look good.

"Played for Notts County, didn't you, Andy?" Dad had followed his career. Dad had kept me abreast too.

"That's right, Roy," Andy said modestly. Not bragging. When you did it, it's not bragging. Both me and Dad were a tad jealous. But you couldn't help but like Andy Lunn. Little Sammy went off to play with my kids, showing them the pink and blue plastic slides.

"How many years did you play for 'em, Andy?" Dad said, leaning in like his old coach, wanting everyone to know the answer.

"'Bout four and a half years – before I done me knee in." He patted the side of it. It was too dark to see the scarring. But you knew it was the right one. The right one that unleashed shots like David's rocks pelted Goliath, with deadly forces of accuracy. If you played on Andy's team, your job was to get the ball to him with an ounce of space. Like Jeeves, I delivered. I was good at that.

"Roy, you haven't changed a bit. That's why I sent our Sammy over; I hoped it were you." Andy wanted to change the topic, and we wanted to keep it going. His highlight reel was our new movie; we wanted to see it, and he was tired of replaying it.

"You were and are still the best kid I ever saw play the game!" me and Dad said in unison, like we were his cheerleaders. Andy probably blushed; it was too dusky to tell.

"You still in America, Ad?"

"Yep. I love to come back as a tourist!" I joked, but I'm not sure it sounded funny anymore. Some things just sound funnier in your head, right? "Love to come back and see everyone, visit the old haunts."

"Not much changes 'round 'ere!" He was right about that, except maybe the pink and blue slides.

"And that's how I like it," I nodded, and Dad was pleased, I think. We took pride in Andy's achievement. I mean, Notts County, they were legit. We watched them play Town; that made it legit!

"I woulder like to 'ave played for Town, but offers never came in," Andy lamented, the way me and me Dad did.

"Yeh, but you nearly played division one! I remember seeing you when County were on that great run years back – you scored from outside the 18 and no one saw it but the back of the net." Dad had been there. Well, he was always there, so it was kind of automatic; it just needed Andy Lunn to be there.

"It killed me to score agen' me own team!"

"Don't think the keeper saw it! He might still be looking for it!" Dad had us all laughing. "Seen you do it a million times on the park, Andy – it was just great to see you doing it at Saltergate," he paused "– even if you were wearing those ugly black and white stripes!"

"You were too good for Town, Andy!" It was true. Andy had real class. And just like now, he charmed my family as everybody gathered to be introduced to our celebrity. He politely nodded. He remembered my sister – I think they went out once together when they were like fifteen. Whatever that means when you are fifteen.

"You should'er made it too, Ad!"

"Now you are just being kind, Andy, and we all know it."

"Nah, that school tryout – Jock didn't like you – probably cos you were small—but I scored seven that day." Good God, he remembered – Andy Lunn remembered my highlight reel. "Jock should've given you a chance, mate!"

"He did – later in the season." I paused; not everyone knew what really happened. "When we were in the cup semi's, Jock asked me to play."

"Yer kiddin'? But you din't play – I would've remembered that. We were Woodward and Curry!"

"Nope, I didn't – I turned down my one big chance," I said rather nonchalantly about a wound that took years to heal.

"Why, Ad, you could've had a winner's medal?" And that's why it took years to heal. "Why did you say no?" Andy was genuinely shocked. "It was from that same championship game I got picked for trials by t' County coaches." He was rooting for my past efforts the way a tandem rider cheers on the flagging pedaler behind them.

Ouch! It had been painful enough saying no to Jock, who I know it was killing him to even ask me. I wasn't one of those kids who would have said "I wouldn't play for him if he asked me" after being rebuffed. But this new information blackened a dark spot of my past. I didn't know that Club's scouts would have been watching. I couldn't breathe now. Even more so than when I couldn't breathe to tell Jock my decision to not play. As I told them in the pub garden – I relived a proud and painful moment, now even more painful with the "regret" that kicked my shin-bone for good measure.

"The game, Andy, was on a Saturday afternoon," I worked through the re-emerging pain to retell the story I'd buried with a therapist's help."I remember," Andy followed along intently, caring – he was always a good bloke.

"Most normal kids would have jumped at the chance and said yes right away. But I told Jock I had to think about it."

"Is that why he didn't play you? Because you had to think about it?" I almost sounded like I was defending Jock.

"No, that's not it at all, I told Jock that I would have to check with Mrs. Irwin if it was okay to play."

"Why her?" Andy looked and sounded equally perplexed.

"She was the director of the school play and I had the lead. *Stirrings in Sheffield on a Saturday Night*. I had my own stirrings and asked her if it was okay to play footy just on that one evening. Our conversation was frank; she treated me like an adult which was a rare moment for a thirteen-year-old. But I was an old soul. She asked me to take my time to think about it. To imagine my team with or without me and to imagine the play with or without me. I wanted Solomon's sword to hack me right in half. Her question was too good.

" 'So, you're saying I can play footy then?' I said quickly, naively.

" 'Take a minute to imagine both scenarios.' She got up and walked to her coat, folded it over her arm, and left rehearsal, prematurely."

There was no one to witness the tears streaming down my face as I walked home, passed the playground where I dominated lunchtime footy, then by the field where the seven assists put Andy on a path to being a school legend, then under the small tunnel for the main road where my screams of frustration echoed back at me, around the maze of estate roads to my house. Mum was asleep and I had gone to my room, squeezed my eyeball sponges into the tear bucket. All that remained were just dry heaves of eyeballs, knowing my high school footy chance was gone forever.

Suddenly it was very cold on top of the slide. The wind of my history had picked up and carved right through me, the polished slide mirroring the ghosts of my childhood. This impromptu séance of my childhood spirits chilled my mind the way a black hole forms mid-sentence, when your life voice loses direction and time drifts around its galaxy like a Tardis sequence. Spinning, gyrating between obscure memories good, bad, indifferent invoking random dialogues between unhinged histories. Today my mind's kaleidoscope twisted and turned Forrest Gump's box of memories into a single unappetizing chocolate patty.

"Oy, mister! You gonna slide down or no?" came the voice of Christmas present, awakening me from my time travel.

"Yeh, I'm coming down!" I replied like a snotty teenager. "Wait your turn." Then the kid was echoed by his entourage. I inched my bum forward through Franz Klammer's starting gates, expecting the slope to take me away. Nothing. I ended up working my way down the polished steel the way crampons would scar a curling lane.

"Ye' now fuck off!" one of the posse yelled from behind a Roman cocoon of parkas. "Yeh! Yeh!" followed the chorus of young hooligans, even from the pink ones. This was indeed real time travel, as I felt threatened by these adolescent ASBO's. I paid them less and less attention as I walked away. This part of the park's territory I didn't miss. Ju's place wouldn't be far, but I was curious to see if there was a rope swing at our 'rope swing tree.' so I headed towards the taller willows, ignoring the path of the crows.

My phone rang—not a solicitation at this time!

"When are you coming home, Dad?" My son's croaky but chirpy voice was a welcome comfort. He must have called me right away after waking up.

"Soon, sunshine." I beamed back at him with the brightness of an open fridge door.

"Like today?" he said, much too hopefully.

"No—sorry, kiddo. Soon. I'm gonna stay with Grandpa a little while longer," I pledged.

"Is he sick? I had a dream that he was sick."

"Is that why you're up early?"

"Yes, kind of." His spirit tailed away.

"Yes, honey, he is, but the doctors have ways to make him better, so I'm gonna stay a little longer," I said with rising optimism.

"To rub his head when it hurts!" he blurted out.

"Yes, just like that, just like when you get a headache,"

"Then he can go to sleep like I do." He'd had far too many migraines for a little kid. Could he be so stressed out, or was he sneaking red wine behind our backs?

I'm not good at walking and talking and found myself entangled in the tentacles of the enormous willow tree.

"Yes, then he can go to sleep." Sleep is such a great remedy.

The willow walls of our childhood palace protected the inner eye of calm. I had napped and daydreamed so often in its protectorate. Through the waterfall of Willow I could see our tree swing; its huge knot for your bum to ride on had been added to by a Goodyear tire, likely from a Ford Fiesta. The distinguished oak from which it hung wore it proudly like an army officer would wear a medallion from the discos of the '70s.

"Go back to sleep yourself, honey; it's way too early. I miss you, CLUM!"

"Clum," came the sleepy little voice from the end of line as I passed beneath the willows to the rope swing oak. CLUM was our thing – I somewhat stole it, or rather was inspired by the words of Gil, a short-term former colleague of mine whose casket was emblazoned with "LUM" – we all had wondered what it stood for as we gathered around the gravesite. The thirty or so onlookers in darkly themed attire, heads down in prayer and thankfulness, stared at the oblong hole in the ground, then back up to the gurney and casket carrying Gil, the brass letters glistening their secret message in the flickering sunlit morning. I suppose the others were trying to guess its meaning too—or did they just know, because they knew him better?

I played with the letters – "Live UnMatched," "Love UnMatched," "Live, Uplifting, Magnificently"—my father was the crossword puzzle expert; he would have loved this. "Life, Unity, and Majesty"? Between prayer and gratitude, I couldn't help but think what a good turnout this was for Gil. I'd read somewhere that you could count on two hands the number of people who would watch your final passage back to the earth and dust. Gil would have been pleased and likely would have handed the reluctant audience his signature calling card of a long-stemmed red rose. Perhaps his good turnout was in part his premature and untimely death or the respect of a small village or more likely the larger impact of a generous life. The small country village minister, passionately, gently rounded his graveside homily with the words of his friend – "Love U More." This had been my colleague Gil's response to his kids' "Love you, Dad!' "Love You More," he would chirp, and everything would be right with the world. He was sixty-two.

The love was profound, and the tears of that morning would have rusted the letters right off the oak.

So, I took the moment and added "Couldn't," and thus the word "CLUM" came into our family's being. It was a secret code word we proffered at night before bed, at the departure before work, in the moment before a recital, at the sideline before the game, and at every special moment in the day. The laundry was switched, CLUM. The dishwasher loaded, CLUM. The dog walked, CLUM. The garbage taken out, CLUM. A cup of tea made, CLUM. Teaching a friend the in-swinger, CLUM. Teaching me how to kick with my left foot, CLUM. Putting up this rope swing, CLUM.

The phone rang again. The reception inside the "Willow Tree Palace" was excellent, like a land-line or two cans strung together with string as in our childhood; it was the only way to reach us.

"When are you coming home?" It was Dad.

"I'm stopping by Ju's; the shop was shut."

"Alright, but don't forget the tea and we need milk too!"

"I won't, CLUM"

"What'd you say?"

"Nothing, Dad, nothing."

CHAPTER 9

This must be how a mollusk lives. In the shelter from the storm, protected from the driving ocean tides, battering breezes, and weathering elements. I hung up my string phone, opened and closed the tasseled doorway, and made my way through; exiting, the wind grabbed a few of the willow's stingers and swept them across my face like a clown fish leaving the coral. "You're leaving me now, you're out there, expect pain," stabbed the message from my willow tree.

The park hoodlums in the distance stood on the very edge of the hurtling roundabout, hanging ten, and screaming new-age profanities, attempting selfies with their truncheon sticks.

I could still hear them streets away as I came to Ju's house. The Wildgoose and Son cookie cutter had baked her a house that resembled the entire estate. Like Dad's place with a worse view. Wildgoose and Son had gotten here late to the table—or kitchen, if you prefer.

"Number 5!" That's how you knew it was Ju's – every house they had lived in, three of them, had been number 5!

"Hia Ad!" She could and would sing a welcome to everyone, so you always knew the key of her mood. Today she was thrilled to see me with an undertone of curiosity and worry.

"Hi Ju." I was excited to see her, but through the pain and cold, I was having a hard time expressing it.

"What happened to your face? Let me get a bag of peas!" Like the magic icy wet sponge at a football match, the bag of Birdseye Peas was a remarkable cure-all! She scurried off like she would to help one of her pupils. She was always the practical caring sort. Not the lovey-dovey, fussy sort, but reliable, generous, caring in a matronly way. Accepting of the responsibility, enjoying taking charge without having to pet the patient.

"I'm fine, really, Ju!" I called after her as I followed her to the kitchen, then the garage. "Where are you at?"

"In the garidge, bought a new deep-freezer," came the voice from the darkness. I must remember to say it right. Not that our Ju spoke real Chezzy; she was better educated than all of us. But "garidge" for garage was a Chezzy special.

From the darkness, a hand holding a bag of peas emerged, with Julia not far behind.

"Light went out last night; bloody creepy in there. Thank God there's a light on me phone!"

"Still afraid of the dark, then?" I foolishly started the verbal joust, proving the swing and the racket hadn't indeed knocked any sense into me!

"Yeh well, I'm afraid of getting taken by zombies with your face!" She parried my first strike and we were off. "You look like you got the silver medal in the who can force their head in a shredder fastest competition! Or lost a battle with Gascoigne's Heavy Weight Boxing Champion Tabby! Or worse – you were inspecting the chimney when Santa came bundling down! No, no, I've got another!"

"Really?" My swollen head and puffy eyes waited for the ringmaster to send me back to my cage. Or the white towel to be thrust high into the ring.

"Yeah – or worse still – you fell off a kiddie swing and face planted into the ground!!"

"What the? Who told you?"

"Rob, of course! Thought it was hilarious and Snapchatted this!" She held her phone to my face like it was a hand-mirror– it was ghastly. Looked like an advertisement for wearing your seatbelt! "Bloody hell! I do look like a frigging zombie!"

Julia put the elixir of peas on my cheek.

"Hold this while I get the bag of mixed veggies too; it's worse than I thought!"

"Not the mixed veggies! Anything but that!" And she was off in the darkness, led by the white light laser on her phone. Growing up, you knew you were hurt if the "mixed veggie" bag was needed! Our fridge freezer growing up never emerged from "refrigerator kindergarten" the way American refrigerators are today – like, the size of our kitchen growing up that is the fridge of today with ice dispenser, cold water dispenser, crushed ice, measured pours, "graduate refrigerator" stuff. Ours growing up had been stunted in its early childhood, probably from all the smoking Mum and Dad did. To be honest, it's a wonder any of us grew taller than the kitchen table, as we lived in the halo of smoke the way earth lives in the halo of the Milky Way. Our abortion of a fridge-freezer was too small for American college dorm life. The freezer section was smaller than a mailbox—enough for two empty ice-cube trays, the aforementioned peas and mixed veggies, and the balance of the polar ice-cap.

"Here you go; slap that on the other cheek!" Boy, she was in a good mood. I don't think she could have been happier if she had inflicted this hiding on me herself! Siblings, eh? Just can't wait for them to fall down, can you?"Cup of tea would be nice?" I said sorrowfully.

"Yes, it would – milk and one sugar if you don't mind? Almond milk," said Ju, like I was at my house.

"Alrighty then? I'll put the kettle on." Ju was not one for taking orders, requests, or pleadings from anyone and certainly not on half-term. She was chief delegator at home and school. I juggled the veggie icepacks and got the fixings for tea.

"Down in a minute," she called back as she went upstairs. "Gonna put me face on. I suggest you do the same!"

As the sugar dissolved, Ju arrived back.

"How's Dad doing?"

"Mrs. Millward, I think!" That was not the answer she was looking for, apparently.

"What?"

"Nothing; sorry, off in my own world!" It was my regular get out of jail card, and frankly, my regular absences from their world gave it credence! Living in your own world has its privileges for me and those around me. It allows them not to feel so guilty when they roll their eyes at me! For me—well, I don't know any other world, so good or bad, it's mine anyway.

"Like a pine cone!"

"What, Ju?"

"Your face. It's like a pinecone, with evergreen or ever grey sticking out of it!"

"I thought we had moved on?"

"No, I'm still working on it!" She grinned at me like I was her little brother who had never aged beyond his shoe size! As the first born, I often liked it that she took the lead every now and then. Like a Tour de France leader likes to give up leading and let the pack take the brunt of the wind. So now I could slipstream behind Julia.

"So, what's the status with Dad?" she said with a soft "a" that rhymed with "date us."

"In full recovery mode! Physical therapist says he could play for Town!"

"So not good then!" Ju was on a roll today. "No starting lineup for West Ham then? So not as good as we'd hoped! Anyway, you idiot, how did it go with Dr. Doran? That's what I meant!"

"You mean Dr. Death, right? God, that's a depressing place! He's like the grim reaper in tweed."

"Yep, I always hated going there with Mum back in the day – but what's up with Dad? That cough that doesn't want to go away, like a woodpecker in your soffit!"

"So… Dad didn't call you then?" I stalled. "Is the tea ready?" I needed the nurse on standby.

"Yep, here you go! Still no sugar, right?" She was proud she remembered, but politely confirmed. "So, Dad, what's up? Is it walking pneumonia? I told him to get it seen to before Christmas, but he's like you; he doesn't listen." She was now a frustrated mum to us both. She sipped her sweetened tea with almond milk and nestled into the low-back high chair at the kitchen counter, leaning in, ready to catch a library whisper. The brightly lit kitchen stood out against the dreary backdrop of her window like Hopper's "Nighthawk." I sat one stool over, like a guy entering a urinal giving her some personal space. The library quiet continued as I brought myself back from little brother to big brother.

"Despite Dad's appearance--" I took a sip, scalded my tongue, backed away from the cup. "Despite Dad's appearance," I began again. "He's really sick, Ju," and I lost it. It was all I could get out. The "tea-nurse" couldn't help, and unrelenting tears streamed down my face like rain on a Manchester windowpane. The salt felt good on my tongue, like liquid crisps, as the tears collected where the tea was supposed to be.

"Come on, Ad, it'll be alright." She moved closer, put her tea down in the personal space of the countertop, and embraced me. "We've been through worse, right? He'll be alright, right?" she said hopefully, and concerned. I started over with heavy heart, and heavy breath.

"Dad has stage four lung cancer." The last word drifted away like rain in the gutter. I had whispered the words and she tightened her embrace. I could feel her shaking rhythmically like an offset spin cycle. Her whole body reverberated in mine, shaking the whole house. I gripped her tighter as I stared blankly at the windowpane, wrapping around her to stop her coming apart like the pretty paper on a Christmas cracker. Rain now lashed at the window the way a willow's branch lashes at your face. The rain masked a battleship-grey exterior. The vibration became worse the faster it got; the less water in Ju's tumbler, the greater the syncopated pounding. Tears ran down her face, I had to presume, as I felt their wetness through my shirt the way a faulty pen bleeds into your shirt pocket. Brock had had a similar diagnosis only a year earlier. Our sadness grew alongside the dampness of my shirt, and the library silence deafened us.

Her husband had done a really nice remodel job, I thought. This kitchen had been moved three or four times; even though they had never moved house, it felt like it. The crisp, modern, clean lines of the glossy metallic cabinets had replaced Ju's cozy cottage phase. The seriousness of the black exterior softened by the coral-schemed glassy tile. The canned lights gave pock marks to the black sheen. The kitchen sink was back in front of the window after a short repose by the back door. An interesting idea had given rise to frustration, so this was their redesign. The wind picked up, throwing pebbles of rain at the picture window. Ju held on to me as you would hold on to a lamp post in a tornado. The rain tried to break in, whipping itself at the window like a slave begging to be freed from the Colosseum.

I pulled her up and into me, her late-winter jumper bunched up. I could feel the warm softness of her back shaking. It felt odd to touch her there; not since we wrestled as kids did we have any real contact of skin. My autistic staring out of the window continued while sensing the fine down-like hairs on her lower-dimpled back slowly perching with the sudden exposure.

"There are treatments," I hissed through the rain. Someone had taped over our snorkels and made breathing impossible. Ju began talking underwater abandoning her snorkel – I couldn't make out what she was saying through the rain and the pain. Our embrace was one, the way twins would exit the womb together if they were given the opportunity. I again tightened and gripped her the way a can opener would right before the first twist. I could feel the debris of our childhoods being brought to shore with the threat of an orphanage.

I held on to the back of Ju's jumper, straightened it a little as she continued to drain. The crashing tumbler slowly regained its equilibrium and started to bounce less frequently, slowly leaning into its natural spin. The rain streamed down the window the way sand moves across the desert, slithering a film over the outside world, disguising what lies beneath until that becomes the new reality.

"There are treatments," I repeated, unsure if she had heard me beneath the water. Still no response, but the spin-cycle started to wind down; her rigidness began to wilt like day four of a daffodil centerpiece. I held her a little more tightly, unsure if she was fainting or deflating.

"Surgery." The word sliced out of me, suggesting optimism. I felt her nod a couple of bumps into my chest. These were things we knew. We knew the standard of care. Toe has a verruca, doctor slices it off. A wart on your hand, laser removal or bio-freeze. If it doesn't belong – hack it off.

"Radiation," I continued with the cycle. More head bumps to my chest. Like an internal bio-freeze we can zap the offending cells. The head bump moved like a puppy in a pillow. We are going to declare nuclear war on these imperialist cells, annihilate them and their borders.

"Chemo," sounds so innocent like a Hawaiian Disney character but it is like the use of chemical weapons on your body – strategic poisoning – a breach of the Geneva Convention but approved by the FDA.

Tragic that we know the routine like the wash cycle. All of us are touched by cancer's victims, many in remission, few are cured. We didn't need a refresher course; Uncle Bill had the same schedule of events presented to him not that long ago. Medicines and treatments are kinder these days, in the way that fifty lashings of the whip are easier than a hundred.

The black cabinets, the coral tile blended like a watercolor in the dismal rain of pain. I had nothing to offer as we stood awkwardly, the way siblings never do except in times of misery and death.

"God, Ad, what's that awful smell?" The connection was broken.

"My armpit? I dunno; I was running at tennis then sweating in the dentist chair, then worked up thinking Dad's house had been broken into; then I fell off the fucking swing, walked here in the rain like a porous duck – it could be that!"

"Or the dog shit you've carted all over my new carpet!"

"Crap! Really? This lack of olfactory is really depressing. I'll clean it up – hand me that towel."

"Like hell – there's kitchen roll over there."

"Kidding! Of course I'll use paper towel; white carpets! Really who does that?"

"People without pets who insist on having guests leave their shoes at the door!" She pushed me away, in the chest, on the wet spots.

"Now don't go walking around; take 'em off!"

"I will, I will, stop shoving! I'll wash them in the sink."

"What is wrong with you? Are you mental? Outside with the hosepipe!"

"But it's raining cats and dogs?"

"And I hope they both shit on you! Look at the bloody mess--it's ruined!"

I rinsed off my crap-caked brogues in the hose and noticed the scuff marks from the talons of the park zombies. I shook an angry fist at the falling cats and dogs and thanked them for this good fortune! As I walked back in from the washed-out Lowery canvas, I wondered how soon it would be before the citizens of Chesterfield evolved back to the "Man from Atlantis"?

"Stop right there!" Ju was playing kitchen policeman or something.

"What the hell now? I'm drenched, me shoes are ruined, and my prayers to the Sun Gods have fallen on deaf ears."

"Socks off."

"If you were an escort, this might be fun, but honestly sis this has been a rough morning."

"You're right by the washing machine. Take your wet stuff off and I'll get you some jogging bottoms of David's."

"Now we're getting somewhere."

"When you're done, call Zoe to come round; she should hear it from us first."

The deputy head was back. She had mangled dry her eyeballs on my slightly bloody and sputum polo shirt, and now school was in session and time to restart with an assembly. We couldn't imagine Zoe being this strong, so it was best we were together. In my mind, though, I knew Dad was either being strong or in denial and probably could have held court with us all. But for now, he was enjoying the freedom of his new flex hip; he would worry about the cough at later time. From the outside he had the flexibility of a bungee cord, and inside the lungs of a coal face.

"I'll put the kettle on again." The MASH unit was once again being prepared for more incoming casualties. Zoe landed after twenty minutes of my scrubbing the white carpet. My efforts were greeted with:

"You fucking moron, Ad!" I'm cleaning up her anger for gentler ears. "You scrubbed so hard – now it's whiter than a Crest commercial! You've ruined it!"

Even when I clean up the shit, apparently, I'm still in it. I sat there on my haunches, scrubber, Resolve and a bowl of warm sudsy water around me like chess pieces in for the kill. I was as guilty as a puppy sitting next to a pile of poo, to quote Blackadder. And that was my position when Zoe walked in.

"Wow, Ju, you do have him well trained! Cleaning carpets on his vacation! Can you send him round to Hoover me stairs when he's done?"

"Not sure you want him; he might suck the fibers right out of the rug!"

"Hello, you two; I'm still in the room!"

"Sorry, we're not used to you being around!" Zoe's knuckles and words dug into me head.

"Yeh, you can leave that carpet; it's ruined as it is, but at least it smells better! I'll take you to B and Q tomorrow see how we can fix it!"

"Thanks!"

"Come on, Cinderella, make us a cup of tea!" Zoe was the third musketeer, the good-looking one and now apparently the funny one!

"Still two sugars, Zo?" I remembered "So not quite sweet enough yet then?" I wasn't giving up my funniest guy in the room title easily!

"Cinders, are these your shoes? Can we expect the prince at the door?"

They were ugly-funny sisters! Ju's kitchen with renovated soapstone island gave host to the morning show of news. The formalities of family catch-up and a review of last night's *Coronation Street* tease of an ending behind us, we now had the awful task of telling Zoe the truth about Dad's cough. We teased it through the needle's eye. First, we greased the lunchtime news with the hip recovery; then not even the whole sugar-cane plantation could make the medicine of Dad's cough go down any easier. The news came to Zoe like the cut of the North Sea at Bridlington. Ju and I each took a hand as if to reach out in prayer, connecting the three siblings. Zoe stared like a middle-aged woman receiving the news that she will be expecting triplets (much later the reason how I know this, if we have time). Then a Manchester rain of tears rolled down her face, briefly pausing at her lip where they waited for more to gather until they were all ready to jump off. Ju became the tear-sponge this time. News like this rekindles a sister's lost love. Common pain bringing uncommon closeness. Their muted embrace lasted the length of my tea. I sipped quietly from across the expansive countertop.

"Soapstone, eh?" I asked, wondering if one day this counter would disappear like a bar of Dove. Lamely I swept my hand across it like a rotary phone dial, slowly at first but then a little quicker, in a counter-clockwise direction. Smooth and hard like a baby doll's back. Lowery's painting behind them became even sadder, as it often did when you stared at it, the weather taking on the mood of our morning, as opposed to the other way around.

My sisters embraced with the tightness of arm-wrestlers, until they simultaneously tapped out on each other's back.

"I need to go fix my face," said Zoe, "and Ad, you should do the same!"

"Hey, not fair!" was all I had in response and then I quickly brought her up to speed on my morning. Well, not all of it.

Moments later, composed with fresh make-up, Zoe and Julia re-emerged like Academy Award presenters. I, myself, well—I just used more of the frozen food items from in the freezer.

"We need a plan of action!" said Ju, opening the first envelope. She wanted to proclaim a list of nominees.

"How's he doing?" asked Zoe. That wasn't in the script. She was supposed to suggest courses of action.

This time I refrained from poor comedy, though tempted of course.

"Honestly, a little quiet, but otherwise kind of normal," I informed her.

"Denial, he must be in denial." Ju's social work training came in handy while I refused another easy lay-up of a punchline.

"We should go round right now and see him," Zoe announced, wanting to commandeer the troops and put a war plan together.

"We should wait a while," I jumped in, not having an envelope of my own, for obvious reasons that I didn't want to share. Zoe had probably seen enough of her kids for the time being. She didn't want to delay; she had always popped round unannounced and Dad had always been over-enthusiastic to see her. As I have learned, there's a gaping hole in a home when the kids grow up. So, Zoe's proximity to Dad and her constant impromptu "popping round" gave him someone to cater for, someone to feel needed by, someone to talk to, someone to discuss the cricket with, someone to complain about the weather to, someone to share the extra Greggs' "buy-one, get-one free" creamy donut with, someone to hope for. The problem with being the favorite child is that you reciprocate by sharing equally high pedestals.

So, to protect Dad's potential fall from grace, I added:

"We should have a plan before we go over; I'm with Ju on that one." That was rare of me indeed. But war makes for strange relationships.

"Right. We can't just barge in and ask him to bare his soul. We should do lunch, just the four of us."

"I can get a sitter for tomorrow," said the favorite one.

"Perfect. How about the Red Lion? We used to love going up to Stanedge of a Sunday afternoon."

"Sounds like a plan."

"A normal kind of plan," Ju added. "We don't want to cause alarm; he's been through enough already without us melting down on him."

"We must be strong."

"And funny," I added. "Try to act normally!"

"Except try to be nice." Zoe threw in one more jab before accepting the white towel from the opponent's corner.

"Who's gonna call him?"

"Well, you of course, Zo," Ju and I said in unison. "You are the favorite one!"

"No, I'm not!" she said, aghast, mouth open for dental cleaning. Ju and I looked at each other and laughed aloud, knowing that the "favorite one" couldn't be either one of us!

CHAPTER 10

The Red Lion had many identities throughout its evolution from farmhouse to public house. Currently it offered a great "Carvery Lunch" special, as if the farmer's wife was preparing to feed a hundred or so of its farm hands. Two meals for twelve quid, so the four of us could really tap into that bargain. But, also at night, this was a romantic couples haunt. A popular first date spot—high on the bluff overlooking the town, with many a country road to divert one's attentions, on the way back home, if the occasion arose. Or if the Red Lion was too crowded, there were back-up plans. For most, it was the right distance for the first date's initial conversation as you sat next to each other trying to be your best version of yourself as the familiar Matlock Road wound its way higher. A road that was never too busy so that you could drive it a little distracted if you liked! If you were really distracted, as I mentioned there were country roads with lay-bys of gated fields – because sometimes you need to stop and smell her roses.

The Red Lion, with its fortified sandstone walls and slate roof, stood majestic above the fields it once owned. Currently this old country farmhouse was in its sixth generation of re-build since it emerged from the late 1700s. A monument to the brutal work of farming, it weathered quickly, unprotected alone on the plateau. Every ounce of moisture hailing in its direction it brushed off as a cliff face beats back the perpetual ocean. But each passing squall kidnapped particles of its substance in the way an old lover always takes a sliver of your soul with them, neither visible to the naked eye, though over time the wounds reveal themselves. In a photograph, the public house sported a new slate roof, in keeping with its history, the way hair-plugs of an old lover blend in at a reunion. Her skin of sandstone bore the scars, large and small, of centuries of living. The liver spots of the industrial revolution had been sandblasted clean decades ago, and now she was starting to age again, the way a facelift eventually sags.

Her weighty oak double doors hinged to bring a horse carriage through were deep enough to absorb a musket ball; today she only smiled a half smile for these punters armed with Ford Fiesta keys. Modern carpentry skills of laser precision had replicated the look of old photographs. Multiple small lead-lined windows the size of the Mona Lisa circled the building to bring in light to each alcove. These proud native sandstone walls sponged in the odors of the past, sucked up the tar of fireplace and cigar smoke, having grown oily like the sheen of an aging cricket bat. The interior had its own industrial imprint, juxtaposing the light of day with the grime of life. Her sturdy walls indented at the windows, leaving a bay for flowers and photos. Enough streaks of light entered so that you could see the ancient pavers at your feet. In a pre-recycling age, the floor consisted of worn-down tombstones. Horses, sheep dogs, lambs, pigs all had played their part in honing the stone of its forebears. Only in a few untouched corners of the old farmhouse could you make out the names and occasional dates of the long gone. Persian rugs of rich pinot noir reds and Tuscany field ochre had been scattered methodically within each alcove, warming the stone of the dead and softening the stride of guests. Today those exposed corner slabs lay hidden below refurbished pew bench seating with tapestry cushions. Weighty oak throne chairs continued the theme of formidable longevity – difficult for one person to move. Groups of five had a terrible time of adjusting the furniture to meet their dinnertime eating needs. Replicas of the Bayeux Tapestry adorned the stone walls to soften its edges, inviting one to the alcove of intimate conversation. Oak beams the width of hundred-year-old trees bridged the gathering places, cut down at a time when no one had seen them planted. As strong today as the day they left the forest border, witnessing, like silent immortal gods, the ephemeral life beneath them, chapel lintels eavesdropping on the fleeting lives of its taller inhabitants. A workplace room of function and protection had become a function room of fun and recreation, a place to share innermost feelings, made easier by Stella and Jack. A place to air laughter, wit, and somberness. A place to vent misery, depression, and sarcasm. A place to join, cajole, and separate. A place to prod, poke, and joke. A place to eat, drink, but not smoke. A place to decide the rest of your life.

The renovated farmhouse was centered around a cave of a fireplace. You could park a Clydesdale in it. One could easily imagine the dripping, slaughtered pigs, sheep, goats, and chickens hauled in from the shed roasting on the manually rotating, medieval spit, a gravy of blood and innards puddling on the stone slabs, farm hands and family alike taking their prized knife to the burned, crispy carcass, juices running wild between slabs like guttered rainwater, the head of the carcass staring in dismay as the surviving animals licked at the slabs. Lard- smothered logs were now long replaced by a natural gas line. The farmhouse's Inhabitants, workers, and slaves of the land were replaced by modern-day surveyors. Hikers, for the fun of pain with a promised ploughman's lunch versus the pain of hiking with clumsy scythe, harnessed plough, wayward sheep, and a hope for food. The farmhouse's many iterations gave way to this cozy, historical haven for secular celebration high atop the bluff, remembering the ghosts of its caretakers.

So, it was here at the Red Lion we met for lunch. Dad drove, his hip being fine, and it was his car and he "wasn't dead yet"! It was a fair comment. I'd been happy to drive with him when his hip was crappy and in need of surgery, so why not now when it was healed? Still a fair point. The lung cancer wasn't going to impair his driving--not today, at least. The day we had chosen was one of brilliant blue sunshine, the kind of day you never see in Chesterfield in summer! The kind of day that sixty-five days from now would make you rush to your back yard, unfold the slightly rusty-edged deck chair, and plonk down for an hour to cook up a pink lobster tan! Unattractive in every way--openly showing one's panic and gratuitous stupidity for warmth and vitamin D!

Easter was early, and Good Friday meant that everyone was off. Well, except the staff of the buffed-up old Red Lion.

"The usual, Jan, if you don't mind." Dad's Olympic-sized hip strode ahead of us all – patriarchal pride, I suppose.

"Got it right 'ere, duck! Saw yer car Roy pull in through t' winder." Jan hadn't been born for many centuries when the place was built, but you would but know it. She'd been there as long as I'd been going there; like an unrequited lover she took great care of Dad, poured his pint of Tetleys with a half inch lip of head just the way he liked it. A servant who wanted to be his queen.

"Champion, that, Jan!" he announced to her, taking a sip like a chef's new soup recipe – he approved. They both smiled and winked – their calling cards for forty or more years now.

"Honestly, Jan, if I didn't like your 'usband I'd be sneaking off to the Fox and Goose with ya!"

"You like 'im mor' 'an I do then!" she chuckled. But she knew he didn't like her that way, and yet, she loved him.

"See you've got tribe with yer today, it looks like. Come over all religious, 'ave yer?"

"No!" Ju was short like an affronted atheist, agnostic, or whatever. "Just happen to be all off today."

"Right." Her one word filled a sentence and Jan felt a little put in her misplaced place. Roy cringed a tad, like he'd invited an unappreciative member to his club. "What y'havin' then, duck?" She resumed her frothy welcome like sheep back to the fold.

"White wine and soda, please" Zoe - efficiently polite. Something sacrilegious in my mind about diluting wine. Some would say it's sacrilege to offer crap wines, therefore deserving of the affront. "Don't forget you're driving, Dad." Zoe was favorite and mum to him.

"I'm celebrating, I'm fine, I'm only having a couple," he answered with the pride of a club champion.

"Wha' yer celebrating, Roy?" Jan chimed in.

"New hip, Jan – I'm as good as new!" he beamed, and the beams above him acknowledged it.

I choked on my unordered drink. He was celebrating, and we were contemplating his demise. We could be in for a very long lunch. Receiving and discussing bad news on a Friday, never mind a Good Friday, was never a good way to go into the weekend. But my time in town was running short and, Ju and Zoe had other family to enjoy at Easter weekends. This was our dark day, our dear goodness Friday, our "oh God Friday."

"Soda and lime with a lemon—oh, and ice too. I'm driving as well." Ju was curt, grateful, and apologetic with her order.

"I'll just have a Stella, Jan, please." I didn't know it, but this would be one of the last beers my stomach could manage.

"Off yer Fosters then, Ad?"

"Bloody good memory, Jan." I beamed back at her like another club member.

"Well I ought t' bloody remember; you've ordered barrels of 'em in t' past."

The spout spluttered puked out its foamy brain into the pint.

"Barrels gone. Back in a minute." Jan was gone, headed to the former coal basement and former salt meat storage, which was now the home to aluminium barrels of refreshment.

"Let's grab a seat then," I offered, since I was gonna be without for a while. Pointless, I realized, as Dad was already off to his favorite "sitting" spot like a cat to its favorite window!

Zoe and Julia squeezed into the corner benches, their feet just about touching the gravestones below. Dad and I part lifted, part dragged, the heavy chairs as if they were anchored by two-inch tethers to the floor.

"Primo – this corner, yer mum an' me always tried to find this corner if we could. Sunsets over here."

"Not planning on being here that long, Dad!" laughed Ju. "I do like that it's quite private in this corner, away from the bar, tucked away from the toilet traffic—you can really talk here."

We all stared her down with rolling eyes checking out our frontal cortex.

"If you took away the pews of a church and put in a bar and fireplace it would look like the Red Lion," I added. "Pubs are like churches, aren't they? Little confessionals of private chatter around every table."

"Thank God there's no vicars listening in, though!" Ju cracked off. "It's enough that God is watching!"

"Or is it Santa watching?"

"No toys for you this year, Ad!" joked Ju.

"Normal then! What's weird now I'm older...."

"You mean Old!" Zoe always enjoyed the opportunity to spot me some years.

"Seriously, though, it's weird, in't it, when as a kid all you want from the God in the red suit are toys, and then one day, clothes are no longer a regrettable waste of the Christmas pile but actually sought after! We stop playing and become self-aware! Now I'm even older I could care less about self-aware – so where's me fuckin' toys? That's what I want – to be a kid and get toys!"

"What kind of toys you 'naner?" asked Zoe.

"I dunno – how about a new Subbuteo team?"

"Stopped making 'em years ago, Ad," Dad said. "I know; I tried to buy them for your Billy."

"Come on – must be able to find them on eBay! Whatever – toys – like George Bailey I want to live again! I want to play again. Everything is so adult these days; I want to live my inner-child!"

"Well that's because you are one!" Zoe poked, rolling both eyes this time, already fatigued with the brother who wants to be a child while she is piled high at home with children.

"Hardly!" said Ju.

"You're always doing fun things, Ad." Dad was concerned; there was a little depression coming into my voice.

"I dunno – maybe it's having a January birthday, so when I get to Easter this is really my last outside chance of getting a present… of getting a toy!"

"Okay, you are five years old! I knew it!" said Ju.

"What's wrong with wanting to be five again or always? No mortgage, no bills, just a random life of play, of toys, of creativity—what did we think of back then?"

"I can't remember yesterday!" said Zoe. "But I've got kids. I can ask them!"

"So crazy how the mind would find a constant place of hunger to search out and play, to draw or build if it wants to, or slam fire engines into skirting boards, or line up dolls, teddys, and Action Man for school time when it didn't even go to school!"

"Yep, you're an old git, Ad! Give me a glass of wine and Coror' and I'm good!" said Ju. This was her Tuesday Thursday play time.

"We laugh at those saddos who still collect and play with their action figures!" said Zoe.

"I still have some of yours in the loft, Ad, if you feel the need to…" said Dad holding off, worried his son's sadness would return.

"Chance to play would be a fine thing," added Zoe.

"Enough of your rambling, Ad," said Ju. She was getting anxious to start the day's agenda. She hated the school meetings that went off on tangents like this one her brother was taking them on.

"Is this for you, Ad?" It was Joe – an old neighbor of Ju's son. Great kid, good footballer in his day. Apparently, we were peers and friends now, as I wondered I stopped being "Mr. Griffiths" to him.

"Yes, tar Joe – still playing footy, Joe? When did you start here then, Joe?" I hit him with questions like it was Prime Minister's Question Time.

You could see Ju winding into her glass her fingers tongue and grooving around her tumbler of soda. Joe had been her neighbor and her student. He had the looks and manners of a Simon Cowell-produced boy-band.

"Where you playing at?" added Dad.

Joe smiled at our little conclave –

"So, one at a time," said Joe, catching his asthmatic breath. "Yes, playing for the Badger at Barlow on Sundays, and I started here a couple o' munths ago."

"You likin' it?" added Zoe politely.

"I'll have to come and check out a game if you're playing that close – usual Sunday at ten in t' morning?"

"Yes, Mr. Griffiths – we're at home this weekend, if ya like?" Joe had nice manners – Dad had apparently gone back to being Mr. Griffiths, if he was ever Roy. "Tickets are available on Ticketmaster!" Joe was cute funny. If we didn't know him, I think my sisters would have the kind of girl crush you have on a kid who is a full generation younger. Put a microphone in his hand, and I swear they would swoon.

"Joe, can you help with this tray?" Jan, being short, needed Joe's height behind the bar.

"Coming, Jan. Yeh, I'd love to see yer at t' game Sunday – me mam and dad might be there too. I'm sure they'd love to see you too," he said with the manners of a choir boy.

"Cheers, Joe. I might just do that!" said Dad with sincerity – he liked young people. I don't think he ever grew up. He was always your mate whether you were twenty-three or eighty-three.

"You know, if he wasn't Alan and Andrea's son, I could really fancy Joe!" blurted Ju.

"I know what you mean; he is really quite a dish, and that perfect bum!" Zoe couldn't resist adding her sixpence worth which seemed like a quid's worth, since we had all known Joe since he was filling nappies.

"He's like Shaun *of Coronation Street*, Deidre's grandson," Ju went on, like Dad and I weren't even there.

"To be fair, I couldn't pick between them."

"Well, at least Joe has a stable job while Shaun is just an actor!" I had to break the nonsense, as it was starting to sound like a hen night and the sister version of my Thursday night out with the lads. Who honestly ever cared what occupation the girl bursting out of the tank top was almost wearing like an accidental life ring thrown from a raft by her father before she left the house.

"I shagged Jan's sister once," Dad said with the nonchalance of opening a packet of cigarettes. Randomly his memory bank tapped on his hand, and out popped a cigarette of memory.

"Shut the front door!" laughed Zoe, who like the rest of the world had a hard time imagining their parents shagging – I used to… but not since the morning with you know who! We knew our parents had been young, because there were fragments of their lives captured in black and white photos at Nana's house—little smartly dressed figures with unknown relatives and friends emerging like smartly dressed ghosts from the rolling fog brought to life by the silver-halide crystals. Nana never had a stack of random pictures, or boxes of them like we grew up with. Any photo ever taken was prized and framed, all posed, no spontaneity, couldn't waste a shot, think of the expense. Candid was for royalty and the nobles. The "wasters," as Nana would call them. Being Scottish, she had never gotten over the murder of Queen Mary centuries before.

"How was it?" is what I wanted to say regarding the Jan's sister shag – you know, like mate to mate, discussing the game."Dad!"

"Really!" One after the other, Zo and Ju protested the information that was like toothpaste out of its tube; once out, you couldn't get it back in. Might as well brush and smile on.

"I'll be dead one day," Dad said as he sipped into the diminishing foam of his pint, looking over the glass like Humpty falling backwards. "Not any time soon, I hope; not at all, preferably." He put down the pint. "But at some point, I will be one of the ghosts that haunt this place after closing time." All three of us stared at Dad. He was serenely calm. He must have thought he was talking to three statues or gargoyles of punters planted in the pub corner to garnish curiosity.

"See that cricket match over there?" He pointed with his pint to the three lost ramblers who followed his directions intently, out of the south-facing window. Sunlight illuminated and fired up the pastures and in a couple of hours the mid-sky sunshine would fire up this corner window like the open engine door to a steam train.

"I remember watching me first cricket match over there. I mean, we played all the time as kids, but aged about thirteen I actually watched a match for the first time sitting on the grass, close to the boundary rope for the closest view. I remember lying on my belly, like a sniper, hands shielding my eyes like binoculars, trying to focus in on the game which seemed so far away, further than any movie screen. Out in the middle was Brock, Uncle Bill, sporting his Old Baileans cap, traditional gleaming whites, his v-neck jumper emblazoned with our crest. Geoff Wildgoose at the other end. You all know Geoff," Dad nodded to us, took another even, and deliberate sip of his beer, the evenness was measured by the foolscap lines remaining in the glass. "The Geoff of Wildgoose construction who you've all known for years was a fine batsman. Geoff and Brock stood out in the middle of that pitch over there like John Wayne and Alan Ladd, a fierce-some pair. Bill and Geoff would slash their cricket bats like Zorro, carving imaginary

'Zs' into the wine-colored balls. They defended the crease like Butch Cassidy and the Sundance Kid. Their speed and skill was effortless—better timing you wouldn't find in a Rolex factory!" Dad spoke sometimes like he was recording a historical novel. He transported us back in time – we pictured those carefree kids in the school photo, all shades of grey, smiling animated like Disney cut-outs planted in the fiery green meadow, a few hectares over from the pub window, ambitions running over.

"Bill and Geoff were revered by all their classmates – they opened the batting intent on leaving their teammates on the bench for the rest of the day. Brock and Geoff deftly blocked and turned the ball away from them; occasionally swatting away a pesky high ball like it was an errant fly. It was here at this less than perfect pitch that Brock missed only one of a few in-swingers. It clipped the inside corner of his bat, shot straight up, and split his lip, hard enough to damage a nerve, which is why from that game on he always had the little 'V' in his lower lip. The little 'V' didn't ever get better; it looked as though it had been dented by years of pipe smoking. Girls wondered what it was like to kiss it. Many girls wondered; few ever learned. Brock did all his bragging on the cricket pitch, daring the ball and bowler to trick him. The uneven pitch beat him that day; his wicket remained intact even if his lip didn't. The tomato soup of blood spilled down his whites like poppies on a Normandy cross. You could hear the coach yell – 'You should have kept your eye on it William!' I lay there baffled by the remark thinking then his eye would be bleeding. Bill bled his way to an unbeaten 65 runs that day – he and Geoff had an opening partnership of 103, only Albert Dobson got to bat the rest of the afternoon. The team declared they had enough runs, and they proved it in the two hours after tea."

"How do you remember such detail? I can't remember what I had for tea yesterday," laughed Zoe somewhat nervously, only then taking a sip of her soda and lime.

"You'll start to remember your childhood in greater detail soon someday," Dad said matter-of-factly. "I can feel the warmth of that day seeping into me jumper like a toasted Hovis slice. I was warmed on both sides by the earth and sun in some kind of pagan homage to that memory. I remember thinking I wanted to be just like Brock – always calm with focused vision. He always held a very patient view of his present and future. On the the other hand, I wanted to tear the world up. Learn as much about sports as possible – yes, maybe I will become a sportswriter someday. I had a dream, an anxious dream to recreate this day for Bill, so I started a school paper."

"I never knew that, Dad!" remarked a surprised Zoe.

"Well, the dream died, along with my metabolism, years ago. Didn't seem any point in bringing it up anymore. Nightly I wrote for hours, submitted endless strips of articles to my paper – I handled sports and left the news, mostly cafeteria complaints to the rest of the board. But what I think is how quickly a life dream can shift."

"You were in the Air Force though, right, Dad?" Zoe, like his favorite cheerleader and lawyer, reminded him of his alibi.

"True enough – and maybe that's where the dream went to die. I can't say for sure, but time served and my mission was derailed or deplaned! If you like? Even those buried visions keep resurfacing, like New Orleans coffins in a flood. Tragic how my life is over and the dreams flood in, like the outtakes at the end of a movie where lines are missed or improv abounds and we laugh at how it spontaneously fell apart but in the movie it was re-shot and edited. Life isn't like that. Life is the out-takes, all of the captured film—there is no dress rehearsal, as they say, and there is no editor either to piece it back together to have it make sense. Life is a running film, one director one actor, one colorist, one sound manager, one costume designer, one envelope with several nominees for who did the best job."

"I see what you mean, Dad, but where do we go from here?" I hadn't been drinking, just meandering with Dad and his memories, picturing him watching Uncle Bill the way I had watched him as a youngster. A memory collision.

"So now these dreams are once again hammering at my door as the Academy Award Envelope is about to be presented. Death is a great motivator, and I want to bring life to a few last memories, a few last goals. I had told Brock after every time I got in trouble for playing footy that I would play for Town one day ,and I would like him to see it – I would be representing team Griffiths. That all his childhood years of covering for me would be worth it. He believed in me with that renegade football – I can't let him down again." Dad took another measured sip. "I can't have that memory of his disappointment haunt me again, as I know it will. I want to play for Town. I want to do it for Bill." One more. gentle sip. "I want to show my parents what it meant to me when those memories return." Another sip; they were coming at a faster clip. "I want for you to know I honored my brother Bill and that life is honoring your 'self.'" He put the quotation marks there himself whilst still holding his pint. "Honor the pieces of you, the essence of you, the memory of you that you live with the moment you awaken. Wake up with those pieces of you intact not hurt and regretful. Wake up knowing you honored your promise to yourself and those around you as if you had declared and shared them. We can't go back and edit the film, we can only turn the projector on anew each day, run the film through, make sure it shows what you want it to show." And with that he set down the empty glass. It was lined like the painted stripes of a lighthouse.

Our gazes moved from Dad's glassy eyes to the glassy lines, each demarcation like a commercial break in his life story. We all became heavy in our chairs, like little trainee Buddhas unable to move because of the words of the master, waiting on our next instruction – which, if we rewind the film, we knew was in there. Dad had given us his "thing to get up for." In his passive request, he let us know he needed a supporting cast.

"Is that your bucket list then, Dad?" Ju went first. Dad shrugged. "Just one thing? To be sure? You don't want to see the Taj Mahal, the Pyramids, the Great Barrier Reef, the Empire State Building? The Northern Lights? The Eiffel Tower? The Parthenon? The Colosseum? The Canals of Venice? The Grand Canyon?" Ju sounded kind of disappointed, like a travel agent whose client had instead opted for a "staycation." For someone with a fear of flying, Ju would have had Dad flying all over the world for one last glimpse of humanity's great achievements and the Earth's most remarkable destinations.

"Yeh, Dad, I'll go with you!" Zoe chimed in. "I'll take you wherever you want to go! Make a list."

"It's a generous offer Zoe, Ju," said Dad casually, looking at her like she hadn't heard a word he had said.

"Joe, if you don't mind, can I get another pint?"

"Right away Mr. Griffiths." Joe's politeness was almost as cute as his bum. In an age where manners constituted rolling your eyes up from your phone to respond to a question, it was nice to hear someone being addressed formally, with kind respectfulness. So often that respect, unless earned by reality TV, is left out, abandoned like Facebook was for Snapchat. Merely being older didn't command much respect these days, unless of course you had gender confirmation surgery or hosted *Britain's Got Talent*.

"Tetleys, wasn't it?" How cute; Joe even checked with the knowledge that he already knew, just to let my dad know he knew. To let him know he was important, important to have his preferences recognized.

"God, he's good!" Ju jumped at the chance to praise him.

"I know he's a friend, but I would love a WWA roll around with Joe!" Julia had gone from great wonders of the world to small wonders like Joe's bum.

"Hello! Ladies! Focus! We are on Dad's bucket list, not yours!" I cut the tension like a machete on a bungee – the fears crashed harmlessly into the river below.

"So, you don't want to travel, Dad?" Ju confirmed.

"I would love to see something – get out of this village, anywhere really, not Scarborough perhaps, but anywhere, not Cleethorpes. In fact, I'd rather stay in bed than visit those places!" Zoe was on a roll, a nervous roll. Dad had raised the spectre of his not being here one day, and we knew she would take it the hardest. He was good to all of us, but she had more recently been there for him, taken care of him, rode shotgun with him; they were confidantes. Their closeness had grown and matured together like an only child, whereas Ju and I—especially me—had the closeness as toddlers. Ju, as she would note often, as the middle child had been cheated at both ends!

"Don't you want to see the Great Barrier Reef?" Zoe had the beauty and majesty of the reef positioned in her question.

"I did once." He paused. "I wanted to see it all once." He paused again. He flipped the beer mat in his hand, checking both sides; they didn't match. He put the beer mat half on the table in front of him and half off. He lined up his left hand underneath the hanging edge, closed his eyes for a moment, and flipped the beer mat, catching it neatly in his hand. The beer mat protruded from his hand like it was in a naked Muppet's mouth. He opened his eyes nonchalantly.

"Still got it!" he said. "Not dead yet!" and he laughed. He had all his faculties and cognitive talents.

"Okay, Dad, what's your record?" I said, competitive as ever.

"Thirty-seven in both hands with my eyes shut!" Dad was more competitive than anyone I'd ever met. It wasn't until his body started to break down that I could beat him at any sport.

"You sure? That's a ton!" I looked around the room; there weren't seventy-four mats in the whole pub.

"Yep. Had to ask Jan for extra mats from storage. It was easier then - I was still smoking!"

Our corner went quiet for a second. The cigarette revolver's hammer had been cocked – it had taken fifty-plus years to finally catch up to him.

"I loved watching all those Jacques Cousteau documentaries, so I'll just have to make do with that. It would have been nice to swim with the clown fish, or Nemo as he is better known these days. There was a time I would have dared to climb the Pyramids or the Eiffel Tower, but …." There was no need for him to finish the sentence. He had gone to the end of his paragraph.

"Here you go, Mr. Griffiths." Joe placed the pint on the mat and Roy took a very long quaff, the way one might inhale your first cigarette following a trans-Atlantic flight. For all the nicotine he'd inhaled during his life, I still believe he could sit at the bottom of the swimming pool longer than his children, the way he had always done when we were facing our fear of the water. He had built his lungs as a high board diver, to calm his nerves, and to hold his breath as he dove deeper and deeper into his pool. Diving deeper, taking all the velocity gravity offered and still touching bottom. Holding his palms up and gently flipping them like Nemo's friends – treading water. Echoes of splashes above – solitude below. A thinking corner by himself behind his imaginary anemone. There is safe serenity in the depths of the pool's amniotic fluid. Eventually no light, sound, or smell can penetrate its comfortable clutches.

A bullet can only penetrate the water so far; and sitting there you can look up and see the bullets whip into the water, stall and fall to the pool bottom. The blustering snap through the meniscus quickly silenced, its intent broken and laid to rest. The sprint of a bullet's youth halted by a snapped hamstring, rendering it harmless, limping to its inevitable finish line.

A second quaff and the pint glass was empty.

"You in a rush, Dad?" asked Zoe.

"No, Zo, just wanted to see if I still had the breath for it!" he cracked.

"Impressive, Mr. Griffiths," said Joe, noticing the pint was empty in seconds. "Play rugby, did you?"

"As a matter of fact, I did!" puffed Dad proudly.

"Then I'll be right back; hand me your glass, unless you want a fresh one?" offered Joe.

"Barely used this one!" and Dad proudly handed it over to Joe.

With both hands empty he took two beer mats, put them on the edge of the rock-solid table, placed both hands under, flipped and caught them.

"See, I haven't lost it yet!" bragged Dad, now holding both mats like two aces at the Black-Jack table. On a different day I—actually we—would all have had a go at beating Dad or at least matching his little show.

"Right about that, Dad!" applauded Ju.

"The thing is, I don't want to travel any more. I'm at the cul-de-sac of life. If I travel, it means time away from someone, one of you. Seeing more of strangers in strange places—well, it's not so appealing any more. Don't get me wrong; with more time, I would have loved to see it all, but the color of travel has greyed with my hair and as it has thinned, so has my desire." He paused.

"Thanks again," he said to Joe, who had quietly this time, placed another pint in front of him on the mat he'd brought. "The wonder of the world has nothing on the wonder of seeing my family, remembering the places where I loved, lost, and won. It's about purpose. We lose a lot of it as we age – our identity dissipates with our looks – our identity goes away with our kids to college or to wherever they end up – we are left a little shell-shocked – lots of life filled raising and providing for a family, raising funds for bills and food for all, like running from the bulls – you can't stop until one day the bull quits running – leaving you at the end of an unknown street wondering how you got there – you knew why – but not how – avenues passing by in a blur while the bull's breath charged your ear– then the street broadens into the cul-de-sac of the future – a little bit of street left but emptying into a bowl. This narrow view of homes and places unlike a delta, with everyone and every memory back down the street."

"You sound sad, Dad; you alright?" Zoe asked cautiously.

"Ha—well, I have been better!" and he lit the table with his smile and familiar wink.

"So, looking back down the street, the one thing you want to do is play for Town? That's it, right, Dad?" Ju looked at him disappointed, as you'd look at a bright kid looking only for a passing grade.

"Shouldn't be hard to do," agreed Zoe in a not so disappointed tone.

"In a real game!" Dad added.

"What, like in one that matters?" Ju questioned.

"Yes, one that matters," he confirmed.

"Well, how the bloody hell do you think that's going to happen?" Julia was unimpressed by the idea to begin with and now rolled her eyes at what she saw as the ridiculous.

We quietly sipped our drinks. All I could think of was "Booking dot yeh!" There's no travel site for this wish.

"Do they even do open tryouts?" asked Zoe.

"Doubt it," said Ju. "It's all meticulously calculated these days. Speed trials and strength measures and that's for t' nippers!" She was starting to drop back into her old brogue. The one that decades in front of kids had been polished up and hidden.

"They're not bad enough to do open casting! This is not like the movie *Invincible* about Vince Papale."

The rest of the table looked at me like I was an Arabic speaking Muppet.

"Don't know that one, Ad," Zoe mocked.

"The Philadelphia Eagles?"

"Okay, need the sat nav! What are you talking about, Ad?" said Zoe.

"Doesn't really matter – but anyway, the Eagles had been bad for years, so they put out an advertisement that they would do open calls in the hope to get someone who wasn't in the system, hadn't been through the system and was unknown."

"It's a movie, right?"

"Yes, but it actually happened!"

"Was the bloke in his sixties?" Dad added.

"Well no, but..." I paused. "No matter; it's not gonna happen anyway."

"So, that's it, Dad? That's what you want to do with the rest of your life?" Ju was angry at Dad, I think me, and the cancer, but mostly the cancer and the world.

"Yes, my hip is right again, and I've always said I'm still twenty-three in me head," the C word was left out of the conversation, like a Victorian child, seen and not heard. "I've been working out at physical therapy and at home, my legs are as strong as when I stopped playing six-a-side!"

"But Dad, that was years ago!" Ju was getting frustrated. She had been happy the day he'd finally hung up his trainers. She had been the wife and mum figure for many years – she had "reason," middle-child reasoning, middle child balance. "Dad, you can't go trying out for Town; it looks pathetic...." She hadn't meant it to come out that way, and the world paused for a split second allowing the trio to stare her down.

"Dad, you're not forty anymore! Or even fifty! Jamie Vardy syndrome doesn't strike blokes in their sixties just because they have made a wish!" She paused. "I'm sorry, Dad, but this seems like a colossal waste of time!" Ju stood up to leave, the heavy oak of the table unmoved as she slid her legs out of the bench like exiting a kayak. It paused her movements, tearing at her emotions as she needed to leave.

"Sorry, Dad, I need some air." She abandoned her drink and strode through the impressive doorway, her heels echoing a speedy typewriter clip along the gravestones, until a sweeping draft told everyone she was gone. Once outside, she ran across the gravel lot to her car. Didn't get in, just leaned on the driver's side door, releasing a jugular of tears. She whispered to herself, "It's no use, it's no use, it's not fair--" and this was why she hated God – this God was going to make her an orphan, and even though she was in her early forties, she still wanted to be someone's kid, someone's proud daughter. She reached for a tissue, then realized she had left her handbag and keys under the table. Her sleeve would have to do. "Why do you have to take him?" she asked in her alfresco chapel. "I'll confess anything," she continued. "Why him, why now, why ever?" She used the other sleeve, leaving matching snail trails of tears and mascara. She kicked at the gravel, little ghosts of powdery dust spilled up and over her black Mary Janes like mushroom clouds. She was overdressed to be outside. Some of the gravel found its way into her shoe, like little silver balls finding the holes in a child's puzzle. She tried to shake them out but only succeeded in shaking them further in. The sun warmed her back and the breeze chilled her face. She raised her chin high above the car as a puppy would, reaching for more air, capturing more of the breeze. Soft scents of heather floated to and beyond her from yesterday's rain.

Closing her eyes, she wanted to inhale the moor's zephyr and be transported back to the camping days in Abersoch where she played her father's Little Miss Sunshine long before her sister came along. She had been the baby of the family for almost a decade. She was Daddy's little girl with an older and massively annoying, sweaty brother. He had Dad's attention for all things sporty, but Julia had him for the rest of the time. He was hers for most of her childhood. He always returned from work trips with parcels of goodies. He walked back into the kitchen like an unveiled Santa. He made no apology for spoiling her on his return. Sure, her brother got stuff, silly stuff like football cards. She got real presents, Cindy dolls and matching ponies. She got big-girl hugs. Found herself running through the kitchen to meet him. "How's my little princess?" he would announce. "Daddy! She's much happier now you're home." Ju loved to jump into his arms while they were full of trinkets. She wrapped her legs around his waist, and he would hook his arms under hers. She loved the scratchiness of his skin as he held her close and she popped a kiss on his cheek. He would always be her king. She pined for him when he was gone. Her mother never really knew how to play with her. "I don't do playing," she would respond when asked. She wasn't mean about it; it wasn't something she was given to. Whereas Daddy made everything a game.

Back in Wales, the rain poured hard the entire way through the Welsh mountains. Your only guide that you were in the mountains was that your ears were clicking and popping as you were taking the line around the darkish brown bits on the map. The mountains themselves could have been any hill of any denomination, thought Julia.

"The hills are all clouds, Daddy!" the young Julia said from the back seat. "Keep on this road until you come to a crossroads; then go left." Julia was an excellent map reader even at six years old. Her mum had declined the request to do it last year when they went to Bude and Julia had said, "Let me try!" eagerly trying to please her father. In the same way, she learned to ride her two-wheeler for him as well as for herself. She wanted him to be proud of her.

"Alright, Juey, are there any numbers on that crossroads?"

"Don't know, Daddy! I'll try to find some!" Julia was navigating our way to a farmer's field in the northern Welsh peninsula. I was older, and I guess I could have helped.

"Found it, Daddy! Take the A487 toward…toward a town with a capital P then lots of 'l's' and a 'w'!

Mum sat there, quietly emotionless, staring through the drizzle.

"She's right, Dad," I said, looking over her shoulder at her tiny finger following the line. It helped that Dad had marked up the route beforehand, but she was navigating and following his lead.

"The town is Pwllheli!" Dad announced. "And that means we're nearly there!" which was parental speak for we have at least another hour of rain-soaked, brain-crushing, winding roads and bank holiday traffic. The bleached candy-floss clouds never parted like in the movies as we arrived at the farm. As was typical, the farmhouse was stationed in the middle of the farm, down a winding tractor trail that had been worn into the fields so as to reach the main road. Tractors had no problem negotiating the craters and puddles; our Hillman Hunter, on the other hand, struggled like a geriatric marshalling his first Zimmer. Inch by inch we flopped forward, the tyres grinding at the wheel-well. At last, wider swaths of mud made a grand entry way to our "hotel" destination. The crumbling stone farmhouse perched at the top of its sheep fields had recently seen tourists, and specifically campers, as a new source of income. Very recently apparently. The door to the lobby was locked or seized up, since the rusted hinges must have been inches thick.

The campsite was a field and up until last week had been a campsite for sheep. They had probably booked it for the impressive views of the village that lead down to the beach. The sheep must have known the persistent rain was likely to continue into this week and had transplanted themselves to lower fields for the remotest possibility of taking in the scenery.

"Good morning--Mr. Griffiths, I presume!" inquired my dad with Ju by his side. Mum and I stayed in the car. The puddles were too numerous and potentially hazardous to Mum's footwear, so she had remained behind. The favorite child had gone along with Dad. Her feet too small for stilettoes. She had her wellies and was proud to use them.

"You can call me Dai?" said the stereotypically dressed Welsh farmer. He'd emerged from the back of the farmhouse after Dad had repeatedly knocked at the door.

Dai Griffiths, a man of infinite charm for a farmer who had spent decades as a child herding sheep around the hillsides, pointed in the general direction to where we should park and plant our tent.

"We share the last name, Dai – I'm Roy Griffiths," said Dad, expecting some royal or family upgrade.

"Nice – you'll find half the village is named Griffiths," said Dai and offered his scaly hand as a counter on which to put the payment.

"Thirty pounds," said my Dad in his for some reason an adopted posh accent, like he'd just arrived at the Ritz.

"Toilet an' shower are round the back," said Dai.

"Easy enough," thought Dad, but it came out.

"Sorry?" said the half-listening sheep whisperer.

"Nothing--"

"You can set up anywhere that's open," sang Dai, and he returned to the back of the house through the brilliant Mediterranean sunshine, leaving us to head to our cabana. At least that would be how our holidays shaped up in later years. For now, we headed through the still- bleached candy-floss clouds through an open field, surrounded by openness and an audience of sheep.

"We can pick anywhere," Ju announced to me and Mum when she got back to the car.

"I pick Spain!" whined Mum.

This was as close as Mum had come to camping, this sitting in a car in a field. Usually if she was sitting in a field in a car, there would be a lover in her embrace. Her sisters had married farmers, and yet this was as far as she had ventured on to any farm. The heavy mist stuck like mercury balls to their clothes. The mist would have fallen as rain, but it was too close to its source. Dad stopped in the middle of the field, his decision encouraged by the sinking of the tyres.

"This is perfect, Dad!" Ju announced.

Mum half looked back at her as she jumped out of the car. Ju and I were thrilled to be out of the back seat after rolling around the rolling hills. The Hillman was too old, and we were too young to realize the benefits of being strapped in.

From the side of the car we stared at the blob of orange on the car roof. This great pumpkin, a Santa's sack, contained our holiday home. Responsibly, Dad had tied the sack on really tightly—"Don't want it to fall off on the motorway," he'd announced as he demonstrated his Eagle Scout knots. He had to be regretting all those perfect knots as we were drenched by the time he dragged it off. Mum was perfectly dry and would only get out when there was a threshold to be carried over.

Family-sized tents were the Rubik's Cubes of the '70s—ordinarily smart people taken to task by something so outwardly simple. Our father, a man who could rumble through tough crosswords daily over toast and tea, had been rehearsing tent erection on our lawn for days prior to taking this trip. Ju and I would return home from school to see the alien orange blob, like Dad's Stonehenge, perfectly centered on our lawn. Excitedly, we had waited for Dad to get back from the job site. Three days we honed our skills as Dad's pit crew.

"Guide ropes?" Dad would call out the checklist.

"Got them!" Ju responded – they were her responsibility. One Across.

"Tent pegs – twenty of them?" Dad paused to let me count them out.

"All present and correct, sir!" I flattered him with my little military knowledge. Two Down.

"Orange Blob?" Dad called to attention and we all yelled out:

"GOT IT!" Three Across. Mum stared blankly from the kitchen window, puzzled by the excitement of taking what was sure to be a miserably uncomfortable holiday. For a woman whose only stay in a hotel had been on her honeymoon, she was insistent on high standards. Four Down.

"Ground sheet?"

"Have it here!" I shouted. It was 12 Across and 8 Down.

After practically an hour we had the checklist completed, including the beds, the cooker, the sleeping bags. We were ready for our mission. For some reason, mallet wasn't on the list – whether Dad had it remembered by osmosis or not I don't know – I didn't think to second guess our team leader.

The timer was on, and we unpacked the blob. Dad wrestled with the tent posts; they were – Five Across. It was like watching a chimp wrestling an octopus! Legs and arms everywhere, misdirected and twisted in some contortionist duel.

Dad called to each of us to hand him pole after pole until the mechanical spider was complete. He draped the tent shell himself; he was the only one of us tall enough to reach the center roof and tie it off! Once the shell was on like marzipan, it was our responsibility to line up the guide ropes and pegs with their respective hooks. We ran around like a doctor to a nurse – Ju calling for the pegs to her ropes. Dad followed after with the mallet. He tugged our lines and pounded the peg with one blow, like a fisherman making sure the fish was dead. We moved in a clockwise direction around the tent, like a rotating village clock ornament – standing up bending down, Thwak! standing up bending down, Thwak! Standing up, bending down, Thwak! The last one given just a little extra like it was an extra knot or something.

We were ready for Silverstone. But even in Formula One, there are weather safety codes.

The rain in Wales spits like its proverbial dragon. Like it actually wanted to really hurt you. Where water stings like fire on your skin. Heavy, too, like it's trying to push you into the earth.

Part of our failing was we had only done dry runs. The other part was that the mallet, which lived in the garage on peg board and not with the orange-blob, never made the check-list. The force of the rain kept the marzipan shell on the mechanical spider; we did as we had rehearsed and laid out the guide-ropes and pegs, our wellies marking the broader area where we had stood.

"Where's the mallet, where's t' mallet?" Dad was getting frustrated as he foraged in the orange Santa sack, looking for the last present.

"Must have put it in the boot, Dad," offered Ju helpfully.

"Right, right." Dad was chilled – looking down at Ju through his matted '70s locks and sideburns.

The Hillman Hunter's boot was not listed on its highlight features, and so when Dad opened it to see that it was jammed, any hope of quickly finding a mallet soon faded.

"Damn it!" spat our own Welsh dragon into the boot. Leaning his bum on the boot, he closed it back up.

We looked at him horrified as he came back empty-handed.

"This'll have to do!" We stepped back startled. Then we heard the familiar sound of Thwak, Thwak, Thwak! Dad had removed his platform shoe and was driving the pegs home with its heel! Thwak! Squelch! Thwak! Squelch! could be heard as he worked his way around the tent!

"Now for the ground sheet!" he declared, as if we were laying the foundation stone to our home. The origami tarp was unfolded and placed corner to corner and attached on the inside. Stepping on it was the same as walking on a yogurt lid. Dad carried Mum from car to tent, standing her up like a lamp in the high part of the tent.

"There you go, love!" He smiled with worship as she landed, and her stilettos, like tent pegs, went straight through the ground sheet! Mud bubbled up like blood through a bullet hole.

"Ah, crap!"

"Yes, Roy, and I'm stuck – these shoes will be ruined!" shrieked Mum. Dad dived down like a pearl snorkeler to unbuckle them as Mum teetered.

"There you go! Free at last!" Dad tried to joke but you know when someone has a firm hold on the serious it just etches the stone deeper.

"I'm going to the bedroom," said Mum, with a disparaging huff which was a common response since the incident.

"What shall we do! What shall we do! We're sinking, Dad!" Ju had mild panic.

"Let's lift it up at that spot, wipe it off, and tape it up!" said Dad. The tape was number 17 Across and easy to find in the blob.

With all of us inside the tent, it was as if we had been shrunk into an asthmatic orangutan's lungs. Dampness and tension fogged up the castle as Dad directed Mum to help him with the interior compartments that would become the boudoirs. We had our own room, just like home. Meanwhile Ju and I attended to the rest of our "inside" list.

"Will it ever stop raining!" Mum was feeling claustrophobic quickly. Rain hammered down and mud splattered the outside like a kindergarten paint fight where all the colors mixed to brown. Ju and I again broke out the Chinese checkers and played squatted on the cots we had erected.

"I don't know if I can stay here," called Mum from the cotton-walled bedroom. "I think I'll go back in the car!"

"No need; I'll open a window!" said Dad as he unzipped for the great reveal. The mesh net of a window opened to a sinking Hillman Hunter and let in so little light that even Bob Cratchit would have been unable to work.

"Give me the keys!" she insisted. Dad held out his hand and Mum walked straight into the hanging night light.

"My eye, my eye! What was it?"

"The paraffin lamp," Dad answered.

"I'll get the peas," said Ju, her natural reaction, not realizing this castle had no fridge or freezer.

"I'll rinse off a tea towel and run it under the stand-pipe by the farmhouse." Dad was soaked anyway, and left to find even colder water while Mum's eye swelled like a puffer fish.

"My feet! My feet!" Mum had tripped on the tape and the mud was coming back in. Mum danced around the mud like it was hot coals. "My hair, my hair!" She had removed her cellophane hair protector once inside. "Oh my God!" Mum looked up in furious disdain – drops of water smacked her forehead like some water torture! "It's raining inside now! I knew this was a bad idea, never wanted to come in the first place, don't know what your dad was thinking! My perm is ruined!" Her voice stamped its feet where her own could not without sinking. The mud once again pumped through the tarp like the swelling on Mum's brow—not dissimilar colors, if I remember correctly.

"Got it!" announced Dad as he ducked into the tent and stood upright, not expecting to see Mum right behind the flap. He caught her under-chin with the top of his head and she went down like Ali in Manilla! Like straight out cold. Barnum and Bailey clowns would have been proud of this farce. Dad tried in vain to catch her, but he was coming up as she was going down. Opposites don't attract, in case you were wondering. The flowers of Mum's floral dress were laid to rest in the mud from whence they came. "Is she dead!" Ju panicked.

"No!" Dad lost his cool.

"Daddy!" Ju was in tears – probably not because of him yelling, but because we would be privy to more rows and the likelihood that our holiday would be over. The tent's membrane couldn't hold back the torrent of precipitation – and it dripped on Mum as Dad tried to sit her back up. It looked like an adult christening! She came around from the temporary sleep and looked lovingly into Dad's eyes.

"Are you alright, love?" Dad pleaded. He grabbed the wet cloth he had dropped as he entered. He gently dabbed Mum's face, pocking it with mud like he was a creating a faux-finish on the living room wall.

"Not good," was all she said, as a drip started to land on her forehead once more. Ju and I returned to our Chinese checkers.

"Roy, I told you I didn't want to come! I knew this was a terrible idea. I've never been camping before, and this is why! This is a bloody disaster! You only wanted to come because Jean and Trevor are coming! I've seen how you are with Jean! Always cuddling up to her!" This old rant had been percolating since crossing the Welsh border and the imminence of a campsite.

"No different than you and Mick!" battled Dad defensively.

"Mick and I were friends in school—that's different. We're just friends, that's all!"

"First friends!" It was their code for their first sexual encounters.

"Mick and I will always be close. Our mums are neighbors. So, leave him out of it. I've seen the way you and Jean are in the pub – don't think I haven't seen the way she looks at you!" Whether it was the crack on the head, the lack of medication, or pure fury, Mum's glare electrified the orange pressure-cooker.

"That's silly – she's Trevor's wife. Trevor and I have been mates since primary school. Why would I mess with Jean?" It didn't make sense, but these things often didn't.

"Like that ever mattered with you!" Mum's voice grew loud enough to push back the rain.

"What does that mean?"

"You and our Iona! Don't you deny it!"

"I don't! There's nothing to deny!"

"You're a bloody liar! A bloody liar!" Steam filled her gills and she fixated on Dad like Jack Nicholson in *One Flew Over the Cuckoo's Nest.*

"Why don't you lie down? I'll put the kettle on," Dad offered.

"I think it's your turn," whispered Ju to me. This had become a familiar scene – we played on like we weren't there. We played on like we weren't theirs.

"...and they say we'll have some fun if it stops raining!" I couldn't resist letting it run through my head and out of my mouth. The chiming of the "Camp Granada" song had rallied us through the mountains.

"Go to hell! You lie down! Like you did with Iona!"

"What the bloody hell are you talking about, woman?"

"My sister! I know about you two!"

"That's insane! There's nothing to know!"

"Don't deny it, you lying bastard!" Where the fury came from in a woman of barely five feet was incomprehensible.

"You bastard! Don't lie to me! Don't you bloody lie to me!" Mum grabbed Dad's shirt collar like a prop-forward, dragging her nails across his face along the way.

"You bloody bitch! You're crazy, you are—bloody crazy!"

"Well, if I am, it's because of you, you bastard!" Arms flew like propellers, hitting the ground. "Get off me, get off me!" Mum screamed as Dad tried to catch the harvester blades coming at him.

"Chris, stop! It's not true! It's not true! There's only you, there's only you!" he caught her wrists and put his thumbs to where the scars were, the tiny ridges now barely perceptible. "There's no one else; there's only you!"

"Don't you lie to me, Roy! Don't you lie to me!" The fury had taken over Mum; it came and went often. Only the three of us remember the fury. Mum never did. There were no videos or Snapchat in those days.

"Precious, it's only ever been you. Surely you know that?"

"Jean, you and Jean? I know something's going on!" She tried shaking Dad's hands away, but his thumbs compressed her pressure points; she felt herself trapped, safe.

"There is no Jean, there is no Iona – there is only you, only you my precious!" the plane crash ground into the ground, taking in all those around it.

"Get Mum a towel," said Dad to one of us, keeping his thumbs pressed and pulling her close.

"And a paracetamol!" Dad added.

"The box is in my handbag!" It was Mum's daily double – tea and painkillers.

She ate them like a child sneaking candy in a classroom. The lid started to slide off the pan, and as often happened, as quickly as it reached its boil, the bubbles stopped. The pan boiled without pattern or cause and cooled by the same manner. I can't say if that's what caused Ju's night terrors, but my letting her win at checkers didn't prevent it. That night, Dad came into our side of the tent. Ju and I were awake, bolt upright in our sleeping bags. Mum slept on. Ju had screamed through the nightmares; it always scared the crap out of me—the talking I could manage but the freakish hallucinations where she yelled at the wall to get off her were paralyzing.

So many nights, Dad would take her pink-fringed tatty blanket, the love-worn blanket, and wrap it around her shivering shoulders. Ju twitched like darts were being placed repeatedly in each side of her neck, eyes fixed on the walls that moved to crush her. The blanket helped. Dad swaddled her tightly from behind, bringing warmth and calm. Her breathing once again slowed to a simmer, her eyes slowly closed out the horror, her spasms subsided. Dad and I looked warmly across at each other. Only we knew her torment; she would never remember. It was Dad's and my little secret. Dad always protected his little princess.

"Come back in the pub, Ju," Dad offered as his denim-shirted arms held her tightly from behind. "You haven't ordered dinner."

"I'm not hungry. Thanks, Dad." She was calmer now – she was protected from the elements, and softened into herself.

"Ju, it's okay; it's okay. We'll get through this. We always do."

"But Daddy!" She was six again, turning into his hug.

"We've been through worse," he whispered. She needed to hear the lie; she hadn't been through worse, and she buried her head into his chest pocket where the cigarette packet once sat.

Dad inched her away from the car the way he had from the brow of her mother's grave a few years earlier. The night terror, so dramatic at night, poured ice through her veins, paralyzing her in moments of trauma. "I want to jump in and be with her, Daddy," she had told him that time. Nothing prepares you to be an orphan. Nothing prepares you to look out of your crib and know there is no one coming to pick you up and soothe your soul. Your crying aching being simply throbs of lonely empty selfness. Who would wrap her up, hold her tight, when it was his turn to stare from the bottom of his crib? Who would steady the cocktail shaker of her life, a bundle of cubes bouncing around the steel, chipping, splintering, melting with each shake? What would be left of her after he was gone? Who would pull her from the grave's edge, smile, kiss her forehead, and with warm comfort tell her everything was going to be alright when it never was?

Out here in the car park she imagined the breathless wind as his whiskers, as the coat hangers were forced into her limbs. Tension ramrodded through her anxious body. She was entering a panic attack; soon enough she would be shaking like the Tin Man tug-o'-war. Ju wrapped her arms around him, crushed him into her the way you would a seat cushion in an airplane water evacuation: for dear life.

He felt her head burrow like an armless mole into the pocket where his smokes had been. The smokes that had allegedly poisoned his lungs, the smokes that had always settled him in periods like these were the reason for their pain. He could really use one about now. As soon as he was able, he had begun to smoke. The Captain had settled the nerves of his energy. Every day since quitting—or as he preferred to say, "retiring" from smoking, since no one likes a quitter—every day he craved a smoke. "I wouldn't have quit if I'd known I was going to get this diagnosis," he said later. Every day, he craved the solace and the calm of his smokes. Rebuffing the craving drained his daily quota of willpower; by the end of his marmalade toast, his willpower for work, exercising, loving, wanting, was emptied like a smoke-alarm battery. Just enough juice to power the reminder for a new battery—this had been his day for nearly nine years.

"Beef sarnie is the best in the village, Dad." Ju spoke, a fragment smile – he nodded at hearing his refrain come back to him. His life would live on in her, his gentle Julia, the original baby of the family; she would be the one to carry his essence forward, but he worried who would cradle his baby from her edges.

"That's my girl!" He lifted her chin from his chest one last time, smiling down on her, shoes fully covered in dust. "A beef sarnie au Jus!" And they laughed together at their lifelong pun.

"Come on, Ju." Dad wrapped his arms around her like a human shawl. His body ran hot, and Ju could feel the safety of his warmth. "Come back inside, Ju. I know, kid, you've seen a lot. I'm still here for you; it'll be alright," and he handed her a hanky. He was still part of the last "hanky generation."

Julia turned into his embrace one more time and held on for his life, like holding him would keep him alive, squeezing the death of the cancer out of him.

"Let's eat," he said through the apple trapped in his throat.

Ju just held on a little longer, like gripping the edge of the comforter on a wet November Monday! In rejoining our party, we could see the tear stains on the pocket that once held Dad's smokes. Once Julia returned from the ladies' after clearing the dust from her eyes, Dad leaned in once more to the group.

"I promise not to waste time with you; some of it may seem fruitless and frivolous, and I get that, but this is the time I have left with you. I ask you not to judge. In my head, I will always be the soul of a twenty-three-year old. Dad and grandad to my family, the best titles I ever earned, but on the inside, in my head, where the me lies, the me wants one more try; the me wants that child to be just about him again, one more run at being me. One more run, where you see the me, the me that I know, the me that was and is me before I made you. You are the best part of my life, and I'm not changing that, but the 'me' wants one more go - the 'me' in me refuses to stand down. I want you to see the me the way my parents could have. See me just as me." And he punctuated his moment with an emptying glass. He reached to his shirt pocket, but the smokes were no longer there, like someone had removed the gun from his holster.

Dad had made himself and us a real a promise a last wish—but there would be no open call for players in their sixties. My only hope was to somehow find a reason to blackmail Brian! Not a pretty thought. Dad gets a wish and to visit his son behind bars."I'll talk to Brian. He was always a big fan of yours, Dad," I said brightly, knowing I'd already somewhat put the wheels in motion, if you can call being stranded in the equivalent of a Yorkshire bog, motion!

The group seemed happy with my comment – it was at least something, if it did sound hollow-ish. No one had any real hope, and I think secretly we all wished Dad would change his mind and opt for an all-inclusive trip to Barbados!

To all, his was a unique unicorn of a request, and we all returned to slowly sipping and staring at our respective drinks. Dad eased back into pensive sipping; Ju wanted to pull up Expedia for some international bargains. My mouth, still sore from my injuries with Brian, juggled both ice-cubes around my gums. Zoe was sitting on the best and worst news of all.

"I'm pregnant, Dad." Zoe was matter-of-fact; as young as she looked, we all knew she wasn't. Dad's baby girl was having another baby.

CHAPTER 11

"Good morning, Chesterfield Football Club!" answered the bright-sounding respondent.

"Ah yes, sorry, I didn't think anyone was going to pick up. It's been ringing for ages and I thought I was going to get voicemail like last time."

"I thought so too!" responded the young lady, who sounded no more than eleven. "I'm just waiting for me dad to pack up his stuff. He's the manager, you know." Her sunshine voice beamed through the receiver.

"And what's your name, angel?"

"Daniella." No stranger danger in her voice.

"Daniella, would you be able to get me the secretary?"

"I'm afraid, mister, everyone's gone home. Dad says they've all been sacked!" She said it cheerfully like the administration were inheriting a bag of early birthday presents or Santa's back-up consignment.

"Oh, I'm sorry. Is there anyone else I can talk to?" I was a little at a loss. I hadn't expected anyone to pick up, but to be chatting with the coach's daughter was surreal.

"Nope, I don't think so." Daniella paused to think. "Just me dad, and he's in his office, I think?"

"Would you be able to get him for me, Daniella?" I knew I was taking advantage of the situation. I needed to talk to someone in authority and someone who might be able to help fill my dad's bucket. Then as I hung on to the receiver, I could hear a commotion in the background—men's voices, one older one, my age, and I think a woman screaming. I was glad I was at this end of the phone. A voice came into range and clarity.

"Daniella! What are you doing? Hang that up right away! What are you even doing in there? – I told you to wait outside!" The voice was firm, with love, and slight disappointment at being disobeyed. Daniella cocked the phone. It was odd to her how it was shackled by a pigtail cord.

"It's for you anyway, Dad!" Daniella pointedly offered the phone to her dad.

"What? For me? Hello, this is Danny Wilson," offered Danny, not used to taking un-pre-screened calls, a little anxious in the way that you inadvertently pick up a sales call from an insurance salesman. He was tempted to just put the receiver on its cradle.

On hearing his voice, I cleared my throat.

"Danny, I mean Mr. Wilson," I spoke like a fan begging for an autograph.

"Call me Danny. What do you want?" He was a little short in voice and in real life.

"I wonder if you can help me?" No hesitation – I went straight out with the begging bowl. Good people find it hard to resist helping.

"I'm not sure I can," fired back Danny with puzzled impatience.

"You're one of the few who might be able to!" I was fishing, of course. Blindly, without a hook.

"I doubt that very much."

"You see, my dad isn't well." I went on anyway; nothing ventured….

"You need the hospital – you've reached Chesterfield Football Club – though it is like a bloody infirmary around here." Danny was having fun with this.

"I know, Danny, sorry, very good."

"What, do, you, want?" Danny regretted taking the call, but Daniella was still standing by him, watching him proudly.

"It's serious, Danny." I tried to find gravitas – it was hard to choke back my excitement – I was talking to one of my childhood heroes. This was the man who was part of the Anglo-Scottish Cup winning team, and here he was, yakking away with me, a nobody, a fan. He'd gone on to play and coach for Ireland – he was a real small-town legend, adopted by the village and loved like an orphan with seven thousand proud dads, a couple of mums, and some horny girl cousins – you know the type.

"Very serious, Danny." I found my adult voice.

"Then perhaps the emergency room? I'm sorry, mate; I've got to go. They're showing me the door."

"Redecorating?"

"What do you want?" Danny's frustration blew at the phone.

"Daddy, don't shout at the nice man," I heard in the background.

"My dad is dying, and I need some help." That was it. Danny had the information. Silence descended like heavy snowfall.

"I'm not sure how I can…."

I cut off the great Danny Wilson mid-stride.

"My dad is dying, and he wants to play for Chesterfield Football Club!" I practically yelled into the phone.

"I'm sorry, mate, but I don't see how I can help."

"You're the coach, Danny – you pick the squad – you can make it happen!"

"I'm not bloody..."

"But Danny, it's really important!" Through the frog spawn in my throat I yelled at Danny Wilson, the Danny Wilson—*the* fucking Danny Wilson!

"I'm sorry, I can't help you." Danny wanted to hang up.

"You must—there isn't much time!" I screamed at the phone like he had the antidote.

"Who are you?" I had sounded deranged and he frustrated and confused still hadn't hung up.

"You Must! Help, Danny! Don't hang up, Mr. Wilson." The formality caught Danny off guard, so he stayed on the line.

"Danny, I'm your biggest fan, but my dad's an even bigger fan, and he's dying!"

"I'm really sorry." Danny was calm; he could smell the pain of forced retirement from life in my voice.

"Danny, don't be sorry; all he wants is a chance to play for Town. It's stupid, I know. God knows my sisters are ready to kill him because of it."

"It's not stupid. I get it; I lived that dream."

"You know him, Danny." I was pulling that card.

"I do?"

"It's Roy from the Olde House." The snow fell harder, quieter.

"Story Roy!"

"You know him?" I was in shock. I thought Dad was bragging all these years. Like he stood in the same side-room of the pub as Danny but not actually in Danny's group.

"Of course—drinks Stella, no head, filled to the brim."

"You do know him!" I was startled and thrilled; Danny Wilson had my dad's MO.

"I do; takes the longest time to tell a story. I'm really sorry to hear he's not well, and I'd like to help."

"You can, Danny, you can—just give him a chance."

"No, you see, it's not up to me."

"He was a hell of a player in his day. Got signed by Wolves but never played. Had game, you know! A left foot to rival yours!"

"No, you don't understand--"

"I do, I do – he's old but he's in good shape, new hip and everything!"

"No, you don't...."

"Danny! He's just looking for one more shot! For one minute of time, for one golden moment to put on the 'Blues' kit, trot out with the team on to the hallowed turf. Be announced, take his nod, and play one minute."

"You..."

"He just needs one minute, Danny; just one minute, Danny; just..." The great Danny Wilson interrupted my stride this time, like one of his famous sliding tackles.

"I'm not sure I could have or can." A pause in time, the way a defender would slowly realize Danny was gone in the opposite direction. "I've been fired!" I could hear his daughter's tears of shock. This was not how he had meant to tell her – she wasn't supposed to get it as a bystander with her daddy talking to a stranger.

"I probably could have..." Danny wanted to go on but was struck by the flood of his daughter's tears. He would have been struck worse with the tsunami of mine. Like lava on Pompeii – the dream was over.

I heard the click on the other end. I could only imagine the grief he felt after being let go as coach of the team that made him. His own dream shattered moments before, then not having to take a call but taking it anyway and euthanizing someone else's dying dream in the same morning. I had made the worst day of the great Danny Wilson worse.

I hung up Dad's phone, put the receiver back in its hammock and sat on the bottom stair looking through the opaque glass front door to the garden in front. Dad had pruned the roses, clipped the hydrangeas, and trimmed the bushes. The imaginary mid-morning sun cast bright light behind the white on grey clouds illuminating the tiny foyer. A floor-to-ceiling, velvet, carpet-like curtain stood to attention, pushed to one side ready to cast a shade in the unlikely event it got too sunny. More often than not, it was a mere draft excluder, blocking the wily gusts from the south and the Matlock Road. You read of characters carrying their heavy heads on their hands, so imagine that. The sleeves of my Next grey quarter-zip jumper were a little long, even for my monkey arms; the cuffs acted like half knit gloves, comforters for my chin to rest in.

"So that was it then," I mumbled to myself.

If Dad were sitting on the stair with me, he wouldn't have heard it. If Ju or Zoe were there they would have berated me for mumbling. I think it's a writer's trait to always be mumbling – talking to someone – don't you agree it's a career I should consider, then?

Dad was in the garage. Where a shed might suffice a man's needs to house his tools, my dad had a garage, with a little extension on the back that looked like it would be a shed. So, when someone in Chesterfield tells you that they love you "shed loads" or just "sheds" as it's commonly referred to, then likely they are referring to Dad. Dad and his garage and shed of tools. Multiples of necessities, drills, hammer drills, hand-helds, with and without cords, their battery back-ups. Extension cords – must be nearing a hundred. Linked together, they would stretch for miles. Buzz Aldrin held one end while Dad held on to the other. "I'm at the moon, Roy," I'm sure he said, confirming with ground control in Houston. If the extension cords stretched to the moon, he had enough buckets of sandpaper to carpet it when he got there!

Then there were the saws! Hack saws with their gormless expressions hanging on the wall – various sizes from small enough to work on a doll's house to as long as your arm to work on Robin Hood's tree. Smallest at the bottom – so it looked like a shoal of bass with their lazy jaw open-mouths were swimming right at you. Then he had to have saws of a regular kind – the ones that slice up two by fours – which if you have ever built anything, beware – a two by four is actually three and three quarters by one and three quarters! That's a big difference when you are finishing your basement! I'm just saying! Saws that could trim to saws that would look natural in a magician's act. Then there were the circular saws and "Sawzalls" – it was hard to picture the jobsite in his thousand-square foot home where you would need seven circular saws on the go all at one time! I questioned him once – "They were on sale, it was too good of a deal to pass up!" So he fell prey to the Sunday papers inserts once in a while, I guess.

His garage hadn't seen a car since the previous owner; during the open house you could see it was spacious enough for a Toyota Land Cruiser and room for a work bench at the side. "Perfect," I remember him saying.

Garden tools – they were in the shed – you just couldn't get in the shed to get them. He had enough rakes, spades, and shovels for all of the Seven Dwarfs to personalize their own.

The side door of the house banged to a close with a familiar assist from the west wind – the good-tempered glass never lost its cool.

"I'm thirsty, Dad." I rose to meet him in the kitchen.

"I'll put the kettle on!" Counting his rakes, shovels, and spades always seemed to put him in a good frame. "Still no sugar?" he asked. Actually, he asked a dozen times on my stays, like I was gonna change my tea preferences in America.

"No, Dad, I drink it the same way as you now!"

"Good man!" he added like I'd graduated sugar college or something.

It's true we both enjoyed our tea with a splash of milk no sugar. As a kid, I had troweled in the sugar. But once in college, I realized the true cost of the white indulgence – and since no one in my dorm was going to share in the expense, I decided to go without. I have to say, it took the whole semester before I really enjoyed a cup of tea! Dad was right proud though when I came back for Christmas break. "Like your old man now, eh? No sugar in tea!"

"No, Dad, I think I need a real drink."

"What's up?"

"Nothing. I just feel the need to get out. Mind if we go to the Olde House – for old times' sake?"

"I'll wash the grease off me hands and we can go then."

"I'll grab our coats."

"And the lights!" Dad reminded.

They were easy to locate; they were the outer layer of the coat hive that decorated the foyer where I had been sitting on the phone earlier. Dad turned out the lights anyway, before washing his hands. It was a strange reminder that I was back in Chesterfield. The odd phenomenon that even during summer months our house needed lights on—and the heating, too.

Dad moved easier now into his RAV 4, a car that on leaving the dealership was thrilled to be having one careful owner but then disappointed to learn it would never see the inside of a garage. Where Dad's parents' retired generation enjoyed the luxury of saloon cars and cigarette lighters, Dad enjoyed the transition from truck to this SUV with its moon-roof and phone charger. Dad was relieved to see that the cigarette lighter, rather like himself would have a new identity since he quit. In practically every photo since our birth, the few photos that we had with Dad showed him clutching his adult pacifier. He wasn't in that many photos, since neither Mum nor Dad trusted Mum with Dad's Zeiss Nettar camera. By the time we kids came around, it was a relic with many miles and many stories on it. In today's world, we would have airbrushed the cigarettes out and smoothed out Mum's imperfections. Mum, though a chain-smoker herself, was keen never to be photographed as one, instead maintaining her model poise in front of the Zeiss. Dad's deliberateness allowed for the make-up and hair team to come on set and do their thing.

Dad slid easily into the driver's seat. The Sport and Utility were synonymous with the elderly being able to practically leap like Dick Fosbury into the higher accommodating seat. Very useful! The only off-roading this SUV ever did was clumsily backing down Dad's narrow driveway. Dad always reverse-parked into his driveway – like a bank-robber's lookout, as though he might one day have to make a quick getaway. A quick getaway geriatric style, looking both ways and then a second time looking up the hill, to confirm there were no mums with buggies, as there were a lot of young families on the street where we had grown up. The kids like me on that street were all grown up. Except for Tony Martin; he still lived across the way with his mum and dad. He was their full-time child-minder since life had thrown them the double blow of early onset dementia. Living in the same house, he had grown from child to parent without ever leaving.

Dad removed the parking brake and we were off at a speed that surely would have given a snail whiplash.

"I'm not even sure it's open at this time, Ad?" Dad said as we drove around the maze of the cul-de-sac. "I've never been this early! Usually if we're knocking on the door it's at half five, not eleven in the morning."

"I'm sure they're open—well, not that sure, but it'll be soon either way."

"Bugger! I forgot to change me trainers! I'm still in me gardening trainers—they're all covered in mud still."

"Don't worry, Dad; we can scrape 'em off when we get there. It's an old farmhouse, remember – they have one of those boot scrapers outside the front door. The one that looks like three toothbrush-heads."

"It looks closed!" said Dad as we pulled in.

"No, there's one car there round the side—see?"

"That'll be Mike's, the barman."

"If it is, I'm in the wrong job! That's a BMW 7 series with new license plates on it!"

"Probably left from last night then!" reasoned Dad. "Anyway, I don't see any lights on!" He was right; the nearer we got, the less likely it looked to be open. I yanked at the door while Dad brushed off his trainers with ballerina leg swoops. Showing off his new hip to the teacher, I suppose.

This old converted farmhouse was now surrounded by our housing estate – it had once stood proudly alone amongst its fields like the Red Lion; now it was an anachronistic stepchild, renovated time and again by foster parents.

"It's closed, Ad. There isn't a light on."

The door's open—come on – there's a light on behind the bar at least! I can hear voices."

"Not that again – I thought you were taking medication for that!"

"Good one, Dad. Sounds like a girl crying."

"Even she's upset by the price of a pint in this place!"

The latest rendition of the Olde House had made it more open plan like the newer houses on the estate. "Open concept," so everyone's house became the venue for a rave party – a party barn!

"The crying is coming from the old part."

"I can't tell; it's still dark in those little alcoves. Back in the day I can't tell you how many girls I kissed in those lovers' corners!" Dad sounded like he was bragging. He championed me on the girl front the way he could beat me at most any sport my whole life. The girls loved a winner.

"Let's see if she's alright."

"Okay, Dad, but we're not prying."

"Not prying – she might be hurt." Dad talked and walked like he owned the place – and perhaps coming here for the last forty years or so may have given him some progressive squatter's rights.

"What's up, duck?" Dad dropped into a child-approved vernacular. And the crying stopped. The girl, of about school year six, looked at Dad, oblivious to me.

"Y'alright? Where's your mum?"

"I'm here!" came her dad's voice from behind us. We would have spilled our drinks if we'd had any he came up on us so quickly. "These two bothering you, Daniella?"

"No, Daddy," she just managed to get out.

"You're Danny Wilson's daughter!" I almost yelled at her.

"Yes!" she screamed with delighted pride.

"That would be right," came the voice from over my shoulder. "And I would be Danny Wilson!" loud and authoritative – bringing us to a halt the way a referee's whistle would.

"Danny, how ya doing, mate?" Dad greeted the football star like they'd bumped into each other on a beach holiday.

"It's not Roy, is it? Well, that's weird – I was just talking to some bloke on the phone about you!"

"Hi Danny, I'm the 'some bloke' you spoke to—Roy's son Adam. Can I get you a drink?"

"Jack and coke would be nice."

"Can I get an H2O, Daddy?" chirped a calmer Daniella.

"Usual for me, Ad, and whatever you're having!" He sounded like he was buying me a drink but went to sit next to Daniella after Danny had sat down beside her. When I returned with the drinks, I heard the words "Anglo-Scottish Cup" get louder as I approached. They were living their glory days. Daniella sat with pride eating the salt and vinegar crisps I dropped in front of her which had invited a "look" from Danny. Most kids liked ready salted, but in our house that was the bag left until last in the multi-pack of choice. I couldn't ever understand why you would pick a bag with so little flavor.

"So, what's new with Town, Danny? Are we gonna make a late-season run and get promoted to the same division?" I hadn't told Dad my news yet or the reason for the need to be here. Under most circumstances, in fact in almost every circumstance, it would be a highlight reel moment to be visiting with Danny Wilson—local, national, and international football legend. Any day except today!

"Well, I suppose your son filled you in a little, no?" said Danny, perplexed.

"Actually, Danny, Dad knows nothing, and the idea was to come here to break the news to him, but you seem to have had a similar need to come here."

"Well, Roy, the news is that I just got sacked about a quarter of an hour ago!" Danny gulped on the Jack Daniels. Daniella started to cry.

"Don't worry, angel, it will be alright." Danny pulled his daughter in close to his hip wrapping his arm around her. "Mummy will be here soon to take you to dance."

"Aren't you taking me to dance, Daddy?"

"Not today, angel, not today."

"Why did you call Danny?" Dad asked me.

"Obviously, I didn't call meaning to get Danny, although he would have been my first choice. I didn't expect anyone to pick up – I usually get the phone tree nightmare. I was just hoping to find someone in The club who might be able to authorize your, entertain your wish of playing for Town, Dad."

"I picked up the phone," beamed Daniella. "It wouldn't stop ringing! It was starting to become annoying."

"And that's how I ended up talking to Danny. I'm really sorry. And I'm really sorry about, you know …." I halted my double apology, not wanting to trigger another round of tears for Daniella.

"First one of the day! In this glass!" Dad raised his glass and for some reason we all followed suit. "Cheers!" But we had nothing to "cheers" about.

Danny's phone vibrated on the table – a photo of a pretty woman about his age showed up on the screen.

"Mummy's here. You can take your crisps; she's in the car park waiting. Have fun at dance."

"Town is a right mess. Injuries have killed the team this year, and all the losses turn into reduced numbers at the gate. That puts pressure on everybody. The board has put up millions and borrowed as much just to keep it afloat. It's gonna be like taking a barge on a three-point turn in the canal."

"What are you going to do next?" Dad wanted him to stay in town, of course.

"Don't know – I mean I'm not surprised and all, but I certainly wasn't looking. My dream was to take these lads to the FA Cup Final to win what was stolen from us in 1997!"

"That's what I'm talking about!" yelled Dad. "Cheers!" Dad had affected the American twang.

"But that's gone now – and you, Roy – you wanted one last crack at playing for Town?"

"Not dead yet – still do!"

"Don't know if that's gonna happen or could happen – players going, board members resigning. I'm gone, and so will most of my staff, I assume! It's pretty dire over there, Roy. I was their golden boy, and they let me go!"

"Sorry about that!" I interjected.

"If money were no object, what would you have done to stay up?" Dad sounded professorial – looking for the empirical answer to a failed experiment.

"I'm not sure money is the answer; I mean it's obviously a big part. But you need a single-minded club whose only goal is…." And he left the sentence for us to fill in the blanks. "You can't have conflict and many directions – people wanting a return on their money, even if it meant middle of the table performance. It became obvious and pressure come down from around that certain 'steady' players were needed to play – that the lowly goal of status quo was acceptable. If I had the cash, I would search high and low for players who only wanted to play for this club – that this was their soul, not a stepping stone or a YouTube moment for them." And with that, he finished his drink, sucking on the lemon slice as punctuation.

"I have cash," said Dad.

"Dad!"

"I might have enough to buy The Club." He laughed jokingly. Then dropped to a serious tone.

"It's my retirement savings – but according to the doctors, retirement may be a shorter rather than longer plan. Who can I talk to? Whose numbers do you have? No lackey, mind! Who are the decision-makers – they're the ones I want to talk to."

"Decision-makers are getting harder to find! That was the straw they pulled when my name dropped! With the chairman gone and the rest of the board's share value toppling, they needed a scapegoat!"

"So, they picked you!" I queried.

"It's what you do – you sack the coach, manager, whatever you want to call me. You know it when you get the job. We are a researcher's slide – always under the microscope!"

Danny was in good humor for a man just given a red-card and marching orders.

"When money is tight, love flies out the window! No matter my love for The Town and their love of me – the love of their money is number one. Advertisers stop returning calls when The club slips down the table. It's like an election cycle – you're always running for re-election and trying to find new sponsors at the same time, just in case!"

"It's a real tail wagging the dog story!" Dad said. He'd watched some late-night movie apparently and left Danny and me in the dark.

"The club may be 150 years old and a season of 46 games, but in reality, as a manager you're under a 90-minute review by everyone: the players, the board, the advertisers, and most importantly, the fans. It's a what have you done for me lately lifestyle? And lately means in the last five minutes on Saturday's pitch. It's what you hear on game day after a week of training, strategizing, repair and repeat. I love it. I get to see a lot of great kids on their way up, hopefully, and I get to see some old friends on the way down."

"People want to be entertained—a club might be struggling, but the supporters want to see a show! These fans will get behind anybody with a bit of speed or skill and really get behind a crunching tackle!"

"Your team is like a classroom where former pupils get a do-over!" I jumped in.

"At least the teachers get a year for peer review! I may only get the first fifteen minutes of a home game if I'm lucky! It's like a baking reality telly show every Saturday afternoon—come see what I cooked up for you now!"

"I must say, Danny, you are taking this remarkably well! I thought you'd be crying in your beer! I would be!"

"Gutted inside, mate. I hate the song and dance of looking for a new job, but maybe I can find a group who will follow this Pied Piper! Luckily the new bosses, if they are out there, look at the whole CV and not just the last ninety minutes! After all, Don Revie was the manager of England!"

"So where do I start?" Dad sounded rather eager.

"You're not serious, Dad?"

"Serious as a heart attack!"

"Not funny, Dad!" he always felt he could go there, now he was a member of that club.

"I can get you in the front door, Roy," said Danny, holding up his key.

"They were in such a rush to have a statement for the papers they forgot to ask for my keys. I got a nice box for my stuff, mind!" Danny grinned his trademark smile after dancing by opponents' defenders.

"Will Daniella be alright?"

"Probably, though it's like starting a new school for her every time! A new job for me, a new school for her, so I'm sure that's what she's most upset about. She's got friends all over Britain!"

"I bet! No, I didn't mean it like that. I just meant, can I get you another pint, Danny?"

"Yes, and you'd better get your dad another too if he's thinking of buying Chesterfield FC – you don't want to be sober for that experience!" said Danny.

"Cheers to that," I added. Dad just smiled the low-radar smile as he nodded into his Stella.

CHAPTER 12

"Well, here we are, lads," announced Danny in front of the side door reserved for employees, staff, and concessions volunteers. We didn't need buzzing in.

"This is as far as I can take you," said Danny beneath his Spireites-blue umbrella.

"What, you're not coming in?" I said.

"No chance – I have my box – be sure to give them these keys when you see them."

"You alright with that, Dad?"

"Who are we looking for, Danny? Who do I need to speak to?"

"Damned if I know – it was random when I worked here, and it's absolute chaos now! I got on with most of the board, but they're not involved in day-to-day ops. Brian Banner's a good bloke – most of 'em are; they just don't like to bleed cash. I suggest you head to my old office on the second floor – you can see the window from here looking out over the Mega-Tesco. Just so you know, there are no players in there to buy – believe me, I looked!" Danny laughed us off and went back to his huge Beemer, parked next to a Barbie-pink Porsche Boxter. He never looked back once, not even as he closed-up his umbrella and tossed it on the back seat. Probably didn't give the rear-view mirror a check, either.

"Alright then, Ad! Let the games begin!" declared Dad. The key rotated twice, and we were in! Not breaking and entering, but definitely entering! Not completely uninvited – Danny had invited us. And, well, we were providing a service – we were returning his key for him. So justifiably, we were free to roam the halls!

"They might save some money by switching off the damned lights; it's like a bloody Christmas tree in here! When I'm in charge, it'll be different!"

"Dad, you're a long way off from that! We're here to just talk – there's no one who is gonna have the ability to make that call for ages."

"You never know!"

We took the stairs to the second floor, and halfway up we could hear people coming out of the lift down the hall. The place wasn't empty as we'd been led to believe. A good start! Two ladies, one smart, one casual, each carrying an oversized mug of tea. One may have had a One Direction picture on it. Neither of them looked young enough to be a fan – the casual one looked like she'd just walked the dogs, dogs plural now the kids had left the house. A dog to replace each of the kids. The smart one, crisp white blouse, cut fit, to match her cutting tongue. They turned and walked away in heavy conversation before tripping excitedly into the third office on the left; one of eleven, we counted and followed. Dad and I looked at each other – we had no idea what to do next. So, we waited outside the office like *Starsky and Hutch*, without the training! I know, who could be less prepared than that? We had our backs to the wall and looked down the hallway left and right – that much we knew from *Starsky and Hutch*. We propped our umbrellas on our shoulders like sentry rifles standing guard outside the palace gates. We listened in like "scientists" listening for aliens in deep space. Which might have been what Town were looking for to rescue this terrible season.

"They're just bastards – I 'aven't bin paid in weeks, and now they hand me a box and a thank you—fuck-em is what I say!"

"I 'ave another job. Start in couple o' weeks. Don't need the screaming an' yelling; I can get that at 'ome!"

"I had to go t' bank for a loan just to pay our Charlotte's dance lessons. What's it coming to, eh?"

"We'll be cracking open a tin of spam next!" Both ladies burst out laughing.

"If nothing else, having no food around the house, I'll lose weight!"

"They'll probably take credit for that and want payin'!"

It was all on for me and me Dad to not walk in on these ladies. It was like listening to Wood and Walters.

"Guvner, himsen could do with shedding!"

"Dun't look like he's missed a meal since he threw his bottle out t' pram!"

"He's always first in t' queue for t' communion cracker, that one!"

"Bet 'e's 'ad more free samples from Tesco's than a pimp and a new recruit!"

"Oh, that's a good'n Marge, well funny!"

"If he were any shorter, 'e'd be a space-hopper!"

"And he's got the ears for it! Oink oink!"

"Fran, you're killing me—right nearly spilled me tea!"

"Reminds me of Les Dawson; does he you?"

"I had 'im down as a Roy Kinnear type, like in Willy Wonka – flustered like!

'Is wife is like Veruca Salt, for sure!"

"I want an Oompa Loompa now, Daddy!"

"Want another cuppa? That's all we've gorr on t' agenda today!"

"That, an' them new fellas are coming."

"Who's that then – friends of t' board. Not due in for ages yet."

"Yeh put kettle on agen – we can get our wages in tea-bags, I suppose!"

"Yep, new owners 'ad be'er 'ave loads a cash!"

"I don't drink that much tea, Marge!"

"I'm thinking we're rate buggered – sacked Danny yesterday!"

"No! While I were gone for t' day! I missed saying goodbye – worse, missed me goodbye kiss! Love that lad – I could watch him run in them shorts all day!"

"I'm with yer there, Fran--worra bum he's go'."

"I heard local judge is punishing criminals by givin' 'em season tickets to t' Town!"

"That's a good one!"

"It's a bad sign tho', intit! Most o' team is gone, managers gone, only one physio."

"Tony, yeh, he's looking for another job – I heard Sheffield United offered 'im a job – but he said wanted to only work for a men's team! Ha!"

"You are a guddun! Well, if this gig dun't work out, you could always do t' comedy clubs!"

"You've got to laugh—right? Bloody change from a couple o' seasons ago – all we go' left is memories."

"Don't know how Tony does it. He'll be gone soon, I'm shooer."

"All we'll have left is t' hot tub, ice bags, and steam room."

"And plasters! Worra 'bout Lego? We can get truck loads into rebuild t' players?"

"I think Les Dawson's working out right now!" She used her hands for the universal sign of quotes around "working out."

"What, in the steam room?"

"Yep, boiled bacon for breakfast! We should bloody check on him – he could have a bleedin' stroke in there!"

"Yep, we don't want him gooin' out on us. Who's gonna not sign the checks we're not ge'in'?"

"Ooh you are good, Marge!"

"Anyway, steam room's usually knackered."

"Griff Griffiths – plumbers – come to check out the steam room!" Dad had rushed in. Just like Starsky to go in without telling his partner. Now I really empathized with Hutch!"Ladies, my name is Roy. Me and me son are here to fix the hot tub."

"You're not the usual fellas?'

"Nope – I guess we must be much cheaper! Which way should we go?"

"Where are your toolboxes?"

"In the van. Now which way did you say we go?"

Fuming, I was following Dad in and he was exiting almost as fast as I was coming in! We really were Starsky and Hutch! I wanted to shoot him with the wrench I didn't have—not even the wrench in the van, in the van we didn't have!

"Tek the lift downstairs – you can't miss it, at t' end of the hall – marked 'locker room.'"

"We're on it!" I said on entering and exiting in the same motion, faking teamwork.

We synchronized our marching and headed to the steam room for a showdown.

"What are we gonna do when we get there? He could be ages in there."

"Don't know, Ad; just making it up as I go along! Exciting, isn't it?"

"Well, kind of, but you could just go to a board meeting!"

"Have you ever been to a board meeting? Really should be 'Bored Meeting'!"

"Very punny, Dad!" He was juiced with dad jokes, a trait I had apparently inherited. And now we were hustling down the brightly lit corridor, at a fast clip, his hip clearly mended. Since we had authorization, we didn't have to hide. Just two completely inconspicuous plumbers half-sprinting down a *Star Wars*-lit hallway. Like Hutch, I followed Starsky's manic lead just off his right shoulder, like Sebastian Coe ready to pass Steve Ovett on the last bend of the Olympic 800 meters.

"Out of order! You've got to be kidding me!" I said, a little sweaty with weighty breath – the former chain smoker was unfazed, breathing normally. "It's a sign!"

"I know that, you moron!" said Dad. "I can read."

"No, I mean a sign we shouldn't be here!"

"I know that too! Let's take the stairs. They probably used all the electricity on the lights and left no power for the lift!"

I followed the modern-day Fred Astaire down the stairs, feeling a little second fiddle as he swung his umbrella and tapped each stair with flair, wholly unnecessarily in my opinion.

"Here we are!" The sign read "Locker Room"--the ladies hadn't lied.

"Now what?" I looked at him like a puppy had chased a rabbit into the woods and suddenly come up on a bear!

Barely had the words crossed from my brain to my tongue when I almost bit them off, following the mad ex-smoker into the locker room. Every light on, of course. You could see the light pollution was starting to irritate Dad.

"No wonder ticket prices are so high!" at home, Dad lived in a state of permanent darkness except for the halo of television pixels. Even the day-glow green clock on the microwave annoyed my dad – "If I wanted to know the time, I'd check me watch, not the bloody microwave!" This became a mantra of his.

The club had saved money by not putting a sign on the steam room wall! Wisely, they had just let the players figure it out for themselves. So, dressed in anoraks, we piled into the scalding corpuscles of steam and sweat – it was impossible to determine the percentages of either!

"I can't breathe," I whispered to Dad. "How does anyone like this?"

"Don't know. I'm trying not to open my mouth in case I inhale clouds of pee!"

"Can you see anything? What's that tapping?"

"I'm using me umbrella like I'm Helen Keller! Keep your voice down? You go that way around and I'll go this." We each slid the tips of our umbrellas around the walls like we were maneuvering around a maze of fog. The tip of the umbrella gave off a tiny scraping sound each time it reached the grout of a new tile, like a metal detector signaling that we had found… yet another new tile! Our newly bruised knees told us that there were ceramic sitting benches around the walls, about knee high. "We should have expected that one," I said to myself, wincing from the cutting corner of the seating. The sauna came to life with hissing and wheezing as more steam released from the chrome snake heads above us. Next to the serpent heads, its eyes of opaque lights, like you might see at the bottom of your swimming pool, failed to illuminate the room, its rays clouded in this recycled microcosm. At arm's length I could barely hear the scrape and tap of my umbrella. The sound from Dad's had disappeared almost immediately. I was gushing sweat from every pore – warm rivulets ran down my thighs like I'd peed myself! In seconds, my hair was soaked like I'd been flipped upside down and dunked in a mop bucket. "I'm gonna have to take me anorak off," I whined to myself. I didn't want to risk the synchronicity of our maneuver, but I was melting like chocolate in a pan!

The cold steel of Dad's umbrella tip touched Mr. Newall at the side of his rib cage, and he leapt up like a blast from an air-horn. Instinctively Dad kept the cold steel of the umbrella on Mr. Newall.

"What the bloody hell is going on?" came the Yorkshire middle-aged voice.

And just as he said it, I was taking my anorak off—I couldn't have timed it better. As I was pulling down, he was standing up. I jerked the anorak up off my sopping, sweaty body; it initially clung to me like pie crust, but once it came, it came off like an archer's bow, snapping up over my head, and by complete accident I had bagged the portly director in an anorak straitjacket!

"We ask the questions!"

"I demand an explanation!" Mr. Newall's blood was boiling both literally and figuratively.

"Mr. Newall, what is it?" came a sweet young voice from the floor. I wasn't expecting that. "Are you done already, sir?"

"What's going on? Who's in here? What do you want?"

"Just me, Mr. Newall. Are you finished?"

"No! Yes, for the moment," Mr. Newall could feel the light-headedness creeping on as a result of the heat and Viagra.

"Not another word!" Dad's voice had gone all gruff and Mancunian suddenly.

"Who's in here?" asked the young lady, from her knees.

"Get this thing off me! What do you want?" asked the rising panic in Mr. Newall's tone. His heart and "mind" had been really pounding just moments earlier; now at least one of them was ready to explode.

"Thing? Mr. Newall? I hardly call myself 'thing,'--don't you love me anymore?"

"Sweetheart – we can talk about this later – there's someone in here with a gun in myside and a bag over my head!"

"What!" screeched the young girl.

"That's right, miss – I didn't catch your name?" Dad persisted with the accent like a bad audition for *Coronation Street.*

"Janie Alcock," mumbled the trembling girl.

"My personal assistant!" mumbled the director through my anorak.

"Very personal!" Dad joked like a bit part actor on the soap.

"Not Janie Alcock the counselor's daughter?" I guessed. I had broken my silence but copied Dad's marginal accent.

"Don't say a word, Janie. This is a shakedown! What do you two fellas want? My wallet is in the locker – take it and go!"

"We're not 'ere for your wallet!"

"Are you from the syndicate? Did my wife send you?" The director was panicking, probably sweating twice as much now. Dad and I retained our radio silence. "I demand to know who sent you!"

"You're in no position to make demands," Dad said, then remembered the young lady kneeling somewhere down on the tiled floor. "Well, not of us at least!"

"What is it you want, mister?" Janie was nervous and sounded clearer now that she had cleared her throat.

"Your dad's the one that approved the relocation of the stadium, isn't he? The one that allowed Carter and Butts to build on the prime location on Saltergate?"

"I don't know about those things?" claimed Janie innocently.

"But Mr. Newall does—don't you, Mr. Newall?" Dad was in his best Detective Columbo mode having switched out old pervert mac for easy to pack royal-blue anorak. It was looking less royal and more navy as the sweat poured out and the steam in.

"Who sent you? I want to know!" He would have remonstrated and tried to wave his arms, but the anorak, which was tight on me, was closer than a mummy's bandages on him. Plus, it was doubly hard to move with his membership in Janie's hand and mouth.

"Can't say." Dad was very cool, for a man his age wearing an under vest, plaid shirt, tidy V-neck sweater, and an anorak.

"Mr. Newall, what's going on?" said the young girl with the voice of a polite receptionist.

"Nothing, my angel!" Mr. Newall could feel anger and tension riddling his nervous system as he tried to placate his confused secretary.

"Nothing, Mr. Newall? I beg to differ! You are standing naked with a young lady between your legs. A young lady who is not your wife." Dad paused.

"A young lady who is not your wife and whose father was the deciding vote on the most lucrative real estate deal in the town since the Romans replaced the shepherds!" I added for dramatic effect.

"What is he talking about, Mr. Newall?" Janie wondered.

"I'm sure Mr. Newall has been very kind to you, Miss Alcock!" I said, fishing.

"Yes, that's my Porsche in the car park!"

"The pink one?"

"Yes! How did you know?"

"I couldn't miss it – you don't see those every day!"

"Mr. Newall gave it to me last year!"

"Stop it, Janie, stop!"

"I'd say you're in a spot of hot water, Mr. Newall," Dad added with a dad joke.

"What do you mean? You can't do this! You'll find that I've done nothing wrong!"

"That will be hard to deny when I take this recording back to the people that sent me!"

"Give me that – I – I" Mr. Newall couldn't fight through the anorak and Janie wasn't moving, mostly because she didn't know who had the gun.

"Our people suggest you announce your resignation from the board and sell your shares on the cheap."

"Your people?" queried the director, who was now stuck in the anorak by the glue of his steamy sweat.

The spout hissed some more, and no one could see.

"I don't feel well...." The director's voice faded.

"Mr. Newall!"

Dad jabbed him in the ribs one more time then took his umbrella again to the wall – tapped it and I obeyed my signal and walked my umbrella tip against the wall to exit, leaving Mr. Newall in the capable hands and mouth of his mistress Janie Alcock. Janie wanted to scream but then realized she couldn't draw attention to their situation. Mr. Newall passed out, sliding down the tile of the steam room. The medication bottle was correct as it accurately listed the side-effects of Viagra – nausea, light-headedness, a drop in blood pressure and even fainting! All the blood had run from one head to another as he stood up.

CHAPTER 13

"It was announced today that Chesterfield Football Club director Andre Newall was resigning from the Board and selling his shares," said *Look North's* Harry Gration.

"Would you believe it! They're all leaving the sinking ship," said Zoe.

"That was a fun day out, wasn't it, Ad?" Dad winked at me.

"Yes, we met the head of The club, but couldn't get any information on how to proceed with an investment in The Club!" I added smugly.

"You'd think they'd be lining up to take your money?" said Ju.

"And a further development in the story – Mr. Newall said it was for health-related matters. It is unsure whether The Club will seek new investors or go into receivership. The Club has a storied past but has been under a black cloud for many years. Mr. Newall was not available for further comment – and when we visited The Club earlier today the doors were locked, but the lights were on. Now for the weather in the region—over to you, Diane."

"Thank you, Harry. That black cloud over Chesterfield is going to bring continued rain to the region…" said Diane, the *Look North* weather professional, picking up on Harry's metaphor.

"They left the lights on! Damned waste! At least they won't have to water the pitch!" Dad was frustrated at the TV, as usual! If it wasn't for Harry Gration delivering the news, he probably would have used expletives!

"Things really are imploding at Town in a big way!" Zoe continued.

"Been like this for fifty years! Can't seem to get it right. It's proper frustrating when you see the likes of Watford, Bournemouth, and Hull in the EPL! You can't help wond'ring why no' us?"

"Yeh, Dah, why is the culture so bad?" I had no idea why I dropped into using the Welsh "dah" for dad. Probably conflicted as to which dialect to readopt on my return to the homeland. "Seems like ev'ry time we have a team on t' cusp of summert great they fuck it up!" now the Hasland was really coming out in me.

"Whoa! Ad, they took you out t' village but they couldn't take village out of you, eh?" Dad chuckled.

"Worra y' talking about?"

"...hmm, summert, eh?" said Zoe.

"Well, you didn't grow up there, so you wouldn't know."

"No, I grew up in England, where we speak English!" laughed Zoe. I had been raised for the first decade of me life on the other side of town. It had its own dialect! Zoe was a late arrival to the family, raised by our aunts her first year, so by the time she rejoined our family we had moved to the posher end of town.

"So, what do you reckon they are gonna do with The Club, Dad?" Ju knew how much it meant to Dad – they had been going to games together for years. Our Ju was one of the minority girls at the game, always insisting on going to the Kop and standing versus sitting in the stand with others on their daddy-daughter day. Like me she had spent her youth on Dad's shoulders – he always wanted us to see the world that way. His construction arms and shoulders were broad even as he aged. Being on Dad's shoulders was as solid as riding a horse. He probably would have galloped around the pitch with us on his shoulders like he did our back garden when we were growing up. He'd raise us up charge around like the Lone Ranger's horse Silver, depositing us on a willow vine so we could swing like Mowgli back on to the lawn!

"Town have been on t' brink since I don't know when, but they always find a way!" said I, sounding like me dad.

"Meks you wonder who now? Investors on t' sideline? Who would get behind a ship that regularly sinks?" Dad had a point.

"True, they never did name a *Titanic II*! Did they?" I gestured."It teks a special kind of courage to take on t' responsibility!"

"And a lot of money, Dad," Zoe offered. "This out-going chairman, never can remember 'is name – put loads o' cash in. Where's the return on your investment?"

"I would argue where's the personal touch?" said Dad. "If all business is personal, then why does this team continually fail to grow?"

"I don't know," said Zoe. "They do a bang-up job of getting kids and families involved from that standpoint."

"Yeh, it's way more civilized than when I was a kid! Practically gang-like on t' Kop in them days! Now it's all so politically correct! But at least you can buy a pint in the ground again!"

"Kids' sections, family sections, it seems like its loved more than ever down there, the ground is great – a brilliant place to watch football. And I can only imagine what it's like to play on. It's as smooth as a Subbuteo pitch!!" Ju went on with pride.

"Hello – when did you play Subbuteo?"

"When you weren't looking! Me and the girls got pretty good! Ha!"

"What the..."

"I don't think the problem is The Club?" Dad postulated.

"What do you mean?" Zoe and I were like synchronized twins in our response.

"The Club does a lot. They are involved in the community. They do charity work, they have local advertisers, they have cheerleaders, there's brilliant marketing, there's a mascot, The Club is everywhere – so why does it fail?"

"Leadership?" said Ju from her position as head of personnel.

"I got nothing," said I.

"It's the players!"

"What do you mean, Dad? They've got way more talent than when we were young, faster, stronger--" I became the player's union rep for a minute.

"It's not the skill, the quickness – I'll give you that that they are better players and most days they play like a team. What I question is their 'why.'"

"Their 'why?'" Zoe picked up on Dad right away. "I think I know what you mean. I just read this great book as part of a course I'm doing for work. The players are sound, some are even good, many have big hearts and get involved locally. But there is something missing."

"As sincere as it seems, it's all a little fake – too organized. Like all kids' sports! There's no pick-up games anymore – its spontaneity is gone – the players have on and off field schedules like movie stars doing their film promotion." Dad had noticed a qwerk. It was his thing. Qwerk spotting! He should have been a scientist!

"The players give their best, periodically have chemistry, but it seems that beyond this elusive goal of Chesterfield winning a division or trophy – there is an underpinning that is missing. Individually, there is a different mission. Maybe it's driven by them, their agent or significant other. Some are on the rise in their careers, others are on their way down looking to keep playing as long as possible. They have different 'whys.'"

"You may be on to something, Dad!"

"But how do you build a team of like-minded, skilled players with the same why?" Zoe wanted to know.

"Money talks!"

"But it..." Secretly Neil Diamond had always been one of my favorites, thanks to Mum. And his refrain would live with me all day.

"If everyone was paid the same with the same incentive – only one question need be surveyed – 'Why do you want to play for Chesterfield FC?' Right?"

"Go on," said Zoe, leaning into her tea.

"You find a squad of players who answer the why the same way – everyone else you let go or eliminate."

"So, what's the answer, Dad?"

" 'I want to win the FA Cup!'" he declared. "It's the only thing that really matters in football. No one ever plays for the FA Cup prize money. They play for the history and the glory of the game. You play because you have beaten the best – and every level regardless of origin is given its chance. Underdogs have a real chance. A limited amount of games means the odds are somewhat with you!"

"But that's ridiculous, Dad!" said Zoe. "What about all the other games – the rest of the season? The week in, week out?"

"Every other match is a training match for the FA Cup game. Why not even have two separate teams?"

"Because you have to pay for them, Dad!" I was finally a realist.

"But they are on a different pay scale," he added. "Their mission is a different one – they are the same team that shows up each Saturday, same as today."

"But what about their FA Cup dreams?"

"They answered the question wrong – but still get to play and fulfill the other part of their 'why'!"

"That seems mad, Dad!" Zoe was bemused.

"The FA cup honors the tradition of participation – it recognizes all levels – and on a Saturday afternoon in early May, the world is glued to see who is the best. It's as romantic and pure as it gets! It stands above all other competitions in the world. A season all of its own, with the drama of Shakespearean quality. Pitting world 'All-Star' teams against underdogs who have earned the right to be there. Players who border on amateur status have the chance to go before the world and play against the lottery winners of the sport. Probably golf is the only other place where amateurs line up on the same stage as the greatest players in the world."

"Yeh, but Dad, it's a different deal – to have one player have four good days is way different than having a team have a fairytale run. Each game is like a golfer having a sudden-death play-off round!" Ju knew her sports. She was her daddy's couch caddy during the golf majors once I had moved out! Sat with him for hours watching golf, then cricket.

"Golf is the only game I'd rather watch than play," I added. And was duly ignored.

"But Dad – be real," Zoe ignored my vacuous comment as if I hadn't returned from the States.

"Dad may have a point, Zo!"

"Come off it! What two teams? In one club? That's madness!" Zoe was not convinced by her own skepticism.

"Think about it, Zo. You have one team that plays every week – their goal and mission is to get The Club promoted – more money – weekly recognition by other teams' coaches and managers."

"They're called the 'first team,' right?" Dad was liking the build on his idea.

"The others," I went on, "are the practice squad. The first team has the traditional goal of getting points week in and week out – getting style points so that sponsors return."

"You may have a point," Zoe continued. "The B team is usually the group that does all the PR crap – sometimes it's the first team, but usually it's the non-starters that play mascot through the town!"

"Come meet Chesterfield player so and so – who you've never heard of, right?" Dad was in his element as he had taken me to many a car dealership as a kid to get autographs! I didn't keep any, for obvious reasons!

"So, what you're saying then, Dad," asked Zoe who was growing into the idea. "The B team in your mind is the A team – with its own private goal, undeclared to the rest of The Club players, management, and fans?"

"Exactly, Zo! The Club declares its goal – promotion or bust! The usual stuff, the usual contract signings with that goal in mind. Keeping everything the same. We pay them a different salary—a completely unique contract. They would be sworn to secrecy."

"It's like in the States – they play the season for the playoffs – which in the basketball nearly everyone qualifies."

"Probably?" Dad had no idea and didn't care, obviously.

"Or football – the Chicago Bears played most of their season last year with their practice squad after so many starters got injured – and because they had all played every week and practiced together they almost made the playoffs."

"You bring up a good point – what about injuries? What do you do then?" said Zoe.

"We have to tek a chance – there wouldn't be any money to replace them." Dad had clearly been thinking it through. When most in his situation would be thinking chemo schedules and radiation therapy, he was mapping his fantastic vision.

"So, you're saying you wouldn't take a player from your practice squad to join the weekly team?"

"No – tek a kid from high school, or wherever, whatever, but don't interfere with the B or rather A team's—mission. 'One Goal, One Mission' winning the FA Cup – the dreamers cup, the most glorious team competition in the world, the most glamorous trophy, on the most historic stage, where legends are crowned."

"Dad are you alright?" I asked. His eyes had rolled back in his head like he was summoning the footy gods.

"Just picturing it, Ad! That and the cup of tea I've been waiting for that you promised, since we walked in the door!"

"Ah yes—I'm right on it!"

"Milk, no sugar, in case you forgot, Ad," said Zoe, who was now a chain tea drinker apparently.

"Yep, got it!"

"So, what's next then, Dad?" Zoe wanted to know, needed to know.

"We are born with t' gift of time and t' not knowing how long it would be." Dad paused. The apple of time caught him by surprise in his throat. "My time is a lot less, but it's been less every day for some time. My equinox is long past, and we never have too much time. There is no landmark or statue to mark my time – I never thought in terms of legacy, I was never afforded the luxury of time to consider greatness. For me, greatness was in paying t' bills and time with you kids. Now this idea might sound soft, but there aren't many things that can be accomplished in just one year, let alone ten months, but this would be fun—an old man's childhood dream."

"Crazy old man!" Zoe laughed through her emerging squall of tears.

"I know I must be soft in t' head, but it could be an 'ell of a journey."

"Teas up! All for one and one for all!" And to that we raised our mugs, clinked, and looked straight on at each other. We were really going to do this thing!

"This just in." Harry Gration was back on the telly. "It has been reported that Chesterfield Football Club is being investigated by the FA. It is alleging there may have been corrupt real estate dealings with regard to the new stadium – we'll have more on this in the days to come!"

"It looks like the Musketeers are being called to the rescue!" smiled Zoe.

CHAPTER 14

"Where is he? I'm gonna kill him!" The fury of a father back from the war was like no other. "No son of mine is going to play that pansy-assed game!"

"What are you talking about, Bill?" Roy's mother loved all the men in her life, but this one she needed. Although since his return from India he was different—still handsome and all in one piece but very different. Nights were shorter for both of them as he wrestled with his nightmares and the enemy in his sleep.

"That young'un! Your son, he's been at it again!" The peacock on the wallpaper took the full force of the front doorknob as Roy's father charged into the house.

"Roy? What's 'e been up to?" said Liz brushing off her apron, flour still on her hands.

"Don't tell me you don't know?"

"I'm sure I don't, and you'd better watch your mouth – this is no way to come home! I won't have you using foul language in my house!"

"Your house! I'm the one who pays for it! I'm the one who fought for it!"

"Thank you for that," Liz shut him down. "But I'm the one who maintains it, loves it, fills it with food, and fought for it while you were gone!"

"I wasn't gone by choice, was I? Anyway, where is he?" He was starting to take off his work belt. Smudged fingerprints of oil smeared onto the leather.

"Don't you dare!" screamed Liz.

"Where is he – no son of mine is playing football! We are a rugby family!"

"He's not home."

"Where is he?"

"He's probably off with Billy somewhere – probably looking for bombs in the woods!" She reminded him of her war, the fight and fear of night raids. He never talked of his war.

"'Bin a hell of a day, and now Mac tells me Roy is getting caned for playing football! I won't stand for it! I'll damn well cane him myself too!"

"I'll talk to the headmaster! Mr. Rhys, I think," Liz knew Mr. Rhys well – she was the one who begged him to take Roy in early. Now she might be regretting it. She knew full well Roy was playing football and getting detentions for it – but for some reason it had slipped her mind and never reached the dinner table's discourse.

"You don't sound surprised?" He paused slightly to wind up his rage. "He will rue the day he ever lied to me! It's your fault! I'm gone fighting for t' king and country an' you let these boys do anything they want! Football! Bloody football! I'll kill 'im!"

"Bill, no swearing in the house!"

"It's my house! I'll swear wherever the hell I like, woman!"

"No! You won't! This is my house now!" she said, emasculating him further. In her favorite pre-war patent heels, like on the dance floor she stood up to him, chin slightly raised in anticipation of the first trumpet chord.

She never saw the hand, just felt the burning sting, trails of engine grease like Indian face-paint marked her quickly swelling cheekbone. He'd never hit her before, so she had no reason to evade him. An apple-sized welt puffed out her grease-streaked chin."You bastard, Bill! You're nothing more than a fiend since you came back! Like an animal!"

"A crazed animal!" And he pulled no punch with his meaty left. She swatted at it blindly as it landed its force on her shoulder, heaving her across the tiny kitchen table toward the Aga, its steel handle cushioning her head as she fell against it. Stunned by his own strength, a fiend she had called him right before he thrust his beloved rag doll. She now lay fetally at the base of the cumbersome family stove.

"Liz! Liz!" screamed the fiend, waking from his fury. "What have I done? What have I done?" Bill threw chairs and table to one side, her tiny frame still not responding to his gesticulations.

"Liz! Liz! Liz!" he howled at her and scooped her from the floor like a child with a new puppy. "What have I done?" What have I done?" He couldn't sense her shallow heartbeat or delicate breath.

He carried Liz, rocking her gently, as though she were a baby already asleep. The fiend couldn't seem to wake her.

"Mo! Mo! Help! Call the ambulance!" Yelling, he ran next door with his precious angel in his arms, motionless as an empty dress.

"What's a ma'er, Bill?" Mo stepped aside as he brushed by her to sit in her parlor. She didn't need an answer – she could see her childhood and wartime ally unconscious in his arms, limp like a used tea-towel.

Running to the phone – "I'll call an ambulance right away! Did she fall down them damn stairs again?" Mo and Bill looked at her fancy shoes, with larger than normal heels.

"I need an ambulance right away! Now! Number 6 Fairholmes!" she screamed into the receiver. "I told her them shoes would be t' death of her!" turning back to Bill, whose wartime hands had never been awash in so much blood. Mo didn't realize the prophetic nature of her words. "Why she wears them, I don't know!"

"What number?" came the voice of the operator.

"Number six!" Mo yelled at the operator like she was yelling for everyone to head to the bomb shelter. "She lives at 5 but she's here at 6!"

"I'm patching it through now!" the operator yelled back.

Feeling the warm syrup of Macbethian blood on his hands, he knew an ambulance was going to be useless and his Judas tears blessed her fading cheeks where his gladiator hand had struck. The color of life bled through the canvas of both, like a bleached-out pastel, hardly leaving a stain.

The coroner confirmed her injuries to be consistent with those of a fall, the heavy bruising to her shoulder and head where the bannister base had injured her temple. Bill's head forever sullen, forever in prayer, the last time he raised his fist or his head was to carry her coffin. And just like that, their life was gone. The aroma of freshly made bread no longer blended with the weakest hint of pre -war Chanel, the latch of the door no longer welcomed the cheery "Oh good, you're home!"

The reason to ever leave the work-shed was buried with the reasons to go into the work-shed. The boy's hatred of him exceeded his own. Blaming him for not catching her; blaming him for going away and for coming back; blaming him for the quiet and the constantly drawn curtains; blaming him for the family and neighbor's constant presence; hating the man who saved England yet failed to save their mother. Blaming him for the house of darkness; whose drapes lined the coffin of their house where they each slowly died with her.

Seasons passed by the house, never peaking into add warmth or cold. A constant temperature of darkness prevailed inside. The family home as intimate as commuters. Boys to men in different directions, with little heed of the other. Toting their misery to and from every endeavor. Bill's work lunch lost its variety and spontaneity. No treats from the continent he had "helped save," no tasty leftovers rescued for him from the night before. A long-opened Marmite jar became the center of his lunch, spread thinner than his smile. His hopelessly devastated sons ran off leash and lash. His pride, Billy, depressed himself into his schoolwork, the key to college and an exit door from number 5 Fairholmes Avenue. Roy thought the same but with footy; taking joy in now telling his eunuch father each time he was off to play. He delighted in telling his father he was playing football even if he was off to captain his school at rugby. He showed his father, a man who couldn't swim , his County High-Board Diving Championship winners medal the day after it happened. After school each day, Roy wanted to close the clasp of the lock to his father's shed with him in it. At the now wobbly table, three tea-time place settings of sandwiches lay ready. Billy had clearly been home and gone or was hiding behind his homework in their room. Roy ate from the plate prepared by and for his father, being sure to leave waste the crusts. Roy and Billy's passive fight, cruel in its ingenuity, formed an escape tunnel from their living tomb. Fashioning an exit the way an Egyptian Pyramid slave might, fearing he would be left with the dead.

Like any June day, the Tourette's syndrome rain followed patches of cloud, coolness and intermittent Punch and Judy sun. Their dad stared at the daily nibbled crusts before him.

"I got into Oxford University," Billy began. "I shall be starting in October." Billy enunciated clearly as though he were a graduate already.

"Your mum would've been very proud, Bill," acknowledged his father, swallowing hard, the strawberry-sweet news wedged by his larynx, unable to pass, gagged in the knowledge that he had taken this momentous occasion from her, from them both.

"And you, Dad? What about you?"

"I couldn't be more…" He was cut off by Roy's entrance.

"I've got in, Dad!" Roy blistered in the way he ran rings around defenders.

"In what?" reeled his father, thinking he joined up in an effort to further smite him.

"Wolves, Dad, I'm goin' to be playing for Wolves next season!"

"Over my dead--" The scrape of the chair as he pushed back from the table like the proverbial fingernails on a kindergarten chalk board cut him off. Bringing his guilt and helplessness to the fore. Their father had created his own hell and here he sat in a purgatory wait.

"Your mum would be...." Still the strawberry lodged deeper as his second son would be gone. He wanted to say proud; cakes would have been made, champagne celebrations too perhaps, promoting her joie de vivre. Billy looked at Roy, stared with him for a while, a hint of nod, a job well done, there was a crack in the tomb, and they would be gone from it. Looking at their father as they left, they each grabbed the last of the sandwiches, went to their room, opened the curtains wide, inviting the lightning in, cracking a window to let in the nitrogen air.

Their father remained as if restrained by the newly created scratches in the floor. A knowing thin streak of kaleidoscope light from upstairs glinted off the bannister base where his wife had supposedly hit her head. Had he not been such a good soldier, a stalwart defender of his king's realm, this misery he felt would instead be a streetwide celebration.

CHAPTER 15

"It's a lot of money, Roy. Then again, it's not." Leo Katz did the weighing of scales with his hands as he spoke.

"What?" said Dad with his usual straightness. He hated the hedging that these advisor folks spoke with.

"Granted, you have saved a lot of money. But have you considered future health care needs? The impact of taxes? Once it's gone, it's gone!" Leo slanted his head knowingly, offering concern for his client's future needs.

"The same can be said of me! What's the best way to pull funds?"

"Well, if you are going to go through with this,"

"I am – what do I need to do?" insisted Roy.

"I'll get you a form. It allows for regular and ad hoc withdrawals. I recommend taking the funds in smaller amounts minimizing your tax burden."

"Ta very much – where do I sign?"

"This is quite a change to your original plan, Roy. What made you change your mind?"

"Death, son, death. It can be a great motivator. God apparently had a different plan. I have lung cancer, stage four." Dad was calm, clear with Leo like he was ordering a new pair of dress shoes. Leo was someone he had known for years; they had planned a retirement vision together for years. It was fuzzy back then – goals of paying bills were a dominant theme. Not owning a boat or a summer home or a Bugatti were all goals. His savings had been squirreled away, learning from his ration book days. Ration book days and rainy days. He could afford a few toys, but the heart attack a few years ago changed all that. Roy had gleaned great clarity from the elephant on his chest. Dumbo's sitting there had squeezed any want for a boat and holiday home right out of him. As the weight grew heavier, his only thoughts were to the family he'd got up for every Monday morning feverishly trying to feed. Through the tea strainer of life, the only flavor that poured through was family; family and the memories with his family.

"I'm really sorry, Roy. I had no idea."

"Life can make a mockery of our plans—eh, Leo?"

"But still, with drugs and treatments..." Leo maintained his usual optimism, the way you do in these situations. Dreadfully sorry for your friends – eternally grateful it's not you.

"I can be miserable, tortured for longer. No, I will do those things, if only to get me family off me back, but God gave me a deadline and I'm gonna honor it." Dad stared a little longer across the boat-shaped desk into Leo's eyes, like a captain receiving the king's orders to go forth in the name of king and country. This was it, there was no going back, like your birthday.

"Let's make it happen then, Roy. I'm a planner; it's what I do. Then whatever else I can help with, you only have to ask!"

"Thanks, Leo. If you have the combination to the bank's vault, that would be great, as I think I'm going to need it!"

"I'm sorry – do you mind my asking what the funds are for?"

"I'm buying Chesterfield Football Club, and we are going to win the FA Cup!" and like Yul Byrnner, Dad stood, pushing the plush black leather chair back, reached out, and shook Leo's hand. "God and Dr. Doran gave me twelve to eighteen months; there is no time to waste!"

"Come on you Blues, then!" chanted Leo as he held Roy's hand just a split second longer than was customary.

"Thanks, Leo; from this day forward, we are gonna be busier than the day before our vacation!"

"Paperwork and funds will be processed. Expect the money to be in your account by t' end of next week." The code of the slang slipped out.

Outside, Zoe was waiting for him.

"That's that, then," he said, matter-of-fact.

"You sure you want to do this, Dad? I mean there's a lot…"

"Sure as onions is onions. Where's Ad?"

"Meeting Brian. He wasn't needed here, so he trogged off to find out what our next move should be. Cup of tea?"

"Sounds like a winner."

"Joplins? I'll tell Ad to meet us there. Like old times, eh?" Zoe was as on board as she could be. With the same conflictions of the only eyewitness to a crime! On hand, ready to help more if Dad should change his mind. She hoped to God he would change his mind.

CHAPTER 16

"Honestly, Adam, I don't have much time today," fretted Brian.

"I know, I'm sorry. We're all a bit short on time at the moment."

"Yes, sorry; I didn't mean to be insensitive, Adam."

"You're not, Brian; I just need some cell phone numbers of people we can get in contact with. Dad is actually going through with this."

"You did hear that the FA may regulate Town further, right?"

"No, but what a stroke of luck!"

"Luck? That means less revenues, less advertising, less promotion money, less crowds—it's a fucking disaster!" I'd never heard Brian swear before. The crescendo of agony in Brian's voice reflected the sucking vortex on his funds and time into The Club.

"My bad. Buy low, sell high, was what I was thinking – I was forgetting you had shares."

"Yes! I thought I'd already bought low enough! Now those funds are in the crapper!"

"We'll see. All markets rise eventually."

"How long is eventually? And what the hell are you talking about? It's going to take a mad man to take on this sinker."

"I think I know such a lunatic. But I'm gonna need your help with the Board and procedures. Who do I call?"

"I can give you names, but there is a scandal brewing. Payoffs and fraud are involved. We might even lose the ground."

"That would suck! What are you into The Club for?"

"About half a mill." Brian's voice tapered away like the zeros on his investment.

"And what's it worth today?"

"Don't know. Whatever anyone will pay, I guess. Why?"

"So, you'll get basically nowt for it, right?"

"Well, yes."

"So why did you buy in in the first place?"

"I wanted to see the Town get promoted."

"Or was it 1997?"

"Okay, you're right, it was 1997 – there was magic, the buzz around Town; everyone I spoke to through gauze and rinse had Town on their minds."

"That's what we are talking about too! Getting the buzz back and we have twelve to eighteen months to do it!" My iPhone had its signature ring replaced by the theme song for *The A-Team*! "Sorry about that, Brian—hold on, that's Zoe calling,"

" 'Sup Zoe?"

"Got your American accent back, I hear! We are at Joplins in town, if you want to join us?"

"On me way! Brian, Zoe and Dad are in town—want to join us? We can go over the plan."

"Fair enough. Two more patients to check and I'll meet you there."

CHAPTER 17

"So, Roy – you're getting the band back together again I hear!" said Brian quoting from *The Blues Brothers* and still wearing his sunglasses in the dimly lit coffee bar.

"Something like that, Brian! Any word on who or how we contact the Board?"

"On my way over I talked with Dean Robson, the head of the largest remaining syndicate." Brian left a pause.

"And?" sang Zoe, Dad, and myself.

"They are very interested in meeting you."

"Like rats abandoning the burning ship! They want off."

"And you have the lifeboat!" said Brian.

"What about you Brian? You staying on?" asked Dad.

"I shouldn't—I mean fiscally speaking I should take whatever you offer and run for the seven hills of Sheffield like the rest of 'em."

"But you're not gonna, are you?" Zoe asked, smelling blood in the water. "You're a bigger fool than he is!" She pointed to Dad, who was adding a third sugar packet to his coffee.

"Enough sugar there, Dad?" Zoe diverted herself.

"Never really liked the taste of coffee, to be honest. Only drank it without sugar because I thought refined sugars were really bad for you. Doesn't seem to matter much now, does it?" He coughed, suppressed it with coffee.

Zoe stopped the flow of her mind which wanted to add, "I'm sure you're gonna eat lard on your bread next" but instead just handed him the sugar packet from her saucer.

"I'll take some of that too," said Brian. "Never sweet enough!" and he looked piercingly with affection at Zoe.

"So, you're not out then, Brian?" I added.

"I'm very much in. I din't invest in The Club to make a killing – it would have been nice! Don't get me wrong! but I want, well my 'why' was to see The Club do something special like Hull City, Bournemouth, and ruddy Huddersfield!"

"Right on, brother!" Caffeinated and sweetened Roy recaptured his '60s self.

"I'll be working on Monday whether Town win or lose – but I'm happier when they win. And it's been twenty years since that great FA Cup run." Brian smiled again at Ju as Dad looked deep into the foamy coffee. There would be no more work on Mondays, win or lose, for Dad.

"All for one and..." led I.

"And what the hell are you doing?" yelled Joan at our little gathering. "Were you going to tell me or..."

"Joan – sorry – it's been an 'ell of a week. How did you find me?"

"Julia. She said you would be here. Discussing something about Chesterfield Football Club! What are you thinking?" Joan was on fire, not like the Arc but symbolically. "What the hell are you thinking?"

"Why do you care?" Dad shrank back from his sugar with coffee added.

"Because you damn fool – I like you – so what is all this?"

"It's really none of your business, Mrs. Millward." I spun the wheel of the conversation like the *Titanic* captain.

"Young man!" The soprano decibels were definitely ringing in my ears. "Young man, your father and I have been widowed friends for years and I'll have you know we've shared a lot—haven't we, Roy?"

"Except this, apparently." I pushed my chair back anticipating the soprano whiplash.

"Adam!" Joan found it and cracked the whip above my head.

"Mrs. Millward, if I may make so bold, please take a seat," said Brian, trying to harmonize with the frenetic Joan.

"Who, might I ask, are you?"

"This is Dr. Brian," Zoe announced with newfound affection. "He's on the Board of The Club."

"Soon to jump ship, I would imagine – going to take your ball and go home, are you? Trying to sell my Roy your shares so you can go galivanting off to the south of France!"

"Mrs. Millward!" Zoe and Brian joined in song.

"Mrs. Millward!" we all chimed in, hoping to slow her tirade.

"Call me Joan; or I think people are addressing my mother-in-law!"

"Right you are, Joan." Brian paused. "I'm not selling Roy anything. I'd like to turn this *Titanic* into an ATV."

"What are you talking about, young man?" Joan was flustered still, but her voice was becoming sotto vocce. And she spoke of middle-aged men as young, as her seniority dictates she should.

"Joan, I want to take this sinker of a club and turn it into an All-Terrain Vehicle. One that can come through its watery grave and take the world by storm."

"You are, as they say, delusional!" Joan folded her arms and borrowed a sip of Dad's coffee.

"You may be right, but it's his money and his dream." Brian jumped in like a professional skydiver.

"And you want my Roy to throw his good money after your bad, Brian? Is that what you want?" Joan anchored him to his statement.

"I see it differently, and I think Roy does too." Brian was calmer, almost to a whisper.

"Joan, we've tried to stop him!" Zoe threw out the words with despair.

"Seriously, Joan, we all wish Dad would just go around the world with you, and maybe us…" added Zoe.

"But this is my dream – and – my money." Dad rose from his quiet place. "Joan, I have given up so much recently. No one likes a quitter."

"You're no quitter, Roy; you're a trooper, that's what." Joan wanted to defend him.

"Retired, then. I've retired from a lot of life. Work has gone by, along with those work mates, my footballing days are gone but the pains remain, friends are gone laid to rest before their time."

"But Roy, why this?" Joan was softer now.

"Because it can be done in twelve to eighteen months. Goals have less time to stew; there is no present like this present."

"So? Why does that matter? We are young still, and somewhat active. You're as old as the woman you feel," Joan said with a gaining wry smile.

"Joan, this isn't the right time – but there never will be a good time or right time for what I have to say." All around, in this dimly lit corner those present were suddenly moored to his every word. "Joan." Another pause of breath, a feature that would slowly grind more into his daily conversations. "I can't wait– there is no more time; I have lung cancer and it doesn't look good. That's all the time I may have. The goal, the distraction; it may sound stupid, like an idiotic, pathetic old man, but the reminder, the freshness of that childhood dream, well—soft as it sounds, it will help me fight."

Joan had no words. We all have a time, a slot we are given.

"Oh, Roy." Joan went to him, stiffly lowering herself to him, resting her head in his lap. "But why this? Why now?" Her words were imperceptible to anyone else.

"Because…I'm still a child."

Tears leaked out of all our eyes except Dad's. He had cried over many things, mostly people, but not himself.

I had never seen this softer side of Joan, the brisk tone, the stiffness, the firm British upper-lipness of her wasn't present. Joan nestled into my dad's lap the way my sisters had growing up. Sitting on the floor, arms around his legs, head resting on his outer thigh. I would never have believed this of this woman, this childlike woman, this compassionate suddenly whispering child was Joan; where had all her brashness gone? I couldn't help staring at her and noticed that Ju and Brian in their quietude were staring too. Joan held on to Dad's thicker Wrangler jeans, more denim than leg these days. Joan's fingers curled easily into the stiff blue cotton, taking a better grip of him. How odd it seemed to see him being loved so deeply.

CHAPTER 18

"Gentlemen, this is the man I was telling you about," announced Brian. "This is Roy Griffiths."

"'Ello Mr. Griffiths, pleasure to meet you. Mick Spencer, club treasurer." Mick's black-pudding-sized hands looked like they had many times been jammed in the till.

"Call me Roy." He sounded as firm as his handshake.

"Indeed, mate," said Mick informally.

"Good to meet you, Mr. Griffiths," said Eric Bloomer, thrusting his fencing hand forward. "Acting president since—well, I'm sure you're aware of the situation, otherwise you wouldn't be here, would you?" Eric's blade of a hand retracted. The incongruous pair, stood side by side as a modern-day Laurel and Hardy.

"Thank you, nice to meet you too." Dad's formality shrank him a little like one's first job interview.

"We'll need a quorum," said Brian.

"The rest should be here momentarily," said Eric. "You're early!" Eric's pointedness was not lost on Brian.

"Not by much," said Brian. Pare riposte!

"So, you're interested in joining the Board then, Roy?" inquired Mick.

"Well of a fashion, yes, I suppose." Dad was remarkably composed. Probably comes with age and finiteness.

"What do you mean exactly?" Mick found himself a little disposed to his back foot.

"Oh, I dunno," said Dad, also backing off. "Tell me about the shares of The Club, if you don't mind? Who has what and all that?" Brian had informed Dad, but Dad was taking that knowledge as back up – and to find out the nature of the Board members in front of him.

"Well, Mr. Griffiths, much is in flux, as I'm sure you are aware if you read the papers!"

"I've informed Roy a little too," added Brian, emphasizing Dad's first name.

"Many shares are outstanding since the Chairman's departure, and with that the valuations are…?"

"Not outstanding," Dad prompted.

"Ah yes, very funny. But not so; many of us have had a vested and non-vested interest in The club for years," Mick went on.

"And you'd like your money back!" Dad was shockingly driving the stake home: "Mind my asking how much you have at stake?"

"Well, of course, but more than that we'd…" Mick blew by the question, addressing only the first part.

"Like a profit," said Derek stabbingly.

"Not a trophy, then?" jabbed Dad, poking their eyes out with a stare. "What's the update on the Saltergate scandal, as it's been come to be known?" If Dad had had his walking stick back, it would have been jamming into the chests of Derek and Mick.

"Not much news, really; nothing to report. All still relatively new since it broke only last week!"

"Not good, though, right? Likely it will shrink your profits, eh Derek?" Dad's metaphoric stick impaled both Mick and Derek. Brian had been right – getting here early to tackle any Board members would hopefully divide and conquer. So far so good, if you're looking to buy lower.

"May I remind you we did recently win the Johnston's Paint Trophy at Wembley! Not every year can be a golden one!" Derek batted defensively and with a point.

"It may prove difficult to discuss much more with you, Mr. Griffiths." Mick moved closer to Derek.

"Again, you can call me Roy," he insisted softly in low tone, almost a mumble.

"There are many pressures mounting – not least of which being the investigation by the police and I'm sure subsequently the FA. Ultimately, we may not be in charge of any decisions going forward." Mick started to twitch as he spoke; you could see a bubble of anxiety above his left eye, flickering like a strobe."Our meeting here tonight, still shy of any quorum, I might add, could be moot if the FA decides to follow the course of penalizing The Club. In fact, I'm not sure how much we can share. Our dealings with the stadium project were left mostly in the chairman's hands, but I can see how we might be asked to resign in light of the impression of impropriety!" Derek's directness reflected the direness of The Club and the redundancy of any decisions.

"The impression of scandal is often worse than the action for damage to our reputation! My voicemail is already filling with requests to reconsider advertising contracts, even the lease agreement. God knows it's not unforeseeable that this time next year we could have nowhere to even play our games!" Mick's blood pressure and twitch were sweating out of him like a vindaloo. Image can be everything.

"Trust is paramount, and with results not happening, questions are being asked—isn't that right Mick?" Derek pointedly backed the treasurer to his own corner, like two gerbils facing a pit-bull.

"Thank you, Derek, I'm fully aware of the situation, and as treasurer I know my feet will and are being held to the fire. My professional practice and my livelihood are both on the line here!" Mick could feel the drool of the pit-bull on his shoes.

"Mine too, Mick – you know how bad this looks! It's not just the investment; it's my family's life! Already my Angela is asking me questions and looking at me differently! Clearly, she's worried."

"Charlotte is riding my ass every day I come home from the office! There's no break. And now the Derbyshire Times reporters are following me around like a cheap criminal! One even followed Charlotte around Morrisons as she did the weekly shop!"

"Some days I feel like I'm in the shark cage and bleeding out. Everyone is starting to want more and more from me, and I don't know where to turn! The phones ring constantly with either season ticket holders canceling their renewals or our sponsors wanting modified or out of their contracts!" Mick's veins in his neck showed like flex-hose expanding out with his blood pressure.

"The books are clean, right, Mick?" The two gerbils squared-off eye to eye; where was the exit light?

Mick, under Derek's passive accusation, just nodded full flush with borderline panic wishing he'd taken his Viagara.

"But none of it seems to matter. Losing advertisers will mean more scrutiny and red ink like blood in the water, all the sharks, the investors, the fans, my clients all will be wanting answers devouring my time and reason. It feels like a death spiral with only the ground to break the fall."

The air had gone out of Derek and Mick's superiority. All the brassy glamour of being on the board of a professional football team had tarnished. Needing a constant polish and no funds for a butler. No one in the room wanted their name on the headstone of Chesterfield Football Club, you could see that, and none could afford the further public shaming of scandal.

"I fear we are headed to receivership!" Derek said aloud—in a mumble, but aloud, and his despondency filled the room.

"Then what? And who takes over?" Calmly, Dad's vulture eagerness was palpable in a room of carcasses, like the moment you see a goal-keeper move too soon on a penalty kick and all you have to do is slot the ball into the empty corner.

"A little harsh there, Mr. Griffiths; you sound as though you want it to happen!" Mick took a few steps towards Dad, his temple vein popping a few short jabs in Dad's direction.

"Are you looking to join the Board or not, Mr. Griffiths? That is what you've come here for, right?"

"Actually, no; I don't want to be part of any Board, I just wanted to get a good look at the faces of the men running the show when I realize all the staplers have been nicked!"

"What the hell are you talking about, Roy?" Brian was a little miffed.

"I hate committees and Boards, and when I run this show there will be none of you! There will be no stipends for trips, no lights left on, no car allowance and petty cash available; there will be no…."

"What the hell are you implying, Mr. Griffiths?" Mick took another step closer. Dad never looked more frail; his muscle tone did not match the current crepe paper of his physique. Though not in bad shape for his age, Roy's toned athleticism was thinning.

Mick strode into Dad's awkward space, like a crowded elevator, towering over Dad as he would have done even had Dad not aged smaller.

"I'm not sure what you are insinuating, Mr. Griffiths… Roy! But you can get the hell out if you think we are to blame for what's going on around here! If you think for one minute that we have had our hand in the till, I'll take you outside!"

"Pretty aggressive for an accountant there, Mick!" Dad kept on baiting him. "Looking to take on this old man, are you?"

"I don't care how old you are!" And that was the last thing my dad heard for a while.

Finally, someone switched out the lights, all of them.

CHAPTER 19

"You stupid old fool! What were you thinking? What were you thinking?" Joan charged in.

"I was thinking-It's nice to see you, Joan!" Dad inched himself up on the hospital pillow, wincing from the sharp pain in his shoulder where he had landed.

"I see your ear is swollen and bruised—is that where he hit you?" Joan was unsympathetic.

"It's hard to tell, I hurt in so many places. I'm gonna have to get back in the ring and spar some if I'm gonna take on the Town's bosses!"

"You are a total arse, Roy!"

"If I had been, I might have had a softer landing!"

"You're worse than that. You need to give this thing up, Roy. These thugs aren't worth your time."

"Come, sit next to me. Shove that drip stand over by the chair." Roy was trying to soften the verbal blows.

"No need – I won't be staying."

"Joan, come on – it's just a little swelling; it'll go down in a matter of days. Besides, the sheets are clean and I don't think the nurses will be back for a while. I'm no longer in a critical condition. Well, at least those parts of me aren't!"

"Well, I am – been up to my neck in worry, Roy – you can't keep doing things like this to me, Roy. Not in your condition. It's a fool's dream!"

"Joan, settle down. Come sit by me. I need you here by me."

"Roy, no – hearing about your cancer was hard enough, but knowing you want to waste the rest of your life chasing this stupid dream, this stupid..." Joan turned away, unable to get the words out, unable to look at him. She looked at the clasp on her purse, snapped tight together. That's what she wanted for her Roy. "Snapped together," not this mad rush of childhood fantasy.

"Joan, I'm sorry." Roy squirmed in his pajamas, rearranged the collar to have it stand like a '50s rock star.

Joan turned to see him in his Elvis pose. But it didn't soften her resolve.

"Roy, you fool! I just don't think that I can go through this with you. It just seems like madness – and put your collar down, you're not a child!"

"But Joan, aren't we all just children inside?"

"I'm not, Roy! I don't have those dreams anymore!"

"So, you did have them then?"

"Yes, of course I did, but I grew up and entered the real world."

"Did you like it there?"

"Where?" Joan was losing herself a little.

"The real world – the place as children we were in such a rush to get to. Adulthood like, grown-ups!"

"What are you going on about? Honestly, Roy, I'm losing my patience with you!"

"Said the doctor to the nurse!!" Roy's attempted humor threw fuel on Joan's fury.

"I can't believe I came here. I can't believe I came to see you, I can't believe…"

"What can't you believe, Joan? Spit it out."

"I can't believe in your dream, Roy." And she sat next to him staring at the exit toward the ward station, beyond which dreams and dreamers died on a daily basis. Joan was there but gone in the same place. There was a paused silence, like they had both taken a potty break during the movie.

"Where's your childhood dream, Joan? You can't tell me it's gone away!"

"But I can, and it has. I don't need to live in the past, Roy – I was there already. I want to live in the future. And for a mad moment there I thought I wanted to live there with you." Joan quietly unclasped her handbag and found a tissue, secretly dabbed her eyes, her mascara left a barcoded message on it. A price too high to pay.

"This is my life too, Roy."

"I know that, but…well, you don't have to… but well it would be great… to have you on my team."

"I thought I was already on your team! I thought that I had made that quite clear the other morning!" Joan turned to him stoically, no hint of faded eyes. "Roy, can't you let this child rest? Can't you just let it go?"

Still attached to the drip, he took her hand.

"Joan, I've let this thing go so many times, but it's like the cancer, it gnaws at me constantly, eating me inside and out." He exhaled more rapidly than he anticipated and had to catch his breath.

Joan too paused. In her mind she was channeling the lyrics of Mary Hopkin of days that would never end. And now her own Mary Hopkin soul charmed the tears from her eyes.

"Can't we stop and smell the roses, Roy? Can't we just enjoy the garden of our lives?"

This time she turned back away, her marionette shoulders dancing morbidly with her quiet sobs. As the song says Roys's dreams were the same - Mary Hopkin sang softly to her.

"I want to live the life I want to choose," she said softly.

"So do I, Joan; so do I. I get it that I may sound like a crazy old man, but for a few months I want to live like that child again, like that bright blue-eyed, blonde-haired kid who wanted to grow up but didn't know how and now still doesn't. I see it for what it was. A happy core of me that I let go, and I want him back. Not just for me, for my kids; for them to see the way I was before they knew me, before growing up got in the way."

"But they love you so much – just this way – that should be enough."

"It should be, but it's not, Joan. I want them to see the person, the kid, the young man of hope and dreams – the footy star, the rugby captain, the joker, the me their mother fell in love with—the…lover."

"You old fool, you are so much more than that, more than the who you were. You are their rock. And what about me, Roy? I love this you – this stupid, foolish you. You want to live in a past I wasn't part of?" Deliberately, Joan placed his intravenous hand upon the hint of mint-green bedspread. Caressed his fingers to their very tips, like Michelangelo's Sistine Chapel, she pulled her hand away and left the room.

"Joan, Joan—come back! We can work it out, surely. The drip bag acted as his anchor and he could see her sailing away. "We can work this out," he said mis-quoting from McCartney then moved on whispering to his chest the words:

"I never promised you anything – just me being me. You have to live with all seven stages of me. That's how love is at this age." And he'd said it – if only to himself. His tears yelled angrily at her sunset silhouette.

CHAPTER 20

"It's for you, Dad!" I said, rushing into Dad's room and accidentally kicking his puke bucket. The sour smell hit the air, as did its contents. I wanted to puke.

"What the hell! I can't, Ad; this chemo has kicked me for six." Dad rolled over, burying his head in his pillow. The room was dark at midday. "I just want to be left alone."

"It's the bank."

"What do they want?" Weariness ebbed into frustration.

"To talk to you." I emphasized with a whisper.

"Look, I'm an old man; I haven't had a mortgage in years. Can't you leave me be, Ad?"

"I would, but It's the third time they've called today. This time it's the senior vice president at HSBC! So, I thought it must be important, sorry."

"Well, obviously it's a mistake. I don't have an account with them. Has Joan called?"

"Dad." I paused, looking at the back of his head a thinning wispy crown of white hair staring back at me like a feral eye. Above the whiff of vomit juice, I could smell the air of age in the room. I could feel a hopelessness that I hadn't felt since the days spent with my grandfather at Valleybrook nursing home.

"Let me rest, Ad, please," came the whisper smothered by the pillow.

"Alright, Dad, rest up, sorry," and I grabbed the bucket, emptied it of food remnants, carrots that I didn't remember cooking, wiped off my shoe and returned it quietly. It was then that I realized I had left the bank on hold this whole time.

"My God, I'm dreadfully sorry!"

"Mr. Griffiths?" asked the patient voice on the other end with an accent not from these parts.

"Yes…I'm Mr. Griffiths." Dad was too tired and I was too curious. "How can I help you?"

"Well, I'm calling at the behest of the Chesterfield Board of Directors." He definitely wasn't from round these parts! No one here had used the word "behest," since English Lit homework for Shakespeare. And then, as now, I'm not entirely sure what that means other than pompous, so I let him go on anyway.

"As I say," he said in a rather plummy yet eloquent way, "it has been brought to our attention, that you, Mr. Griffiths, have shown a certain interest in acquiring shares in Chesterfield Football Club."

"Nope, ta' very much!" it was a rough Chesterfield accent but the best I could do on short notice. A local would have known how fake I was right away, but a Harrow boy wouldn't know fake northern if it came attached with a map. So, I hung up. "Sorry!"

The phone rang again almost immediately. I picked it up, ready to hang up again.

"Not interested, at this time!" I went to hang up until I heard a woman's voice on the other end! "Ah, Joan, very sorry – been getting a lot of pestering calls." I tried to recover.

"Is Roy there?" Joan was back to being Mrs. Millward.

"He is, but he's sleeping off a rough morning – I'd rather not wake him."

"Just let him know I called, would you?" There was a patient haste in her tone.

"Of course," I said to the phone tone. Her receiver had made it back to its cradle faster than a bad poker hand. I checked it, rolled my eyes, and popped it back down. It came back to life like a crying baby waking as it nestled in its crib!

"Hello, Joan!"

"Mr. Griffiths?" not Joan, then.

"Er, yes? Which one are you looking for?"

"I think we were cut off? I'm from the bank. I called a moment ago then again, but the line was busy?"

"Bloody BT – rubbish, aren't they?"

"I can't speak to that, sir."

So, I hung up on him again just for kicks! The baby cried right away!

"Mr. Griffiths?" the caller had immense patience and obviously a great need to speak to me; I mean Dad."Yes – you've found me again. What terrible service we are having!"

"Then I'll be quick and to the point. As you may or may not know, the Board of Directors is under terrible scrutiny and shares are being relinquished and sold back to the bank. Of course, we are reluctant to take them back given the nature of the financial crisis."

"And their de minimis value." I was nonchalant in using a word I was unsure of.

"Well certainly, sir," the banker paused probably wondering why he was holding the phone at all.

"So, you're looking to find someone you can palm a leaky boat off on to? Buy low – sell high!" and once again I went to cradle the baby. However, I think the voice on the other end could smell my intent."Don't hang up again, Mr. Griffiths!" Bugger! He was on to me. "Sir, I believe we can find common ground!" he yelled into the phone in the event it was headed towards the cradle again.

I paused. "I'm not deaf! Yes, what is it you would like to say?" *Check!* I thought.

"Yes, we understand our boat has lost its mooring, but I'm assured that we can keep the Chesterfield Football Club afloat."

"With my money?" I tried to age up my telephone voice which I'm sure was making its way up the steep stairs to Dad's room as we spoke.

"That would be part of it, of course."

"So, give me a little update. Where are we at now? What shoddy mess are you trying to sell me?"

"Well, Mr. Griffiths, let me begin at the beginning…"

"I'd rather you start at the end, so we can get to a new beginning!"

"Most definitely, if I may continue?" Our banker sounded like a Catholic selling a Gideon Bible –

"Yes, yes," I interrupted. "Please do!"

"The club is largely without a Board – there is one standing member—Brian?" the banker's momentary lapse allowed the ship to board an iceberg.

"So, The Club has no Board or quorum?"

"Correct! Again, if I may continue?"

"Sure, sure," I interrupted again. Gosh, this was fun.

"We need to show good faith to the world. We at the bank, that is. Without a Board, advertisers will want to renegotiate with The Club or renege on their contract, given the scandal and chaos. Sir, image is everything in a case like this. As you know we must present a united front in face of this abandonment. We must cut them off at the pass. We need a fresh face on the Board; we need a hero!" There was fresh concern in his last statement.

"Call me when you're desperate," I almost shouted into the handset—and I hung up. Power and money, money and power do strange things to a person – especially me when it's not even my money! But this last statement "need a hero." Dad had always been a hero to me; was this a time for him to be a hero and get what he wanted, too? Did I hang up prematurely this time? Apparently not--

The phone rang again.

"That was quick! So, you are desperate, then!"

"Desperate? What are you talking about, Adam? Is Roy there?"

"Joan? No, still sleeping. Can you hang up? I'm expecting a call, sorry!" I nodded my head in apology. Not very effective on a phone, I'll grant you.

"Sorry?" Joan was a tad put out. I hung up and presumably she did too.

Almost immediately, the phone buzzed to life again like the beeps leaping off a patient's flatline!

"Mr. Griffiths! Do you have any interest in helping Chesterfield Football Club?"

"Yes, Mr… what was your name again?"

"Harold Stanley Boris Charlemagne!"

"Quite grand – I'm sure I would have remembered it? Anyway – you were saying?"

"HAVE YOU ANY INTEREST IN HELPING CHESTERFIELD FOOTBALL CLUB?"

"Yes, I believe I do. Let me check my calendar." I paused and stared at the imaginary calendar on the textured, magnolia painted wall paper; that should be long enough, I thought, having no particular schedule. Then I remembered there was a calendar in the kitchen.

Dad had the Wildgoose Calendar pinned to the side of the cabinet, so I took Mr. HSBC for a walk around our castle of a house before checking it out! Ninety seconds to go about nine feet should seem about right? Wanted to give the right impression, you know.

"Ah, there we are – sorry, Mr. C it was all the way in the south wing!"

"How does Wednesday at 10:15 look? You can meet me here at the market location in town?"

I checked Dad's calendar again – wide open that day.

"Sorry, Mr. C, I have an appointment with my attorney to go over my trust."

Thursday Dad had a follow-up meeting regarding the chemo.

"Thursday?"

"Sorry – quarterly review of my accounts with my financial advisor!"

"Friday, then?"

"Let me see…." It was wide open. I mean, Dad probably had to do his daily shopping in town. "I might be able to move a couple of things around – what time were you thinking?"

"11:15?" Mr. HSBC threw out optimistically.

"Make it 1:15, and I think we should be good!"

"I'll check my…" was all I heard as I of course hung up! Those with the money who live in castles like the one we do have all the power! Okay – Dad's money, Dad's castle; well, he is English and it's his home, ergo his castle! And by my extension, he was now gaining in power.

CHAPTER 21

"The papers, Mr. Griffiths!" said Mr. Charlemagne. "Here is the Chesterfield Football Club offering!" Mr. C was a worse poker player than my dad, or me for that matter.

The papers were an advertising brochure on the cover of a Profit and Loss statement – where the "profit" part was missing. Red ink was just a euphemism, but the parentheses around the losses were very real. That number was likely to get larger, and no parentheses were going to buoy that!

"You okay, Dah?" I looked over his hunched shoulders as he labored through the reports.

"I can't tell if it's the chemo or the numbers, but I feel nauseous. Could you get me a… " Puke has a strange consistency, like that of an unfinished half-cooked omelet – chunks of food floating amid a swell of yolk. Turning in a violent fashion, Dad sprayed both Mr. Charlemagne's and my brogues. Trails of omelet hung from the cuffs our trousers like carrots suspended in napalm.

"I'm so sorry." as Dad heaved further, you could see sweat pouring out and drying. He was already in his back up suit given the morning's earlier misfortunes. No, he hadn't been sick earlier. I just hadn't seen him behind the lounge door as I brought him a tie. I wasn't to know he was about to get more creamer for the coffee I'd just made him. There really is no way to disguise a coffee stain on a fawn suit.

"With any luck it's not ruined," Dad lamented. I thought the opposite. It would be decades before fawn suits with flared bottoms would return to the height of fashion. I hope to be dead before having to witness that debacle. His back-up suit was much more appropriate. Even though it was his father of the bride suit.

"I never feel like me in this suit," Dad had said as he slipped the jacket on before the trousers – first of all, who does that? Jacket on before the trousers? Old people, apparently! Not that he was even that old! I'd aged along with Dad, so it never seemed like he was that old, until recently.

"Why does a slim suit make me look fat?" He had a point, and I had no answer. Zoe's wedding had been a long time ago, and Julia's was well before that. So, this was the suit's third outing in almost as many decades.

"Navy suits look good on everyone, Dad. Now put your trousers on; you're not in a home yet!" I used to dread that thought, but this latest diagnosis made that "fade to grey" look like a Barbados sunrise.

"Funny, Ad!"

"I try to be, thank you! You might want to try less bread with your sandwich, Dad!" I mocked as he forced a muffintop over the waistband. "Good job low-waist is back in fashion, eh?"

"Not sure I can wear this for long! Might end up sounding like Minnie Mouse!"

"Can you at least button the jacket?"

"Well, would you look at that?" Rhetorical pleasure swept over him and rhetorical relief over me, as he could do at least the all-important top jacket button.

"Alright, let's be having you then!" I quoted my nana, his mum, to him. That was just weird, right? "I'll grab the fawn jacket and drop it off at the dry cleaners on the way home."

"Don't worry, Ad, I never liked that suit anyway!"

"Really? But that's the suit you wore to my wedding!" Slightly miffed, I grabbed it anyway.

"You alright Mr. Griffiths?" The bank chairman was anxious to get the paperwork reviewed and signed. The necessary witnesses and attorneys sat impatiently bored across from my dad.

"Bin better." He took a tissue from his pocket. "Toilets close by, are they?"

Dad left to freshen up, passing the janitor coming in. Dad looked so pale when he came back. He popped the ubiquitous red-white swirled mint into his mouth, pocketing the wrapper.

"Has Joan shown up yet?" is what it sounded like as he rolled the newly skinned mint around his mouth. Not since his near-death experience following a routine wisdom tooth extraction had he been able to open his mouth very wide, often sounding rather regal as a result, except when he was trying to manage a conversation and a boiled mint simultaneously.

"No, Dad – sorry, not heard from her. She was talking of taking a holiday, so maybe she did. We can stop by on the way back if you like?" Our side-bar ended with the reinjection of the bank's chairman.

"Mr. Griffiths, would you like some water?" The chairman was clearly relieved to see Dad back at the table.

"Cup of tea would be nice." Dad grinned. The tortured witnesses rolled their eyes mentally, counting the extra time needed for the tea.

"I'll take one too, if you've got the kettle on!" we were a team, me and me dad.

"This is like watching *Jaws*, Mr. Charlemagne!" said Dad.

"How do you mean, sir?"

"I just keep looking around waiting to be eaten! Then the head drops out of the bottom of the boat!"

"I'm not sure I follow, sir."

He had good manners, did Mr. Charlemagne.

"Well, Mr. Charlemagne, assuming the worst-case scenario – Town being penalized and dropping out of the league officially – all these advertisers' contracts are null and void. The payroll debt alone is killing The Club. It really is rather worthless, isn't it? Like the serenity of a sunken rowboat, until the head drops out of the boat!"

"How do you mean, sir?"

"Well, Town may own the stadium – but that's pretty useless if you don't own the land it sits on!"

"Standard contract, in most cases, Mr. Griffiths."

"Fair enough. Who owns the land?"

"We do!"

"I don't like the way this is shapin' up, Mr. C. I've heard of people buying and naming stars but never black holes!" Dad had Mr. Charlemagne locked in his gravity.

"I'm buying a tarnished name, and pools of increasing debt that will likely drown us in a couple of years."

"I'm afraid you are correct, Mr. Griffiths – it may get worse before it gets better." To his credit, the bank chairman was honest, to a fiduciary fault.

"These are all the shares, then?"

"The ones outstanding, outside of Mr. Banner's of course."

"Okay – the deal is done." Remarkably, Dad signed where highlighted. Witnesses shuffled awkwardly as Mr. Charlemagne backed into them.

"This is the worst deal of my life. Only a very sick man would do this. You're not taking advantage of a sick man, are you, Mr. Charlemagne?"

"You have my word, sir – all the good news is right there in front of you!"

"Then I never want to 'ear from you again. Sorry about yer trousers."

"Nothing a dry cleaner can't fix, sir!"

"Dad are you shoower?" I affected some weird colloquial accent! Don't know why.

"I wish Joan were here," was all he could say.

"Probably best she wasn't!" Sometimes thoughts come out as words, don't they? Without deference to the sensitivity of the moment.

"What d'you mean, Ad?"

"Well I think, Dad… secretly she's a Sheffield United fan!"

CHAPTER 22

"So, what do we do now, Dad?"

"Well, Ad, the first thing we do is celebrate – we are the proud owners of Chesterfield Football Club!"

"I'll call Brian – we can have a meeting of the Board – at Joplins, perhaps."

"Yes, and I'll call Joan," Dad said excitedly. "She's not really a Sheff U fan, is she?"

"I think so, Dad – you'll be surprised how many round these parts are!"

"Well then, it's time we gave them a new bandwagon to jump on." He flipped open his phone. "Joan are you there?" He paused; both of them rarely carried their phone on their person, so they would need time to locate it. By the same token they were the only two people I know who ever left their ringer on! "No answer."

"She's like you, Dad; probably never carries it with her and then can never find it! Probably 'not charging' down the side of the settee or something!"

"Very funny. Well, we can pop round her place on our way home, then?"

"Hi Brian, it's Adam and Roy. The deal is done, mate; it's just you two now."

"Well, mostly Roy, actually." Brian had settled into his stepsister role nicely.

"Could you meet for a drink? Thinking a mini-celebration before we call to gather the troops!"

"Of course. Got a couple of things to wrap up, but I'll walk into town in a little while."

"I'll call Ju and Zo to tell them the good news—on second thought, it's probably better coming from you! Herr Director!" it was surreal that I was standing with the new director and owner of Chesterfield Football Club. It felt like a lottery win, when in reality we should have felt like runners-up on Bulls Eye. "Come and have a look at what you would have won!" That is to say, we could be staring at three Ferraris, the lion's share of a Bugatti, a London condo? A thousand round-the-world cruises? A small island off the coast of Oregon? A thousand weeks at an All-Inclusive hotel in the Dominican Republic? The list was bloody endless; instead we owned Chesterfield Football Club, a club that, like the *Titanic*, created its own vortex of problems in the waters around it.

"I'll call the girls to let them know right after I let Joan know."

"I think you should call the girls first," I insisted.

"There was a fairy! Her name was 'Nuff' - Fairy Nuff!" Dad loved this line. And I'm sure I'll use it endlessly when he's gone. Gone? Which, obviously, would be never.

"Joan, are you there? I have some news to tell you!" Dad was yelling into the voicemail. Not very effective, but it did affect a certain passion, even concern. "Damn it, Ad – can we go round to Joan's first? Plus I could use a change of clothes before seeing Brian – I think I may have splashed myself with puke earlier."

"Joan's not home, Dad. I don't see any lights on!" We drove by almost back to his house.

"She's just being cheap – she never has the lights on; I like that about her. Go'round the back see if the telly's on."

"Nothing back here either, Dad," I lied. I could see Joan curled up on the couch sitting in the afternoon darkness of a house that faces north, staring at her mobile. Dad must be calling her again, I thought. I saw Joan startled; she had seen me, my nose to her picture window. Tissue in her hand she waved me away, closed her phone, and buried her head in the couch cushions. I had no idea she had any vulnerabilities or clearly how much she cared about Dad—or Sheffield United?

"Not back there, Dad – lights are off; there's nobody home. Like I said, she's probably off with her sister – Bridlington, I think she said?"

"I miss her, Ad. I want her to be part of this great adventure. Already I feel I have more energy. Strangely most people would feel more sick at owning Chesterfield Football Club than going through chemo! That bloody chemo. It must be the power of a lifelong dream. It's hard to think of anything positive when you are hurling your scrambled food into a bucket, especially when you have nothing but time to think about it! Now we have a mission."

"I know, Dad – we have so much work to do."

"And not much time – I'll be quick – keep the car running I will be out in a jiffy." For a man on chemo and a new hip he moved like a garden imp, I couldn't help but notice. "Keep the car running" would become our mantra. He ran down his driveway, found the flowerbed at the side of the house, added a splash of color, planted some carrot seeds, and returned to the car.

"Are Julia and Zoe coming?" Brian asked, huddled around his Joplins coffee mug.

"No Brian, PTA meetings – one hosting, the other attending. Both would rather be here than there, that much I do know!" I brought Brian up to speed.

"Cheers, Roy! You are a brave soldier in so many ways! Tackling chemo and something even more physically debilitating, Chesterfield Football Club!"

"I'll drink to that! To the new owner 'Roy, my dad, Griffiths'!" as I said it, I looked hard at Dad, the way you stare down the miracle of your child's birth. He probably hadn't smiled like that since—well, I don't know when. Those are his memories, not mine.

"I don't have long, gentlemen – I don't mean that lightly – I know I'm a sick man, maybe even desperate, given this latest venture. I have no time to waste; those days are all behind me. So, we need an agenda."

"And a team!"

"No time for flippancy, Ad; we need to have a water-tight plan. There is no time for plan B! Or money, for that matter."

"Roy, you should start by introducing yourselves to the staff."

"I think we did already," I whispered to Dad.

"Sorry, Adam? Didn't catch that," said Brian.

"It's alright, Bri, just an inside joke."

"Okay, then – I think you'll find that there are a lot of nice people running day-to-day ops at The Club."

"I think they might be even nicer if they got paid too."

"Sorry – I'm not following," said Brian.

"Just something we overheard that, well, The Club is perhaps behind on its payroll."

"Brian, I will start there – I need good people, and if you say they are good we should keep them on. The backroom stuff needs continuity – but I would like someone to watch the lights! Brian can you visit with accounting and have them let me know how much we owe the staff? I don't have time to change them, hire new; we need good faith effort, and changing these folks won't be the difference in us winning the FA Cup!"

"FA Cup? What are you on about, Roy?"

"Brian, can you keep a secret?" Dad huddled Brian into the uneven circle of three; somewhat awkward as we had chairs for three others who were supposed to be here. Brian collapsed back into his chair on hearing Dad's goals.

"So that's it in a nutshell!" Dad threw his hands behind his head and grinned like the king sending the *Titanic* off on its maiden voyage!

"Well, Roy – I don't know what to say. Having been in the weeds of this swamp for years, I think you are out of your mind!" Brian wanted to be onboard, hesitating like a Wright brother. My sisters would have agreed with Brian, were they not getting criticized at their respective PTA meetings.

"Not much to say, Brian – we almost pulled it off in '97. We will, as I said, have essentially two squads. An A and a B – two separate missions. We will advertise locally and nationally, looking for players to try out for our 'practice squad,'" Dad used the finger version of quotation marks like he was a sixth-grader. He wasn't thinking of cancer, chemo, or radiation – there was no room in the conversation, and I know that's what he wanted.

"Dad, I'll visit with the social media and regular media department of The Club tomorrow?"

"What's wrong with today? There is no time, Ad. Finish your drinks, boys; we have work to do! Cheers!"

"Meeting adjourned, then!"

You should never slam Stella Artois like it's a cheap shot! All three of us simultaneously siphoned beer through our noses! Not exactly the Three Musketeers; more like the Three Moustacheketeers!

CHAPTER 23

Brian led the way through the halls, which Dad and I were already familiar with, and Dad turned out lights as we went.

"Follow me, gents!" I called ahead to let everyone know the new chairman was on his way so hopefully some at least stuck around!" Brian breezed in like a Persil commercial – all white flowing sheets smelling of the morning dew.

"Glad you're on board, Brian!" I said briefly, not trying to stain his sheets.

"Of course, I am! One life to live!" and Brian pivoted into the room with us in tow.

"Ladies and gentlemen! I give you your new chairman – Mr. Roy Griffiths."

The half-dozen or so employees crammed into the chairman's brightly lit corner office offered polite applause as Dad took his bow. More of a stoop than a bow. He had bowed over many buckets in recent weeks and felt the need to stand straighter as a result. The onlookers were a mix of generations dressed casually: track suits, Nike trainers, orthopedic shoes, one pair of heels, a couple of pairs of sensible pumps, a more seasoned pair of Mary Janes, Doc Martens with red tights in them, flip-flops (unacceptable, he would have to be spoken to), Brian's brogues, gladiator sandals with gold buckles. It was quite a mixed bag of unenthusiasm.

"Well, this is a moment I dreamed of," said Dad and the room quieted with anticipation – or bemusement that someone should be excited about owning shares in the modern equivalent of a DeLorean! Most in the room they seemed to be staring Dad down to find his sanity perhaps hiding in his shirt pocket, fly zipper, or on the top of his shoes. This to them, was like buying more stock in bargain-priced GM during the "financial crisis." It wasn't going to end well. All in the room had newly updated their CV's and had them posted on various job sites; not much reason to stick around.

"For some of you this might be a nightmare, but I want you all to know as a kid I dreamed of playing for Chesterfield Football Club. My son even joked with his friends that he would one day own The Club. Well he may have to wait awhile for that one!" Dad was enjoying his moment, but only half smiles from flip-flops and Mary Janes greeted his words. Questioning folded arms raised higher to the chin of the sensible pumps, almost in unison. Like they were keeping their heads above the waves. They must work in the same department – probably accounting, human resources—or worse, payroll.

"I may sound crazy, but that's reserved for my son here."

A ripple of smiles started with Doc Martens with red tights and spread to Brian's brogues.

"God, it's bright in here! Sorry, I'm not big on speeches and I'm not crazy. What I am is... dying." And like a Shop-Vac Dad sucked the air, light, and sound out of his newly assigned office. Nikes, flip-flops, pumps, and heels started a shuffle in unison, not something you see very often. The sensible pumps even rolled their folded arms less in their sorrow rather than disgust as a temporary measure. Turn-over was already a problem at The Club. You could practically hear the printer churning out page one of the CV. Previous experience – Chesterfield Football Club, unemployable.

"I don't want sympathy; after all, you don't know me. But I promise you this, I will give you every ounce of my time and patience." Dad shuffled his Clarks to attention. The parade ground was now motionless. "Additionally, I will pay you what you are owed by The Club this morning; I need you all and I want us all on the same page."

Page Two was on pause with writer's block.

All the shoes twitched a little with relief; for the Mary Janes, a smile cracked. There was finally going to be food with the meal.

"My singular goal is to win the division and return to the rightful place of recognition back in division two where we rightfully belong – then set course to be like Huddersfield, Hull, and Bournemouth into the mighty English Premier League."

Delusional! Page Two of the CV printed out. Or not. Brian finally looked away from his shoe eyelets to look everyone in the eye. This wasn't the goal he'd been told.

"Here! Here!" yelled Brian's brogues as his heels clicked together with Michael Flatley flamboyance. And the cacophony of shoes shuffling to Dad's Clarks gave the impression of a room united. A room united by the need to get paid first, then move on to the English Premier League.

"You did say we would get paid today?" asked the Doc Martens, closely followed by the flip-flops.

"Give Mr. Griffiths a chance, would you!" The sensible pumps needed to confirm with the payroll service first.

"So where do we begin then?" the Nikes seemed eager or anxious, or both. It was hard to tell, what with them being so brightly colored and all. Apparently, they had missed their morning jog on account of the breakfast rains. Like a chain-smoker on a trans-Atlantic flight, they shuffled furtively in place.

"Some players would be nice!" said the orthopedic shoes, and the Mary Janes nodded in agreement.

"Who's in charge of PR?" I asked as the shoes settled back to leaning on the desk and surrounding windowsill.

"That would be me. I've been volunteering that role for six weeks now," complained the Doc Martens with red stockings, his toe caps a little scuffed.

I raised my eyebrows but should have known that all PR is social media now. And that unless the millennial is taking endless selfies, Doc Martens and red stockings are quite acceptable in the workplace. God, I sounded old, perhaps even a little demented. The inserts in my Hush Puppies were starting to pinch (and don't be so "judgy"--they are very comfortable, otherwise – my collapsed arches require me to have inserts, and the extra height kind of helps too…where was I?) and I could feel the blister popping and seeping through my socks. That's probably enough about that, though.

"So, you're in charge of PR—social media, then?"

"Yes, that's all me. I'm an entire department." The Doc Martens and stockings rolled their millennial shoulders. "I'm Zach – I do it all!"

"He's the best!" The Mary Janes tightened their buckles for emphasis. "He's an intern from Sheffield University, on loan, as you footballers might say!" and the buckles chuckled.

"On loan! Not free! So, you're saying I will finally get paid too?" the Doc Martens and red stockings scuffed with tempered excitement.

"Everyone will get paid. Zach, we will start with you, since you will be our first order of business."

"I'll get the ledgers, Mr. Griffiths, and see who is owed what," said the sensible pumps.

The Doc Martens and red stockings remained uncharacteristically enthusiastic given their punkish history. It was shocking to see how my Air Force father didn't bat an eye at this goateed youth in yellow-black plaid kilt, Doc Martens, and red stockings. I would have been buried alive for sporting that get-up in public when I was Zach's age! I was disowned for months following a single ear-piercing, for God's sake! Times have changed! Huddersfield are in the EPL – that's just ridiculous! Can all this really be normal? Dad owned the Town!

"Take a seat, Zach – I'll tell you my plan. Brian, you can stick around too, if you like?"

"Not my bag, Roy; I've got teeth to pull in my office. I'm done pulling them here! – see you at the board meeting!"

"Oh Brian – just so you know, there won't be any, so stop by whenever you like!"

"But the bylaws, Roy?" Brian's brogues needed a little polish.

"Don't have time for them, remember? The by-laws didn't stop us getting where we are now, so I don't think they're going to help us going forward!" Dad put his watch on the oak laminate desk, using the black leather strap to hold the watch face towards him.

"Zach, let's go; we have exactly one hour!"

"Okay, Mr. Griffiths, what do you need?"

"Start by turning out the light and calling me Roy!"

"Tell me what you need, and I'll post it."

"Post it?"

"Yes, online – blog it, Facebook, Snapchat, Twitter… you know all the usual stuff." Zach was ready to go and could have done it in his sleep.

"So, you're not sending out letters and calling the papers then?"

"No, your letter-box is reserved for your junk!" The Doc Martens gave their knowing wink.

"Moving right along – okay, we need players; rats have donned their life-vests and jumped overboard! Let's find a way to make them regret it. I want an open call – we will do a series of open tryouts. The normal channels have been exhausted, I'm sure, and we don't have money for fading stars." Dad took a breath and turned to me. "Ad, can you get me a cup of tea?"

I looked around for someone else. There was no one – my CV said I was suitably qualified – especially about the part where it says I work for free.

"Be right back, then," I said.

"There's a little kitchen four rooms down," added Zach, affirming my position, or lack of it.

"So, Mr. Griffiths – to clarify – we are gonna host tryouts for Chesterfield Football Club as if we were in high school?"

"Yes, but no high school coaches are allowed. I draw a line at them!"

"How many events? And what age are we looking at?"

"We'll run tryouts the next two weekends. Open up the gates of the stadium – the top thirty recruits will play a one-time playoff match for a place on our squad. We'll invite the world! Fill the stadium! So, contact Harry Gration."

"Harry Gration?" Zach was confused.

"From *Look North*! He's famous – he'll spread the story!"

"Sorry, I'm lost. Is *Look North* a travel show?"

"Forget it! I'll take care of Harry – you do your Face-chats and what-nots! Radio too!"

"Radio Two?" Zach looked at the dying man rattling off dying industries. "Dude you want young players, right?"

"Seventeen to thirty-seven!"

"Thirty-seven? And their Zimmers? Don't you think that's a bit old?" Zach had no filter, which to be fair, given the timeline, was the exact feedback Dad needed. "What about a coach? Danny's gone, and his whole team aborted once the rumor of his departure was confirmed. It's gonna be hard to recruit a team when The Club has one foot in the grave and the other on the pyre!" This millennial honesty was going to take some getting used to.

"You've got a serious point there. We're a little cart before the horse with that one!"

"I'll say. I'm headed to Starbucks – you want anything?" Zach grabbed his 1970s satchel, swinging it, looping it over his head.

"I think that is actually my satchel from Hasland primary school, Dad." I laughed. Zach was out of earshot!

"I heard that!" said Zach. "Yes, it was me dad's – found it in the attic!" not so much out of earshot then!

"Wanker!" I whispered.

"And I heard that – maybe you should take up smoking or something. You sound a little tense!"

"Thanks, Zach – how about you bring me a grande skinny mocha instead!"

" 'lright will do – and they call me a fag!" Zach's honesty set me back on my thong.

"He's gonna be trouble, that one," I added, now convinced he was out of range, still whispering just to be sure.

"Oh? I rather like him," Dad said pointedly accidentally checking for my thong.

"Anyway, he is right; we do need a coach – and I've had a thought running through my head."

"Finally!"

"Wow, settle down, super-supportive Dad. For any of this to work – it has to be unique – we have to create the longest football-high any team has ever had. We need to build our own football nation. A nation of agnostic fans. Those same passionate patrons of *Dancing with the Stars*—people are glued rooting for the underdog. We need to capture their attention from the get-go."

"A gimmick?"

"Well, sort of – the hard thing is that we need to keep the FA Cup goal quiet but not secret. We need to have everyday TV watching folks glued into the team."

"What are you suggesting, Ad?"

"I'm suggesting that each week we add a celebrity player!"

"That would be a frigging circus!"

"Yes, exactly—a media circus! Dad, don't you see – you only have so much cash. And with all the will in the world, advertisers have been tapped out and won't come back quickly or easily. We have to roll a snowball in June."

"Not too hard in New Zealand!" Dad offered. "You're right, I suppose. But gimmicky circus, is that taking away from the purity of the game? Is that just making us a mockery?"

"Not if we only invite them to play on the first team our practice squad the FA Cup team. We ask celebrities the same question! Who would want to play in an FA Cup match?"

"They don't have to play for long, right?"

"Of course not. Everyday fans will be happy their team is practicing as normal – usual footy stuff. But our team – the practice squad will have the hoopla! The buzz that will put us on the map. We even have the Saturday fans pick the celebrity player. Announce it at the match's end – even away games – only those traveling get to vote!"

"Should any of them even want to take part in this charade! How do we know which celebrities play footy?"

"Dad, drive me over to the library and we'll go to the reference section and pull up the microfiche!"

"We can't go now; I have checks to write. Or we could check Google, you smart ass!" Dad gave me the look I was after.

"I'm already on it, Dad – the obvious ones like Gordon Ramsey."

"Don't forget Rod Stewart – he still kicks out balls at his concerts." Dad was a fan, but he was really mum's guy – if you know what I mean?

"Look at this list, Dad – Tom frigging Cruise! Are you crapping me! Jon Stewart! This is great."

"Who is Jon Stewart?"

"A has-been comedian – I'm sure he would love a comeback!"

"Bob Marley played."

"That's not a comeback even Chesterfield can offer!" and me and Dad lost it right there, our ribs bursting with breathless Jell-O!

"You boys alright in here?" The sensible shoes were back, payroll ledgers in hand. "Are you ready for this, Mr. Griffiths?"

We both answered with nods – our chests aching hard as if needing an urgent bowel movement.

Sensible shoes added:

"It's good you're sitting down!"

Dad and I remembered the last time we heard those words together.

"Good God, that's a lot of zeros!" Whatever pent-up gases were being held back aerated the room! Sensible shoes – both pairs—exited the room in haste, leaving the ledger on his desk in front; my Sperrys weren't far behind the sensible shoes.

"Sorry about that, ladies! Dad's taking a lot of meds."

"Oh, that's alright – we thought it was you anyway. You're Andrew, right?"

There was no air left in me to feel deflated!

I returned to Dad at the desk looking all presidential in the way that JFK must have when faced with pushing "the button" in the 1962 Cuban Missile Crisis.

"You alright, Dad?" He looked pale and serious. Not sure if it was the gases, so I forged on.

"We're gonna need a bigger boat!" said fisherman Dad, having stared down the mouth of Jaws.

"I'll get on to *Dancing with the Stars* right away. This is an impressive list, though, Dad—look: Matt Smith – the 11th Dr. Who – there's a crowd of geeks you don't usually see at footy matches! They are junkies for memorabilia – we could fill stadiums with Dr. Who fans!

Channing Tatum! All-American GI Joe! His fan club would bring an army of American fans – GI Joe in a Town kit! Imagine!

Johnny Marr! Are you frigging kidding me! Eye-liner Marr – all the Goths and those who felt socially outcast by the jock crowd – think of it, Dad – flocking to see The Smiths' genius. Maybe he'd play a riff of that let me get what I want song? Dad, that could even be our theme tune!"

"Yes, every love story, every movie needs a theme tune!"

"Dad, look – even Julio Iglesias!"

"He's got to be older than me!"

"Yes – seventy-three, but he doesn't need to play for long—imagine every granny following the Town!"

"Steady on – Granny? Those grannies are my age!"

"Enough said! He played goalie at Real Madrid! This is awesome!"

"You're such a Yank these days, Ad!" His eyes rolled with whatever he was feeling at the time! I couldn't get a read on him, even as well as I knew him.

"Always was, I think! What about Boris Becker? – he could use the exposure! Just filed for bankruptcy – so we have that in common! Maybe he can help our cause! And his!"

"It's worth a shot!" Dad joked.

"Louis Tomlinson! God – even a hint of an appearance, and we'll have girls lined up around Tesco and back!!

"Olly Murs!"

"Who's that?"

"Don't know but it said he scored twelve goals in thirteen games – we can certainly use that talent!" Our fever grew – this was taking on a life of its own.

"Dad, look--Chad Ochocinco!"

"And?"

"He played 'football' in the states – both kinds! American football fans here are demented here– they'd fill Wembley even if its someone else's team!" Dad and

I were like kids bartering over kids playing cards mapping out who could play. "Mia Hamm as well!"

"I've actually heard of her – the American team captain – brilliant. I wonder if she would play?" Color rose again in Dad's chops.

"I wonder if she would coach?" was my thought.

"That would be insane, Ad." Of course, it was all insane.

"Yes, it would! Everyone loves an underdog."

"God knows we've got that down!"

"We need to keep thinking big, Dad! We have to give the people of this town a reason to get out of their mind excited – we don't need to be pushing tickets we need to find a way to be holding them back! A 'take-away' sale. I have some contacts in the States but no personal connection – we may have to Twitter this and hope for the best. The key in this PR-soaked universe is to be unique – and this is certainly that!"

"We need t' get Zach back in 'ere right away – he might be our only chance of locating these people. He'll probably need some support. You could be his secretary. And get me another cup of tea while you're at it! One more thing, Ad – I looked at payroll – apparently the groundskeeper hasn't been paid. Could you mow the lawn?"

"Lawn?"

"Yes, the one over there!" and Dad pointed eagerly at the hallowed pitch.

"Aye-aye, Skipper!"

CHAPTER 24

"Mrs. Millward – thank you for hearing me out – so that's the plan. What do you think?"

"I think Roy's gone mad!"

"Well, I blame you, in part. See, you haven't returned his calls and now I think this... mania, if you like, is a cover for the absence, for missing you."

"He knows where to find me. You're—you're just a pair of little boys playing tin soldiers, moving people around on a board."

"Yes, exactly! Don't you still want to play with your dolls? Well maybe not you, but I'm sure other women do."

"Get out! You don't know the first thing about me! I can't believe I let you in in the first place. You're just a light-headed child like you always were. Never far from your mother's madness – we could all see it. Now maybe I'm thinking it was on your father's side instead! Give my respects to Roy, but I still won't be answering any more of his calls." Joan's air of royalty clipped like a polar zephyr, laying a meniscus-thin frost in the room.

"Joan – this may be mad." I began to plead – which is exactly what I was trying to avoid.

"It is!" Her frozen lake comment sealed me in. I banged on the ice above me one more time.

"But this madness, as you call it, will one day be over; all the living and loving will be over, and when it is, love will live on. That is how we are remembered—for the love, not the madness. Enjoy the Hobnobs!"

"I will, thank you. You can see yourself out."

"I was doing." I was not the right man for this job, and I should have taken the Hobnobs back with me.

Why won't she see him? He's doesn't have long. I thought for a minute there, she actually liked him; I thought for a moment Queen Frostine had thawed but she was exactly the mother of my mate I remembered – a curt tongue laced with Botox – she froze you in your place. I shouldn't have gone. She was right – this football thing was madness. But what she didn't realize was that there was no cure! There is no cure for life, only in its living – and loving. *Forget you, Mrs. Millward – Town marches on with or without you. I still can't believe I had to give up my tickets for the Joshua Tree tour in '87. I wonder if Bono plays football?*

CHAPTER 25

"Got him!" yelled Zach down the hall! He had set up camp outside the ladies' bathroom – apparently we were having WiFi issues and he needed to get closer to the router? Or whatever bullshit these kids come up with – can't follow them anymore. I need a bloody dictionary. One that updates every ten minutes!

"Who? Who?" Dad squeaked with excitement.

"Ramsey! Gordon Fucking Ramsey!" yelled Zach getting his stockings in a bunch – green today, with swirling patterns, if you were interested?

"That's 'rad,' man!" Dad yelled back at him. Apparently, he'd got the hang of Google and its urban dictionary.

"How much?"

"Didn't say – just said he's 'on fucking board'; loves the idea. Loves helping lost causes!" Zach retreated to the men's room to fix his eyeliner.

"So, cart before the horse then, Dad! How about some players and a coach?" I quipped.

"Open call – first round tomorrow," Zach yelled from the men's room mirror. Or boys' toilet, since we are in Chez-Vegas. Yes, that is how its known locally. Chez-Vegas."Alright then – festivities ready?" I asked.

"Festivities?"

"Yes, don't we have to put on a show? Can't just expect them to show up. Who's gonna run the drills – we don't have a coach!"

"So, no word from Mia, then?"

"Kind of a long shot, don't you think?"

"The whole thing is a long shot. Well, let's start the drills there!"

"What? It's like talking to a madman sometimes!"

"First drill—who can shoot from the center spot!"

"We have nothing else – we'll go with that. Cones? Pinnies? Oh, and balls—do we actually have any balls?"

"I'll say!" said Zach. "Not my aisle, luvvies," he said, affecting a fake effeminate accent.

"Accounting is on it!"

"Accounting?"

"Yes, well—since we will need them eventually, we have to keep them on—but right now they are all out of red ink, so I put them in charge of running drills," said Dad, coming back from his cliff-edge of insanity. "All hands on deck – can't have 'em sittin' around counting beans we don't have. Everyone is paid through the end of the month. Lawn looks nice, Ad – so visit with sensible shoes, Mary Janes, and let's get ready to see what rammel runs through our doors in the morning."

"You know that this is mad—right, Dad?"

"Yep! That's why it feels so good!"

"What are the Nike trainers, flip-flops and heels up to then, if you've got sensible shoes and Mary Janes running drills?"

"Media day! Doc Martens and stockings has Harry Gration on board, and *Look North* is televising it. Plus, we have our own cameras streaming live for internet voting!"

"Internet voting? Are you seriously mad, Dad? When did that vote get passed?"

"Yesterday afternoon while you were mysteriously gallivanting off!"

"It's called lunch, Dad!" I couldn't tell him where I had been, obviously. My trip to Joan's had been a disaster.

"Most of us eat here these days, Ad."

"I know, Dad. Sometimes – I just need a breath you know?"

"More than you know!" and he grinned when he could have been morose. The puke bucket was never far from his desk.

"Well, at least if this thing doesn't pay off, we'll have embellished our CV's! What's next on the agenda?" Doc Martens and stockings jumped in.

"The inflatable ball will be here any minute – so be ready!" said Dad, looking right at me.

"For what?"

"The inflatable ball that you'll be rolling around intomorrow!" Apparently, Dad had been having random ideas that were voted on in seconds. If you were out of the room at the time, you were likely volunteered for service.

"What, the football! When was that decided?"

"Yesterday at lunch!" we said in unison. My eyes rolled to meet Dad's, whose were grinning like an FA Cup winner. I'd never seen this post-game face before.

"Kilt and stockings says we can make money if people watch us in numbers online. Something about a virus?"

"You mean viral. Dad. Close enough!"

"That's right, Mr. G. We'll have thousands watching – we can turn it into millions!" Doc Martens and stockings had clearly been energized by Dad's mission or madness. A real test of what you can do.

"Bums on seats, Ad, that's all I care about! Bums on seats! That and about fifteen players or so. The questionnaire is ready – Premier League title or FA Cup? Name, cell phone, and email is all we need apparently?"

"What have you got there, Dah?" I was curious.

"It's the Johann Cruyff biography – I always remember what a big fan you were of his. I well remember seeing newsreel of him as a youngster; and, well, the World Cup in 1974 was his coming of age party! I thought I'd see what we can take from arguably the greatest player and coach of all time. What I'm learning is it's hard to coach attitude or passion – a player has to have that for themselves. Cruyff had that in spades and apparently looked for it in his teammates and acquisitions."

"I like your thinking, Dad – wouldn't it be amazing to find a guy like that tomorrow? To find someone who for no reason was overlooked by talent scouts or happened to be on holiday the day the scouts visited their high school!" I was rocked to see Cruyff on the cover – he had been my childhood hero—the moves, the flair, the speed, the balance; the speed, that was it. We need blazing speed, Dad!"

"What's on your mind, Ad?"

"You're right, you can't coach attitude or passion, in the same way you can't create speed. Sure, you can make someone a little quicker. But flat-out speed is something more innate. Regardless of skill – tomorrow I want a prize for flat-out speed – the fastest guys over forty yards from a jogging start. As Sam Walton said, you can teach someone the job, but you can't teach attitude, and we should add 'speed'--that's just who you are!"

"Who is Sam Walton?" Dad was excited right along with me and lost in the same breath.

"Started Walmart, Dad – built stores of lowest-priced goods – went where no other retailer would go initially. 'Swim upstream, go the other way, Ignore the conventional wisdom.' Like us, no one would do this; this is our circus and now we have to get some monkeys!"

"Impressive! I'll keep reading this, if you don't mind." Dad happily waved Cruyff in my face.

"Alright then, I'll be off."

"Can you take this, Ad?"

"Sure, what is it?"

"It was a sausage sarnie, but not anymore." And Dad handed me his puke bucket.

CHAPTER 26

Training day tomorrow– weather forecast pouring rain – of course! But for now I was enjoying a misplaced summer's day.

I had kind of an epiphany as I was quoting Sam Walton – it is all about the customer. And ours were firing us in droves. Not that they were switching brands; they had just merely decided to overlook our luxury items. We weren't bread and butter, and we weren't nicotine, either. We needed to create that nicotine need – for our fans to once again crave us like a morning smoke. To create that magical pairing of coffee and a fag. The breakfast of champions. We needed to be the Kardashians of football – something that you knew you wanted to avoid like a car crash, but couldn't help looking at every minute on your phone.

I drove by the old "sports day" track at Queens Park – I remember the day we competed against other schools – I might have been ten or eleven. I remember being one of the fastest kids in the school. I also remember how big the track seemed back in the day. One lap seemed like a mile. I took off after the gun – lane six – it was difficult to see everyone at the stagger – I was leading but couldn't tell. I had passed the outer lanes after the first 50, feeling really strong, but by the 200 marker I was cramping up, thighs burning with lactic acid, and I had a stitch that tacked my stomach like a steel staple in a refrigerator delivery box!

Reminiscing, I decided to pull into the car park of the track. It looked run down, weeds growing out of it like a first-day patient of "hair plugs for men." It was no organized "sports day" – kids, adults, and families alike just jogging or running in random order—some even running clockwise, outrageous anarchy! Siblings picnicked on the grass bank of the hill to the east of it. Not so odd when you think about this area – terraced houses broken up by a chip shop and nail salon. Not much park space close by, and this outpost of nature was lined by 50-foot elms and oaks. Athletes hid here like they were in quarantine.

Not wanting to draw attention by sitting in my car, I jogged over to where the starting line used to be. Not the four hundred, but the one hundred. I walked down to the approximate 50-yard marker and took off. It didn't seem so far, but I'm not sure I could have swum it. I dipped at the finish line. I caught my lung before it introduced itself to the track. Slowly I walked back – I should have stretched; and tried to do so as I walked back to about the 70-yard marker. I set my timer on my watch – I mean phone. At the 50, I took off again – phone in hand trying to time my 50-yard dash. I don't remember how fast I was, and I guess it doesn't matter – but what does matter is seeing if any of these runners out today are enticed to try to beat the middle-aged guy over 50-yards.

Eventually, kids came over.

"What ya doin', mista?" They weren't sniveling but easily could have been.

"Want to race?" I asked.

"Sure, mista' – how far?"

"Did you see what I was doing? Jog, then run – I'll race you!"

I lined up with a couple of youngsters – not being very good at gauging kids' ages, I guessed they were probably nine or ten. Twins, so I only had to guess the age of one!

"On your marks, get set, GO!" I yelled as loud as I could. The goal was to attract the picnickers and other strangers. The twins were really quick out of the gate, but like a sore loser, I closed the gap dipped at the end and beat them; it almost looked spiteful, passive-aggressive bullying. That was my goal. I'm not puking a lung so I can recruit year-five kids to Town's tryout. Their dad came over—tall and skinny, walked deliberately toward me as though I had just taken his child's ice cream, licked it, and given it back.

"Best of three?" I called to the twins. Was it me, or were there a lot more twins around these days? Wouldn't surprise me. Everything is more efficient and instant nowadays. Instant coffee was as immediate as it got when I was their age. Ready-made family in this case; boy and a girl – one of each – done. A dancer and a footballer – I'm not being sexist; a lot of girls play football, and a lot of boys now dance.

"Alex, Sophia, well done—you almost beat him!" Their father's pride made them smile. The word "beat" resonated with me, as did his military-like stride.

"Yeh, we're gonna do it again!" they replied in unison, like two halves of the same brain. Like a 99 - two "Flakes" in an ice-cream. Or whatever twin cliché you want to choose here.

"Your twins are really quick, mate!" I said, in my attempt to befriend him.

"They're not twins." The dad was somewhat muted. So not a "99," then.

"Well, they sure do look a lot alike."

"Kids, will you keep an eye on Brian while Daddy goes for a quick run?"

"Sure, Dad," they said with a slight echo. Alex and Sophia took off up the hill to where Brian was playing on the tartan blanket.

"They're triplets. A bit odd that you are racing kids, isn't it?" the skinny man stared through my forehead like a Botox injection. There was an accusing scowl in his tidal-wave-furled brow. As if I were some pedophile or child-snatcher.

"I used to come here a lot as a kid to race," I said. "Grew up not far from here; this was the only open space to run without a car on it."

"Fast, are you?" the Botox needle was pushed further in.

"Not bad. The Hush Puppies and jeans probably not the best attire! But I was coming from work and--well; I reminisced – caught my childhood self and decided to have a go for old times' sake?" It was believable bollocks. "Is your third child a runner, too? The twins are quick."

"No, he has Down Syndrome. He runs with Alex and Sophia, of course."

"Sorry to hear that." I fumbled – the Botox must have caught a nerve in my face and I could sense gibberish about to flood out, like it always did when faced with compromised kids. I'm like most, sympathetic, not empathetic, and as I fail to get wiser, I realize that families aren't looking for sympathy.

"No need to be sorry." His tone was as quick as his kids' feet.

"Sorry, I didn't mean anything by it, I--"

"He's a blessing – he's definitely had his struggles, but his laughter is infectious, his effortless smile is the tonic in every day. We are all truly blessed." The skinny man looked over at his triplets playing on the blanket laughing uncontrollably as they rolled down the embankment.

"We doing this thing, or what?" The skinny man towered over me like a basketball hoop – he must be at least six-four or more. Not intimidating in the fact that we probably both weighed twelve stone.

"What?"

"Racing. We doin' it or what?" He stuck the needle in further and I could feel my face locked like a constipated mannequin!

"But you're in flip-flops?"

"And you're in – be quiet – Hush Puppies," grinned the man on stilts.

"Fifty-yard dash?"

"I'm in." Lowery's entry in today's race took a glance back at his heap of kids giggling on the lawn of weeds, covered in litter and dust.

"Jog twenty yards together, then go?"

"If you like? Meks no diff'rence." The Botox nurse had a certain arrogance I didn't care for.

"Start from here then, twenty paces, then go!" So we did. We jogged nicely in unison. He kicked his flip-flops aside so he could show me the soles of his feet as he took off. Like crispy fried eggs, they were. White with brown outlines, blurry, on account of being ten yards ahead in a fifty-yard dash. Tanned edges, on account of his frequently wearing flip-flops.

"Best of three?" I wheezed at the finish line. He strode like a queen's guard back to greet me.

"Good enough," he said. He marched to the vague starting line, saluting his cheering kids, Brian leaping up and down as his number one cheerleader.

"Ready!" And we jogged again until the sprint. Like an imperialist chasing an aborigine, I was left behind. Twelve or fifteen yards he had me by this time.

Brian, Sophia, and Alex ran down the hill to the track to greet their sprint champion. Their smiles wrapped around him like Usain Bolt's cluster of gold medals.

"That's some speed you've got there, mate!" I had to jog beyond the finish line just to catch up to where his momentum had taken him. His kids circled him, and I swear they would have carried him off if they'd had the strength. He picked up Brian, and he was right, Brian could illuminate a damp November depression.

"County Champion in year two of sixth form!"

"Thank God for that – I thought I was a decent runner until I saw you!" I addressed the trio: "Kids, your dad's got great stuff. Wanna be like him one day?" Sohia and Alex doubled down on Brian's big grin."Teks me mind off t' grind o' looking for work, comin' 'ere – reminds me I were good at summert once upon a time."

"Dad, Dad—race us, race us!" Alex and Sophia launched at him excitedly.

"I'll keep an eye on Brian," I offered stupidly. The beanpole rolled his eyes and I watched him and his family race like a family of gazelles. They all turned at the finish line to greet Brian, whose form I thought might one day win him the Special Olympics."I'm Adam," I said rather formally. "There's a football tryout at the Proact Stadium tomorrow. Would you be interested in coming?"

"Footy? I 'aven't played since school."

"Good! Then you're not injured then!"

"Can't, mate – got to watch kids; wife is cutting hair all day."

"I'll watch your kids. How old are you, Mister…?"

"Macintosh, Mike, Mike Macintosh. But I don't play football."

"Let me be the judge of that!" I could feel the Botox easing. "Eight a.m. sharp – how old are you, Mike?"

"Thirty!"

"That'll work – you know where the stadium is, right?"

"Yep we all know where the Proact Cemetr'y is!" he scooped up the balance of his children and left to polish off his picnic.

"One down, fourteen to go," I whispered to myself. "They'll never catch Mike Macintosh in a million years!"

CHAPTER 27

"Good God, Dah, look at all these people! To think I barely slept a wink wondering if anyone would show up!"

"Its what we thought, in't it Ad? The game is like a religion. They must be queuing around Tescos!"

"Probably nearly to Sainsbury's! Zach and his social media – what a discovery! We could never 'ave done this with newspapers, radio, and a hint of television!"

"Roy! Roy, are you ready? Harry Gration wants to do that interview now!" said Dr. Martens and Chesterfield blue stockings, anxiously wanting to keep up with sensible shoes' and Mary Janes' schedule.

"Dad, this is brilly-ant!" my local-boy accent was primed, just in case Harry needed more fluff in his story.

"Can't believe I'm goin' t' be interviewed by *the* 'Arry Gration!" He wandered off like a winning lottery ticket holder – I swear he dyed his hair last night.

I sidled up to Nikes, stilettos, and orthopedic shoes, who were all checking people in, taking down cell phone numbers and names, emails and Facebook accounts.

"You're in t' way, Mr. Griffiths. Anyway, aren't you supposed to be o'er thee'er?" Orthopedics pointed to the first event.

"Sorry, you're right – my bad!" I was American again, non-local boy. Or local boy gone bad or mad.

"What?" She looked at me like I was a stupid cat, and in truth I was behaving like one, without schedule and searching for a warm sunspot to rest in. I really should have taken the melatonin.

"Ad! Found you! Here's a coffee; you look lost, love." Zoe was on the spot with Ju behind her, both excited but worried about Dad – chemo was running its course right through him, but forcing everything living thing out of him.

"Thanks, Zo – Dad's off getting interviewed by *the* Harry Gration!"

"He is? He'll be made up!" Ju, at least, understood.

"This mad idea is coming to life, isn't it? I'm so proud of him." Zoe admired Dad in the way that only the youngest sibling, who lived like an only child with a much older parent than your school friends, could. Her version of "Dad" was closer to their granddad than dad. He was all three, as she never knew either of her granddads.

"Can't believe it, I just can't believe it!" Ju actually clapped like a monkey with its cymbal.

"I've never seen so many people in trainers and football shorts! There's more Town kits here than on a Saturday match day!"

"Dad's in his element 'ere! I want to listen into his interview."

"You can't do that, Ad; you'll throw him off!" said Zoe.

"Besides, you can watch it all on *Look North* tonight! If you ever get out of here!" Ju was right; it was going to take hours to process all these people.

Harry Gration looked genuinely excited to meet our dad. "So, Mr. Griffiths, did you ever expect such a turn-out?"

"Harry, what a privilege it is to meet you – call me Roy." Dad had his calm director's telephone voice on. "I have to say in me wildest dreams we din't expect this kind of turn-out. The response has bin incredible."

"There are swarms of people all ages, young and younger! We have a lot of young ladies even, too, I noticed – not sure how the FA would address that?"

"If they're good enough, they'll play; that's all there is to it! Like t' playground days, Harry," said Dad pronouncing the "H" remarkably well, probably for the first time in his life.

"Indeed, for the FA to decide," and Harry paused letting that sit with tonight's future audience. "So why did you do it, Roy? Clearly, you're no spring chicken, if you don't mind me saying so!"

"Right about that one, Harry, and this chemo is giving me a right kick up the arse!" Dad's telephone voice clicked off briefly, and that last bit might be edited from tonight's airing.

"Chemo?" Harry couldn't have looked more startled if he were faking it at the Disney Haunted House.

"Yes, Harry, I have stage four lung cancer." And you could hear tonight's TV audience lean forward toward their goggle-boxes with sympathetic sighs.

"I'm sorry to hear that, Roy." Harry gave the universal sympathy on behalf of his audience, an audience he knew would be lapping up this even bigger underdog story.

"Thanks, Harry. In a strange way, I have it to be thankful for."

"In what way, Roy?" Harry maintained his gentle tone, afraid to break Roy.

"Well, I plan on getting be"er; but..." Dad caught sight of Ju and and Zoe caught his breath. The stray golf ball in his throat once more was cutting him off.

"Tea, Dad!" and Zoe ran between him and Harry.

"Ta, love." Dad smiled, and his squint forced a barely perceptible drip from his eye; after all, it was very windy today. "Well, Harry, you just don't know how long you've got until a doctor tells you." And Dad's words swirled around Proact Stadium. Dad liked Harry, so he bailed him out – seeing his "TV-pal" a little lost for words. "We meander through life paying bills, but we are all kids inside with dreams; or at least the kid we were had dreams and many of them die with the adults we become. Well, the doctor didn't give me long, 'though it could be longer,' he said, wanting to give me hope." Dad paused again as Harry hung on every word. This was going to be better television than he could ever have hoped for. "So, my retirement is getting cut short; and as a kid I always dreamed of playing for Town – so owning it is the next best thing!"

Harry let that sit with tonight's audience before moving on. "And this today, what a turn-out! There must be a thousand people here?"

"This is incredible, Harry! Truly mind-blowing, totally mind-blowing. And I just want your audience to know how grateful we are and that everyone who tries out today, whether they get asked back, or not, will be given a voucher to come see us play in the upcoming season." Dad went totally off script! Zach looked down at his notes, flicking up and down the screens of his iPad for the paragraph he must have missed when typing up the Evite! Not finding the note, he stared Dad down from behind the camera. He wanted to slam his digital clipboard down like a frustrated coach but held off, realizing how many hours of raking lawns and weeding at the old folks' home he'd put into pay for it.

"So, no one leaves empty-handed then, Roy!" Harry said excitedly in a festival tone.

"No, Harry, we want this to be everyone's club—young, old, boy, girl, able and compromised – if you love the underdog, then let us be your club. We are going to rise up with the help of these wonderfully dedicated folks here today and put this town back on the map like it was in Roman times!" And behind the camera with arm around Dr. Martens and royal blue stockings, gladiator shoes leaned in and hugged her colleague.

"Well, Roy, I hope you find the team of your dreams! And we look forward to following you throughout the season!"

"Cheers, Harry – I know we will, I know we will! Come On, You Blues! Over and out!"

Harry turned to his cameraman and said his goodbyes to his audience for the later viewing. Harry's grip rolled up the cable, the camera light went dark from its lively flashing red, and within seconds the whole television crew was packed up and off to the next story or home. It was Saturday, after all.

Ju came rushing over. "Well done, Dad – you were totally brilliant! You feeling okay?"

White and blue kilt, royal-blue stockings, and Doc Martens had shrugged off the hug to come running in too! "I was wondering the same thing, Roy! You never told me about the giveaway! How are we going to figure over a thousand new tickets for everyone? Tell me that?" His sensible voice cracked slightly. Using his tablet as a steering wheel, he turned away, not waiting for the response which was likely to be "You'll find a way, Zach; you'll find a way!" Zach thought this new work family might just do him in. At least it would look better on the CV after today's television interview.

We—Dad, Ju, and Zoe—all tracked behind Zach to where stilettos and orthopedic shoes were still checking people in. Cell phone numbers and names, emails and Facebook accounts had reached over a hundred since the gates were opened. Dad was walking slowly behind us like the last Olympian being lapped in the 26-mile walk, gradually falling behind, sipping tea from his mug like it was a champagne-filled FA Cup. Gladiator shoes caught up, running by them all, grabbing Zach's arm and leading him from check-into the starting line of sprints. Seeing this, Ju and Zoe slowed a few steps to catch up back to Dad. Ju looped her arm inside his, and Zoe's, careful not to spill the tea she had just brought him, wrapped her arm around his waist. I pulled out my phone and took a picture of Christopher Robin, Pooh Bear, and Piglet.

Check-in was going well – an e-voucher would be emailed. Life could be so much simpler now with technology, especially when it works as designed. IT have replaced car mechanics. The shooting drill was in full flight, shots raining in from the halfway line, both corners of the eighteen-yard box, the penalty spot and corners; iPads recorded the result and video-bursts captured technique. Here, video reported back a couple of early standouts, mostly because they were both over six foot two tall. I made a note of their pinned-on numbers – 14 and 15 – they must have gotten here early. While Christopher Robin, Piglet, Pooh, gladiator sandals (she did also have ballet slippers, but they would be ruined by the showers predicted for the afternoon) and Doc Martens all sat in the dug-out. I went to the Director's Box – I wanted a better view and shade. My iPad was dark in the morning sun, which shone like a stage spotlight on these would-be players. From this vantage point I had a little quiet and could see the drills; players jogging like Sporty-Spice ants, weaving across the field, except for a few bystanders in the opposite goal-mouth, who must be the budding goalies. All shapes and sizes, Morcambe and Wise, to Laurel and Hardy – that would be interesting video later.

For now, the towering 14 and 15 had my interest. In the shade of the Director's Box I could pull up their detail: brothers Hatt, the taller one was younger by a couple of years, reports in at six-foot-four, his older brother six-foot-two. Wayne, the older, would be thirty before the season started and his taller brother not yet twenty-eight. On the old side, but? I checked out the video which had been linked to them both. The younger one, Nicholas, cracked the ball from the halfway line with cobra-like venom and accuracy. Similarly, from the corners of the eighteen-yard box – using both feet – they looked small on the video – probably the camera angle. No problems from the penalty spot either. Nicholas could pull in-swingers and out-swingers from either corner flag too. *Not bad.* I nodded to my iPad. I looked up at the pitch before checking out his brother. The two were at the sprinting lane. Wayne, the older brother, ran with Nicholas for about thirty yards until pulling away easily, seriously quick. *I hope they're serious about playing.*

I checked out Wayne's shooting – fine from the halfway, his taller younger brother being much stronger from there. But from the penalty spot, he had my attention. He sprinted from the arc of the "eighteen" and scooped the ball back over his head bringing it sweetly down in front, flipped his left foot over and under the ball before drilling it top right while leaning left—incredible! Illegal penalty, of course, but he had the speed and control of Buffalo Bill. I could see it now – the brothers Hatt – a lot of us enjoy a sibling story. But for one sibling, that is, it was going to be as convoluted as his penalty kick, as we would later learn.

As youngsters, the tallest always have an advantage of standing out, and so it was today as I echoed the responses of coaches past that I despised. I ran down from the Director's Box, not as comfortable as I thought it would be, and dashed across the halfway line behind numerous contestants to catch up to the twin towers before they started our next drill.

"Wayne! Nicholas! Hold up a minute, can I have a talk with you?"

CHAPTER 28

"Where do you think you're going at this hour?" Michelle had their nine-month-old perched above her spit-up-stained right boob. The stain had ruined her favorite Top Shop blouse – her black ruffled halter-top had been her staple Saturday night "trapper" shirt. After her first girls' night out since Madeline was born, she had been still wearing it the morning after. Wayne had been up all night with Madeline, so she gave him the early shift off out of motherly guilt. Michelle had pumped the night before, so she gave Maddy her bottle. It was like trying to do surgery with a bendy straw. Maddy fought her mum off, knowing that the real thing was within inches. Maddy gave in; suddenly it was easier, the bottle took less effort, she gulped with rhythmic ease. Michelle's guilt doubled down; the post-drinking depression and the ease with which Maddy took to the bottle. *Please don't like it too much*, she could hear herself pray through her pulsing eyeballs. When Maddy finally ate so quickly she spit-up, Michelle was glad, but her favorite shirt was ruined. God had a way of prioritizing your decisions, she thought. So now she wore it as a badge of honor even months later. *Sexy momma*, she thought of herself.

"I to'd yerr, I'm goo'in' wiv our Nicky t' tryout!" Wayne was frustrated. But the blouse reminded him of her both sides, and he loved them equally. He never got over meeting her in that snooker hall, a cathedral to men. Wayne stood there frozen, he'd promised his brother, and argued with his dream girl who once scored an eighty-nine at snooker. He loved her more at these moments; even though she had chased him downstairs after grabbing Maddy from her cot; even though the hedge was apologizing profusely for what it had done to her chestnut locks; even though she cupped Maddy over her forearm with a yellowy plump nappy; even though her mascara from Wednesday clung to her eyelids like a French cedilla; even though her Thursday thong had mislaid its calendar.

"Maddy misses you already! Don't you, Maddy?" And their daughter grinned at the Chesterfield Ladies' snooker champion before burying her head into her mother's neck.

"But I promised our Nicky; vis might be 'is one chance t' ge' back t' where he was duck. 'sides verr 's nowt goo'ing on 'round 'ere vis mornin'!"

"Nowt," she mocked him. Wayne and Nicky had grown up on the other side of town, raised by a father too busy trying to feed them to worry about their execution of the English language. Their mother would not have approved, but once her breast cancer had metastasized and leached her of life, her defeated husband had all on to not kill the Red Label and her boys.

Wayne hated to be mocked; he was the funny brother but being out of work for a couple of "munfs" as he would say was driving him mad. No houses to build or porches to add "it were like all-on-'em 'ad closed verr wallets at sem time."

"Worra 'bout Maddy?" She was mocking his accent more. Growing up in Dronfield, she had always looked down on the people of Unstone; literally they were below them, in the valley and socially. But Wayne had rock-star looks and physique, lithe and strong the way you have to be to build walls at speed between rain squalls, popping up and down scaffolding like a crackerjack slinky, hod in one hand, and an Action Man vice-grip on the poles as he slipped like Tarzan through the iron tubing.

"She won' miss me for a couple 'ours! Will yer, luv?" He tickled her under the chin that was nestled above the crusty spit-up. His little, crusty finger slid along her blouse; he wanted to remove it as he had done so many times before it had been hit with baby mortar-formula. He had seen splashes like it on his brick fascia; he knew how hard it could be to get out!

"Careful, you! All of us girls are mad at you for wanting to leave—aren't we, Maddy?" Michelle snuggled Maddy's head to her neck, now knowing this was another of Wayne's favorite places. "Go off with you, you big kid; it's for Nicky, not you, and don't forget we're out of nappies!" Which explained Maddy's current Sumo wrestler version.

"Like a sed, am on'y goo'in' fer our Nicky!" He was adamant about that. He'd had his chance and turned it down when he was sixteen. Preferring to get a job, any job, laborer as it turned out. He was tired of being poor, and playing for Town would have always kept him there even if he was one of the lucky ones. Nicky had taken his chance – played for Manchester United academy, then their first team which played a few divisions above Town, which was probably why he stood out to me from the stands. Where had he been for the last couple of years? Rehab would have been done with ages ago.

"Maddy and I will be waiting – neither of us have any clean underwear, so don't hang about after!" Michelle's pinky removed her Thursday thong whilst pronouncing her queen's English. This was how she seduced him years back, sans baby of course.

"A won't, a promise!" *Damn our Nicky!* screamed the whisper in his head. But childhood promises to keep promises run deep forever.

He left Michelle surrounded by a half-plastered but newly added foyer. Electrical wires dripped from the ceiling like Twizzlers; the outside looked in where the shims held the windows in place. *Still a lot of work to be done around here,* she thought as she closed up her Thursday thong for the day.

CHAPTER 29

"Lads, hold up, I want to have a quick word!" I'd made a bee-line for them.

"Ye'?" Nicky turned around eager while Wayne smiled knowingly at a job well done, unless this bloke was scrounging a few quid."I know you're in the middle of drills, lads, but I couldn't help but notice from the stands back there that you have great stuff – have you played professionally before?"

"Ye'," Nicky added keeping it short and modest.

"Excellent. And who for?" after a curious pause.

Nicky's tone fell away. "Man Uni'ed." There was something lamentable in the answer, like he was trying to hide his past. Like he wanted to be seen new without history or baggage. He wanted the sense of being discovered, like he was twelve years old again.

"That's great. What did you say your name was?"

"Nicky, Nicky Hatt, an' this is me bruvver Wayne." His name fell away as if it tumbled down a mountain.

I'd never heard of him. "I think I remember you,"

Nicky's doubt was clear "Really? Most o' first team reg'lars 'ant 'erd of me and I were in t' line up!" I was disarmed by his charm and grin. However, long he'd been in football, he could spot the panderers and the wannabes.

"And you, where did you play?" Wayne was starting to wander off – his much taller younger brother always got the attention.

"The playground!" Wayne loved the tease and both brothers cracked up. They know it's the truth.

"No, seriously, where did you play? You've got great stuff," continued the panderer-in-chief.

"I 'aven't, not since high school – well a bit on Wednesdays we our Nicky 'ere, bu' uvver van vat, nuffin."

Sounding a little effeminate, I followed up with: "I'm shocked! You have quite the touch, mate."

"Girlfriend thinks so too!" Nicky laughed at Wayne.

"Partner, if yer don't mind? Practically married!"

"Except she won't 'ave nun of it, right? Yer 'er toy boy!"

"At least we've gorra a 'babby,' yer eunuch!"

Their backhanded support for each other was both off-putting and endearing.

"Lads – lads, if I might…"

They cut me off – "I'm only 'ere to keep our Nicky comp'ny."

"'sright, tha nor interested in playing, are yer, Wayno?"

"'ad me chance yonks ago – said no then and said no nar. Puff's game!" Another brotherly jibe.

"No, seriously, Wayne – you have to come to the next round at least," I said weakly, like pushing a piece of string rather than pulling it.

"Our Michelle would kill me. 'sides, 'ave got a business to run."

"Y'aven't bin busy in weeks, Wayno--'sides, you was always be"er player."

"I've all on t' come 'ere today. Tha's no idea wo' it's like. No work, more bills than a Donald Duck store. Michelle is mental on me nar. If I come agen, well I might as well 'ave not put them new winders in – cos she's gonna frow me righ' frew em!"

"Premier league title or FA Cup?" the decider question. "One, two, three, shoot!"

Each of them in unison – "FA Cup!" no hesitation.

"I'll see you boys at the next tryout. Go home early today, lads, start training, and Wayno tell Michelle this job will pay should you get it!"

Two down, the rest of the squad to go; this mad idea might have a chance!

Now I had to go roll around in that bouncy ball – the things we do for love!

CHAPTER 30

I ran over to Dad. "What else have you seen today, Dad? Owt or nowt?" my "Chezy" was coming back!

"People don't take care of themselves is what I'm noticing! Not like in my day. There's too much food, too much talk of food!"

"Dad, what are you going on about?"

"Look, Ad, I've never seen so many young people out of shape – most can't even run the fifty yards. We should be sponsored by McDonald's. Or Bayer Junior Aspirin! This mob is gonna keel over in front of us. I wish they'd never moved Royal t' other side o' town; it's gonna tek ages for t' ambulance to get 'ere!"

"Well to be fair, Dad, we have come a long way since rationing! And besides, you buggers were all smoking at twelve; no wonder you never got fat!"

"I guess wars weren't all bad, then!" Dad mocked me back. He leaned on one of the training poles, acting as a defender/player to go around. He wanted to trip up a couple of the attendees – it was just his instinct as they went around him.

One two three, trip.

He settled into just shoulder charges – even the little kids, he shouldered them as he had done me as a nipper. He was less solid now and he smiled before and not after the challenge.

"How many have gone through here, Dad?"

"I'd say about fifty or sixty."

"Any thoughts?"

"I told Zach about a few young'uns. But its shockin' how kids today still can't play with both feet. That's why I came over here. Well, to block a few, but I wanted to see their left feet. I always made sure you could use your left, Ad! One, two, three…."

"Shoot! He scores! One touch left, nudge with right, finish with the left!" I put my hand on his, like a maypole; with footballers running underneath our arms in and out, weaving through the poles. Nothing new about this drill—that was until we decided to run players simultaneously from each end. Head down, head up, look left, look right, and watch out for oncoming traffic.

"Have you spoken to Joan, Dad?"

"Look, Ad, you may have a winner here – unless he's not old enough to pass his cycling proficiency test!"

I looked over at the scrawny, pock-marked adolescent with the balance of a ballerina. He massaged the ball with his feet, the way a clairvoyant massages her crystal ball. A scuffed-up, chipped old Mitre ball, a little soft on the inside, definitely not one of the practice balls we had provided. He avoided Dad's body check like he knew it was coming; he controlled the ball in a way that told you when you have very little, you hold on to what you have very closely. He weaved by like a river torrent around rocks, frothing slightly from his tongue; the trip from behind was another story.

"Sorry, kid, not many pass me an' get away with it." Dad shrugged.

"You're a dick, mister." Not the language we'd have expected from a ballerina. But we needed a little attitude. The crystal ball rolled on ahead, stopped by one of the poles.

He jumped up foaming like rapids on a rock, pitching right up, and went after me dad, grabbing him by the collar, his fist cocked like a rabid dog he was in Dad's face, spitting something inhuman out of his mouth. Dad lost grip on the pole, stunned like he was wearing a police dog—then from nowhere, he was!

"What the fuck!" new language from Dad indeed. The Alsatian had bolted from the sideline after seeing his owner tripped. Dad lay terrified as the 90-pound animal growled, drooled, and barked in his face. Dad suddenly looked very old. We were all very afraid; the Alsatian had teeth of a land shark and the menace of a crossed mobster. Dad didn't move. Dogs can sense fear. It was all around. The dog's jaws faked like they were gonna bite my dad's face off time and again. The Alsatian's paws had claws out, impaling dad into the turf. Dad rolled in terror, the dog digging in for better purchase with every movement. Jack looked on. We all looked on. Dad grabbed the animal's front paws, pulling the canine-ski poles out of his chest; the dog went mental – frothing frighteningly like his owner had, tight in his face, its angry saliva dropping all over Dad.

"Gerr it off me! Gerr it off me!" Dad struggled to breathe but could scream enough.

I went forward to grab the collar, right up until the savage teeth snapped round at me. Jack watched on.

"Little fucker!" It missed me – like it knew I wasn't the problem. I went back at the dog – again – it snapped at me like it could break my arm off at the elbow.

It might have been a few seconds only, but this dog was in psycho mode. We backed off when we should have gone in. Dad went in when he should have backed off; the barking coursed like an approaching train with Dad tied to the tracks. He was shaking in fear. Jack watched on. A small crowd gathered round the horror movie unfolding, the Jackal and Jack watching the old man squirm in fear.

"Patch! Release!" yelled the kid, and the drama was over, Dad's face plastered in sweat and frothy cappuccino saliva. Fear left his eyes.

As he lay there, his heart racing, he turned to the acne-faced yob. "FA Cup or Premier League title?" "I wanna be Captain Fantastic! FA cup all the way. Come on, you Reds!"

Patch sidled over to him like a puppy, leaned into Jack's shins, hugging him in a fashion, looking up to him as if to say, "You'll be alright now mate, you'll get no more trouble from that old man," And he was right – smart dog, that one.

One, two, three – ouch! Captain Fantastic Steven Gerrard single handedly beat my team West Ham United in the 2006 FA Cup. It was the stuff of FA Cup legend. Not quite Sunderland beating Leeds United, but it was the proof of soccer magic as Steven Gerrard – aka "Captain Fantastic" led his team to a miraculous comeback. The announcers let the viewers know there would be four minutes of extra time as West Ham cleared their box to Steven Gerrard, who took one look as the ball came on the bounce to him. When most of us mortals would have put the ball over Millenium Stadium, Stevie G drilled it like an Exocet from thirty-yards out into the bottom left corner, to take the game to extra time with less than a minute of regulation in the game. You can't write this stuff – no one would believe you.

The kid looked up at me with his baggy Liverpool kit on, Carlsberg emblazoned on the front. He couldn't have been more than seven or eight on that legendary day.

"Who are you, kid?" Dad the "dick" picked him up even though neither of us liked Liverpool FC.

"Jack, Jack Bleacher, like Jack Reacher!" said the spotty refugee as Dad lifted him up. Dad looked over at me – at least this kid had passed up a few donut shops. We had no idea who Jack Reacher was – probably some player from X-Box.

"Son, you've go' some nice moves, except with your mouth!"

"Lucky I din't knock your fuckin' block off, mate! No one teks down Jack Bleacher and gets away wiv it!" Not quite the manners of the charming Captain Fantastic – me and Dad said telepathically as we watched the runt recover his ball.

I looked hard at Dad. "We're gonna need spunk." Dad still had pupils of terror filling his half smile. We didn't grow up with dogs, thanks to him, and as a result we had no concept of them. Guinea pigs and fish we knew—not much loyalty there, though.

"What's the dog's name?"

"Patch!"

"That's right, you said that already," forgetting the command to release.

"He's not my dog; we're just a couple o' strays. Neiv'er one of us 'as a collar."

"Strays? So, where's home, kid?" I asked a little dimly.

"Ev'rywhere, ma'e. We live all over."

"With friends? Family?" Dad probed gently, knowing we'd want to be getting hold of him.

"Nah, by t' river or tracks mostly. A real-life Chezzy refugee – me an' Patch don't answer t' no one." Standing over the dog, petting Patch under the chin, we could see his lack of nutrition. He wore the Gerrard jersey the way a snowman would wear an apple tree.

There was a difficult childhood behind this acne-skinned, sunken-eyed kid. Probably a drunk parent, probably a beating, probably irregular meals and an absentee at parent-teacher conferences. An abandoned kid gone to live by the rails, just as he started to come off them. Since no one cared once he left school at sixteen – there was no punch card – no timetable – he led a life of truancy.

"How did you know about today's tryout?"

"You woke me up! I were sleeping wi' Patch under that lorry in back o'er thee'er!"

"Good God – you've got to be kidding!" We stared out of the stadium to where the Hilton lorry might be.

"All this fuckin' chaos – me, Patch an' me pillow had to check it ou'!"

"I'm glad you did, kid, apart from the attack on me dad!" No one smiled except the dog. "How do we get in touch with you?"

"You don't – I get intouch wiv you," he said, serious as a dog attack.

"But kid, you've got stuff, moves we could use, maybe," Dad started to plead.

"Ta', but me an' Patch are just fine."

"Then why did you come out here?"

"Dunno. Nowhere else to be, prob'ly." He questioned himself in a life of no reason. He and Patch started to walk off.

"Where are you going?"

"Food stand – you've got brekky 'ere!"

"Then where?"

"No place – we like it like that." At sixteen, or however old he was, he was living the life of a retiree. Without the pension, of course. He was no one's understudy. You can't be a substitute in your own life; you have to be an everyday starter.

Frustrated, I said, "So that's it?" I hate wasted talent.

"Take a shower, son." Dad's patience shone through. "We'll be here tomorrow and every day here after. Can I let you into a secret?"

"Sure, mate." He addressed my father as though he were junior to him in school. Not sure what Dad whispered in his "shell-like," but an agreement of some sort was made. Dad had a way with kids, like a Macchiavellian child-catcher; they gravitate to Dad—whether it's the plain talk? The pauses to listen? Or his sincere eyes – all of us kids listen to Dad – he found a way to everyone's marrow and now Master Bleacher-Reacher or whatever the hell is name is had come under the Roy spell.

Bleacher and the dog wandered off – to the river or the lorry – he didn't care and we shouldn't either would be his response. But you do, don't you, when you see a kid in trouble, out of the ordinary, on his game but out of society, feral.

"That's sorted then." Dad marched off to the other goal without a word of explanation, looking quite agile for a cancer patient who was one "release" from being mauled as breakfast. I followed – I was getting more used to that now.

"Yes, let's see what we have in store there, perhaps a Yeti from the forest or an ape from the jungle!" Things spill out of my mind when they are meant to stay in. In fact, they're meant to be out because no one should keep that junk in. *Goalies are mental – maybe I should have been one*, was all I could think.

"This is the breeding ground of exceptional goalies!" Dad was proud of that fact. He made no mistake of telling us at every game whenever a miraculous shot was blocked. "They seed the field with great keepers here!"

My childish thought was, *Well, they ought to be damned good; they get more practice than any other goalie!* Childish but true. And true, great goalies have passed through the royal blue of Chesterfield – or rather the field-green goalkeeper jersey!

"Into battle—eh, Dad?" But he ignored me. He marched on like his Ritalin had kicked in, full of purpose. Maybe he could read my mind after all and took offense to my flippant thoughts.

One, two, three—shoot, Ad!

I couldn't think straight; too many balls rolling around in me head.

CHAPTER 31

D*addy'll be home soon*, thought Joan to herself. But he rarely was; neither was her husband, and now Roy. All too busy with their lives.

"Daddy'll be home soon!" soothed Michelle to the baby. Michelle and Maddy shared the bathtub; following the nappy explosion, they had both worn the contents. Michelle wanted the luxury of a bath not a shower. Wayne would be gone for ages she figured. She and Madeline played row, row, row your boat in the tub, singing loudly like you should when no one is listening, they giggled together, laughed until they both peed in the tub, then laughed some more! They would need to shower now anyway, so would rubber ducky, who watched on without a quack. This was easy accounting – one love. And she started to sing the U2 song like no one was listening, hating the idea that balance sheets, cash flow summaries and a mortgage would take this away from her again on Monday.

"Daddy'll be home soon!" She was mostly right. Soon is very vague.

"Daddy'll be home soon," Mom had forced herself to say through the darkened room from under the eiderdown. It was like she sleep-walked through her answer. "Where's Dad?" was a common question. Ju always knew where Mum was – it was daytime; she had to be sleeping.

"Daddy'll be 'ome shoon, Jack." Her once-endearing lisp was now shaken and stirred with her morning martini. "Daddy's on the train; he'll be arriving at the station any minute." His mum hadn't seen the point in putting the vodka into such a tiny glass. So much easier to add tiny amounts of vermouth to the Svedka bottle; it already came as a cocktail shaker. She was most sober at breakfast; still her period leaked through her panties. It dribbled down her thigh, over the bruises like an unaggressive suck on a rocket-lolly leaves trails on preschooler's chin. Daddy, John Junior, the love of her life, the architect of her life; he planned her modeling career. She was beloved in the Littlewoods catalogue. A lingerie model, she shared her ample bosom with many an adolescent. But then Jack came along, and the Caesarean scar breached her career. *Just move into swimwear and teddys*, she thought. But her agent struggled to convince the agencies of that. John Junior had impregnated and tainted their golden goose; Jack was a good-looking baby, grannies would coo over him – it was in the genes. Baby Jack started to get more work than his mom. But never enough to pay the bills. John Jr was failing to sell his wares and opted to visit Dr. Smirnoff instead. They would toast to the good doctor every morning. Jack became a ping-pong ball between them, each giving him a tiny slap back to the other. Until that fateful morning when John Jr decided to take a train to work. He leapt from the bridge to catch the 7:38. Now Jack's mom just plays ping-pong alone, against the wall, wondering why John Jr's commute is so long.

One two three, shot – not long now....

CHAPTER 32

First thing you need to know about goalies is that they are mental. So, it was no surprise to find Marcus hanging by his ankles from the crossbar – what was incredible to me was how the prosthetic leg didn't rip straight off! Or him slip right out of it and land on his face?

"So, ape man, what's your name?"

"Marcus Banks, great-nephew of the famous--"

"Jeff Banks?" I called to him, staring at his Muppet navel. Ever talked to a face upside down? Thought not? – it's creepy, alien like, with the mouth on top of the eyes. First time I snuck up on my wife dozing on the beach, I had a surprise 99's, the Flake would make a perfect funnel to drop melting ice-cream on her boobs. Her sunglasses lay on her belly under the boob line. I came from above on my knees like a cloud. The disappearing sun disappointed her, so she opened her eyes to see how long before the next blast of warmth. Her open eyes and upside-down mouth freaked me out – she squealed and the 99 landed face down into her mouth, plugging it like an ice-cream and chocolate plunger! Anyway that face just before the 99 settled in – freaky – don't try it at home; it's a Stephen King moment.

Marcus the monkey swung like a trapeze artist waiting to catch the next flyer.

"Gordon! You moron!" The tune ran through my head – it would stick to and be with me all day. Jilted John from '78 a one hit wonder. That's exactly what we needed from this team! A one-off, a "never done before" moment, a "first time for everything" kind of year. A one-hit wonder.

"You're the great-nephew of the legend himself? Not possible!"

"Possible! Distant relative; both grew up in Sheffield. I was a fan of Town ever since, because of great-uncle Gordon! No good at footy, though!"

Well, that was what I didn't need to hear. A one-legged football player confessing that he's no good at the game!

"So, what brings you out here if you're no good!"

"Played rugby for Chesterfield, so I was driving down t' bypass when I noticed the car park filling up – thought there must 'ave been a game on or something so

I stopped by. Here I am swinging from your monkey bars."

"And your leg?"

"IED – Afghanistan …"

"Enough said – thank you for your service."

"You're welcome"

"So you want to be a goalie?"

"Played number 15 for Chesterfield Rugby club before taking a bomb to the leg; I've got pretty good hands!" and he dropped from the bars catching himself now walking toward me upside down – the Muppet mouth still staring me down. Even freakier to see the mouth moving, chatting whilst walking at you. Definitely more Stephen King than Barnum and Bailey.

"So, you can catch – but what abou' yer leg?" His good humor led me to believe I could address it.

"Not much good for kicking, but it never was; I'm a righty." He snagged a loose ball and punted it clear to the other eighteen, where it leveled a pot-bellied optimist. The beer drinker rolled like a bowling pin, then got up and yelled something rubbish at the Afghan veteran.

"Not bad, monkey-boy – what else you got?" The six-six vet stood like an inverted Blackpool Tower – titanium and iron.

"Check this out!" He was not lacking in confidence, for someone so traumatized. "Come on, lads, tek some penno's then!"

We all lined up. Some of the youth team took shots first. I whispered to them to mix it up, even have them in quick succession before he could get to his feet—foot. The blade, runner's blade, à la Pestorias might be an issue, but we'd cross that footbridge when we came to it.

"Got it!" Marcus slapped away shot after shot, yelling, taunting us with our best efforts. "Weak! Harder!" High, low, straight at him, his Eiffel Tower frame came with bear-like paws, on the end of cobra-tongue arms.

Dad had watched the whole thing, settled the ball on the white paint the size of a salad plate. Took three paces back and almost took the skin off the ball. Like a side-winding firework, it scurried into the bottom left corner, grazing Marcus's finger ends on the way. The only one of us to put a ball past Marcus "the great-nephew of the legend" Banks, Dad calmly walked away.

One, two, three, goal!

The three-step drop makes it hard for the goalie to read your hips, settle and pounce. The blade on the left leg was the stronger; this would make his right the weak side. *He will have to cheat an inch that way in games*, thought Dad. The crew was growing more motley by the hour. Dad spoke to Dr. Martens and stockings, and gladiator sandals as he left the field. He needed to both eat and puke, his crustless egg-salad sandwich was waiting for him in his office. Soft to eat, protein packed, easy to puke.

"Who's that guy?" asked a stunned Marcus.

"That would be your new boss! I believe he just told Zach to add you to the list of callbacks."

"Few people put one over on Marcus—where did he learn to shoot like that?"

"The Air Force."

One, two, three, shoot!

"I can go home then?" He was questioningly triumphant. He punched the clouds.

"Yes, Marcus, you can."

It appeared that the keenest ones with the most talent came early. The dad from the track the day before was in the early group, Mike McIntosh – I was glad to see he came. He brought the tribe, a picnic hamper (who has those still?), the buggy and a "nappy bag." He was fastest by far. Didn't see if he could kick a ball – I was too enthralled by our army veteran.

One, two, three, fire!

A cluster of players made the list – mostly because our list was looking really thin. The advert had brought out the circus in everyone, Marcus included.

There were a lot of men here whose clear ability for soccer remained on the Subbuteo pitch, Foozball (as we Americans call it), or X-Box. The defibrillator remained close by for the sprint section. The medics worked harder than a nodding donkey sucking the last oil drop from a Scottish well. Up and down they were taping ankles, icing knees, backs, and temples. This must have sounded like a good idea to a lot of lads after a dozen or so Boddingtons – the bet was made and here they were reeking and wreaking havoc—doubled-over, doubly dehydrated, and doubly annoying to our medics, emanating alcohol like a Tiki torch wick.

There was no sign of our Sam – a talented kid in his day; fireman now – I thought he was off today, though. Tryouts would end in an hour. We had maybe nine candidates at a stretch. As exciting as a day as this was, and though the PR had captured the town, we needed more actual players unless we fancied volleyball instead.

One, two three, blurp, blurp, blurp sang the alarm clock.

CHAPTER 33

Joan watched the live feed with Harry Gration, both hands wrapped around her china tea cup, slipping her middle finger through the delicate handle—no point in saving these for best she thought. Every day was "best." The kick of the burnt-orange tea sans sugar burned her tongue, stinging it and rendering it senseless.

"You bloody fool, Roy," she whispered under her breath, hoping to cool her tea with her chill words. She was honest, like the ring of an alarm clock. She had no time to be foolish. Her tea was still too hot, just the way she liked it – so she cradled her best china to its saucer that rested on her silver tray. She could have been expecting the queen at any moment. But hers was a house where few had visited since Eric died. Not that many dropped by even then. Now the gaps between visitors grew ever longer. She kidded herself that she saw people when she wanted to. Convinced herself that people don't just drop by anymore; that was old-school. And it was sort of true.

One, two, three—answer the door, would you?

Growing up, people were in and out of one another's kitchen; her mother had a constant flurry of people. Neighbors offering gossip with the sugar; old wool was shared to darn Dad's socks; suet borrowed and returned to make pudding. Conversations about rationing – sacrifice, scarcity, strife—brought people together. Needed each other. Now people just order online or off the TV, practically anything they want, even prescription glasses. Gift cards abound where gifts used to be. Nice little envelopes to be forgotten and misplaced instead of newspaper-wrapped trinkets in boxes held together with string. There was so much surplus you couldn't possibly know what to buy anybody. They probably had it, and if they didn't, well they could get it simply by pressing the right combination of buttons on their phone.

If the door knocker was redundant, then the house phone was not far behind. "I'm sure I hated the day every house had a phone." Joan spoke to the teacup welcoming it back to her lips. Strong, rich, full-bodied—like herself, except for the last part. She prided herself on the last part; even though she like Marie

Antoinette could afford cake with every cup, that was not her way.

"You're a bloody...bloody... damn fool!" She spoke to the television now. She was the only person I know who ever called it a "television," addressing it always by its full name even when an abbreviation would suffice. The television failed to respond the way that they can now.

People stopped coming around once the phone was installed. Much better to communicate from your own home; it was hailed as a breakthrough. Everything can be done from the convenience of your own home. A world of hermits living next door to one another. Anonymous packages arriving at doorsteps, soon to be dropped by radar toys so that even the postman's "sign here" would be eliminated. Your facial recognition from your biometric scan would be recorded and the toy helicopter would deliver your order. Thanks, eye in the sky!

Joan took another sip. It was bitter, stronger than normal perhaps – perhaps like herself today. The well-thumbed book next to her silver tray was finished – *Lady Chatterley's Lover* – banned in her childhood, it had taken until now, until ordering online to have the courage to buy it. Not bad, she thought, for a cheesy romance novel – to think D.H. Lawrence had grown up not far from here. Her perfectly polished pinky finger held out rigidly pointing to an imaginary butler. After all, that would be "just a silly expense."

She missed Roy and their frugal shopping, having the delicatessen girl take off that extra slice of ham so that it was no more than the quarter pound they had asked for. Or Roy's complaining that the fat on the ham shouldn't be included in the price.

Joan picked up D.H. Lawrence's finest work – reread the dog-eared pages – folded for their sensuality, leaving the bookmark to note where she left off. Smiling at the words, thinking it was rightly banned—the television had timed out and its sudden quietness caused her to glance at the screen's blackness – it was almost noon – seeing her naked shameless self, she thought it time to get dressed. After all, what would the neighbors say if she answered the door like this! But no one just stops by nowadays; even the gas meter is read from outside.

One, two, three, ooh la la!

CHAPTER 34

"Who are those guys?" About half a dozen well-tanned, black-haired thirtysomethings were sprinting over to the stadium, cigarettes in hand. All but one threw them down and stepped on them as they came through the gate.

The one with the cigarette stepped forward. He was the translator for the group.

"We are hheere, hheere for ze tryout?' hissed and weezed the confident foreigner. The others sort of gathered around, looking in different directions at the surroundings as if fireworks were going off in either direction. Over their shoulders I could see Laurel and Sam.

I rolled my eyes, having gone through a long day. "Go see the man in the skirt." I pointed to Zach, who was in the midfield circle by now. "He'll check you in."

"Verrry goodd." And he kept on smoking. Then he dictated something in a language that I would later learn was Romanian. His band of merry smokers followed him like he had the last pack of fags in the village. Zach questioningly took down their details – a lot of Eastern Europeans made it to Chesterfield looking for jobs the locals couldn't seem to find, as a tourist might look for gold in a California mine. Being exceptional with knives, this group had been given jobs cleaning behind the butcher's counter, stocking the slabs of carcasses and disposing of entrails. Their resume couldn't be counted on or verified, so it would be years before they could matriculate as the butchers they had been in their home country. Their boots and knives had been lost in the move to Britain, either confiscated or stolen from their luggage. No explanation was given, as seemingly none was owed.

The team leader flicked the somersaulting cigarette out of range, before translating again to his nest of chicks.

Zach put the little detail they had into his tablet. I put the Anadin tablets into my mouth and washed them down with a healthy dose of Diet Coke to welcome angrily my second cousin and his girlfriend.

"Where on earth have you two been? Oh, don't answer – I can see it on your face!" Her mascara was all over his ear and neck, probably from where she had fallen asleep post coitus.

Proudly, "We can tell you if you like?" offered the spunky punk with her tousled hair and glittering piercings.

"I'm good, thanks," I said, a hint of dejection in my tone. My calcified and jealous testicles had long been boxed away.

Her piercings and tattoos seemed to desecrate her superbly well-toned physique. Clearly, she cared about every detail of her form. The carved lines in her shoulders showed remarkable strength of definition. Sam, in contrast, was soft, puffy almost, young with beer excesses. No piercings or tattoos. A body for holding beers rather than dumbbells.

At least they had brought their boots. Their boots? Laurel wasn't trying out as well. was she?

"Check in with Zach in the Doc Martens and stockings, or with Delilah in the gladiator boots," her name wasn't Delilah, but "Andrea" just didn't seem to fit the garb. Why I thought Delilah fit better is anyone's guess. I had misheard her name, and now it stuck.

The Romaniants hadn't brought any boots to change into—or shorts, for that matter. Most were in jeans, some in Adidas sweats, one in parachute trousers from the late '80s. Oddly, they all wore the same Nike grey trainers, like they had been given a group discount?

Some stretched, some whined, some laughed then coughed, some coughed then laughed. Then to warm up they juggled tossing the ball casually from foot to foot. *Not bad, actually*, I was thinking – "circus" is what I was really thinking. They all had their 1970s Cryuff hairstyle – or lack of it. But the balls at their feet started to dance – there was routine to their casual stance. This group had done this together before. A system emerged; first the right foot was woken by flipping the ball up off their toe-tips, rolling it on to their instep, holding it there for a second before flipping it again sideways into the circle of Eastern European visitors. Each player similarly flipped juggled and tossed it right, anti-clockwise around the circle, once it reached its beginning, the left foot was awoken. All the while, there was casual chatter of an impenetrable language. Always strange how when we are presented with a foreign language, we listen intently like that will open up the Rosetta Stone of understanding! In the same way, we yell loudly to be understood. We lean into listen harder, like the code of language will be broken with no more effort than better hearing.

More gibberish and the ball was elevated to knee juggling, then shoulders, that one had to be seen to be believed! Then a quick flick of the shoulder and now a heading drill commenced. This was a circus until their leader cracked a joke, and laughingly they all stopped lining up their grey Nikes on the midfield circle, waiting to be called. One after another they were given the nod by their translator, who had gone first; they each crisscrossed and curled the ball sweetly fifty-plus yards to the goal. Balls like floating kites landed deftly under the crossbar and down the back netting, as one might brush a child's hair.

Dad had missed their earlier arrival but saw the darkened skin of the Romanians and curiously looked down from the Director's Box. He had given up trying to puke, after ten minutes of dry heaves. *Who are those guys?* he thought. The only skill he'd seen was the last of the group, who had swept the ball from halfway the way an artist might color-wash a life-sized canvas. Now this little pack of men stood strangely close, like a pack of burnt-tipped Woodbines. Was someone actually lighting one up on the pitch? *For God's sake, they are!* it angered him to watch this clique, but not for the reasons you might think like: "They are disrespecting the trial," "It's so unhealthy!," "It's a non-smoking area"—no, he was angry because he was not part of this clique any more.

He still craved a smoke every day since his heart had weighed in, he wanted, needed his nicotine break. Ever since the bike sheds, he'd been on the edge of societal conformity, a passive little snub to the world; now he looked down on the little pack gathered at the center circle, all chummy, hands cupping their neighbor's cigarette as they attempted to light it for them, faces leaning into bowls of hands to catch the flame to satisfy the urge to inhale and relax, take the edge off. Not being able to eat, Roy could sure use a smoke right now. What difference would it make, anyway? But he was a former smoker now and they are as socially acceptable as a former drinker – "judgy" or not, they are assumed to be. Judgy of their old pack – somehow now superior because they could let go of the grip. Dad made his way again back down from the stands to the field.

"Hey, Uncle Roy! How are you?" Laurel's bubble almost burst with excitement to see him. He was a real live uncle – she had never known one – and like all broken things, Dad had a way of taking them in and bandaging them up. Her enthusiastic hug pressed on his bandaged heart.

"Want a fag, Roy?" Essex accents stand tall in Derbyshire like a cough in the cinema, or the crushing plastic of a water bottle at the theatre. No matter how sweet the words, they are tainted, like grating your fingertips instead of the cheese.

"Hello! Lung cancer!" Dad mimicked a thirteen-year old girl's response to deflect the embarrassment of her coming realization.

"Oh my God, Roy, I'm so sorry!" she went back to bandaging him with a hug, as if listening for his heartbeat.

"Yer fine, luv!" He peeled off the koala bear wrapped around him. "So, Sam, are you here to try out, then?"

"I am, Uncle Roy; and Laurel too!" His enthusiasm was that of an alcoholic learning that there are positive health benefits of a couple of drinks a day.

"I am, Roy – played in college for the Essex ladies." Quite the oxymoron, thought Dad. The pompous inner voice of his mother had never truly left him, but his better exterior kept her quiet to the world.

"You're late, where've yer bin?" Kilt and stockings, and gladiator boots yelled at Laurel and Sam. "It's been an epic of a day and we're knackered, so can you get on with i'?" Gladiator boots and Dr. Martens spoke in unison like fraternal twins.

"Sorry!" Laurel's apology came out of her like the squeak of a dog's toy.

Dad could see over their shoulders that I was running the Romanians through their paces; they were all very quick, and as with many smokers, not much extra fat. Whatever they were doing at Tesco's, they were keeping up their strength.

"Come on, Sam." Laurel was hyper, like she'd been injected with energy semen. Sam wobbled like a colonoscopy patient. Laurel dragged him by the ear, the way you'd drag a younger brother, yet soft and playful. Was she filled with maple syrup? Her features were kind of pointy, like Curbar Edge loaded with camalots and carabenas. She peeled off her pillowy North Face anorak to reveal more ink than Shakespeare. Laurel picked up a ball, threw it up with back spin; it landed a couple of yards in front of her and walked like a yo-yo to her instep. At the right distance, she clobbered the ball hard and high right.

"Missed it!" She laughed like a child at the fair whose dart had flown by the target. "Can I have another go?" she said, as if asking for another dart. Zach and gladiator boots had been joined by sensible shoes and Mary Janes. Everyone nodded, intimidated by Laurel's pole-vaulter frame and the grim reaper tattooed on her triceps. Again, she flipped the ball; it rolled back as before, this time to her left foot. She drilled it like an electrician creates a hole in the stud, quickly, accurately, hitting the target and moving on to the next one. And she did, calmly stroking the next three or four with her left foot powered by sprinter's thighs. Laurel was a rock-hard hourglass, who trapped and passed balls back to the center circle as she somersaulted to the sprint lanes. The Romanians were still going through their steps and their roll-ups. They nonchalantly passed the ball and the cigarette at the same time, feet and hands perfectly timed like ballet.

"Can I have one?" Laurel snatched a smoke from the translator who had indicated no.

One, two, three, inhale!

She took a brief drag, and the grim reaper stained on her arm handed it back to him.

"Come on then, lads – let's go!" She directed her enthusiasm at the Romanians who didn't follow her.

"She wants to race!" It sounded intimidating in Romanian – but was apparently funny to the Tesco boys.

Not following, not understanding their hesitation, Laurel asked, "What's so funny? You boys scared?" Laurel must have been fearsome in the primary school playground. Probably had one of those removable tattoos of the grim reaper even then!

She flicked the ear of a Tesco boy with his back to her, snagged his cigarette, and took off. Jumping after her gauntlet he tried to chase her down – the fastest moving hourglass you'd ever seen. She pounded the ground with high knees like a pole-vaulter, the Rizla cigarette her baton; it was close in the end, but he was humiliated by his compatriot's laughter. Laurel bent to her knees, inhaling hard, took a drag from the Rizla for exclamation point, and handed it back to the immigrant. She trotted back to starting line, where the howling hyenas were still taking jabs at their pal.

"Alright, you lot! Who's next? Give me a minute." The translator got his troops riled up and lined up – the London transplant against the Romanian immigrants. *Damn – they were all quick.* Some were gliding like Cruyff, others explosive like Karl Heinz Rummenigge. *I just hope they all come back*, was all I kept thinking. *We may actually have something here.*

Laurel couldn't beat-out all of them – but the chauvinistic Eastern Europeans patted her head like a prize, the translator put his arm around her, and Sam took off like a jail break, sliding between the two, like a train engineer who's a little too late with the brakes, crashing into their platform.

"What the fuckin' 'ell do you think you're doing?" Sam jumped on the translator, taking him down; Sam was out of shape, so with his barrel weight he had the Romanian pinned, his beer-drinking arm on its way to his jaw, before the last second blow knocked him off the immigrant.

"Arsehole!" Laurel knew kickboxing, too. She stood over the pair, angry at her second-place pumpkin. From street brawl to Hong Kong Phooey in one broad stroke of the cartoonist's pen. No one dared laugh.

Kilt and Doc Martens forced his way through like a boxing referee. "FA Cup or English Premier League?" Everyone looked blankly at him.

The translator spoke quickly as you might pepper your eggs.

"FA Cup," said Sam. The others wheezed out an echo.

Watching Laurel reminded me of someone back in the States, so I dialed up. I actually used my cracked iPhone 6 and made a call, a phone call. I left a message. No one ever answers their phone for fear it's someone from Publishers Clearing House or an ex with a new phone! I texted her instead.

"Lindsey, do you coach like you played? If so, I may have something for you. Call me, Ad!"

One, two, three—pray!

CHAPTER 35

"Sorry I missed your call. I was doing a twelve-miler; it's marathon season soon!"

"Oh right. I thought you might have been still sleeping." I not surprised but whispered, "Like normal people on a Saturday morning."

But that would not have been the person I called. I called Lindsey because, well, she scared me on and off the field. Fiery redhead, the beaming smile of a children's TV show host, with the blood-red anger of a mother who'd lost a son to terrorism. On the field she was going to get the ball or else someone was going to die. Well, not literally, but she did break five girls' legs during her career, two of which were on her own team! Like I said, angry. Ubiquitous and angry, like the minefields of Afghanistan. Collateral damage everywhere, like losing the equity on your foreclosed home.

"Saw your text – so what's on your mind?" She was curt but at least returned my call/text. Things had gone sour back in the US between us – for a brief time we had a business arrangement. It had gone badly—not at first, not my proudest moment on the day I fired her. But a necessary one."Playing much?" I asked.

"A little co-ed ball here and there. My knee is strong enough to run with the girls but not enough to play D-One anymore!" There was a slight chuckle. She probably could—not for the team she was coaching now, but for a lesser D1, probably.

"Wear and tear gets to us all." I was empathetic but never in her league, success, medals, and trophy-wise. She had a room dedicated to her successes. I had a shelf in the curio cabinet in my office. A shelf for the one trophy, so it never got overshadowed.

"So, what's on your mind?" The Chicago accent still prevailed through her nose like a missile from a tank.

"I know things are going well for you at Northwestern, but …." Three babies were delivered while I paused. "but I need a coach in England, Chesterfield to be specific. Dad bought a team, my team, our team. He bought Chesterfield Football Club." Then I ran out of air.

"Roy did what? He bought a club?"

"Yep, took his retirement money and bought Chesterfield Football Club!" I was trying to sound enthusiastic, but it came through more in the vein of incredulity.

"I always loved Roy—you, though, you're an asshole!"

"I prefer 'Jackass'"

"Roy needs me? Jackass!"

"The team, The Club, and Roy need you."

"And Roy asked for me, Jackass?"

"Yes!" White lies should be delivered with utmost confidence and precision.

"And you'll pay me, Jackass?"

"Yes!" white lies should be delivered with utmost confidence and precision.

"At least what I'm making now, Jackass?"

"Yes! And enough of the Jackass!" Even frustrated white lies should be delivered with utmost confidence and precision.

"I'll need a passport."

"There's a passport office downtown – you can get one t' same day – just book your flight first and show them your itinerary."

"Give me some time to think about it – I have a great job here!"

"Take all the time you need." As I said - white lies should be delivered with confidence and precision.

"I'll be in touch!"

"Just don't break anything along the way," I whispered to the cracked phone with the red dot on it.

CHAPTER 36

We sat elbow to elbow, almost Starbucks cup to Starbucks cup around the conference room table. "So what are we looking at, Zach?" Dad enquired.

"About eight weary bodies in the midst of a science experiment!"

"What's the number?" "Fifteen that are decent; most are fast, like really fast, especially that bloke you found at t' track t'other nate."

"Oh good!" said I, feeling mildly good about myself for the moment.

"Well, hold on – he's fast but the rest is lacking." Zach was a little down in the sporran today – so many had turned out that the whole day was filled with promise. False promise as it turned out to be. "I think everyone just wanted their fifteen minutes of fame; it's a right pisser! Not even one celebrity came!"

"We can run it again next week and the next!" Dad was enthusiastic about keeping it going.

"We could, but it looks desperate, don't you think?" Zach was right about a lot of things and this was one of them.

"But we have to keep t' town energized, we have to keep them wanting more information about Chesterfield Football Club – we have to be on their radar or the energy will fizzle and so will our FA Cup chances. This has to be a season- long ride of joy!"

"Roy's right!" Gladiator boots licked the foam off her Starbucks. Every other Sat'dy, punters line up to watch t' team give its best. What if we do like Cruyff did and open-up the practices to the public? But go one further – we need the kids and they don't drive, so let's go to them!"

"But they're in school all day, there's no way for 'em to tek time off from t' classroom." Dad was right too – we needed the next generation right now.

"I've been thinking about that too," said the gladiator girl—we'll still call her Delilah. With her arms, she demonstrated to the group. "We go to them – we train on their school pitches – each week a new school. We hold twilight practices so t' parents can watch 'em train, get autographs, mingle. All we ask is that the school provide a little refreshment." The knights of the round table were quiet for a while.

"It's fuckin' brilliant!" said Mary Janes from accounting, blushing at her foul language. Chuckles of agreement flowed through the group.

"Each day we have tickets to be drawn for prizes available on the last day of training. Autographed old socks, or jerseys, shorts, trainers. Tickets for the game. We can have a photo-booth too, for a nominal fee – that can then be autographed." Gladiator boots carved a path of enthusiasm. Suddenly elbows were acceptable on the table as ideas started to flow. The energy in the dimly-lit room shook the table like a séance!

"We are gonna have the Chesterfield FC road show!"

"Think, if we can just get Noel Edmonds?" there was a shine in the smile of the Mary Janes!

"It'd be even better if he could kick a football!" said Zach.

"A season-long party, a celebration of the underdog is what this is going to be." Adrenalin coursed through Dad where the chemo had been.

Mary-Janes grabbed Zach by his sporran – he wasn't best pleased – and went off to make some calls to schools – they would need fifty-two in all. That was a lot of calls.

"We're gonna need a bigger bus!" It was hilarious. I crack myself up. No one else laughed.

"Logistically, this team is going to take a lot to organize. I hope you're ready? One event a week is so much pressure--weekends won't be weekends, schools have schedules too; there's the holidays to think about. Schools have protocols – it's not like in my day, when no one cared who came through the school gates. Gates were to keep kids in, not parents or adults out!"

Plimsolls stepped in. "Teams within teams; that's what we need."

"Explain yoursen', then?" Dad fell into his construction brogue.

"Two teams – same goal of community outreach to schools – like a slinky – one team follows the next into a school, so each team is always working two weeks out. Then you have the home team for events here at Proact and national tournament events!"

"Sounds great, but this table is all there is." Dad knew there were barely funds for the squad now. We would need advertisers back stronger than before – as of now there were renegotiations on every contract. This was before Dad knew what I had just promised Lindsey. Lindsey was going to have to be my responsibility, if she came at all.

Everybody looked at each other – enthusiasm for overtime can be limited when you know your raise is in your job description and not your pay packet. All the shoes looked a little scuffed at the prospect of long hours for little pay—all except flip-flops, for obvious reasons. The microcosm of business sat elbow to elbow, suddenly quiet, eyes rotated, pointing to the quadrants of the compass as if magnetic north had shifted for each of them.

Then, ironically, flip-flops brought everyone to heel. "We are an internet start-up – we are an IPO – but instead of public, we are private. We are preparing a product relaunch. We are rewriting history, not mired in its monotonous shackles – these are not the stocks of medieval torture; this is the stock of an idea of the downtrodden, the put down, the bullied." He paused, breathless from his run-on sentence. "We need to show these kids a little hope, a little light at the end of the tunnel – that life isn't all tunnel. If we get this right – we'll be bigger than football, bigger than business!" Flip-flops slumped back after high-fiving the group and slid himself off his feet.

"Wow, well said…!" I looked across, searching for his name. He'd been in the group for days, but it's embarrassing to ask someone's name when a time frame has passed, and you have been in their company for a while and you really should know it. He could see my reach.

"Chester's the name! I'm the mascot!"

"Of course you are! No wonder I didn't recognize you!"

"It's what you do with a history degree from Salford University! I'm also the dietician. Currently working on the history of food!" He slapped the table like a tom-tom for added emphasis.

"Pair up, everyone – and figure out who is going to run what – we'll meet at 8 a.m. sharp." Dad was perking up – this group was his espresso.

"8a.m.? It's Sunday tomorrow?"

"Like the flip-flops say – there is no bigger cause than to protect the vulnerable. We keep going – we only have one season; success or failure, we'll have next summer off!"

"Failure is not an option," whispered the Plimsolls.

CHAPTER 37

"Did you see *Look North* last night?"

"Yeh, what a bunch of divvies those eejots from Chesterfield are!"

"Feckin' shtoopid – we'd better not start that crap here at Wednesday!"

"Like a fuckin' circus, it were, 't had everythin' but the elephants!"

"'Rate! Nah, they 'ad them too – did yer see some o' them fat fucks trying out?"

"Din't need t' see 'em – could feel fuckin' earth move!"

"Yer some right, biffers – pathe'ic – like summert ou' o' National Geographic!"

"'swot 'appens when times is desperate; 'ere, pass us me boots wou'dge ya?" The scouse accent settled back into the routine of polishing his game boots.

"Desp'rate times call for desp'rate measures – yeh fuck that shit I'd be off if it came down to that!"

"Ah just 'ope we get a chance to play them fuckers!"

"No' fuckin' likely, they'll be out o' t' fuckin' league be t' time season starts." Laughter filled the changing room.

"Look! Look, Mam, it's dad on t' telly!"

"Where? I don't see him!"

"In t' background – look – he's behind 'arry!"

"I think yer righ' – rewind it!"

"Am shoower it's 'im! Look, it's his England shirt behind the kid with t' Liverpool shirt on."

"I think yer right – he looks a proper 'nana! Prob'ly laid up for a week as a result of this malarky!"

"He plays ev'ry Sundee an' he were ou' runnin' last nate - he's no' in bad shape!"

"Syd – he trogs around on a Sunday mornin' with a bunch of pissheads, he's not gonna mek Town team!"

"He migh'. He's best player on t' team ev'ry Sundee!"

"Syd, it's Sundee league...."

"But Mum – last year they played in t' FA Cup!"

"Yeh, alrigh' son, I'll give yer tha', bu' there's no way yer dah is mekking Town team – he can't barely walk after one match a week, ne'er mind 'bout playing ev'ry day! They don't 'ave enough Lego to rebuild 'im!"

"But wha' if he does, mam? What if he does?"

So rarely does a kid live vicariously through a parent.

"Pint of the usual, Dennis?" Rose called from behind the bar as he stepped through the door, halfway done with his pour.

"Cheers, Rose, that would be lovely."

"'rate Den?" Hollered Rob.

"'rate Den?" Nodded Dave.

"'rate Den?" added the stranger at the bar.

The chorus of Chezzy welcomes greeted the late comer. He was late by his corps' meeting time but military perfect for his own. Which was how Rose knew when to start the pour, following Dennis' military precision timing.

"Delicious, Rose!"

"That's two fifty-eight please, Den!"

"It's outrageous i'nt it – raising prices every week!"

"I know, Den, meks it 'arder to get by ev'ry week, what with the price of petrol as well!"

"Might 'ave to go back to work at this rate!"

"That's why I'm here of a night, Den – one job's not enough, not since Mick lost his job," said Rose.

"Not much work for aging detectives, so I may have to start drinking halves!" Den felt bad for Rose and Mick – they were young – in their forties, likely; at least when he was asked to leave the force, he'd made it to his fifties, his pension was locked in; it was hard to believe he'd been retired for almost as long as he'd worked.

"Gents," offered the direct but soft-spoken Den as his welcome.

"See that rubbish on *Look North*, Den?" asked Rob.

"No, I was over at the allotment – cleaning it up for planting, adding me compost." Den nurtured his private time at the allotment, more and more since Doreen passed. He only kept the television because it fit in the cabinet. And "when things fit, they fit" he thought, like a jigsaw puzzle; he and Doreen had been the perfect picture.

"Oh, you missed a treat; Town had a tryout for the whole town!"

"Harry Gration was in town 'imself covering it!"

"Hundreds showed up – like a carnival there today!"

"Dave tried out!"

"You never!"

"I did!" Dave was still excited.

"They're taking geriatrics now!" laughed Rob.

"And I thought they'd been playing all along!" smirked Dennis.

"Well, if nothing else – I've got two tickets for a match next season – look." And Dave pulled the tickets out of his jacket, held them up with pride.

"At Sheffield United, we fill our stadium without giving seats away! You wun't be able to use that for yonks!" Rob was loving what seemed to be absolute desperation from the local club, that of his home-town now. Sheffield United were on an upturn, headed back to their glory days of the 1970s – Chesterfield were on their way out completely. And Rob seemed to delight in the fact. Chesterfield Town's glory days had been Sheffield United's nightmares. Until of late, Sheffield had struggled to fill their state-of-the-art stadium, built on future revenues of projected successes. Town's new stadium was built on them just doing what they'd always done. But even that low bar was becoming too high.

"Come on, Den, looks like we'll have to play trivia without Roy again tonight," said Rob, still glowing with the seemingly pathetic efforts of his local rival.

"He seemed real busy when I left; media types everywhere. Looked pale and thinner to me," said Dave. He was beaming that he'd had chance to run around on the hallowed ground. Dave didn't seem to mind whether Roy chose him to come back for another trial or not. Besides, how was he going to tell the headmaster that he wasn't going back to school next term? Then he thought more seriously about it – less money, no job security of any kind, and he could easily be replaced at school for less salary. *Art teachers are easy to find*, he thought and with budget cuts he always sensed the Sword of Damocles being swung by the board of directors since the music department was chopped two years ago.

The group sidled over to the quiz machine – this had been their routine of late. Trivia gambling, testing their knowledge on everything.

"Looks like we are gonna be hurting in the music-history category without

Roy again. He's not likely to show at this hour." And they all checked their watches – there was still time to complete their evening of three pints and Dennis' two.

Rose would keep an eagle eye on the state of their pints, looking to reload them the moment the cartridge exited the barrel. *Service like that would be well tipped in the US*, she thought. A small dream of escape kept her going.

"General knowledge to get us going then, gents." Den leaned in and put his two-pound coins in. It was long established that the last to show was required to be the first to fund the quiz machine. Den had honored the code even since Doreen passed Keeping things the same. He had always waited for her to go to bed before he would make his way to the Highfield. Now that she was at permanent rest – he saw no reason to change that thinking. He came out at the usual time, to the usual place, to the usual friends, for the usual drink as if she were still waiting, lightly snoring, on his return. She was not. But her cats were, and that seemed to be enough right now. Just enough to be needed by something. A small routine of buying their food, cleaning their litterbox, refreshing their water bowls. Doreen had done all this before—first with the kids then with the cats. Now it was Dennis' turn to take care of the kids...I mean cats.

"Come on, Nan, we're gunner be late." Robbie hustled his grandmother to drive faster.

"She can't drive any faster; cars are in the way, son. Honey, don't listen to him, the selfish brat."

"John, don't call him that!"

"It'll be over if we don't get there; it's half-two and the trial ends at three."

"We should make it, sweetie. We are only at Baslow; we can be there in no time with a good run." Nan spoke like sugar-plum fairies danced.

"Me phone says we won't get there until five after. This is all your fault. I didn't want to dance in t' first place!"

"Hey, lad, show a little respect for your grandmother – she's driven hill and dale to support you. Think there aren't things in her life she'd rather be doing than taking your sorry backside around t' country every night and weekend!"

"I never asked her to!"

"Rubbish, lad – you have been dancing for all your life – what you wanted to do. Your nan and me have gone to Derby three nights a week since you was seven because you wanted to!"

"You needn't have come!"

"Enough of your lip, laddy, or I'll have your nan go straight home; then there will be no tryout, no Town practice."

"I keep your nan company; besides if I didn't have this knackered hip I'd drive you meself – or not."

"Boys, this constant fighting isn't getting us there any quicker! Aer Lingus couldn't fly the plane any faster; and I'm glad they threw that foreign-looking man off the plane. He was making me nervous, what with all the terrorism these days."

"Nan, they don't blow up planes from Dublin to Manchester – that would be stupid – they want something more dramatic than that!"

"Well anyway – he looked shifty to me." And Nan kept on staring at the "wide-load" sign on the back of the truck. This winding, tree-lined hill took you from the valley to the plateau. The hairpin turns of thirty years ago had been lightly ironed out so you could travel a little quicker, a little safer. The meadows of the valley rose either side; you really shouldn't rush through the Peak District. And laden trucks from the quarries saw to it that you couldn't, with limestone chips dancing off their backs like auditions for *Riverdance*.

The "wide-load" slowed down further and moved over the median. "Oh, come on, can't you go any faster?"

"I'm doing the best that I can."

"Not you, Nan, this stupid lorry in front – what is he playing at?"

"Look, son, not even me with a good hip could we drive any faster than your nan, so just belt up, alright?"

"What if I miss it, though? This might be me last chance to play for t' Town."

"No, there'll be others I'm sure, sweetie," and Nan rolled a hard caramel toffee round her gums. It's how she stayed calm these days since stopping smoking. Triglycerides danced where nicotine used to play.

"Of course there won't—this is it. I missed my chance years ago when were in Philadelphia."

"Yes, because you wanted to dance!"

"I know, but I want to play football too, Granddad – I want to play for t' Town!"

"Son, if my hip were any better I'd come back there and give you a good hiding! You chose Irish dance, and now that's the end of it! You're damn good, son, world qualifier; we've put hours aside because this is what you wanted."

"I know, but I want to play for t' Town."

"But why? They're complete rubbish!"

"John, you know it's always been a dream of his."

"Aye 'Robbie two dreams' – brilliant for some. Worra 'bout us? Haven't we got things we want to do?" He shot from the hip—the one that should have been replaced last spring when the pain became unbearable – now this spring was upon them and no surgery scheduled.

"John!" He was shot down. Not since taking on their son's responsibility of raising Robbie had things been easy. Nan had loved him from birth even if his parents hadn't. He was inconveniently brought into the world and wouldn't know siblings. This Catholic grandmother had sworn off the abortion that her "would have been daughter-in-law" wanted. Neither she nor her family had means to take care of a child and even less desire. Her own son, a "free spirit," she called him. A "gadabout" and "waster," her husband called him. "No amount of church is going to rail that kid in, Nan." "You can't just give up on a child, John; you have to persist." Robbie's father had found a commune in the French Alps – apparently, he was an entertainer to the tourists jamming for tips. Neither Nan nor John could follow his thinking – A's in school, church choir, then Molly, she seemed like a nice girl. *But nice girls don't do that, do they?* she had thought – and then been disappointed twice by Molly.

Raising Robbie gave Nan a second chance to get it right--in her eyes, at least. She was an Irish dance instructor; that's how she'd met John. At a dance. He was ballroom she was Irish. Similar but different. That's how his hip had come undone. Robbie had inherited her and John's feet. He was also slight like his mother; his mother had looming auburn locks, freckles, Shirley Temple cuteness.

The playground kids loved to torment Robbie for it. Then the girls piled on too about his dancing. The same girls who thought he was "amazing" in year three backed away from him now, so they could hurl insults from afar. No matter how far his Nan and grandad John drove him to dance competitions, the echoes of insults bounced off every hillside and cliff edge. That's why Robbie needed football – he needed today – if only to staunch the tide of vicious commentary – today – Town – could turn those girls back around. Maybe playing for Town, those girls could once again learn to love his red-headedness. Just one more time.

One, two, three, drive on!

Robbie slammed his orange fringe into the car window. The cyclist had fallen, clipped by the lorry. A little blood flowed and even less traffic. Robbie's Town dream had been knocked off its bike.

CHAPTER 38

"How are you doing today, Roy?"

"I've got cancer, Doc, and it's probably not going away!" Roy's flippant answer followed the vacuous comment.

"Yes—sorry, Roy; we doctors get programmed into certain opening lines. My apologies; I've seen a lot of people today."

"And a lot of sadness, from what I could tell from them in t' waiting room; I counted seventeen ahead of me all with an appointment within five minutes of each other!"

"Yes." Doctor Doran eked out a "yes" the way a slow leak in your tire is widened by an overwhelming summer's day.

"It should be me asking how you're doin', Doc?"

"Quite!" More air slipped out of the doctor. "You sound fine, Roy."

"I puke a lot – I was told I would – my hair collects in my cap around its ring the way my wife's hair used to collect by t' plug hole, clinging to this side of things."

"Yes, sorry about that – we'll give you something for the nausea."

"Fairy-nuff; the other stuff didn't work, so I keep puking. Most of me hair is gone; seems it took me tastebuds with it too. Everything tastes like I'm polishing t' silver with me tongue." If he'd been born royalty, he might think he was choking on the silver spoon. The reality being he was choking down death with every meal; couldn't taste it properly; better to throw it up just in case.

"Skinny people live longer any road, don't they, Doc?" Dad was brave here and everywhere else, or he just didn't get that he was dying. Hip-cat Roy lived the lyrics of The Verve – his drugs didn't work and they made him worse. In a milder case and a lesser reason to visit the doctor he might have complained. "Need something better than Linctus doc!" 'But Chemo and Radiation are the last straws –its not the doctor's fault there are no more straws."These vomiting episodes are quite normal, Roy, quite normal. Anything else out of the ordinary?" Doctors, or at least Dr. Doran had a way of floating over the vacuous – ignoring Dad and his thinner people comment. The doctor's schedule restricted the banter: "Stick to the facts, please." The doctor was judge. not color commentator – all fodder and no flavor.

"Yes," and Roy inflated his tires. "In a strange way this was the best thing that ever happened to me. Knowing my time is short…."

"It may not be that short, Roy; you're responding well to the treatment."

"But it's still shortish, right?" The doctor's nod followed Roy's nodding. "Because it's short, it's manageable—not this coil of rope hanging in me garidge – it's a shoelace that has to be dealt with properly every day. So, in a twisted way, I'm glad I'm sick; it's given me new life, this dying thing."

"I'm glad to hear it, Roy. So many come in here just trundling on until they run out of track…never having chosen a destination. I've seen you on television, Roy – seems you and Harry Gration have a thing going on a regular basis. Seems you've captured the hearts of the town and the local television."

Maybe the good doctor did have a life outside of his clinic.

"Yes, thanks; am a big fan of Harry's, and he seems to be a fan of ours. Hopefully he'll bring some followers with him. It's costing a bomb to run this club. Like a said – this illness has given me a lease on life – a short one – but at least it's a lease. Are we done? Shall a send the next one in?"

"Yes, thank you, that would be very kind. I'll get you a prescription for the vomiting," the doctor offered through his jealousy, still wanting to feel a little useful.

"'S'alright- used to it now. A tek a Rennie – besides I'm losing weight and getting back in shape." His voice tapered off to the doctor, who thought to himself, *We should all be working to a deadline*—but his treadmill of patients streamed in – like steps of an escalator going underground for a moment then reappearing at the beginning again, knocking on his door. How many is too many patients in a day? Shouldn't some of them be limited to so many visits per year?'

"It's like a medical creche in here."

"Talking to yersen there, Doc?"

"Ah yes, Mr. Hudson – how are you feeling today?"

"Well, I've got this rash I can't seem to get rid of…"

One, two, three and one two three, and one two three and one two three.

CHAPTER 39

"You alright, Roy? You seem a little deep in thought—or are you staring at the dust stains on the windows?"

"You sound like me doctor, Brian!"

"Heavens, not that!"

"Yes, I know it's a grim job surrounding yourself with sick people all day long. I'd rather be here – staring at the carpark where t' tube works used to be."

"Yep, couldn't agree more. I'd rather fix and replace lost teeth than have to deal with the rest of the grotty human body!"

"I'm fine for the minute, Brian – and thanks for asking – don't stop asking, because I know, and the doctors tell me at some point I'm gonna need some real help."

"I just came up from a training session. Looks like you've divided the lads up into two squads quite nicely."

"Our focus is the league, and—well, the rammel that came out of the trials seemed to be making a nice effort on the practice squad."

"I was surprised. I think the whole club was surprised to see you sign on so many from that great experiment of yours."

"Good PR, Brian – good PR."

"Expensive PR, if you ask me. Especially for a man who works in the dark to save a light bulb!"

"Damned expensive. And I'll probably run out of money before too long, but I want two squads, two distinct teams. Our league team will only play the league, Brian – make no mistake; promotion is their main goal."

"Understood, Roy, but what about the other cup matches? There's a load of them, and they come early in the season."

"No, no, no – the first team is for the league only. The practice squad can handle the rest."

"If you say so, Roy – that's a lot of prize money to sniff your nose at! At least they'll be in good shape – your Mark and Ad are running them into the ground. It's like watching the movie *Miracle* without ice! Vomit and Gatorade bottles filling the rubbish bins out there!"

"Yes, a miracle – we could use one of those, couldn't we?"

"For now, let's enjoy the attention of it all. After all, you are paying for it!" Brian laughed his way out and into the corridor.

"Eight games – we only have to win eight games to lift the FA Cup – a very short season indeed." Dad spoke to the empty car park, through the gathering dust on the windows.

One, two, three, four, five, six, seven, F8 Cup Champions!!

CHAPTER 40

"Quiet, children! Quiet!" The headmaster was fighting the hubbub of expectancy.

"QUIET!" Julia's voice carried harsher than her soft-spoken head's and the assembly bowed the way a lawn is clipped by a mower. She was the boss's hench-woman – did all his dirty work, meted out detentions, defended the school before government, governors, and parents. She was the face of the school. If kids made it through high school, her tenacity was the reason. Respect was earned and she had a life-long detail of overtime in that department.

"QUIET!" The assembly of blazered hormones had already quietened. Julia was not going to let go a moment to affirm control. Her laser eyes patrolled the crowd below like bank security expecting trouble around the clock.

Robbie and his senior classmates heard the usual whirr of rotator blades from the headmaster--the typical drone of someone wanting their words to land. Robbie hadn't listened all year, distracted by Irish dance, college applications, and football. As a prefect on stage behind the faculty the headmaster's hum of "blah, blah, graffiti, blah blah blah, bullying, blah blah blah, All things Bright and Beautiful the Lord God Made Them all, blah, blah, hearing and vision testing, blah, blah, blah – Chesterfield Football Club will be hosting their training session here on the school grounds."

An email had gone unread, by practically every family without a tiger-mum of a parent. So literally the whole school was unaware that Chesterfield Football Club would be hosting a training session here all week Monday to Thursday. It had been the headmaster's idea to save money by not mailing out the hard copy of the week and month's upcoming school events. Money on paper was saved but time wasted responding to email complaints regarding not being informed of school events: hearing and vision testing – field trip to Twycross Zoo with waiver and permission slip – early closing next Wednesday for teacher training day – blah, blah, blah. The irony never passed Julia, who thought it hilarious that parents who complained by email claimed they never got the attachment! Literally hours of hers and John's time poured down the drain. All parents had to do was put it in their Outlook reminder or, God forbid, print it and put it on the fridge using their own paper! Didn't everyone have an office in their home these days? It's what everyone wants on HGTV. An office in the home—yuk! With wifi, who would want to plonk down in an office at home when, well, the front garden or back garden, the park, or even the driveway to catch the last beams of summer sun would work just as well? Children had been informed for years of the school's ongoing events. It was transmitted in Chinese, apparently, so outside of a couple of exchange students and the Lee family, no one knew what was going on in school. Hormones affected hearing, which is why this week it was being tested; that along with vision, because apparently these adolescents couldn't read bulletin boards or emails!

Robbie had been away in Ireland dancing when all this had come about. The daughter of The Club's new owner had been approached first to "beta test" or "guinea-pig" the idea. Julia thought it stupid and agreed wholeheartedly to be the first. Most of us only get one dad. Some, with more, learn that water is very much thinner than blood.

"What the..." whispered Robbie. The problem with being behind the faculty on the stage is that a whisper can be heard, along with a dropping pin. In a moment the world returned to the Ice Age, and mammoth stares greeted the decorated senior prefect. He stood out like coal on a blushing snowman. If he wasn't in detention for the week, he would have a chance to get up close to his heroes; maybe an autograph or two. He would wear his Town socks under his uniform grey slacks as a show of respect. The headmaster's gaze lit the coal and Robbie hoped to spontaneously combust.

"My office, McDonald," came the whispered response of the head. Robbie wasn't sure there would be anything but embers left for the "head" to chastise further. The head of the snowman rolled off its perch and lay gazing at the shocked assembly. "Blah, blah, blah—you are all dismissed – except you, McDonald."

The windowed corridor back to the headmaster's office allowed the entire school the opportunity to see dead men and women walking.

"Sit down here a minute." The head pointed to the chair outside his office. This was unexpected and annoying. "I have a meeting." The headmaster was frustrated by the change to his schedule and left Robbie sitting at the gallows for all to see.

"Julia, this event today – I have to say it's frightfully annoying – the press will be here, I'm sure – and I'm not convinced this is good for the school."

"John, the kids are really excited..."

"I'm frightfully worried that it will be a distraction; we've already got Robbie McDonald waiting outside for his punishment."

"With all due respect, John, Chesterfield have paid the school handsomely; we have funds for new netball posts and balls, football goals and balls. If it's about Robbie, then I'll be the one to mete out the punishment."

"Would you? I'm feeling a migraine coming on."

"You go for a walk and send Robbie in on your way. Don't mind if I use your office, do you?

"Most grateful, Julia – I'll tour the school – see if there is any more nonsense in the classrooms." And the willow followed the wisp.

"Good idea – send Robbie in then." Julia had the control of a Hawaiian canoeist. "Come in, Mr. McDonald." Julia sounded serious in her gentle tone, good cop and bad cop in one sentence. "Sit down." The naughty chair had been isolated, its sister chair being pushed back in the corner. The naughty chair was placed front and center of the headmaster's desk, behind which Julia now sat with her finger on the switch, ready to electrocute Robbie with questions. Confessions often blurted out before a question was asked.

"I'm sorry miss – but is it true? Are the Town going to be training here this week?" Robbie looked to divert the moment – hoping that familiarity would not breed contempt in her.

"I'm surprised at you, Mr. McDonald," said Julia as if leaning in for a header, ignoring the defender. "What was that outburst all about? Most unlike you!" Julia good cop.

"Sorry, miss; I've been gone with me dancing. I didn't hear the news about Town coming here – well, just got a bit overwhelmed."

"I know, Mr. McDonald, and I'm hoping you have a lot of homework completed for me today."

"I do, miss – spent all Sat'day on it, and Sunday."

"We gave you last week off to compete. How did you do, by the way?" Good cop.

"Top five—so pretty good."

"I'll say—well done, young man," the good cop continued. As good a dancer as Robbie was, he was also the best footballer in the school, had been since the day he transferred in. As team captain, he'd fought off the bullies' gay taunts from his early days in high school. His arrogance became a defense mechanism that few loved and fewer still challenged.

"Thanks, miss – but well, I wanted to try out for t' Town. I know it's your dad running it, and I thought I might have one more chance Sat'day, but our flight was delayed out of Dublin, and well, no matter how fast Gran drove, well—we didn't make it. As much as I love dance, football is like a religion to me."

"I think you should watch your mouth, Mr. McDonald. This is, after all, a church school."

"Sorry, miss, but when I'm not dancing, my world is football. It's like God is coursing through me—the world slows down, and I'm floating."

"That's nice, Mr. McDonald, but it doesn't explain the outburst – you're supposed to be a leader to the other students – that's what that badge on your lapel signifies."

"I'm sorry, miss," and the air left his ball. Missing the tryout Saturday was cutting enough; now he was letting down the school and one of his cheerleaders. He would have shuffled in the chair, but the uniform slacks used his sweat to bond to the plastic chair padding.

"You're gonna spend a week in detention, Mr. McDonald – from those with so much, so much more is expected—and fittingly, your punishment is harsher." And the bad cop rose from behind her headmaster's chair, reholstered her taser, and waited for him to leave.

"But miss, I'll miss seeing the Town practice, that's not...." And he was about to say not fair.

"Not what, Mr. McDonald? Not fair? You're a prefect, and if you want to stay one, I suggest you hold your tongue and your thoughts." Both hands were on her hips, one as if on her weapon.

Robbie's eyes filled like the meniscus on a full cup of tea – any movement would cause a spill down his face. A ginger snap was out of the question – he would hold it together.

"No words, Mr. McDonald. A week's detention will give you time to think about your actions."

Robbie didn't want to topple the cup – air was not forthcoming – he was vacuum sealed. He couldn't look down, either, or the emotion would have dribbled right out of him. Still children at heart, even with the power of the vote and the license to defend their country. Still just children.

"That will be all, Mr. McDonald – you can leave now. You have let yourself and school down."

Robbie remained. He needed pumping up before he could rise from his seat.

"We are done here, Mr. McDonald," Julia insisted.

You know your football career is over at thirteen if you haven't been scouted and called up. Robbie, having moved so much as a youngster between parents, foster homes, and finally to his grandparents who had eventually adopted him, had shown that despite everything, he would not let it get to him. He had resolve beyond his years, fueled by hatred of his parents—he would show them. Football, though, he did for himself. He danced for Nan, studied hard to prove to the chip on his shoulder and his worthless parents that they would regret ever letting him go. But football was where his heart lived, pounded for him, pumped the "him" around. Saturday was his last shot. Watching his team play up close wouldn't have necessarily satiated that angst or need, but maybe it would take the edge off. To watch them play – see them train – to learn if he would have had the stuff of a professional.

One, two three, four, five days in detention.

CHAPTER 41

Meanwhile, on both sides of the pond, decisions were being made.

"I need to move on. Tony Robbins says if you're not growing, you're dying, and I refuse to let that be the case." She looked at herself in the mirror, still twenty-three inside. "Not as young as I was, but I'm still not bad-looking. Ready for a change, a change of destination, maybe that's what I need. I don't need a man; as the saying goes, I need a man like a fish needs a bicycle – funny that Bono, a good-looking man, should sing about that. I bet his wife threw him that line. Who is she again? But I am still ready for a little romance, excitement, the heartbeat of someone to be curious about. To be available to love and be loved; yes, that's where I am now. I shall find a new passion, a new path that might lead to passion; yes, that's what I need now. I'm Georgina Bailey, and I'm gonna shake off the dust of this old town and start a life anew!"

"Well if you are, love, can you leave me your bag o' bread? I'm gonna keep feeding t' ducks, duck!" Mavis wasn't used to hearing so many words out of Joan. Queens Park pond was where they sat, to mourn in silence the chocolate teapots that were once the bread-winners. Gerald, or Ged as he was better known, worked for Eric and died but a week before; Eric had always been the more competitive of the two: "I know I'm not well, but at least I outlived Ged!" It was a race to the finish where the winner came in last. Always counting the ones, our elders who are likely to make the finishing tape before us – giving us a little solace that we are not next. Grandad, then God forbid Dad, then—well, me. Eric had crossed the finish line like Roger Bannister, head back away from the tape record broken. A life with a marker. Ged had lived like the second man to break the four-minute mile, in anonymity. Joan handed her her bread, pushed up the umbrella, tied her cellophane bonnet, walked up and over the footbridge quickly smoothly, thinking she was glad she hadn't been an athlete in her junior years! She marched right into Thomas Cook:

"One ticket to Disney World please!"

Across the pond, a younger lady walked into Apple Vacations and said the same thing.

"Florida or Paris?"

"Florida, please!" beamed Joan. "I'm going to meet my prince!"

"Paris, please!" beamed Lindsey. "I'm going to meet my princess!"

CHAPTER 42

"I can't believe you came!"

"Me neither. Now stand there and smile; I want to show Mavis how I met Prince Charming!"

"Certainly, ma'am!"

"Oh, you really are quite dishy! What are you doing later? And if you say Snow White, I'll slap you with this stuffed Mickey!"

"Ma'am, I'm headed to the ball with Cinderella."

"Of course you are—how silly of me. Now smile."

Almost no one goes to Disney World alone, and her agent had looked perplexed when she asked for one ticket. On the footbridge, Joan had thought about running back to get Mavis. But only for a second.

Disney World is the happiest place on earth and you're not alone for long, it's like they know, like Walt knew somehow some people would come to his heaven alone.

"I can't believe you came—nice tiara!"

"Thanks – Prince Charming gave it to me. Of a fashion."

"Since I didn't hear from you—it's been weeks—I thought, well, that the past wasn't behind us and that the hatchet was front and center for all to see!"

"It is; that's why I'm dressed as Pocahontas. A red-headed Pocahontas – so watch out!"

"I didn't want to say, ask, well…."

"I was in Disney World Paris – thought I'd go to the happiest place on earth before I saw your face again – see if it would give me the strength to get me over the hump of seeing your miserable mug again!"

"Nice to see you too!"

"It didn't, and it's not, and you know it – but you must be up shit creek and paddleless to call me on behalf of your dad. I'm assuming he has no idea you called?"

"Right, right again. Can I take your suitcase?"

"Oh, the irony you want to help me with my bags after you told me to pack them the last time! No, asshole, I've got this – it's a football club. I'm assuming you've got a locker room at least!"

"It's--"

"I'll find it, show myself around. No one needs two assholes, and I've got one already."

"Right…only…." I was going to say that it was a men's only locker room but then again that probably wouldn't have mattered. Lindsey had more testosterone than a rugby brawl. *Mirror, mirror on the wall who is the fairest of them all?* I thought it but hadn't the balls to say it.

One, two, three "poof"!

CHAPTER 43

"Good morning everyone and welcome to Chesterfield Football Club– I want to congratulate you on making the squad!" Dad performed the job of emcee – it was a couple of days delayed, as he had been bedridden. He sounded dehydrated, gravely, as if he'd eaten cat litter. "I want to welcome back our returning players from last season – I know it was disappointing to be relegated. I know that many of you didn't actually play much, but you will now, as a lot of that team has now moved on. Our focus is getting promotion. I've watched you train, and I thank you for your commitment, as you have realized our focus is on speed and stamina. If you are here, it is because you have quickness. Every player here is faster than the starting eleven last year – even the goalies! Everyone gets paid the same now too, everyone gets a bonus on winning – there are no personal bonuses – I want you all to know that there are no individual deals." It sounded like a great egalitarian moment.

Roy continued:

"We have created a little excitement in the town with our home-grown teammates – you might have noticed! So, we thank them, and we need them for this club to be here next year, so we need to keep this energy going. I will be brutally honest with you. I have enough to pay you for this season, but without promotion and full stands, there are no more funds for next year. So, as you sit here, look around you; you are playing for each other and the future of The Club. 1866 this club was founded; let's not see it end on our watch. In a moment I will introduce you to our new coach – but I made a decision a while ago that I think you should be aware of."

Still maintaining the gravitas of history, he transitioned into the present. "We are one squad but two distinct teams. There are thirty of you – that's all I can afford – two teams of fifteen. One group will play all league matches, the other will play all cup matches. I have no plans to mix you up. I expect you both to have long and successful seasons. To preserve our league players, we can't afford to have wear and tear injuries by them playing cup games; it is, in my opinion, unnecessary. Our premise is unique – you will train the same. To you newcomers and non-league players, I ask you this – win the FA Cup. This club nearly did it once. For God's sake, if Leicester can win the Premier League at those odds – surely, we can bring home the FA Cup. Now I want to bring in our coach who is going to get us there: Lindsey Kuzmeski!"

There was polite applause, the loudest mostly from plimsolls, Mary-Janes, and flip-flops. Players, however, were unsure of a woman head coach – it fit with the novelty and circus that had become the modus operandi of The Club in recent weeks.

Lindsey strode in like she'd dismounted Pocahontas' horse – red curls bouncing with each trot, sporting her Northwestern University coaching attire.

"I brought Lindsey here to run you into the ground. Don't let the red hair fool you; she's brutal! This lady is the most aspiring coach in women's college soccer. We are fortunate she said yes. This is a person who as a player broke five players' legs – two of whom were on her own team! This player covered more of the field than the irrigation system! She was ubiquitous as a player and intimidated me as her referee. I'm intimidated by her even as we stand here today! I give you the most frightening competitor I have ever watched play the game – Lindsey Kuzmeski."

"Thank you for that – now let's get to work." She said nothing more. And no voices were raised; she had startled them by exiting the men's stalls having damaged them the way Nelson's cannon would have. Most had thought it was a sporty janitor contaminating the air, hence no one could speak or wanted to take another unnecessary breath. They trotted after her banking on the fact that her healthy vegetarian diet had satisfied its final day's journey.

Mary Janes galloped after her – tablet in hand. "Wait up – Wait up! We have to take the bus to St. Andrews School today!"

"Which way is it?" she called back over the bobbing heads and shoulders, her swinging red curls waving the players on hard through third base.

Mary Janes yelled back with her remaining breaths, remembering that yoga is not the best for stamina. "Take a left out of the car park, and it's up the bypass about six miles."

Lindsey's fading voice said, "Have the bus meet us there in thirty minutes."

Between the accent, the swift exodus, and the pep in Lindsey's breath, Mary Janes thought she said thirty minutes. But that was ridiculous; no one runs five-minute miles for six of them. Then she stopped in her tracks and those of the thirty or so athletes in front of her. St. Andrews was all up-hill from here. *Maybe thirty minutes is more than a half-hour in America!* she thought.

She turned to Zach, clashing tablets.

"Idiot, not so close! Tell Bob the driver to put the kettle on; we aren't gonna be needing the bus for a few!"

"Should we have him follow them, just in case?"

"I'm not that brave, Zachy my boy. Cup of tea, a hobnob, and a safe distance from the Yank, that's what I'm thinking! She's a terrifying thing – one thing's for sure; they'll be scared to come off the pitch!"

"One, two, three lumps for me!"

"And six miles for them!"

"Let's get Bob."

CHAPTER 44

"Harry Gration here at St. Andrews Community School; still awaiting the bus to arrive and the training session to begin. Chesterfield Football Club's opening salvo here at St. Andrews but so far, a no show – a little like last year's performance!"

"Where are they, Julia? They're twenty minutes late – this is embarrashing!"

"I'm sorry, John, what did you say?"

"They're late!"

"No, after that – did you say 'embarrashing'? What have you got in your mouth?"

"It's a plum-shtone, if you musht ashk!"

"Why, John, why? Why a plum-stone in your mouth?"

"I want to shound posh for the televisshon – my mother might be watching."

"I'm going to talk to Harry – I suggest you spit that out or stick in your thumb and pull it out!"

"Mr. Gration – so nice to see you and your crew at our school. You have been so kind to my father and The Club; we all appreciate your support."

"Our pleasure – we love a 'feel-good' story."

"And a comeback story, Mr. Gration!"

"We'll see about that, won't we – I'm a Hull City fan myself."

"So, you can appreciate what my dad is trying to do, then?"

"Well, he certainly has a unique way of keeping up the fan base. Let's hope it translates to points! Unfortunately, we don't seem to have a team to report on and our OB team has to leave shortly to report on sheep that followed each other down a manhole earlier today in Grimsby."

John awkwardly stepped between them. "Julia, shorry for interrupting – Looksh like the team hash arrived!" The cameraman spun around from Harry to catch sight of the team bobbing up the hill, like apples storming the ramparts. "Whosh that in front?" John continued inaudibly.

"I haven't the faintest idea, John, but she's leading them at a fair clip." The cameraman closed in on the red mane charging up the hill like a shot from *Braveheart.*

Lindsey blustered in through the school gates "This St. Andrews? Then we've come to take her over." It was all in stride; no chat with Harry, and the team marched wearily behind their horseless leader. Harry missed his interview but instead got a tagline for the next promo! The schoolchildren cheered them in through the gates and lined the route to the sports fields. No time for autographs; Lindsey was all business, serious, like recapturing her country serious. She would lead from the front using her steel-blue eyes to machete her opponents.

Harry's cameraman tightened his close-up, adding ten pounds of ferocity; she had been given mission impossible. Take a washed-up club, clouded in controversy, stir in some drama, squirt on some frothy hoopla, sprinkle local wannabes into the mix and have the public swallow it. If this was a circus, then the headline was the tigress running it. The cameraman inadvertently backed out the shot, bayoneted by Lindsey's steely stare. Even as a Sheffield supporter, the cameraman wanted to believe—wanted to believe in this unlikely feline.

"Miss Kuzmeski, can I get an interview? Can we have a moment?" Harry of Hull City wanted in – he needed to visit with the ringleader. He followed her down to the fields as fast as Clarks loafers would allow!

A sabered look swung back at him. "I will be available later! For now, we train." The panting, coughing, bleeding pack of footballers organized themselves around her. Lindsey's leadership by example was her whip – keep up or be gone. The cheers of the schooyard faded with Harry's disappointment. It was back to class for the players and schoolchildren. Harry looked on and spoke just loud enough for him to hear: "There's a dark side to every fairytale; she might be just dark enough to pull this off."

"What, boss?" Ben was capping his lens, not catching Harry's meandering thoughts.

"We are gonna keep an eye on that one, Ben; there's a story there and I know it. And we'll be the first to show it."

"Serial killer, if you ask me! I jacked me ankle stepping back from her glare into the camera!"

"Let's hope so eh?" Harry simply winked. "Grimsby it is then, Ben – a story on sheep; you follow me!" Both eyes winked this time.

As the excitement of the school died down the way a Snickers bar loses its prowess after an hour or so, depressions of sadness came like congregating isobars over parts of the town. In various classrooms, heavy thoughts led heavy hearts.

Robbie, Roy, Joan, and Wayne's wife Michelle all sat at their desks with heavy pens in hand:

When the time had come to see the Town train and welcome them to the school, Robbie had lost heart. Homework, biology beckoned still from his week in Ireland; photo-op gave way to photosynthesis. What was the point of any of it? A heavy heart clouds the eyes with premature cataracts. Quiet darkness settled on his page, as others played out their dreams on his football fields to his cheering friends. *That should have been me, that should have been me. I wish I were a plant and I could just switch off that light.*

"My dearest Joan," it said beneath the Chesterfield Logo – this would be his return address, at least for now. "There isn't a day, or a moment in that day when I don't think about you." *Scratch that*, and Roy balled up the paper, pushed his chair back from the rented desk, and drop-kicked another wad of letterhead to the waste basket nestled in the room's corner—supposedly harder to miss that way. The paper snowballs scattered around like acorns of thought. The pen in Roy's hand started to look back in disdain at the paucity of imagination it was forced to write, grateful that each worded sheet had been tossed away. The pen, Roy's Papermate, had tackled so many crosswords over the years—why couldn't he find the right words today, why couldn't he uncross his words today? The Papermate's hearts were breaking for him. "Chew me a little," sighed the pen. "That's helped in the past; or lodge me behind your ear; maybe I can whisper the words you need. Over fifty crossword 'words' a day, surely you can find some happy ones for us to share with Joan." The pen began to sweat, anxious that it was losing its touch. "Come on, Roy—you can find the words. I know you can." And then the pen lay down obliquely on the page like a one-handed clock.

The Crayola note read "Wayne, we need milk, diapers, bread, formula, raspberry jam, arse-cream, tea, Bonjella and a lawyer." *All the usual stuff*, she thought. The acid in her mouth, from holding her thoughts in, had created crotchety canker sores. Smiling through the pain, she looked at the words alternating in colors, leaving the last one and the full-stop in red. The note smelled inviting, looked inviting, colorful. She taped it to the kettle; he'd be sure to see it there. The baby was already at her aunt's, away from the Crayola chaos she was about to cause. She had juggled the crayons with her thoughts for days upon days of training – his being gone for long runs, long hours, long everything. And now it was long in her tooth. "They don't taste too bad, the green ones slightly citrusy – you could never find a pen or a paycheck in this house." Instructed by the purple dinosaur, she had cleaned up as best she could. She had juggled baby food jars and bath toys and had decided that it was going to be less miserable to be an ex-wife than a wife. Her mum would be a better spouse – and Wayne could continue to be the dad, no less hands-on than today. As she signed it, the Blue Ocean crayon broke, leaving a clump of itself and herself mid- surname.

As a recovering Methodist, Joan had found it harder to put pen to paper but easier to make friends. She took the stack of Disney World post cards – separated the Epcot ones – and filtered through them. "Found it – there you are!" a smiling red-faced Beefeater beamed a Disney World welcome amidst the backdrop of the plastic Disney-made Red Lion Pub. She'd even had a Pimms there – pretending with the punters it was Wimbledon fortnight. Yes, this was definitely the card she was going to send Roy. Now what to say? "A brief intro about the weather should suffice." She began to dictate her note aloud to the Beefeater on the front, flipping it back and forth, trying to glean inspiration from him. It was always sunny in Disney World – pointless telling him that – "everyone happy here"—pointless telling him that, too. She wasn't happy, but the Pimms made it so, at least at first. She tossed the card with the pointless words on it, into the garbage can's vicinity. She found another – she was all out of Epcot ones – "Shamu!" she yelled. "Perfect!" She wrote on the back "JOAN," stamped it, looked back at the black and white orca – one of them would be dead this time next year. "There," she said, and stood the card on her Disney World desk with Shamu looking happy. Joan, not being able to stand, wasted no time and collected the dozen or so discarded cards from around the wastebasket, and shuffled them back into a tidy pile. "I'll stick them to the fridge when I get home. No one will notice they had been written on – besides, fridges are illiterate; we all know that!" The Beefeater smiled stoically back at her. "Mother's ruin, my arse!" and she finished her glass. The backward indentations looking up past the Beefeater's grin on the card in her hand: "naoJ evoL."

CHAPTER 45

"Hold on, Juey; I have to take this." I left the corner table of Joplins. It had become our de facto family conference room. "Hey, Billy—how are you doing? How's Emma?" I checked my wrist where my watch used to be. "You're up early, kid – does your mum know?"

"No, Dad – I just, well, couldn't sleep. I had a dream. A nightmare really. So, I just needed to call and to know you're okay?"

"Yes, son, alive and kicking!" I channeled the Simple Minds tune to him and continued to move from the dark, illegally smoky café to the rain-polished medieval cobbles of the marketplace outside.

"I dreamt you were dead, Dad, and I couldn't breathe." I could hear the tears chewing up his face.

"I'm fine, Billy, fine. I know I've been gone a while, but everything will be alright when I get back, I promise."

"It won't be fine, Dad, because one day you'll be dead, and I don't know what I'll do without you."

How do you answer that? How do you tackle that without tackling him and hugging the thought right out of him? I looked up and the rain filled my eyeballs with tears; I looked down at the history of cobbles weathered, worn, withstanding the footsteps of generations, yet eventually wearing down like soap.

"I love you, Billy." My tears joined the confluence of raindrops. "did you finish the Jumble yesterday?"

"Yes, but barely." Not swallowing golf balls was becoming a family talent.

"Miss you, son. Give my love to Emm - CLUM!" Clum is about all you can say when the Titleists are backing up into your throat. I could roll them out of my mouth like a bloody magician.

"Forgot your umbrella then?" Zoe again rolled her eyes at my stupidity. Unless there was vinegar in the rain, there was no need to ask how the call had gone; she could see it all in the redness of my eyes. Parenting pulls the soul right through your eyeballs.

"To business, then." Zoe looked over at Ju.

"Dad's tests came back, and they are not good."

"They told Dad that they're fine. It's the placebo effect; they need him to keep a positive attitude."

There was more, but the Titleist hairballs filled all our throats like baskets at the driving range – there was no room for words.

One, two, Pro V.

CHAPTER 46

"Hey, Roy! Do you have a minute?" Brian breezed in as though he had just shucked half a dozen teeth. He loved the playful resistance of the tooth and its roots.

Looking up from the correspondence in his hand, Roy said, "Sure, Brian; for you, always."

"You okay, Roy?"

"Had better days Brian."

"Something in the ...mail?" Brian nodded looking at Roy's hands. "Mind my asking?"

"No, of course not, Brian. I've had better news, better days."

A door closed behind Wayne. "Baby, I'm home!" It was loud enough to be heard downstairs but quiet enough not to wake a sleeping baby upstairs. There would be no fear of that. He tried again:

"Daddy's home," he repeated as he dropped his kit bag in the dust of the unfinished foyer and walked from room to room like a burglar robbing his own house. The house was empty like the burglar had already been and then tidied up after himself."Must be out walking? Teatime." He had a natural way of talking to himself which he carried through to the kitchen. From across the kitchen table he saw the note stuck to the kettle: a note on familiar paper, in familiar handwriting in familiar crayons. Must be "out walking" is what he expected to read. Though everything about it seemed familiar, the words did not—in particular, her botched signature. Wayne read over the words, hoping that his family had been kidnapped and that all he would have to do is pay a ransom for their return. But it was worse, much worse. The decision-maker had decided for all of them that his being less in their lives was the best option for the majority, including the silent minority.

After staring at the kettle and the note repeatedly, he decided:

"Coffee it is, then." He smiled at the Keurig and left the note on the kettle and went upstairs. He brushed against the drywall picking up dust on his arms. "I'll get that painted ...tomorrow," as he dragged his heavy legs and heart up the narrow winding staircase. The bathtub knobs squealed as he turned them fully open. "WD40 or Vaseline should fix that," but the bright yellow duck just smiled, knowing it would never get done, smiling as if he actually understood. Rubber ducks have seen a lot of our private lives and know us intimately. Their inability to speak is priceless – we only have to imagine what they'd say.

"I saw you on television today, John! You didn't tell me you were going to be on television."

"Yes, Mother, I don't tell you everything."

"Why not, why don't you tell me everything?" John's mother loved to know everything about him, his life. She wanted to know everything; it took her mind off the bed sores, until her mind took itself off them and everything else.

"I thought I did tell you, Mother?" His was a heavy sigh. "So much going on at school; I thought that I must have told you. Funny how we omit the big stuff!"

"I don't find it funny at all – like that *Family Feud* – such stupid people!"

"I'm sorry, Mother. I'll change the channel. You must have bumped the zapper."

"I haven't bumped Frank Zapper!" She was quite lucid in an unrelated way.

John marched on through the routine of his life.

"Would you like tea, Mother?"

"It's not tea, darling, it's dinner. Dinner-time is in the evening; not like those commoners who have 'dinner' at lunch-time."

"Yes, Mother – I made a quiche, bacon and spinach. Would you like some?"

"Oh, lovely, that's my favorite!"

John knew it. He had bought Marks and Spencer's quiche for years now. He had given up on trying to offer her anything different. Never sure who he was going to come home to this seemed to be the one thing they all agreed on. Bacon and spinach quiche. Not without much trial and error, mind. So much food had hit the wall and floor over the years that the house looked like a blender with the lid removed.

"John, your dad's staring again!"

"I'll talk to him, Mother." Dad's picture sat above the mantel next to his urn. John turned the photo around to face the wall. The cleaners would face him the right way tomorrow. John and his mother enjoyed their quiche and *Family Feud.*

"I saw you on television today, John! Why didn't you tell me you were going to be on television?"

"Well, we always seem to forget the big things, Mother; I'm thinking we must have already shared them." A lot of ingredients can go into making a quiche; that's what makes it interesting.

Robbie heard the cheers of his classmates every morning as they welcomed Town to school; even the uncool mascot Chester was greeted warmly, though scorned behind his back. Robbie chose to stay in his classroom, claiming it was part of his punishment as well as the detentions. It wasn't – the churning loss of not being able to try out ground his innards and boiled them up. Robbie chose to remain at his desk, his grandfather's bayonet hidden beneath his history books, football boots, and shin guards. It had been there since their World War Two "show and tell." He couldn't and wouldn't take this disappointment any longer, and by the end of the day someone would regret their actions. Someone would realize that this punishment just wasn't fair, that it wasn't just. They could keep their parades, banners, and vuvuzelas. By the end of today, everyone would know his name. "Coming, ready or not," he whispered to himself, lifting the lid of his desk.

The team had responded well to the training; everyone was fitter than she had expected, especially the first team of last year's pros. What she hadn't anticipated was the assortment of characters that made up the bag of liquorice allsorts. A carnival of characters, so diverse in history and cultures that it made her homeland USA seem a kind of bland soup. She understood the Romanians better than she did the locals, who spoke with coded dialect. At least the Romanians' English came across with the perfection of someone learning it anew, what little of it there was—not the bastardized obscurity of a deaf village. Corners of this town sliced up the language as butchers might trim the fat, only these villagers kept the fat, keeping parts of words that could have been let go and creating a sloppy stew of gobbledygook. A town completely separated by a common yet foreign language.

Then there were the speech impediments.

Lindsey held up training boards that the locals thought were for the Romanians, but in truth she wasn't sure the "Townites" fully understood. If nothing else, this team would be quick. Yet this allotment of vegetables she would have trim enough for a julienne salad. Lindsey was born happy and angry. Thrilled to be born, disturbed that it would end. So it was with that inner conflict that determined how she approached everyone in her life. She was excited by her life in the Roman-founded Chesterfield, with its medieval relics and tongue. The beauty of it, lying upon a plateau, and at the same time surrounded by hiking hills—she loved all of that; how could you not? She was coaching a football team that was as old as Chicago where she grew up. But this team of last season's rejects, hangers-on and lottery winners was a smorgasbord – like making a meal on the last day of vacation. All bought and chosen, but still leftovers. The last slice of turkey in a hot-dog bun with ranch dressing. Excited you still have one last day of vacation, excited you still have something to eat, but emptying the fridge this way was one step closer to packing up and going home.

In the same way, she hated the man who had fired her and she loved the man who hired her. She was here to help Roy. You never know the impact a fleeting person can have in your life. *I have to go – it was Roy who showed me the spinning 360 move, my signature move, the one people knew was coming but could never stop without fouling or without injuring themselves. We won freekick after freekick, goal after goal because of it. He'd showed me at my sister's birthday party. Everyone was in the back yard or around the pool drinking, munching, talking, celebrating, singing, presents, and fussing. I was out under the basketball hoop when Roy, who really didn't know anyone, came to the front of the house; he heard the familiar thunk of a soccer ball hitting the garage door. It took him back and me forward.*"

"So, what are you doing out here kid?" Roy used his telephone voice to be best understood in this foreign land. Everyone who met him said:

"You have an accent – where are you from?" Lindsey had asked. He never heard the accent either here in Chicago or at home.

"Do I?: he paused. "Need a goal-keeper?" he asked.

Lindsey beamed; an adult was actually interested in "her soccer." He was curious that a girl played "football."

"Do I ever – I'm Lindsey!"

"And I'm Roy, Adam's dad. Pleased to meet you. I'm not going to need goal-keeping gloves, am I?"

"You might!" and Lindsey took some paces back and fired off shot after shot. Often there was the echo of the same old "thunk" against the garage door, but every now and then Roy was able to get a hand, foot, or shoulder to some of her shots.

"You're pretty good," said Lindsey with surprise.

"Thank you – I've been practicing!" he smiled back at her, thinking, *For about fifty years I have.*

"Practicing? Are you on a team?" She had the optimism of a child who knows nothing of the effects of age.

He laughed gently, more like a hearty smile that spoke a truth to his own soul than an answer to her question.

"The only way I'll be on a team is if I buy it!"

"Are you rich then, Roy?" again with the energy of a child who's known only positivity.

"My hands are stinging a bit; can you show me some moves?"

"What?" She didn't break through his telephone accent.

"Do you have any moves?" His telephone voice ground out a little slower. She caught the word "moves" and assumed he'd asked about them. She really didn't know about England being the birthplace of her "soccer"--she just knew about her birthplace and her traveling team with a Korean coach. Everyone older than her assumed the English knew a lot about soccer because of its history. She neither knew nor cared and was only interested in the older man standing in front of her showing her a knowledgeable interest. She was the center of attention on her team and the baby of the family, but today was her sister Laura's day. Suddenly she was the center of attention again.

"Moves!" she cheered. "Sure! I've got moves!" Lindsey grabbed the ball and began dribbling; her sixth-grade frame, slight and strong, copper curls bouncing like copper coils! She weaved in and out of imaginary defenders, looped the ball over her foot, brought it back with toe and sole working an imaginary foot yo-yo.

"You're good! Really very good!" Roy was stunned – "football" was a girl's sport in America? He couldn't help thinking back that it was barely a boys' sport in his school when he was her age.

She smiled up at him this slightly greying Englishman – he made a great audience. A knowledgeable audience like a season ticket holder to the opera.

"Have you ever tried this one?" He picked up the ball. She parked herself, a little surprised by him taking her ball. "You start there – you be the defender; I'll be the 'left-winger.'" She smiled at the man with her ball. She didn't understand a word of what he was saying. She understood "left-winger" but didn't know what it meant. He put her ball at his feet. He didn't even turn his nose up at the fact that it was pink. Footballs are a universal code of love, no matter what the color. The older man started to jog then sprint in her direction – she wasn't sure what to do until he got closer and her instincts kicked in; she wanted her pink ball back. He ran full speed at her as though he might go right through her. Right before her, he spun away, turned his back on her, then was gone around her, pink ball and all. Her jaw dropped.

"Do it again—that was amazing!"

So, he did it over and over. "I call it the 'around the world' move. Or a 'panic 360' when I get wrong! Would you like me to show you how to do it?"

She understood that much. "Yes, yes—that was awesome!"

She missed cake and presents and singing and found a friend.

"High five!" She reached up her palm to vacant air. "You hit my hand with yours," she said, seeing his blank stare as her cue. They slapped.

Lindsey owed Roy, and now he owned the team. Lindsey was coaching his team halfway around the world.

One, two, three-sixty.

CHAPTER 47

In Romania, a football team wonders where half of it went. But few are left wondering for long. The curse of European mobility has taken more eligible and able men than Ceausescu did from this village. The communists had lived up to their promise of work. If you survived their death squads and chambers of horrors, you at least had a job. Freedom in Romania was a tasty thing – if you could afford to eat. The pretend communist economy fueled on fear finally met its end with the gunshots ringing in the ears of Nikolae and Elena on Christmas Day 1989. Where Ceausescu bulldozed villages, the European Union left the buildings as open as the borders. The healthy fled the Romanian open prison faster than a geriatric on day-release from an old people's home.

The promise of work, and being able to support their large extended families, extended further beyond Romania's capabilities. For many, this offer also meant an escape from their responsibilities. Generations of the untrusting youth switched colors, preferring unelected socialism to their own revolution. Open borders are death to a nation's pride. The communists' failing was to close borders when in fact they should have opened them – modern-day Brussels and its flatulent socialism – opened them and the brave fled to prosperous nations who had long given up on having children. Britain, France, and Germany at least had Ceausescu to thank for that. Western Europe has been emptied by unwanted children. And Chesterfield Town had Tesco to thank for its talented midfielders. In today's game, there is no limit to how many foreigners can play on your team and no limit to how many foreigners can play in your country. If you ate from a can today, thank a foreigner, because without them your shelves would be empty, and you'd be digging around in a warehouse trying to find your soup.

Vasily was their leader – they were all from the streets of Bucharest, a bald tennis ball their skill-maker. It was easy to pocket and carry through the sewers where they lived. Ceausescu had ordered its women to have five children – he understood the demographics of economics. A later generation may benefit from their demand, but families could not afford the demands of so many mouths. Ceausescu had bulldozed their home and their church to build his "House of the People" in an attempt to build the largest building ever. It came in second, as did the people whom it dislocated. Vasily learned English from his older sister Kristina. It was their mother who remembered life before the bulldozers and sewer children. Carla, their mother, had rescued a Bible and hymnal from the church. In its day it had many tourists, so Bibles were laid out for them. Carla read to her children from both Bibles – they were free. Kristina, old beyond her years, worked with Vasily on his Bible studies in between the street matches. Carla and Ille survived the razing of their city to raise their children in prison-like blocks modeled on the Communist-Korean model. Kristina hated their new home almost as much as soccer, which had taken her baby brother Vasily from her.

Vasily became a player of the streets; his friends Mihai, Marius, Costica and Ionut divided up their team roles. They were, in her mind, "stupid," not like her brother. They were stupid enough to make the reserve team of Rapid Bucharest FC. Stupid enough they could have perhaps played for their country. But open borders took them all from her. Bucharest Rapid's bankruptcy left them skill-less and unemployable, too healthy for begging and too stupid for—well, anything that wasn't already being done by the less talented. With nothing to hold them, and their English-speaking friend Vasily leading them, they all headed west. They were a unit. Their journey took them to Ostend where they would crew and collect mussels; rebuild sea walls, roads, mix concrete until their backs grew solid. Vasily negotiated the work and they all shared in the spoils. There was a roof and food until the summer was over and it was time to move on.

Britain with its miles of coastline, they had heard needed mussel men. A ready-made crew can be helpful when it's not intimidating. Scotland would be better suited to their skills. Their train passage was expensive – "outrageous," Vasily complained. They moved around the trains constantly so as to not get caught – but a sharp-eyed new conductor at Derby station noticed they had paid only as far as Northampton. They would be escorted off at the next station. And that is how they came to be in Chesterfield.

Tesco's security watching CCTV saw night after night how adept these young hooligans were at removing the cans from shelves. Not always the same pairs, but always the same aisles. Canned fruit and vegetables – Del Monte cans. Not understanding English, the pictures on the cans were clear to the foreigners. Not knowing when they would eat next, cans were the best option. Security didn't pick it up at first. They were alerted initially by the cleaners who had noticed soap and paper towels and toilet paper missing. Not far from the train-line and its many bridges, Tesco – a supersized version of it stood like a beacon of hope across the tracks, beyond the six-lane bypass. It was chosen as a warm place to dry off; huge enough that they would blend into a crowd, it had food, clothing, backpacks, and a spotless, well-stocked bathroom! Like ants they would migrate through each aisle, stopping to load up baskets they had no intention of leaving with. After the first day, now clean and fed, they chose to go in three at a time. If three men together was always suspicious, five was a crime ring. Vasily went every time – he was their leader and spoke the native language. Well, English without the dialects of Chesterfield, and thereby a "foreigner" by distinction. They marked their route, divided themselves, even dawdled, pretended to read the magazines and newspapers. For a week, the bathrooms were cleared out. Daily they returned to the bridge, the bridge just down from the train station, the one that was broad enough to extend over both the tracks and the canal. It wasn't so bad, and it didn't smell like a Bucharest sewer. A youth, who looked like he lived there, would play football with them every night. The bridge was a neighborhood. It really wasn't so bad except the youth was a Liverpool fan.

Security ruled out the Polish cleaners who had brought the disappearing supplies to their attention, fearing that they themselves would be accused. When you grow up on an island, you have a tendency to blame the foreigner for everything. When you grow up in communism, you never want to be accused of anything; honesty was a good policy – snitching was a safer one. CCTV didn't extend into the bathrooms themselves. But after a few days – a routine of backpacked young men started to emerge; they would enter and leave around the same time every morning. Nature's call had called them out. The security team then began to trail them around the store. They were good – they went in opposite directions. Meandered and weaved like pros. Left at different times. Placed full baskets in the middle of clothes racks so as not to be seen. Left with only what they could put handily in the newly acquired coats and backpacks. What they weren't aware of was that the security team operated for the whole building and followed them to their teammates waiting out of the rain in the undercover car park. Like a secret shopper – even the car park was under cover. By the end of the week, security had figured out that they all needed a bathroom break around the same time each day. Even their week-long unkempt beards couldn't disguise their routine. The boys from the Bucharest sewers enjoyed and were undone by luxury-soft Andrex.

The SWAT team, as they called themselves – "Security With Attitude"--brought the delinquent foreigners to the Tesco manager's office. This was protocol: return the criminal to the scene of the crime – break down that shoplifting is a crime – personalize it in the manager's office; let them know it's a crime against everyone -"Theft equals higher costs for all," read the poster above with its pathetic-looking family. Cost is not usually a factor for a thief. The poster intended to humanize a multi-national corporation with feelings; those same feelings seemed to be absent when their presence shut down Green's grocer on "Whit moor." Green's had been there since before the coal was even mined in this town, and there long after the pits had been closed down. Tescos offered the wives of the unemployed miners a job. Something Green's could never do. The miners, the miners' wives took their custom where they could get a "family discount." After selling their furniture, Green's realized that a consignment shop was their best future, and still it is today.

The manager's door also had a lock. The SWAT team was inside and out, like Russian mafia waiting for the boss. Mr. Pilkington eventually showed up. He hated, more than anything, these shoplifters—not because of the crime against humanity, but because he hated conflict. His left hand took care of his comb-over before he went in. The sweat pool reached from his armpits to his belt. Mr. Pilkington looked more like the criminal than Vasily and his international band of thieves, and they took note.

"Mr. Pilkington, we have rounded up these hooligans and thieves," declared the SWAT leader, Peter. He'd wanted to be in the RAF, but his glasses were sponsored by Coke.

"Thank you, Peter. Oh, you have done well." Mr. Pilkington dug deep into his left pocket, then his right, he pulled out a crumpled and used monogrammed handkerchief. He mopped his brow, as now he had to lead the meeting – a meeting filled with expectation of justice and punishment. The course on Criminal Studies he had taken was months ago, and he had sweated through those too. The old hanky left a crusty trail of crumbs on his drier brow.

"Now – the police will be here shortly." This was the first line of his course. Let them know the cavalry is coming – this would be a good time to confess – reduce your sentence.

"Peter, would you show them the evidence you have before you." Like a judge on his first day, Mr. Pilkington pointed to the telly. Four of the five hadn't understood a word until the telly came to life. Vasily translated quickly.

"Shut up, you!" Peter pointed at Vasily with a laser pointer, intimidated by the gang in front of him. "Look at the monitor!"...which they all knew to be a telly. When a telly is on, you don't need to be told to look at it. Not men, at least. You just do. It's like a car crash; it's impossible to look away.

After ten minutes of the CCTV – black and white – some images looked confusing, like an ultrasound. The cavalry hadn't come yet. The crumbs from Mr. Pilkington's forehead had become moist—gluey, in fact.

Vasily could clearly see his friends and himself caught in the act. The four stared at the poster of the nice family on the wall after the telly was turned off. They didn't know what it said, but Marius thought the mum was a MILF. The Romanians looked neither guilty nor innocent to Mr. Pilkington—just unshaven. What he then noticed in the video was that the Romanians would actually straighten the cans, logo out. They were seen to be picking up knocked-over cereal boxes, folding sweaters left hanging on the shirt rails and tucking them back on their appropriate shelves. They set aside over-ripe fruit, bringing the better produce to the front. In fact, every aisle they left neater than when they had found it, excepting of course what they had taken. Mr. Pilkington couldn't believe it.

"Peter, take me to the toilets!"

"Excuse me, sir?"

"You heard me! Follow me to the toilets!"

Vasily translated as the two men left – all of them burst out laughing, which unnerved the remaining SWAT team.

Peter and Mr. Pilkington entered the men's toilet together. Someone was going number two.

"Look, Peter; not five minutes ago two of them were in here – it's spotless."

The man behind the door tried to quiet his gases.

"Sorry, gents – you don't happen to have any toilet paper? Only this one seems to be out!"

"Didn't your parents ever tell you to look before you leap?"

"Yes, but...."

"Well, this is what she meant!" Mr. Pilkington and Peter left and went next door.

"Peter, check to see if there is anyone in there first." Mr. Pilkington pointed to the ladies' toilet.

Peter tapped his laser pointer before calling out:

"Anyone in there? It's security!" Peter sounded official. No answer came, and the two of them marched in. Water everywhere. Not like a flood, but splashes on the mirrors, watery trails from the sinks to the hand towels, spare toilet paper sitting on the sink counter, spongelike and warped, having sat in the spills for a while.

"You could wash not dry your arse on that, Peter! Look at the state of this place! It's a disgrace!"

"You should sack them cleaners, Mr. Pilkington!"

"No, what I'm saying is that these flipping foreigners," and Mr. Pilkington flustered around for words. "These flipping foreign thieves have more respect than our regular customers! They leave everything nicer than when they found it! There might be less of it, but these are not your typical criminal, Peter. These are criminals with standards!" Mr. Pilkington stood outside the ladies', bouncing the half-sodden toilet roll in his hand, not knowing what to do next.

He heard mutterings from the men's room. Mr. Pilkington entered dropped the half-soaked toilet paper to the "leaper" behind the toilet door. It slapped like a wet puppet in the leaper's hand.

"What the 'ell am I supposed to do wi' that then?"

"Wash or dry; it's up to you!" and Mr. Pilkington left and marched with Peter back to his office.

When the door opened, the Romanians had stopped laughing and had emptied their backpacks on to the table. Mr. Pilkington could see the cans of fruit and vegetables stacked neatly on his desk.

"Do you speak English?" Mr. Pilkington addressed the group as if he were about to address POW's.

Vasily, the only one to understand, nodded – the others just stared at Mr. Pilkington – well, Marius stared at Mr. Pilkington a little, but the MILF over his right shoulder was something of a distraction.

Vasily translated – the cavalry was not going to take them away. The Romanians nodded humbly. They were in fact going to spend the next week working their fine and punishment off by stacking the shelves. They would work round the clock. They could figure it out for themselves who would do the work. At the end of the week if Mr. Pilkington was satisfied, he would hire them, part-time at first; if not, he would send their photos and the film to the police.

"I'll have me eye on them every step of the way, Mr. Pilkington." Peter stared firmly, looking more like Paddington bear than a Russian bear.

"We will feed you, so you need not take from us. We are, after all, a civilized country," Mr. Pilkington wiped his brow once more, smearing the now liquified snot across his forehead.

Mr. Pilkington had also done a course on Maslow's theory of human needs. He would feed them and respect them and expect as much in return.

Vasliy explained to his teammates how they would work off their punishment rather than be hauled off to jail. CCTV continued to watch them and the manager saw how eager his Romanian team was – the threat of jail can be a great motivator. The fear of starvation and being unseen, unimportant is just as vital. Mr. Pilkington knew that. Peter didn't and kept his security cameras on them at all times.

But in the end, it turned out they were just as good a team on the right side of the law as the wrong side, and the manager hired them anyway.

Rapid's loss was Chesterfield's gain. Yin and yang, right? Maybe not for the Romanians, who went from one bankrupt club to another—well, almost bankrupt at any rate. With Chesterfield, the young men from Bucharest felt like they had won the lottery. They trained hard under the lady American coach: "She could have been a Ceausescu police-woman!" Costica laughed as they ran through town and sprinted hills meant only for goats. "Then she needs to be behind us if she wants us to run faster!" laughed Ionut. The friends had always been one step away from running from the law. Vasily and Marius' fathers had been caught up in the protests. That was how Carla had told it to Kristina and Kristina had told it to Vasily. "The trouble with your life is that you constantly have to get used to people you love not being in it." That is how it was for Kristina now – her pupil and baby brother gone off, who knows where. She chose the sewer life after the police had wanted to interview her mother. Interviews take an unusually long time in Bucharest—they take a lifetime.

Lindsey's Romanian five could not be hurt physically or emotionally – they would not go down. Hours of suicide drills couldn't break them. She ran alongside them. How could they smoke a cigarette after the training? The rest of her team was puking, gagging, or fainting. Lindsey gave Costica that knowing and disapproving look – the one you give a child about to unwrap yet more Halloween candy for breakfast. "Settles stomach, settles nerves, we calm now." Vasily translated Costica's words.

The irony bested Lindsey – "Perhaps we should all smoke," and she smiled a big smoke ring "O." Vasily understood but did not translate. Just blew another ring around her. Silent movies survived for years – this team only needed months. The Romanians juggled balls with either foot while she spoke to them. The balls popped like headless snowmen from left foot to right; effortless puppets comfortable not resting, seemingly attached by the laces. Laces of borrowed football boots from the lost and found. Like the Romanians themselves, lost and found.

CHAPTER 48

That was how Robbie first saw the Romanians – smoking like children behind the bike sheds, on the school fields, no less! In plain sight. The headmaster would be furious! He hated students smoking more than he hated weapons on campus, he imagined. The school outside of classrooms echoed with silence; the hum and click of the oil-fueled radiators could be heard, the gerbil cage of corridors like lake piers facing into goldfish bowls of students. Robbie walked evenly, confidently; every teacher could see him from their classroom desk. The half-windowed door allowed the faculty to see in and out. Robbie was head prefect; it came with certain privileges. He was probably "taking a teacher's message" or asked to recover an item from the headmaster. No one could see what he was holding to his blind side. Kept it tight to his trousers as he marched purposefully toward the headmaster's office.

Outside, the plumes of cigarette smoke from the cluster of players reminded you of a time when Dema glass chimneys dictated the local skyline. An indicator of things being made, brought to life.

The headmaster fortuitously sat with his back to the door, giving Robbie time to strike. The halls were silent—too quiet to get away with it. Robbie heaved at the surprisingly weighty entry doors; the polished brass hinge glared at those below, who dared to exit by way of it. Robbie darted through. No bell sounded, the chilled fresh air smacked, the door snapped back, clipping Robbie's ankle, sending him tumbling to the curb, his hands covered in blood. Instinctively you know the difference in a cut versus a graze. This wound was deep. There's a syrupy redness to blood. In contrast, his hair was nothing like this; blood wasn't ginger, like his hair wasn't red. We don't bleed Lyle's golden syrup.

As much as he wanted to lie there and curl up, he knew he had to keep moving, get away from the building, toward the bike sheds, around the swimming pool with its opaque windows—a perfect escape route. He could be outed only by someone else in the corridor leading to art. He took his chance, wiping the blood straight down his black nylon blazer – his Irish dancing fists clenched tight to his sides. Dress shoes have no grip in a sprint and clip asphalt like fly swatters. After what seemed like a hundred flies had been crushed, he rested in the corner of the corrugated bike shed. Histories of students had proven this to be the one perfect hiding place from school eyes—a design flaw, most certainly. Robbie caught his breath and tears and blood, whipped off his jacket like a second-rate magician, undid his tie, unbuttoned his dress shirt; it was impossible to keep the blood from its crispness, as the blood dried it looked more like the color of his hair. His trousers had a nick in the knee from the fall – a clipped triangle similar to the "V" of an old can opener. His laces had come loose from his schoolyard sprint. They were easy to flip off—too easy, and one sailed over a chopper. *I can leave it – I'll come back for it later.* He slipped out of his torn grey trousers, rolled them into a bundle, wrapped all of his prefect uniform within the black, shiny blazer and tied it with the arms of the jacket. He could see them training in the far-off field, too far to be a distraction from any school window. Bundle in hand, he climbed the green, rust-chipped iron fence that ran the perimeter of the school's athletic fields. Landing on the other side, he pulled his socks tight over his shin guards, laced his boots, and ran to the small smokestacks. Robbie had run this distance every Tuesday and Thursday – this was his home field.

Warm-ups were over. The team was in the heart of six-yard passing drills with a breakout focus on shooting. Balls flew in rapid succession; the blade runner goalkeeper lunged alternately from left to right, his green jersey becoming more camouflaged with each ball he rescued from his goal mouth. Mud caked in the way ink splashes unwantedly from a fountain pen accident, indelibly.

Lindsey rounded the goal mouth and snagged her ball from the inside corner of the goal, looking down on a slightly deflated blade runner. Across the fields in the distance, toward the school and in front of the bike sheds, Lindsey could see a slight white figure moving at speed toward her, like a speck of white frosting on a green cake – moving quicker and quicker in their direction.

Getting closer, it looked like a skinny version of herself – like a lit match, all dressed in white with flaming red hair, leaping like someone threw whisky on it. The figure was carrying a shiny black and red object; the other arm pumped furiously, it too covered in red like a butcher's might be. Its shorts had claw marks down the side.

It continued at great speed in her direction. Lindsey wasn't sure if she should be running the other way. The team continued to train as the eagle fury swooped in on the group. The grace and speed impressed her beyond her concern. The closer he came she could see it, the home team logo and last year's sponsor. As it came running harder at her she stood her ground – his acne came into view – this was nothing more than a student, a school child, one covered in blood, hardly panting for one running so hard. He clutched the pile of clothes tightly, not wanting to lose them having come so far. She could see it wasn't a ball, and with no visible weapon, she stood her ground.

As if running on springs, he ran up to her, as she seemed sure of who she was, while he was unsure of her.

"I'm looking for the coach!"

"Why? Is she next on your murder list?"

"Sorry? What?" His heart was beating too fast for his mind to catch up to her comments.

"Where's the body?" Lindsey went on staring at the blood-soaked blazer and weeping wounds.

For a man who had flown into her presence with such speed and grace, he looked puzzled, as if he had been stunned by an invisible pane of glass.

"The blood." She pointed hard with her whistle. "Murdered someone, have you?"

"No, miss, I'm bunking off school. I cut me-sen when I fell out the main gate. Didn't even notice it. Have you seen the coach? I need to get a trial."

"Who are you looking for? What did you say you were doing?"

"I need to see the coach – I need for him to see me play – we missed our flight – so I missed the trial. I go to this school – I'm the best player on the team here."

"Arrogant too, eh?"

"Well miss, no miss, but I have to get this – it's me life – the coach'll see."

"Alright – but trials are already done – we've been training for weeks. I shouldn't really do this, but I hate to step in the way of a serial killer's goals. The coaches are over there." She said it softly, pointing to the Romanians.

"Thanks miss – you'll see – just watch me?"

"Like I don't have anything better to do?" she hissed at him. "You can leave your bundle with me!"

"Thanks, miss."

"Just leave it on the ground right there,"

And he was gone, the way teenagers leave a parent in charge of their stuff.

She spoke to herself as she waited for the comedy to happen:

"We're gonna have to change this 'miss' stuff – I'm ready to kick his ass when they send him back over here."

Robbie ran excitedly to the Romanians – distinctive by their long black hair, five o'clock shadows that started twelve hours earlier, and the obligatory cigarettes. Vasily was at the trainer, nursing a mild back strain. The four remaining sewer rats from Bucharest merely stood their ground, scratching the balls at their feet.

As Robbie addressed them, they backed away like he was wielding an axe in his still blood-stained hands. The ball remained tight to their feet, and the cigarettes tight in their lips as they stepped away from the youth. He was blurting and pleading with his voice and eyes – it was all so sincere and yet incomprehensible to them. They couldn't understand why the coach had sent the wretch over to them. Since the coach had pointed back at them when they looked up to her – they all offered him the stubs of their smokes. Coach wants us to welcome the fan in last year's kit?

"No, I don't smoke – I'm here to try out – I'm here because I can help the team!" His voice was pleading, and he repeated himself, thinking that an echo might help the information sink in.

With a nightingale's touch, he feathered the ball from Marius' foot – and was headed to goal. A flurry of embers hit the air like the first flurry of Vesuvius' conversation with Pompeii. The "murderer" had cat-burglar speed and quickness. With the pride of Rapid behind him in pursuit, he juked his way toward the practice goal.

"Raspunde! Raspunde!" yelled the Rapid group one after another.

To Robbie it sounded like "Rasputin." Either way, he wasn't stopping; he needed to show them his best stuff. Coming off his latest Irish dance competition, he was in the best shape of his life. There can be no room for excess when performing. The brutal repetition of learning to float whilst kicking, clicking heels with straight legs, forward at head height at full tilt, or rather full speed and perpendicular had taken months to perfect.

The practice ball hovered over his foot like a bubble on a pipe. Bladey was in goal, but taking a break from freekicks. Nicky and Wayne threw down their Powerade bottles at the sight of the birthday-candle figure kayaking toward them, sliding from left foot to right around imaginary defenders, zig-zagging to escape the alligators chasing him. Nicky and Wayne would be much more than imaginary. Robbie continued as if the volcano had erupted an entire police force and he was on the run.

"I'll 'ave 'im!" Nicky had seen the likes of him before. This was his team and his goal; everyone had taken ownership.

Nicky quick shuffled across the top of the eighteen—blue Powerade dribbled down his chin; his black-haired, apish forearm cleared it away. *I'll 'ave 'im*, he repeated in his head with the confidence and resilience of a king's archer. Robbie picked up speed as the Romanian's ball like Velcro stuck to Robbie's dancing feet. Each pace he took added deft pecks, tapping the ball into perfect line. Nicky's huge frame, impossible not to notice, hit his radar. Looking up, the ball in perfect timing with the rhythm of his feet, he could see the defender's intent. It was on. Robbie was glad of the challenge; it would give him the chance to show the foreign-sounding coaches what he was capable of. Their chasing him would give them a close-up of his skills. Further back, Lindsey stepped over the bloody bundle, followed Robbie's line, and strolled on to see if indeed the Romanians would beat up what was left of Robbie once he had run into the wall of her stopper, Nicky. He was quick. "I'll give him that," she said to herself, continuing toward the north end of the field. It would be greeted soon by Icelandic rains and their kiss of grit.

Nicky took off from his conversation and came at Robbie like a blue Transit van had run a stop sign without care or warning. Robbie's radar had picked up the hurtling Tardis, seeing the meteorite had broken away from its previous orbit. Irish dance teaches you to think quickly, meticulously about yourself, the position of yourself in the world around you. The eighteen-yard box was fast approaching, as fast as Robbie could make it approach. A disabled guy in a green pullover had been leaning on the post and had similarly broken away as if it to force a galactic collision with Robbie. Bladey had seen Nicky step aside from his brother; now goal-keeper and stopper would be properly aligned to wipe out the intruder. Their entire midfield had been left in the dust; parked like cigarette butt-ends in an ashtray, they had been, and now they were in pursuit of what looked like an animated version of these cigarettes. The Romanians were hunting it down like it was the biggest prize and last cigarette on earth. Nicky slid into position, as no one was gonna torch his battlements. The slip-jig in Robbie's head took over as Nicky slid in like an eighteen-wheeler screaming, braking, not quite out of control coming down Peaks Trail. Robbie floated up, raised by an invisible zephyr over Nicky's sliding trim but truck-like frame. Nicky could feel himself sliding under Robbie as a barge might glide under a footbridge. The flying birthday candle landed to Robbie's own slip-jig beat—just the goalie to beat, who he could see hurtling towards him.

"Time to go around the world!" Robbie – confident as an airline pilot, poised like a leaping ballerina, took one step—not to elevate this time, but to hesitate his speed momentarily. Bladey froze as the flying cigarette landed in front of him, the ball there but then not there. The cigarette spun before him, like it was on a child's music box.

"Around the world, baby!" Robbie had breath to yell as he effortlessly breezed by this meteor shower – Bladey still frozen, and Robbie tapped the ball home, having gone right around him. The ball barely crossed the line. But Robbie had crossed all of them.

"Take that, you wanker!" Wayne had taken about all he could take at home, and now his little brother had been humiliated by this punk. He slid in studs up, later than a snowplow in April, just as the ball crossed the line, crushing Robbie's ankles, which came up high over his head as the pitch on which he was stood slid away like a rug being pulled. This was no magic trick – he would not be left standing. Wayne hated with the frustrations of a man about to lose everything. This kid, this nobody—he didn't belong in this family, and now from beyond the school fence he'd humiliated his goalie, his stopper, and the entire midfield... teammates who had run the Matlock Road and back, carried each other like Marines over Yorkshire bogs. These were Wayne's only family left – they would not be disrespected.

"Agh!!!" Robbie hadn't seen it coming; the first he knew was the searing pain up his ankle and shin. Why is it every tough tackle manages to miss the shin-guard? The pain, and the lightning contact with the earth, stripped him of sense and breath. He landed at the post, fortunate to miss it. Wayne respectfully retrieved the ball from under the excess netting at the back of the goal just as the Romanians, Bladey, and Nicky came after the "punk-haired dipshit."

"Try that again, you little fucker, and see what you have coming!" Bladey was out of his mind, having been so disrespected.

Robbie's adrenalin stood him quick ready to fight – he wished he had taken the bayonet with him today, he was in massacre mood. His arms like an injured propeller came flying at Wayne, then "Blade Runner."

Pockets of the team ran from their training stations to check out the commotion.

A schoolyard circle developed around Robbie like castle walls, no visibility in or out. The two brothers, the Romanians, and the Blade Runner, stared down on the mite. No matter how you sized it up, thought Robbie as he looked at the anger around him, each one was capable of doing him some serious damage. The coaches with the strange accents were surprisingly angered by what they had just seen.

"But Coach, I thought, I mean, I just…." He stared pleadingly at Marius, having just shown him some of his best stuff. Marius stepped to him menacingly, screamed for about half a minute in Robbie's face. *Must be Glaswegian*, thought Robbie not able to make out a syllable of what was being said! "Are you from Glasgow?" he asked simply. And suddenly everyone exhaled with laughter, except the "Glaswegians," who were clearly still miffed.

Marius snatched the ball back – no one takes anything from a Bucharest sewer rat and gets away with it. Marius prized the ball away with his left hand while giving a dominant shove with his right, similar to a rugby ruck. The shove blew the "flaming candle" into Nicky.

"I want to see you try tha' agen; you won't get away wiv it next time." Nicky stood with both hands on the shoulders of the young truant. Nicky's hands folded like welcome mats over his shoulders, only he wasn't welcome.

"Careful, Nicky—you might snap him!" Brother Wayne wanted in for the "hiding" he was gonna get him initially, but Nicky's massive paws around the irritating schoolboy made him realize that he was just that. Blade Runner punched him right below the sponsorship; Robbie collapsed in a heap, slipping out from the human pegs and falling from the clothesline.

"Sorry, kid, but you had it coming! This family doesn't take shit from anyone!" Blade Runner walked back to his station – apparently one punch would be enough. Blade Runner knew he had it in him to drop the punk with one solid blow. Robbie tried to absorb as much of the blow as he could – but had anticipated the threat to be no more than just that, a threat. Right now, his empty, gasping diaphragm knew differently. Not even the school bullies had resorted to actual violence. The Romanians spit on the child like a sewer rat as he sank to his knees, arms wrapped around himself, trying to comfort his stomach and find air in the grass.

The air had gone out of him with such force that his lungs temporarily thought their only responsibility was to let the air out. Gasping, he vacuumed the pitch, trying to breathe; like an old sheet he wafted on the ground with billowing air pockets longing to be hanging back on the line. As the laundry was already folded, the friends turned to walk away from the tyke, the Romanians babbling violently like whitewater creeks, once again lighting up. Mission accomplished, commotion over – nothing to see here.

Robbie rocked on his knees, hoping to Hoover more air from the football fields. But someone had covered his air hose and his engine was starting to wail and scream. If he could breathe just a little more, he would be angry. It wasn't so bad, he told himself, still unable to stand, not wanting to look up to see if the rest of the team was staring. This Blade Runner guy had been the first person to lay a finger on him. As much as it hurt and as little air as there was to be had, he was still alive, and a smile started to work its way through the fear line. He rocked more, keeping his eyes closed; he worked his diaphragm like a bellows, and air seeped in. More air, the bigger the smile. Blood ran from his shin and ankles into his boots – the stain marked the point of pain. Taking one hand, he smoothed away the Romanian saliva in his hair before it dripped down his forehead. The team had baptized him. This was how it was going to be – them and him – just like in the rest of his life.

"Lost a contact, have you?" inquired the white footy boots with pink piping. Robbie didn't immediately look up. He had a little air, but his abdomen hadn't relaxed out at all yet.

His pathetic frame was lost in the miss-sized Chesterfield away kit. "Would you like a cigarette? I mean fag?" There was no compassion in her voice.

"What, miss?"

Vasily, who stayed around to see if there were to be any further repercussions, flipped a smoke into his mouth and lit it with the match he kept in the top of his socks.

Lindsey, annoyed, grabbed it from him.

"I said – would you like a cigarette, Red?" she asked, pressing him harder.

He couldn't wrap his head around the question – not able to breathe – "I'm too young" – "not on school grounds"--none of it made any sense. *I'm a prefect*, he thought.

She took the smoldering Embassy #1 out of Vasily's mouth and stuck it right into Robbie's, like you would force a dummy on a screaming child.

"I said would you like a cigarette, dummy! Because that's the only rule you haven't broken so far today!"

Vasily cracked a smile at the youth who looked like he'd been given the key to the bank.

"Sorry?" was all he could squeak out. His head remained bowed. The grass was tight knit, not much air to be found. Ankles throbbing.

"I should think so! You, you little shit. You think you can play hooky from school, put on our uniform and join our training session and get away with it. That's not how any of it works, laddy." Her old Scottish coach used "laddy" a lot for emphasis. "You just embarrassed the crap out of my defensive stars! That's unacceptable. Who the hell do you think you are?"

"Sorry, miss." Figuring none of it was acceptable, the remaining breath left him.

"Are you thick or something?" Her American accent came clearer to him now.

"What? Sorry?"

"Apology accepted. Now fuck off with you. And do what you just did here, and do it over and over again! Prove to me that you are no fluke, because I don't have fluking time to deal with you right now."

"I don't understand?" whispered the airless birthday candle. Still not looking up, crumpled like a paper fire-starter, he remained prefectly quiet.

"Thick, you must be thick! You wanted to show me, right? That's what that was all about just now, right? Well, show me you can do it again and again. Then maybe I won't turn you into the school right away." He saw the heels of her boots walk away – on the back of the boots he saw that the number "5" was curiously emblazoned in quotation marks.

"So...." There was a long pause as Robbie gathered the oxygen and hydrogen atoms. "So, you're the coach, miss?"

Vasily choked down the laughter like he'd just swallowed his first smoke.

"You sound surprised? Don't be! And that's another rule you have just broken! Thick – you must be really thick! I don't know if I have room for a thicky on my team! I'm gonna have fun with you, laddy!"

"But they'll beat me up again--"

Vasily grinned the sewer rat grin of a mouse being offered in their direction.

"Welcome to football, laddy—it's not all autographs and perfect hair!"

She marched ahead and he did his best to catch up, fixing his fringe with the Romanians' saliva. He kept Vasily's cigarette as a spoil of war. Them or him – he needed to be with them – the him he knew was too lonely.

One, two, three, four, "5" broken legs.

CHAPTER 49

"Lindsey, you have to see there is no money left – we have allocated salaries, we're running on empty as it is," declared Brian in Roy's absence.

Lindsey massaged her temples. "You must find a way. This kid is special; he floats like… Johan Cruyff." She adjusted her elasticated headband, pushing her bristling copper locks, backsweeping the sweat from the training field with it.

"Have you spoken to his school yet? His parents?" Brian said curtly – distracted, and a little put out.

"Not yet."

"Then you're jumping the gun – we've been going round in circles for over twenty minutes. Roy isn't well, or he'd be here."

"Roy would see to it, I know! He would take care of the lad."

"Roy needs to take care of himself right now. Has he even seen the boy?"

"No, not yet, with his illness and our training schedules." She emphasized the "sch" to be "sh" as if to blend in – as if her being American were the stumbling block. "– I've talked to him on the phone, I've shown him video; he likes the boy."

"Lindsey – you are probably right – from the training sessions I've seen, the team is looking impressive – you know your stuff. I'm actually looking forward to this season. But from a fiscal standpoint, the advertisers are staying away. We are killing it with public relations. But the advertisers, they have been bitten by bad product before – it's hard, no matter how much brilliant PR the crew generates, we still…."

Lindsey jumped over him. "We are getting hundreds to watch the practices, Brian – families, lots of them, the curiosity has them all coming!" One hand was sweeping the lime-green lasso around her head; and the other was air-jamming Brian's chest.

"And that's it, Lindsey – are we just a curiosity? Advertisers don't invest in curiosities – they invest in results."

"We can't wait to see if we have results to determine the future of this kid – we have to be able to tell his family, his headmaster that this is right, that we can treat him as an equal – that's the premise everyone is playing under: everyone gets paid and paid the same." Lindsey's patience was running parallel with Robbie's dream, downhill.

"Lindsey – please! We can't pay him. I can't magically pull cash out of the air."

"Brian – it's not right – am I to ask him to play for nothing? To treat him differently? Give up his A levels and a shot at college – to put his life on hold because of ad revenue?" Lindsey twisted her fingers inside her lime-green headband. It kept the red fury from escaping.

"Lindsey – we have a squad of players – you've done wonders with them… but to take on another, you're stepping over the mark! This was not your decision to make!"

"Not my decision? Not my decision? I'm the damned coach and this kid, Brian, I'm telling you is—well, he's the best player I've ever coached." She stared pointedly at his shoes, hoping to channel her flaming red hair into laser beams – make Brian jump – make him realize. "I don't know how he slipped through all the nets to make it this far and never be in an academy – its Meatloaf's ruby in a mountain of rocks."

"Really? And what about the next kid and the next kid? Where does it all end? Oh, I know, right here!" Brian paused and pictured the empty checkbook on his desk. Brian's fiscal certainty was resolute as his skepticism wavered; there was a certain burning in his brogues.

"The other players know it, Brian – they won't say it, but you can see it. They started out wanting to chop him down, high tackle, late tackle, he danced – literally danced around and over their cheap shots – he's like Michael fucking Flatley with a ball!"

"That's great, Lindsey, but funds are few. Roy's gesture to save The club—well, it was mostly that – we need sponsors. Roy's paying wages, most less than what they deserve, and yet they're still staying on. What few sponsors we have left are too poor to fight their contracts, and they are paying the rest. I spend hours on the phone each week reminding them of their commitment – giving them hope that this gimmick – this community outreach program we call Chesterfield Football Club is going to be worth it!"

"Money, money, money! That's what it's all about Brian! Is that what it's all about!"

"Yes – you're American – you must surely understand that much. Life is sales. Our sponsors bought something – they have buyer's remorse. They want their money back, but we have no refund policy. Just a promise of—well, visibility, bums on seats." Brian sat back, blew his nose – and wiped his brow. Lindsey hung on the door, not letting him out.

"Not all Americans think like that, that life is sales – that you gotta make a buck or two."

"Lindsey, I'm just hoping we have enough coins to put in the light meters! I'm negotiating with the FA to change games to day games – I'm trying to get waivers for Blade Runner to play and for Laurel too. I have a business beyond this – you know how much I care. Like you – like all of us, we need this, we all want this to work; life needs a fairytale. But not all of them are happy endings! And we can't pay Robbie." Brian sighed into his palms, elbows on his knees for support.

"So, you're saying we need a win?"

"Wins!" Brian labored on the "s" – looking up from the palms of his hands like an egg might look out of its cup.

"So, we have to win the first round of the FA Cup? Which is coming up. Will that be enough?" Lindsey started to plead, unknowingly gripping the door more tightly, swinging the saloon door back and forth – a patient cowboy deciding whether to draw or not.

"Probably not, but the FA Cup is only an eight-game season."

"Eight games. We'll be ready." Lindsey repositioned over and over again her lime-green headband.

"We could offer him a deferred comp?" said Brian defeatedly, awkwardly moving in his plastic seat – wanting to offer something and get out of this mini-prison.

"What? Win and you'll get paid?"

"Precisely."

"But that's hardly fair when everyone gets to eat regardless."

"Lindsey – if we lose, and I certainly hope we don't, we all only get to eat for a season! A club that has been around since 1866 will be lost. We are the 'miracle' sauce. We have so much talent even without Robbie, we'll be fine; you've done an incredible job with both teams, especially the practice squad, the FA Cup squad. Are you saying we can't win without Robbie the 'wunderkind' from St. Andrews school?"

"No, I'm saying Robbie can't win without us." She continued to bar Brian's exit.

"Then ask him!" shouted Brian, more hurried now and starting to lose sensation in his thighs.

"Ask him what?"

"FA Cup or College? Tell him he, well…." Brian was so uncomfortable – her glare, her hair, her grip on the door; if his arms were strapped down, he'd think he was in the electric chair. "If he is selected to play, that it's for the love of the game, for Chesterfield! But more than anything—FA Cup or college? But you have to ask him with his parents and headmaster present – no secret pacts."

"His parents are out of the picture." Lindsey knew that much; she knew he lived with his grandparents– Robbie had said so. So now all she needed was the headmaster as a witness.

"Guardians, whoever – we can't be responsible; he has to hear both sides. And do it fast – if he is that good, as good as you say he is, then he'll need to be ready in three weeks. In three weeks we play F.C. Halifax – a non-league qualifier who are doubtless chomping at the bit to play a beleaguered team like us! They're the underdog, and even beating us, sad as that is, is a big deal!"

"I'll schedule the meeting – what will you tell Roy?" Lindsey loosened her grip on the door, removed her headband, shook out her locks like a puppy freed from its leash.

"That we may have a freeloader!" Released, Brian laughed his way out of the men's toilet. Lindsey hadn't waited for him to get done and started her address the moment he entered and sat in the stall.

"Can I go pee now?" asked Zach – who had been waiting outside – not comfortable peeing in front of Lindsey!

Brian brushed by. "All yours, mate!"

Number one and number two.

CHAPTER 50

"The season is upon us – three days to opening day." Roy addressed the League players at the rescheduled meeting. He would speak to the practice squad separately. The entire staff of administration, marketing, accounting, legal, dental, carpark attendant, equipment manager, players, groundskeeper, shop assistant, physios—many of whom were the same person—and coach sat in the Kop end, the home supporters end of Proact Stadium. This modern, comfortable, family-friendly stadium still had its new car smell. The century-old Kop at Saltergate with its standing-room-only terraces had worn through, its steps cratered by anxious segs tapping and scraping at the cement, hollowed at points like the stairways in medieval castles. Generations of boots carved their agonies in defeat, stamping their feet for warmth through most of the season. Where miner's boots ground in the crumbs and gravy of a hundred years of steak and kidney pies. Kids' Clarks, sensible and measured for your foot shoes, bounced hopefully in the spilled Bovril, hoping to catch sight of their heroes.

Doc Martens kicked at away supporters and the cement alike dominating the swath of steps from the goal to the covered stand– progressively aggressive the further you stood from the goal – ratcheting vehemence towards referees and enemy players the higher you stood. Certain that your opponent of the day was clear whose field they had invaded and that they would certainly get a "good hiding" from their hosts, win or lose. Like castle ramparts, you could smell the violence at Saltergate's Kop-end.

Even in times of struggle, poor performance, low attendance, the core and corps of Chesterfield Football Club's military fans remained, and remained defiant behind their goal. It was the supporters that like a geisha fan around them that thinned out as performance drifted. They drifted to the stands where they could sit now as some "regulars" opted to spend their Saturdays differently. For the rest of us – the reality show of Chesterfield Football Club – the taunting echoes of the Kop, the majesty of the white striped lush green stage, the weekly unscripted wizardry of its players, our gladiators, remained intoxicating. This was the pulse of a town represented by a few, envied by all, and ridiculed by the jealous ones.

Your football club was your army, your defender, your representative, your ambassador, your village warrior. Football's rule-based protocols replaced village and family pillaging of centuries past. Now even this civilized weekly confrontation had booked over a century of combat, defeats, and victories somewhat evenly spread – no dynasty of dominance in Chesterfield.

So, it was in the shadow of the shiny new, all-seater Kop that Roy, its dying owner, spoke to our Football Club, his team. This select audience, seated comfortably in rows restricted for families, not clans, listened carefully to my dad whose paleness was kissed by the rising sun above the extended canopy of this new Kop.

"First, I want to thank you all." He paused as if to allow the thousand moments of being a Chesterfield fan to catch up to him. These moments still surprised the heck out of him—that he was the owner. His telephone voice continued:

"I want to thank you for your faith in me – I have been absent more than I wanted to be. I want to thank you all for wearing many hats to keep the doors open and the lights on…and off! You have all kept my light on. When the poison valve was opened into my veins and that first scalding moment of chemo hit me – this is what kept me going. The FA wanted to shut us down and even shut some of you down."

Bladey tapped his leg as if to say, "Right on."

"None of that matters now – you sit where centuries of fans stood and now sit. Behind me is the stage they see, and its actors will soon perform. And I want you to imagine what they will see, what will get them excited, proud. What would you want them to chant, applaud, savor for… life? Etched in me are the performers of the past – visions easily recalled of speed, skill, passion, and heart where the other two were missing. I want you to look beyond my shoulders, to see a landscape--a landscape of players who, like a botanical garden, have been chosen specifically to bring joy and utility to this space. I want you to be the players that the kids in these first rows go home and pretend to be. I want this to be The Club where kids wear these blue and white kits with pride – I want other towns' kids wanting to know where they can get that shirt? I want you to be on little boys' and girls' Christmas lists.

"We have a story here, an important one. You each have a personal history – some tougher than the next – I can see the desire in the way you trained, shined your boots, laundered and even ironed your own gear – and yes, I'm looking at you, Nicky. Who irons socks, for God's sake?" A shuffle of laughter hovered in the family section, in the way that siblings can make fun of each other where an outsider couldn't.

"Some of you without family, families far away, know that you have family here – to you players – you have an older sister in Lindsey – keep listening to her as you have been doing. She is wise … and stubborn beyond her years. Players, be certain today and every day to shake hands with those around you – your stage crew, your physio, your equipment manager, your lawn mower, your janitor—he's standing right there." Allen blushed in his seat at the edge of the group. "Be very thankful. If there is a ball at your feet, remember somebody here," he looked around at his cobbled-together crew, "put it there; if there is a line on the pitch, someone put it there; if there is a flag in the corner, someone put it there; if there is a Powerade on the table and toilet paper in the stalls, someone put it there. Someone, one of you. Take a look how the sun blesses this field; now turn and look at your teammates – look into those eyes of your teammates close to you. Look hard and thank them with your look each and every time you see them. You have all honored your commitment. You have all committed to this club, committed to a goal."

The sun was a little brighter as it rose – Roy squinted into it the way you pause to catch a moment before it drips from your eye. "We have been given one season to make this happen – as in life. Again, I thank you for your support, for carrying my vision as your own, for being family – a toast to you." Roy raised his imaginary glass – the IV Band-Aid on his hand clear for all to see.

"To ONE SEASON!" he called out. And the chant was echoed down the field, over his shoulder, a tsunami of sound that flooded the opponent's goal.

"ONE SEASON! ONE SEASON! ONE SEASON!" It rallied around the stadium like a Mexican wave of belief. Lindsey led them up and down the stadium from corner to corner – they walked each step, down each aisle chanting, whispering, singing, "one season, one season, one season." The Chesterfield Club family walked every inch of the stadium—they could picture, imagine how they would be seen from each seat of the stadium, even the "away-end." Lastly Lindsey marched the Chesterfield Football Club family to the Director's Box – she directed them to sit. And standing behind them, she said:"This is where Roy's family will be sitting – show them and all of the people who have paid, who have given up their money their time – Show them what magic really looks like, show them the miracle. Show them the miracle."

And somewhere, chemicals burned with love. Somewhere a few good cells were sacrificed for the common good.

1 Season, 2 to do it.

CHAPTER 51

Three games into the regular season, the first team had a mix of results. Four points from three games. A loss on opening day at home to last year's losing playoff team, Walsall FC, was a tough start for the inflated crowd and throng of expectation. Walsall FC had finished strong enough to cling on to their better players – convinced that another year of playing together was all that was needed. They had fired out of the starting gate with a mission of shutting down the Chesterfield FC circus. The fans had fulfilled their promise of opening day with a capacity crowd; they witnessed the flyover of six gliders, who later landed on the Tapton Golf Course! Their silent and coordinated buzz, like a computer being turned on, announced the start of this supposedly historic season. Walsall had driven the hour or so to snuff out the party candles and did so with breathtaking ease – winning the toss, taking the ball, and never surrendering it until forty-five seconds later, it whistled by Tommy Lee's outstretched fingertips.

The touch and player rotation synchronized like a Navy SEAL team, slipped two more by the angrily animated Chesterfield goalkeeper, one with a rising revolver hammer of a header from a corner, and the third a swerving rocket from somewhere between halfway and the eighteen-yard box. Tommy couldn't tell, couldn't see it through a maze of retreating legs caught on the back foot. That was how the match ended – Chesterfield's energy snuffed out and Walsall's fireworks were lit. Walsall would run through opponents all year in their historic promation. The second game away to Scunthorpe in sideways late- summer rain and winter winds would have ended goalless except for the generosity of the referee who gifted Chesterfield Football Club a penalty in time added on—the sort of gift a referee usually hands out in a match destined to go into overtime where he has a hot shower and a date waiting for him. The referee lived in London now but had perhaps had a happy childhood memory in Chesterfield to want to hand them this penalty and subsequent goal. A referee's imagination and emotion shouldn't be confused with the facts. There was a foul of sorts; was it in the box? Who could really tell? – The video of these lowly lower-tier games runs only in the referee's, the player's, coach's and fans' heads, and like a schizophrenic, they rarely reach consensus.

The third match at home was equally woeful. The first team had a couple of knocks, nicks, and nibbles taken out of it. Lindsey wanted to reach down to her effervescent practice squad for a refill, but she refrained. Players on both teams couldn't understand it.

Put simply, Lindsey said:

"Each team stands, hobbles, and wins on its own merit. Cup games for the practice squad – League games for the first team – we can't afford fatigue, and we can't afford to not win. We need to keep working on our softness of touch and speed of vision."

By the third game, their stamina had started to kick in – they could play well for longer spells, though still they struggled scored a scrappy toe-poke of a goal that sent the home fans into an explosive pogo-stick dance of euphoria. The season now officially started with the first home goal. But half an hour later, a different referee had a certain penchant for League Two newcomers Forest Green Rovers, gifting them a charitable penalty for a handball in a melee of bodies. The party was over – debris littered the stands of an unhappy crowd. The remaining trash was always a reliable indicator of a crowd's love or displeasure. The trash was mounting week after week, as few felt it their obligation to clean up after themselves. "Trash begets trash" as another fist-sized pie tin, licked clean, hit the ground ready to be trampled like a mini alien spacecraft regretting their decision to land. It wouldn't be long at this rate before "Junk Porters" became their kit sponsors!

Lindsey sat before her practice squad, officially the "reserves," but to themselves they were known as the Cup Squad – this was the double AA team. It had been hard for her to watch the League Team struggle at times, knowing in her heart that players sitting before her could help them immensely. It was worse to know that these players were being kept back, whose own hearts were begging her to play after each exhaustive practice and subsequent underwhelming performance of the League Team. But tonight, in Halifax, was their time. A chance to begin to make amends for all their struggles.

The Reserves, the Cup Squad, had all traveled – it wasn't that far, and they all fit uncomfortably into four cars. Lindsey wanted everyone – their squad was too small to leave anyone out. Roy, myself, Lindsey mostly on the right side – I mean correct side—of the road, and Julia drove them to The Shay, home of their opponents.

Nervously, the players, coach, drivers sat ready for the game to be called. Finally, the tap on the door from the referee signaled both teams were ready. This was the start of the FA Cup Season.

The players randomly shook hands with their opposing number in the tunnel – excitement bristled. Halifax were taking on the big-timers now – no more minnows. They had visions of being in SkyBet League Two next year, likely playing this team. Honorary local businessman Tim Smith read out the players' names as they stood facing their Director's Box. In a twist of tradition, he read his own team, Halifax, first – the crowd loved it – cheered him on. Then he announced the "visitors," and boos echoed around a packed stadium – Chesterfield fans hadn't travelled far, and the light of their sparkler dimmed dramatically as the names of their players were reeled off – each to a chorus of boos. The chilly night brought on a chillier response from the disciples from Chesterfield. They had taken the bus, paid extra money for a "sound nate owt to watch t' Town." They had finished their "tinnies" on the bus, their team had been pre-season curiosities of a nation. None of the "circus performers" had played or been listed in the previous three games. The crowd had relaxed in the notion that it was showmanship, that it was all a public relations stunt. But here they stood at the unwelcome end of an ancient stadium nearly a hundred years old, their taunting home fans comfortably seated in the recently renovated sections.

Having heard the list of players and substitutes, the lads with the empty cans wanted to return to the bus. They were sure of it when the last substitute was announced as Roy Griffiths. Lindsey had listed Roy as her third and final sub for the match. She didn't know how or if this run would go on, so she had put him on the team roster. She had packed a uniform for him, a variety of old boots from the lost and found. He had been reluctant, but the squad assured him it was only right. Even Roy was booed – even as they could see his aging form walking to the center circle. Roy smiled and cried as he was heckled by most of the attendees.

This was game number one of eight. And he wore that number, the number eight – Lindsey knew it was the only number that mattered.

One, two, eight! Forget the rest.

CHAPTER 52

The Chesterfield fans wanted to leave until they realized the bus driver wouldn't be back until the end of the match. His contract dictated that. So, many left their places – this circus was going to go on without them. Heckling and laughing can have two effects: one being to capitulate, crumble, and hide in a corner of yourself. The other is to take your cigarette out – crush the stub with your stud – take the beam of the floodlights, and make it your spotlight. Few things can motivate us like saying it can't be done – you are going to lose - 'you'll never amount to anything!'– you look pathetic – "We'll see you in the clown car!"

Laurel would make them remember her as they laughed and taunted her as she stood over the ball for the opening kick-off. She hadn't carried half her teammates up Slack Hill to be ridiculed. She hadn't left the south to be sneered at by the north. She hadn't pulled the skin off her blisters the size of a Branston Pickle jar to be mocked. Laurel thought of her tryout day as she stood back of the ball. Thought of all the people in her life that had cast her aside. She looked back at her teammates who had gone through their own personal hells. She was the "one" in the "four, five, one" system.

The Romanians had gone from disrespect to disbelief when she outpaced them yard for yard on the training pitch – her strength and stamina was that of a decathlete. The defensive towers were behind them, the brothers swift and polite like a guillotine, the stadium lights like incandescent moonbeams – shadows streaking across the green felt beneath her feet. Vasily met her at the ball; she stepped away as if to let him take the kickoff. He mimicked her, taking out the cigarette and crushing it beneath her boots – pink trimmed like her coach's. Over Vasily's shoulder, she could see the strongest woman she had ever met – her crazy like a young-Einstein hair held back by her reluctant signature lime-green headband. To her right sat Roy – looking intense – nervous likely – in pain likely– could there be an eyelash in his eye? Lindsey was holding his hand – probably too tightly. Next to Roy, Sam looked on with great pride – he too gestured the stubbing-out of the cigarette with his footy boots, then smiled, winked as brief as the flick of the ash. The referee continued with his pre-game checks – acknowledging the linesmen who duly confirmed their preparedness.

They synchronized watches. The linesmen whipped their flags rapidly, harshly, to signal they were disciplined, readied professionals. The flag wasn't bunting; it was policing. The referee checked his watches – both operational – one already in motion, and the other he would time with his whistle. The police chief in black tonight called to the goalkeepers – the visitors first and Bladey raised his bear paw. Laurel knew the sequence, had taken a casual couple of steps from Vasily toward Bladey– she heard the referee call to the Halifax goalkeeper above the hum of the crowd. There's oddly a hush, a pent-up, intake of breath in the football crowd. The anticipation of the first rush of nicotine when you light up. The brief second of adrenalin poised to capture the drug of football. Kops funeral-like, in respect for the minister of the whistle. Tattooed mafia-like thugs pausing as the Popemobile goes by before pressing a victim. Laurel was strong and lithe – she knew where the ball was; it never moved. She knew where the net was; it never moved. The referee's arm went up, and Vasily didn't move. She saw the whistle in the referee's mouth; it didn't move, and in the moment of breath making sound she spun around Vasily. Never taking her eye off the ball, she put it high in the night sky; it captured the moonbeams of the floodlights like a strobe, dark then light, then dark again. It wasn't always clear in the fake daylight. The goalkeeper never moved as the ball slid down the inside of the net like a lint trap in a dryer, snugly dipping over the goalkeeper, under the crossbar resting like the last peanut M&M in the packet. The crowd continued to hold its breath waiting for the blast of nicotine, yet it didn't come, not at either end or either side of the stadium. It had been stubbed out. The pierce of the whistle in the night had barely ended. The circus had come to town and it was as serious as a lion-tamer.

0-1.

Laurel knew it was good from the second it left her boot – her knuckles met Vasily's; she twisted her boot toes delicately in the mud, and with Vasily stepped aside of the center circle. The referee switched sides as the ball returned to the center circle. He blew, and the game resumed. The cheering had stopped except for a small group sitting on the bench near the tunnel and a few lads at the guests' end who had snuck in their own "tinnies" and had no need to leave.

Chesterfield played the remainder of the game on the front-foot – the Romanians dominated the midfield, stroking the ball like a pet on a leash, as relaxed as they had been on the streets of Bucharest. After Laurel's opening salvo,

Halifax began to push too hard, losing shape and rhythm – almost panicking with eighty-nine and a half minutes plus stoppage time to go. Before the half, Nicky had made a late run to the box and fired a header from the penalty spot after Wayne had drilled the corner across from the right side. Timing has to be perfect from set-pieces – it's your free chance to be creative, that rare opportunity that the ball is still and you have ten yards or more to invent something spectacular. Marking Nicky at full speed, laser guided to the ball, was like catching a lamp-post in a tornado. The defender, de minimus in his efforts, the goalkeeper already moving the opposite direction following the flight of the ball flapping like a duck, never truly saw it fly under his flailing left arm.

0-2

Half-time was a muted affair. The typically loud vociferous red-headed coach checked for injuries – nothing barring Laurel's bleeding Achilles.

"Nothing a fag won't fix!" Laurel grabbed her smokes and with her Romanian bodyguards they stepped out of the building, approximately fifteen feet, to be precise. They passed the fag like a ball in the training circle from one to the other. They checked down at each other, saving their breath not for words but for the quick hit coming shortly. The stadium, somber inside, couldn't be heard outside. There's an eerie, unnerving quiet about a building heaving with life making no sound. Standing a few feet from the car park looking back into the lights of The Shay like the inside of the Colosseum, where the latter is now quiet on the inside and throngs of sweaty eager visitors on the outside. Their first forty-five minutes had tamed The Shay. It was a two-fag half-time. Lindsey pushed the door away from the backpack to call them back in.

A second half much like the first, except for a Halifax goalkeeper rather anchored to his goal line. The ball at the feet of the Romanians slid from foot to foot like a ball nominating a roulette slot then changing its mind, going from foot to foot as easy as a cigarette is shared hand to hand at half-time. Lindsey made no changes. Her team was healthy, everyone would be needed. The Romanians completed a "cat's cradle" passing sequence with a sublime volley from Vasily on the hour. The ball dipped and curved; a goalie off his line may have had a chance to narrow the angle – but the goal was as large as it could be, and Vasily had eyed his top right corner three passes before. Halifax had chased hard – pushed well – but tonight belonged to the circus. The traveling fans, through beer haze and cooling late-summer nights, could hardly believe their eyes. No one in the pub back home would get it, that Chesterfield Football Club – the circus of local television—could actually play.

Lindsey's rotating triangle-offense, borrowed from the great Tex Winter of Chicago Bulls basketball fame, fared fabulously in football form too. She blended total football with a kaleidoscope by sliding players in and out of different positions. All stadiums have clocks; the players without signal from Lindsey or the bench could, every ten minutes, change roles. Only Bladey stood his ground. Halifax chased the chess moves of players lost in their responsibilities. Wayne and Nicky as devastating up front as in back, the Romanians flip-flopped from five in the midfield to five at the back – a micro-galaxy rotating again within themselves. As the final whistle approached, Laurel's blood-soaked sock let her know it was time to get sutured up.

Lindsey looked across the bench and back; no one was eager to go in. The work was done—three goals should be enough. It wasn't.

"Roy, take a jog down the touchline for me, would ya?" It was a direction rather than a request.

Roy never felt more in need of a fag than right now. His twisted feet ached from sitting, the boots he wore looked nice – nicer than any pair he'd ever worn before. It had been over twenty years since he'd first laced up his last new pair of boots. Like his last new car, there won't be much mileage on these he thought. He tapped his shin-guards, happy that he'd remembered to put them in – they were voluntary, not mandatory, in his day. His new hip was the best part of him as he stood in the night air. Only the few locals behind him noticed him."Sit darn, you ol' fucker!"

"Watch your language!" Lindsey turned as Roy's advocate, reprimanding the fan. "You should respect your elders – it was nice of you to bring your mother to the match!" Lindsey nodded to the young lady sitting with him. "Roy, you're in; Laurel's coming out."

"Where's she playing?" It was a hasty inquiry.

"Play wherever you like, Roy; that's how we play it here!" She pushed him passed the exiting Laurel, like helping start a kid on a swing. Again, the air rang with laughter, not applause – the announcer recognized Roy's entrance. The lads with the tinnies rolled their lazy-eyes at the news."What next, Noah and his Ark?" The tinnies' chests pounded without breath, as a joke is so much wittier when drunk. Relaxing is easy with a three-goal lead, victory all but guaranteed with ten left to play.

"It's like playing a man down – they'll be fine – we should be able to run the clock out"

They should have been able to, probably could have under different circumstances, but Halifax wasn't about to let their Cup dream die just yet. Roy anchored at the halfway line – he could do minimal damage there. From here he could breathe in the night—the pollution from the lights eliminated the stars. He commented to the lone defender who reluctantly stayed back to watch a pensioner that he could probably catch in a twenty-yard sprint having given him a ten-yard start. Both watched the bombardment of the Chesterfield goalmouth – crosses rained down – Bladey punched them away, Nicky and Wayne towered above heading balls for corners, throw ins anywhere but in the middle. A weak clearance put the ball at the feet of the fastest man on the field. It was chaos all around—legs, feet, bodies wrapped around until he squeaked the ball out – it was in the clear. And like a Romanian being chased by the police, the sprinter from Queen's Park took off – only Roy and a defender between him and the goal. Everything moved so fast – Roy felt like Captain Kirk watching the stars fly by at warp speed. The ball now was headed in his direction, the defender's sweat right on him; in a split second the ball raced on to him, the defender tighter still – no pensioner was getting by him tonight. Almost imperceptibly, Roy opened his legs to let the ball through; like croquet, it went through the posts of the defender too. The Queen's Park Sprinter in full flight could not be caught. The goal-keeper reluctantly left his line, came to meet him, mistiming his dive. The ball slid under him and tucked itself up for the night in the bottom left corner of the net. *Sometimes it's what you don't do that makes the moment great,* thought Roy as he let the ball speed between his legs.

One, two, three, four-nil!

CHAPTER 53

Roy lay face down in the grass, wearing the defender like a kangaroo kid wears its mother. The sweeper had decided to teach the old guy a lesson – standing right on his heels as the ball had come to him – removing skin like a potato peeler from Roy's Achilles'. That's how he knew the non-move, the dummy would work. It was instinctive, not vindictive, of Roy to catch the sweeper by the testicles; as he was forced to the turf, he reached back to stop his fall. It was fortune that he was able to grab on; it was vindictive, not instinctive, that he twisted the defender's sack on the way down, though. You learn some cheap tricks growing up playing in a meadow, in Cromford, with the big kids, during the war, he thought. Some parts of self-defense stay with you a lifetime. There were no roses, but the damp, dewy night grass started to imbue itself with the fragrances more associated with morning.

"Roy – you alright? I'm sorry – I shouldn't have sent you in!" The sweet sound of Chicago rang in his ears above the weight of the Sadam Hussein statue currently passed out on his back.

"I'm fine," he whispered behind the wink of a lover. So grateful to have stood and lain on The Shay's grass mattress.

Back home and elsewhere the story of the Chesterfield Reserves' win, started out in a whisper, a fluke the way you talk about a neighbor's lottery win. Disbelief, jealousy, "it could have been me" close, the excitement of a spinster's older sister has on her baby sister's wedding day.

"Dusn't look like Roy'll be in t' pub tonate! 'e'll be nursing them footy wounds."

"I 'eard 'e wen' darn like a sack o' spuds!"

"I 'eard he went darn we' a sack o' spuds in his hand!" The pub quartet guffawed a two-pint laugh and kept on with their "sack" stories – ye olde social media they were, gabbing away to all them that knew Roy in t' pub. Dennis chuckled as if reading the article, and didn't expound on the nine-year old's humour prevalent in this group.

Mavis excitedly caught up to her friend at the bus stop."Did you hear, Joan? Roy, the silly bugger, was playing football again last night?"

"Yes, I did hear whispers about it, the bloody old fool!" lied Joan, unsure of what to think about a person she was unsure of.

"For t' Town, no less – reserves or not, it's funny, isn't it?"

"Hilarious," offered Joan, suddenly muting herself, wishing the cellophane head scarf would just close up the outside. She tried to picture Roy in his blue and white uniform. It couldn't possibly look right; he must have looked like the last bag of salad on the shelf, sell by date clearly marked as "yesterday."

"Did they win?" asked Joan, showing mild interest.

"I believe so." Mavis never followed football – just thought that it comical that a peer, a neighbor, would be still "playing at our age," that the lonely figure from the bus was the center of her gossip. Gossip FM – the village posting, Mavis to Joan, from Babs to Mavis, from Glenda to Babs. Glenda tuned in to the post office every morning, feeding reports from her sister Patricia, the post office manager. She was told everything, and she posted it and more on to the next person in line for those that didn't hear it from the horse's mouth. The only photos posted in this social media were – well, lost cats, dogs and the occasional criminal – petty theft, mostly; well, it was Chesterfield, not that gangster town of Sheffield.

"Must have been the FA Cup." Joan counted that today was Wednesday, like you have to when you're retired, and every day is a Saturday or a Sunday; some prefer a Friday, but no one thinks it's always Monday. Wednesday in Chesterfield – family allowance day at the post office – like an Associated Press dump in Chesterfield on that day. Gossip from all of the dirty post office corners spreading uncensored, unvetted across the unauthorized town wires. Who needs a town crier when a village whisperer will do?

"What, love?" Mavis had heard, but the language was foreign to her.

"Oh, nothing." Joan was a little embarrassed at making the connection. "Just saying, it must have been an FA Cup match."

"Ah couldn't tell yer, duck – funny though – to think o' that idiot Roy playing footy! He should be in t' grave, not in t' dugout!" Mavis always thought she was the funniest person on the bus.

"So, Robbie didn't play then?" was all Nan said.

"Your uncle Nicky scored last night – open wide – here comes the ball – it's your favorite – bananas and cream – she shoots – she scores." The baby always loved a story before every spoonful. No mention of daddy's assist – he would have to tell his own story.

"One down, seven to go," said Brian to his check-writing pen, which glinted in the free street-light from outside his office window. He'd appreciated the call. He began writing his first check in weeks – this wouldn't bounce – the FA Cup bonus would pay for a lad who didn't even kick a ball. "Robbie McDonald." Remember that name!

One, two, buckle my shoe…three, four, knock at the door.

CHAPTER 54

The Cup run had started – you could practically read the headlines now. Except there were no headlines – no Harry Gration to report on the game. He'd made his way to the opening game of the season provided a nice little blurb on *Look North*, but the fireworks and drama of the pre-season team selection, the gimmicks around town, even the potential visit by Gordon Ramsay failed as the team's so-so start lost its energy. As in a dramatic car crash on the M1, sadly there is little or no interest in all passengers recovering nicely in hospital. So it was with Town – their season had started off like a damp match, and by the time it was dry enough to strike, someone had run off with all the wood. By the end of September there was no wood to burn – the season that began with so much hope now looked as odd as a yearbook photo.

Roy's chemo days at the hospital were fewer now – the first round had been followed promptly by rounds two and three. Anxiety wore on The Club as if it were a post-party hangover. PR kept up the rounds at the schools – the schoolchildren still loved the participation, though with each league loss, fewer and fewer kids showed up to watch them train. The Proact Stadium enjoyed a surge in season ticket holders – families clumping together to buy a seat or two. After a win, family members would argue with each other to go to the game – after a loss or two, calls were made to see if anyone would take the tickets off their hands.

The night chills were starting earlier, as God knows when to lower the thermostat. The three o'clock games are a tougher sell when you know the team is on a losing streak – even though they were just at your kid's school – in the local pubs – at ribbon-cuttings of new businesses – even though they had been on *Look North* back in early August. Fans had fondness but not desire – fair weather determined their performance as much as the players'. Fondness can be enjoyed reading the *Derbyshire Times*' sports report on matches or the cynical rundown of those lads at the pub with little better to do on a Saturday for a couple of hours. Those whose allotments didn't need turning over, or car brakes didn't need bleeding, or gutters cleaning, or variably anything that you could've left to tomorrow if a team's momentum and excitement was headed in the right direction. Season ticket holder seats were noticeably more vacant. You can see a lot from the Director's Box – pock marks of empty seats spread randomly in the South Stand. Fiscally, there was no worry, but atmospherically the Town couldn't afford to lose the energy through this gap in the ozone. Season ticket holders are the magnesium in the firework shedding brightness, they are the "ooh and the ahh" of a team's fan base. Their buyer's remorse this early in the season meant that if there was a next season – these seats would surely be unsold and empty all year, the lads with the tinnies a reliable statistic of unpredictability. Football is a tough business – you have to defy logic with regular appeals to the heart; every week is a Blue Peter special! A borderline charity appealing each week for your hard-earned disposable cash – the difference between paycheck to paycheck and too much month left at the end of the money.

The Reserves had drawn another non-league team away –Framlingham Town – a small village in Suffolk; it would mean a painstaking drive. And again, Town would be expected to win. Chesterfield would be Framlingham's payday. Again, the revenues from the gate would be low. Again, the vendors and local businesses in Chesterfield would not benefit from this fixture. Again, and again, the Proact Stadium would be empty and the Spirit Wear Shop full of merchandise! The spirit of the town itself would surely start to fade, along with memories of the summer and the effects of the chemo.

Each one of us is given only so much willpower each day; there is the will when we wake up to do the things we want to, the things we want to accomplish for ourselves, the will to do the things we have to do, like driving an hour and a half each way to work of a morning. Then there is the willpower drawn on us by family, friends, colleagues – the things they expect of us, like feeding the kids, dressing them, changing nappies, turning up at work, doing the work as it's asked or demanded of us, meeting deadlines, driving home–feeding kids, cats and dogs, spouses, the gym with its guilty call demanding our presence, the waistband of our skirts and trousers insisting we take the call of the gym, the willpower to sit through Britain's Got Talent without feeling remorseful of our wasted life, then the willpower to wake up, get off the couch when it's so much easier to stay there all night. All day long – "willpower" being zapped from us. We go to sleep, hopefully rejuvenated, lie awake for a brief second, check the phone, battery 100% charged, willpower 100% charged – I can get out of bed – 99% charged, then each momentary step drains the battery of our willpower; if we don't attend to our personal priorities it will get hit by others; like their phone calls, emails, Facebook posts, messages, instant and Instagram – willpower being sucked out unwittingly before breakfast and that morning ritual. Willpower down at 50% before even getting in the car for the rally-car commute of stop lights, two-finger salutes, lights flashing behind to go faster, amber lights insisting we go slower, red lights telling us to stop right now on pain of death, then came the writ.

22%, 21%, 20% - Battery low. Do you want to go on low-power mode?

CHAPTER 55

"Middlin'" was all Roy could answer when asked how he was doing. The kind of question you avoid often when you know someone has been critically sick, on the brink of extinction sick. All other species are dead to us once we pass. Roy would have been embarrassed before – an illness? An injury? What? "Me? No! I'm fine!" would be the usual retort when asked about his bout with shingles or his broken leg as a child. You could see where Monty Python got its "flesh wound" sketch from – folks like Roy, his generation and the greatest generation before him. Lindsey of course had no idea what he meant.

"Sorry Roy," was her despondent answer, clearly unaware that "middlin'" was indeed in the ascendancy as illnesses go – "fair to middlin'" being the worse of the two.

"Felt good to beat Framlingham last night, didn't it?"

"Definitely – the Cup team is showing real unity—chemistry, in fact. Passes are moving with the punch of a pinball – it's entertaining. Our freeform philosophy is making it hard for other teams to scout or predict. And I still have a few tricks up 'me' sleeve!" Lindsey unnecessarily was throwing in accents, either trying to blend in or for a hint of mockery. Mockery goes down well in our parts – can't afford a thin skin in our pride of the north; not even the beer is allowed to have a thin head poured on it. So, if she meant to be "having a go at us," as we would say, she should keep it up.

"I'm enjoying my few minutes on t' pitch, Lindsey. You don't have to do that, you know – it'll get harder – it won't be possible to play me an' 'ave t' team keep its shape."

"I'm glad, Roy – and I've even ordered you some new boots. Brian authorized it!"

"Well, bloody 'ell, I 'ope he din't spend much on me – I've seen t' cost of those new boots and they cost a pretty penny!"

"Brian knows ya – he went shopping on eBay – they'll be cheap enough and be something you're more familiar with."

"So, what's on t' agenda today, Lindsey?"

"Field trip – we are gonna celebrate last night's Cup win with a trip to Matlock."

"Really?" Roy's tone went up like a Basil Brush question. Four syllables in one simple word, with a loop on the end for good measure.

"Yes. I wanted you to show us your childhood town – show us the highlights – give us a tour. I've even rented us a mini-bus for the day, so you don't have to repeat yourself over and over and we can all be together. So, put down whatever you're doing, swallow those pills, and grab your jacket—we are leaving."

"What, right now?" Roy wasn't used to leaving or doing anything at the speed of "right now." This must be a totally American thing. He was used to everything being done after a "cuppa tea" or at least tomorrow.

"Yes, right now, Roy – I let everyone sleep in – that was their reward. As we know, the big boys join us in the next round; we have to kick up the training a notch!"

"Can I at least finish me tea?"

"Yes, if you must – we are all on the bus waiting – don't make me come back here for you!" and she bristled out like the last dirt from the last sweep of the gym floor.

"So, this is the house where you grew up then, Roy?" the twin towers almost echoed each other. "Nice." The end-terrace with its spackle exterior had window-box pride of home ownership. The council had owned it when Roy lived there – it was inexpensive, though you wouldn't believe it to listen to his dad. For reasons of his own, he stayed quiet when asked if he'd wanted to buy it when they had come up for sale. And the team van was content that he said he'd moved on – something about a girl. It was enough. The estate was halfway up the valley wall, its creation of simplicity--like many others of its day it had a mold, mix in the block, spackle, plaster and lattice, and you had homes that from the air mirrored the rectangular snakes mocked up on the architect's easel.

At the bottom of the hill nestled in the valley floor rested the town itself.

"Next – we'll head to the Lido. It's where I learnt to swim, where I learnt to dive." Roy left it at learning – it wasn't his nature to tell them this was like home. That he owned it as a youngster – that there were medals in his "important draw" at home. Medals no one had seen, not even his parents. His dad's medals of valor were real – never displayed. So, Roy's county championship high-board diving medal only ever adorned the inside of his pocket, and now the inside of the "important draw."

Everything about the building looked tatty; gone was the majesty of the polished Romanesque copper brick, and the rust in the windows looked anxious to escape its moorings. *Thank God it is still a pool* was all Roy could think. He hadn't been back much since he'd been orphaned – just a little work here and there. He'd not seen the Lido – not gone to that corner of Town, that corner of his history, that corner of his…days of better, days of youth, on the top board, on the top of his world, looking down at the cheering kids, his part-time coach, the shimmering surface of the deep-end a full fifteen feet deep, like an ocean every time he entered the water.

"Okay – everybody out, including you Roy. We are on a training run – back to Roy's house!"

The collective "What?" belly-flopped into the nostalgia.

"Roy – you're in charge of lunch – so bring us some local treats while I take these champions of Round Two back to your house!"

The mini-van emptied of its athletes – relieved that it wouldn't have to drag them back up the hill, for Matlock is nestled at the foot of a valley whose slope matches that of your roofline. The loaded van had lurched painfully the best part of a mile in low gear, concerned that it might bolt from its engine mounting and free-wheel down the rollercoaster of Valley Road. The coils of the gears burned into the clutch, the unmistakable, pungent odor of a van in the preliminary tearing of its ACL. It was a beautiful day for a picnic – unless you had to scale the narrow, tree-lined incline single file. The original town planners had failed to recognize the simpler snaking pattern as a means to traverse the hillside. These footballing tourists could plainly see the top of the hill – Lindsey was not letting last night's win get in the way of her mission, Roy's mission, the reason for them all being together, and now they stood at the foot of the hill that was an everyday training session for their leader. Little wonder he still had the calf muscles of a hippo. Roy was glad not to have to run this hill one more or one last time. The streets looked narrower, worn, bleaker, greyer, the trees fuller, crimping the hiking path of a pavement. The canopy of trees shaded out today's light but not the rain; unfortunately, it was a dry day. Mossy walls couldn't hold back the puffed snowballs of hydrangeas that bumpered the players off the curb into the street.

No room to run without playing in the traffic. *I don't remember them being there,* he thought.

Roy looked at his childhood pathways—weathered, faded by a lifetime, aged and unobserved creases marking times of daily presences, mundanely necessary routines of daily living. Seeing his team disappear up the vertical tunnel, he reflected how he would have led his teammates up the hill, the fastest "squirt" on the team haring back for tea, with only the village clock for a watch. This road was much brighter then, more welcoming, less ominous. His thrilling liquorice-allsorts of players bobbed rhythmically up the channel, to an invisible light; only yesterday, it seemed, he would he have been taunting the stragglers.

This view of disappearing blue jerseys must have been how the villagers saw his Avenue Blues team nearly sixty years ago. Remembering back, he stood and just stared at the familiar hill. *Sixty years is a long time – it never occurred to me that I would be able to say something like back in my day nearly sixty years ago those hydrangeas couldn't even be seen over the school's eight-foot wall.* He remembered in school, this one "just down" from his house, fidgeting in history lessons as the headmaster, who taught history, would elocute personally on the Boer War at the turn of the century – anecdotally confirming the facts of the day with every limp and time-stamp of his cane. The headmaster's history came to life in the tattered texts on their desks – an oddly placed fondness for the books that journaled his youth, a fondness for his fighting teammates, their history making history. The headmaster held his fading text book close to his chest, a Bible of sorts, he would pull it close to his heart beneath his academic robe, look out over the children and see those same snowball puffs just outside his classroom. "If you squeeze them, they disintegrate," the headmaster recalled.

This team, his team, had no stragglers – all had the desire to be first for each other. Lindsey always led the way – she was remarkable – creative in her training – embraced by her players. It was like watching your kids stroll hand in hand down the drive on their first day of school; off up the hill. Lindsey's team didn't hold hands but ran with pack-like closeness and could have held hands if they didn't need them so much to piston pump their way up this valley wall.

Roy had no war – he had been lucky, very lucky.

Hungry; makes me hungry just watching them – an army marches on its stomach – right, I'm in charge of the picnic – Henderson's Bakery – I wonder if it's still here? Probably not, it was in business at the time of the second Boer War – Mr. Henderson and the Head had fought together, shipped out to the tip of the world. Mrs. Henderson shouted at him constantly on account of him losing his hearing in Mafeking. She smiled as she shouted, it was funny to have this deaf puppet to play with – "Mr. Henderson has remarkable hands!" even in her flour splattered apron she would titter and yell behind him as he worked the dough out front, at his counter for prep and sales, his ovens in back.

It should be back around the bottom end.

Gingerly Roy turned to manage his walk to the bakery. Few industries survive the centuries like a baker's shop – always an intrigue and sense of wonder with something created by hand, not machine-tool perfect, gnarled edges on a pasty, an off-center pork-pie, something human in them. At every stage of his life, Henderson's had been there. A cracking, splicing pavement told him he should be back repairing his handiwork – shoots of weeds had found their way to life thanks to the burgeoning tree roots forcing the asphalt apart. Life begets life. He marched on careful not to trip. Relief came over him at seeing it still there. The sandstone structure would survive millennia, but would a baker's shop? a cottage industry maintained in stone cottage-like charm, in an age of doorstep delivery? You can picture buildings aging in a way, but we can never see ourselves that way. A little moss, perhaps stone in need of a sandblast, but mostly the same expectations of time, paint chippings on the pavement beneath a slowly perishing windowsill.

"Haven't seen you in these parts for a while, Roy; What you been up to?" Mrs. Henderson's voice and frame were hidden beneath the counter, reaching for a wax-paper roll.

"How did you know it's me?"

"It's a picture window, Roy – easier to see out than in on a sunny day; lets light in, lets sight out! What'll you have, duck?" she asked standing upright as a shepherd's crook, smiling forward as if to eliminate her chins for the camera.

"Been in Baghdad – cheese and onion pasty or regular?"

"What have they got you doing there then?"

"I'm in the air force, Mrs. Henderson."

"War in Baghdad, is ther'?"

"Not if I can help it? No, I'm just stationed there, back on leave; couple a years to go and then I'm done with the mob."

"What'll you do then love?"

"Gerra job at the airport – air traffic control. It's what I do over there."

"Nice – better than on t' front-line like my Walter, God rest his soul. I don't know why I still whisper—he couldn't have heard me if I shouted!" She crossed herself, at the apron's bow above her heart, her knotty stick fingers, stiffened from a million or more farmhouse loaves, greyish with faded blood. "Don't just stand there like a gormless child. What'll you have?"

"Cheese and onion pasty, please. Your flaky pastry is the best in the land."

"Got that right! I've the hands to prove it!" Holding them up, she played a stiffened version of Chopin. "Got a minute? I'll warm it up for you." Mrs. Henderson never waited for an answer; some things just weren't worth waiting for. She was in the back room setting it in a warming drawer whether you had the time or not. "It'll just be a minute. Better that way. We're all a little tastier warmed up, don't you agree?" Roy blushed from the heat of the kitchen door being opened.

"Not seen you round my parts much, Roy?" came the voice from behind him – sitting, working a little crochet from an upright oak rocking chair.

"Didn't see you there, Mrs. Henderson."

"That's what I'm afraid of most!" she chuckled. She had a new station, not behind the counter but seated in the corner in the window, better able to see a little of the world outside. "I thought that was you out there. Put on a bit of weight since I saw you last! Not in the air force anymore, I see."

"Still as sharp as ever you are, I see, Mrs. Henderson."

"Cheese and onion pasty, flaky pastry?" She proved she was as sharp as ever. "Not that you really should!" her voice creaked more along with the chair, as if the tree roots were poking through her vocal cords. She rested the crochet on her apron, not minding that it would get a little flour on it.

"Ha, ever the wit, Mrs. Henderson! You always did speak the truth."

"A baker never lies – the ingredients of your soul will prove your worth. Michael, would you be a love and warm up a cheese and onion flaky pasty for Roy? He's been coming here since he could climb out of a pram and steal my buns."

"Right-oh, Nan."

"Keeping it in the family then, Mrs. Henderson? It's good to see."

"Well, for the summer at least – then he's like all these kids today, off to university – like you can learn something there that you can't right here. How's the road looking?"

"Terrible! But we're just mending and patching the pavement – roots are starting to show through. Hopefully we'll be asked to do the road as well."

"Two great smells rolled into one day! I have the window cracked so I can take it in – a little asphalt sulphur burning in the breeze – clears the sinuses like an olfactory dose of…."

"Here you go, Roy." The grandson cut her off just in time to prevent his own embarrassment.

"Don't be a stranger, Roy; don't leave it so long next time," she called out through the gap in the window over the sulphur breeze. "But we always do, don't we? Leave it so long." He nodded, thinking he'd be back soon.

"Twenty cheese and onion pasties, please," requested Roy. The building of course still stood; been around for centuries. Since sandstone had been around, well, forever, it stood to reason the building would similarly endure. Mrs. Henderson's ventilation window had been replaced by a single copper-vinyl framed picture window – specially cut to fit inside the non-conforming space. Her solid-paneled door with transom was also gone; it gave way to the modern, copper-encased full-length glass door – you could see all the way to the counter on a cloudy day before you entered. Mrs. Henderson would have liked that. The cracked, carved wooden sign had finally been replaced, having long outlasted its charm factor. Although this garish, modern, ill-fitting, illuminated monstrosity would have to go, it lit the corner like a lighthouse, a beacon to customers and boats if you happened to sail off the River Derwent, through the park, over the tennis courts, by the bowls pitch, and under the street light. Then such a sign would be justifiable: "Henderson's Bakery established 1887." Roy could practically hear Mrs. Henderson's disapproving sarcasm from behind the counter – not that the fresh-as-morning-donut face behind the counter would understand sarcasm. Her delightful, slightly overscrubbed, ruddy cheeks, puffed as he smiled at her.

Roy looked at the "too young to be working" child at the register thinking, was he ever that young? She, being "ever that young," stared gleefully back at the pensioner from under her maid's net bonnet."You do still make them, don't you?" Roy continued, "cheese and onion pasties?"

"Of course, sir – it's just with an order that size – well, you need to call the catering line and give us a bit of notice; we don't have the facility to bake them here, I'm afraid." She was polite beyond belief. "What you see here is mostly what we have – there is some stuff in the fridge in back, but if it's not out here then it's not in back either!" She was proud of her shelf-stocking abilities. "Henderson's" beamed the oversized sign.

"I would like...everything you have here."

"Everything, sir?" she had at least been brought up right in her young life.

"Yes, the lot."

"Cream buns and all?"

"Yes, everything."

"I do have one cheese and onion pasty – let me warm it up for you." It slipped between her tongs, on to a paper plate and into the microwave, her "warming oven." "I'll go in back and find some boxes; maybe there's something left over from delivery."

The last time he was here – you could have reached your hand in the till if she left it unattended for this long. Today though, a little fob around her neck connected and disconnected her access. Mrs. Henderson would have loved that – being able to watch the pies rise and the till stay put would have been a great comfort to her. A small sign above the door to the back gave Roy some comfort too. "Franchise owned and operated by Michael Henderson."

"Is Michael in, by chance?" Roy asked as she came back with an open box for the pastries.

"Oh no; Michael only comes in on Mondays, Wednesdays, and Fridays, in the morning. Then he's off at the main office. We're going national, you know?"

"Main office, going national?" *I approve. Perhaps he did learn something in University after all. A national brand out of little old Matlock—well, I never.*"Yes, in Chesterfield – on Beetwell Street, I think?"

"I know the street. Happen to know how many franchises there are?"

"Not really – you could Google it and find out!" She would have done it, but her hands were busy re-stocking the delivery boxes for him.

"Ah yes – I must remember to do that when I get back to the Tardis!" he grinned.

"YOU A FAN OF DR. WHO AS WELL, ARE YOU?" – a voice so loud and filled with surprised excitement that even old Mr. Henderson could probably hear it even now in his eternal rest.

"Yes – I have been since…." And he left his next thought out in the sweetened bakery air.

A ping denoted his pasty was ready where the pong used to be and with her back to him, she added:

"Who's your favorite Doctor?"

He wanted to answer: "my cardiologist" for saving his life but instead he went with the ever popular "John Pertwee."

"How about you?"

"Matt Smith – but I like yours too! So, what do you think about the Doctor being a woman?"

Roy hadn't watched the show since Tom Baker – Tom Baker was the kids' Doctor. Once they stopped watching, so did he. *A woman as the Doctor now.* It bounced like a sticky bun in his mind. *Not a bad idea, fresh concept, why not?*"I hadn't heard – but I suppose it would work." Trying to sound a little progressive.

"I think its aggressive!" She was buoyant, handed him his pasty and even a serviette. Her smile confirmed to him that "aggressive" was used in the positive not the pejorative. "I think she'll be awesome!" She sounded a lot like Lindsey.

"Thank you for these." He smiled as he awkwardly picked up the box of treats.

"You still have to pay for them, though," she reminded him.

"Right, of course." Time travel hadn't gotten to a place where everything was free yet. He handed over his cash card and the deal was done. Cash cards, no oven in a bakery, windows that don't open to let the smell of a bakery entice you in, tills with fobs and women Doctor Whos – what's next? Across the street, the van was parked, air-conditioning cranked, draining the pace of the engine. Yes, that would be next – driverless cars, perhaps, one day.

Michael's grandmother would be very proud of him still. Roy was proud of him for her, as the tinted-glass door closed smoothly, imperceptibly quietly behind him. Not even Mrs. Henderson would be able to hear you coming in. The little buzzer in the young girl's apron informed her remotely that someone was at the door.

Sitting on the patch of weedy grass at the bottom entry of the Close upon which he'd grown up was the whole team – a little worse for wear. The hill to here was as steep as the angle of pastry tongs. You had to lean into almost parallel to run up the unforgiving pitch, practically crawling like a climber on the sidewalk. The smorgasbord of sandwiches, pasties, pies, cakes, and buns would have made his cardiologist flinch from the overflow of fat, especially that old demon butter. His cardiologist would be wrong – for it was lard that gave the pastry its lightness and flakiness.

Roy was always fascinated watching how people ate. He stood, rested his backside on the ledge at the back of the rented van, carefully capturing each crumbling slice of the pasty. From his little distance away from the team blanket, he stared into the mystery of how we learnt to feed ourselves, how we were taught or not, patiently or hurried, petite or handfuls, clean lips or clown lips of food, spotless or crumbly, serious or smiling, eating or tasting, respectful or hungry, eyes open or closed, smelling or devouring, knives or no knives, pinky finger raised or not, one hand or two on a sandwich, instinctively searching suckling or taught. From a life within the womb of being fed we know instantly where to go for food and survival. Like mini sand shovels, our hands become scoops that wittingly think everything is food. The blankets were filled with the hungry eyes-opened collective.

"Well, the big boys join the draw tomorrow! Let's hope for an EPL team!"

Lindsey was jazzed by the chance of showing them off against the top in the land – see where they really stood. Were they special? Or were they fizzle?

"Yeh. Maybe we'll get Liverpool," sprayed the kid in the Gerrard jersey.

"Or my Chelsea at home!" Laurel choked out.

It would be neither, as it turned out – a home game against Walsall. The first team had already been drubbed by them in the league opener. Win or lose, no rosette of note from that result. Practically a local derby; it would be hard to publicize and generate much extra interest from that fixture!

One, two, three, yawn.

CHAPTER 56

"I wa'n't even sure I were gonna go!"

"Me nie'ver! I were thinking fuck it, another twenty quid down t' crapper, burr i' were brilliant."

Earlier that night, the tinnies had sat in the same spot of the Highfield pub, their recognized and assigned corner, debating whether to include the Proact Stadium in their pub crawl.

"If we gew t' match, it to'ally fucks up t' pub crawl. It's bad enough thee 'ad to move from Saltergate t' fuckin' bypass, nar a cup match on a Chewsdee; 'kinell!"

"Tha' rate, mate, bu' we can stop at t' Badger for a swifty, slide back through t' gennel, over t' Nags, down t' hill to t' Donkey Derby an' then reverse it on t' way back!"

"Worr' abou' t' Goldminers Arms?"

"Alrate, then finish that nar like an' we can 'ave 'alf there an' all!"

"Got t' stay flexible, me owd man used t' say!"

"But Town's first team go' crippled by this team in t' opener; that's why they punished 'em by not playin' in t' cup match!"

"Seemed to have worked – been a bi' be"er since tha' night. Go' a few wins under t' belt – might even survive relegation this season!"

"Come off it, lad! It's more like ge'ing promoted to t' same division each year wi' t' mad scramble every fucking April! It's like our playoffs!"

"I be' thee a fiver Town stays up!"

"You're on, mate!"

Two of the tinnies spat on their hands and shook them.

"I'll tek me winnings in liquid gold right now, mate, if you don't mind!"

"'opefully we can ge' tickets for t' match!" And the tinnies roared with laughter—Stella Artois, the liquid nectar, burst through nostrils like kids at recess! If you could bottle laughter like on *Monsters Inc.*, you'd have to filter it twice for alcohol and snot. Fresh brewed, double filtered!

Town hadn't been able to sell out the Proact Stadium since Tom Jones appeared there!

So, with a couple of pints in them, the tinnies detoured to the Badger; popping into the off license, they bagged a four-pack of Stellas each, for a couple of road beers between each pub. They would never make the mistake of turning up to a Town match sober again! They wore coats like saddle bags and were happy to have these cooler September nights come in. Beer stayed cold in their oversized pockets – not that that even mattered. Shoveling tons of asphalt day after day didn't require rocket science. One of the tinnies' mums had gotten him the job, so out of pride she would shake him and his five Stella Artois up every morning—only five on account of it being a work week. And we all know five means that a couple went unaccounted for, like lost children at the petting zoo.

"Nah – am rate glad I went – we could 'ave sat 'ere all nate an' missed it!"

"It were fuckin' brilliant, wa'nt it?"

"Yer telling me – I thought we were done for after t' visitors scored in first minute -ahgenn. Went 'round us like were standing still. Then I thought coach were fucking bonkers to not play t' regular side – gewing wi' t' Reserves again! This looks like nothin' you've ever seen before. Even t' coach is a bit more fuckin' into i' wi' t' reserves – she teks off darn sideline like a possessed leprechaun. Fucking red, fucking hair goowing every fuckin' where!"

"It's like we're supporting two different teams in t' sem kit!"

"There's summert abou' these reserves though, in't ther?"

"What d'ya mean?"

"Well, like a can't put me finger on it at t' moment, bur' a reckon this reserve lot is as good as regulars!"

"Thar's cracked, thar are! Come on, are ya pissed up already?"

"No, straight up, a think they could tek 'em! Serious – if it wo' t' first team they'd be darn in t' mouf if they'd gid up that goal in t' first minute. But no' this crew. Coach she's fuckin' mad – see – right off she switched t' formation?"

"You cu'nt see shit, mate; you were fuckin' trolleyed befower we gorr' us tickets."

"Nah, come on – that coach, she's on t' summert. A seed, a did…."

"Rate?!"

"Watch next match – see if she does i' again. She put entire back five up front. Wi' Laurel in t' back sendin' long ball, she were able to target t' big lads up front – it must 'ave looked mad t' Walsall players. Fucking, suddenly, all t' Town's defenders are in their peno' box' by t' time they'd worked out who t' mark fuckin' balls in t' air an' big lads are under it. Not sure who gave it flick on, bu' it were like a bullet in t' net. Instead o' ge'in' all defensive like and panicky, t' coach sent in t' heavy artillery. Not kidding; she played a fuckin' 5-5 formation for like five minutes! Then like they all just dropped back in t' starting line-up – watch 'er – coach, she sendin' t' signals in. Am tellin' yer. See her pull on t' 'eadband."

"Thar fuckin' mad, as usual – ja fancy t' coach or summert?"

"Well yerr a bi'." Blushes enveloped his alcoholic flush and wind burn alike. But the tinnies were on to something. This group of back-ups had many tricks, so many formations, always ending with Roy having the last ten minutes of the match. The person coming off was the coach's choice for the noble performer of the game. Recognition given for tackles, assists, goals, saves – you played to have the team honor of giving up your spot for the man who had given it to you in the first place.

"Am not shoower why they bring on t' fuckin' owner every match – rate fuckin' shtupid if you ask me – burr' a' least he ant cost us a game!"

"Must be rate fuckin' embarrassin' for t' player coming off!"

"And for t' Walsall players! Here's t' old codger come to tek piss – we can play with ten men and a fuckin' granddad an' still win! Ha!" The tinnies laughed at their lackluster opponents, who themselves had not sent out the same eleven that had beaten the First Team so handily a few weeks earlier – thinking that they probably didn't need to. The tinnies pushed each other around the little booth already too tight for sardines. Stuck together, spilling beer, laughing at each other, laughing at "schtupid Walsall," they would now have to reroute their pub-crawls, as it seemed there was going to be at least one more game.

"Let me ou', wanker--'ave gorra piss." His mates bunched up. "You wankers--'am gonna piss all over ya!" They crushed him tighter and he broke the seal – he clambered over the table – beers spun like glass Weebles, fell like a Communist wall, flooded the plains and filled jeans with stains.

"You tosser! – You'll pay for that!" One spoke for all – the others added similar lame threats – but were lost in the panic need to pee. All the urinals were occupied – "fuck" was all he could muster. A stall opened up – and pushed in – caught himself in the zipper – pissed all over his hands as he fought to unroll himself – that which hit the toilet formed bubbles of many frothy sizes, shapes drifting together like a jaundiced Aero Chocolate Bar. Weird how these random bubbles all came to one centralized place, collecting like commuters on the Tube. Quickly he wiped up the floor, wall, toilet tank, and bowl – it would be murder if his tinnies walked in after him to find the place like this. He washed his hands like a surgeon – couldn't take the chance of smelling like a distracted kindergartner who'd happily just sunk two juice boxes. "Berkley Illinois" said the label on the hand dryer. *Aye wonder where tha' is', he thought*, reading it over and over as he dried his hands, jeans, and the underwear peeking through his zipper. This was not the way to end a great night. Town were on to the next round – he clasped and rubbed his hands, praying that no one would bother him for a minute or six and that Town's win tonight would bring about a Premier League team for him to watch.

There was no accounting for this team's chemistry; Chesterfield Reserves played for a different "why" – it was their "why not." Why not a team of diverse, languages, height, ailments and even gender? The tinnies were on to something – they were on to the invisible scent of winning. Like dark matter the scent of winning fills the space between – "can do" – "will do" and "well done!" Winning is the imaginary glue of force that keeps muscles fresher, spirits higher, players closer. The gravity of winning is that supernatural force that keeps water globules in place on the mirror – stationary water is a mystical phenomenon squeezed together, unifying, taking the forces that brought it together and holding strong. Winning is a team's gravity, these little wins in the FA Cup a mere bottle cap on the ocean of survival. Gravity, tides, and teams all manipulated by the invisible.

One three! Lost zero!

CHAPTER 57

"Did Harry call?" Dad buzzed in, containing more coffee than Starbucks. It had been his go-to narcotic of late – a poor man's crack!

"Harry? Harry Styles? Which one are you talking about, Roy?" Zach knew which Harry.

"Gration, Harry Gration, Harry Gration MBE - *Look North*!" Too much of a good thing can really get you hyped, and Dad was on the tipping point of sleeplessness. He felt sure that his taking the field in the final minutes of the game would have gotten Harry's attention, or at least the attention of someone in the newsroom. "I've a good mind to drive up to Leeds meself at this rate." Caffeine helped his mood that had been robbed by chemo. "We're all just chemicals, that's all any of us are – and I'm mostly filled with poison!" he'd said on discovery and treatment. "Can't let the bastards grind you down!" Presumably he was talking to the fascist cancer cells devouring his lungs with hate. He'd discovered coffee following his first chemo session. It seemed so civilized, like getting a biscuit after giving blood. The nurse had handed him a lukewarm version in a plastic cup that, had it not already been filled, he would have expected to be filling it with something completely different. It was a hospital, after all.

The creamer he'd requested mostly floated on top, refusing to dissolve, spinning as gently as the Milky Way. "That's nasty!" he'd inappropriately let slip before the kind nurse had left the room. She offered him sugar and he declined – and then his mind started to take a new parabolic curve from his body. Feeling a little clarity up there behind the ploughed fields of his forehead. His straight vines of skin kinked constantly atop his eyebrows of late – you couldn't plant anything but worry in those fields, like putting infantry in the trenches.

Similarly, he lay under the barrage of chemicals that were used to maim and kill his uncles in World War One.

"You wouldn't believe it, Roy, but these chemicals we use initially started out as a mustard gas, not dissimilar from that used in the Great War," Dr. Richardson, a man of similar age, "a brilliant-mind," was happy to tell Roy. Thought they might share a common history, a common interest in history. Dr. Richardson was right – Roy would have loved this kind of trivia on quiz night. Just the sort of curiosity he might even know—today's derivatives designed to kill the encroaching cancer cells the way the plumes of yellow gases were sent to kill the encroaching Allied forces. The same evil killer, but managed, and dripped into the coursing vein, burning its edges, headed to the front lines of our body's evil nemesis. Little plastic pouches attached to mobile stands, filled with irony and now history. Searching and destroying the enemy flowing through those same enemy lines– collateral damage included. Roy was-war weary. The coffee jolt helped, boosted the frontal cortex; the coffee psyched him up for one more push.

"Anyone home?" Wayne yelled loud enough to raise a roof, and the roof already in need of repair looked down with disdain. No car in the driveway, of course; there hadn't been for weeks. He yelled it again. It was enough to awaken the long-gone schoolchildren from naptime in the derelict schoolhouse next door. Empty echoes came back off the unfinished brick walls. He kicked off his footy boots, this same way every night – little cleat marks chalking up another day in the new plaster of the foyer. He'd finished the closeted entryway the first weekend they weren't home, proving that he was a good father. Plastered, painted, trimmed, painted again – a manic weekend. *They should see it now it's done.* They had seen it, coming over when they were sure he wasn't there. *He's made a good start,* she thought with optimism and little intent of coming back.

The heat was turned off still; even the echoes shivered. The new blue-light kettle, quickly filled, quickly boiled water for one. He was never short of tea bags or beer, but milk, on the other hand, easily slipped his mind. The gallon she had left him with lasted well beyond its sell-by date. His tea became increasingly sour with each X on the calendar – soon the whole month would be filled with X's. Carved X's scoring the page repeatedly, as if he were drawing bushels of sticks bound together. He would need a new biro soon, and milk, not things you think about after training. The calendar awaited him in the mud room like a peace sign at a fascist rally. He couldn't believe how many minutes there could be in his hours of waiting for them to come home. Minutes on top of seconds piled on like fresh flowers on a gravestone marking a former life. Kettle was on and done already; not enough time to shower when you boil enough for one—no waiting.

Wayne peeled off his favorite clinging training shirt steaming like the kettle. He'd rejected The Club's offering of a training jersey. It was an odd stance to take. And when something doesn't make sense, there's usually something else going on. So, he wore a bib in practice over the favorite shirt. Like a freshly lit cow pat, his shirt landed in the pile of previously worn tee-shirts already starting to chemically react with each other. The mound expanded between two large unopened drums of ready-mix plaster. He had yet to get to the kitchen/family room combo, since there was no family to fill either room.

The first night, the tee-shirt landed there following an angry explosion between himself and an imaginary foe. Not even drunk, he was yelling at her absence: "How dare she leave? How dare she take my baby from me? How dare she....How do I get them back?" The first tee-shirt flew into the imaginary net between two five-gallon drums of compound, each with twin trowels on top. That was days ago when the biro cartridge had a full magazine. He was one X short of wearing his favorite Nirvana shirt – the pile on the floor already smelling of "teen spirit"! "Come as ..." he screamed the lyrics at the pile, taking aim with each sweat-laden sock, either trying to knock off a trowel or bounce the damp sock ball in off the bucket-post.

The kettle's aggressive bubbles cut him short so he would wail on after, during the steeping of the tea, a reddish cranberry tea – she had left it behind and he'd finished anything that resembled regular tea; they both steeped, both of them turning darker and darker. Then he thought of Cobain's shotgun and his own; both owned the Remington 1100, more than enough to get the job done, apparently. He kept it close by his side, when before, when the house was full, it was locked under the bed. Now there seemed no point to locking it, so like a grouse hunter he wandered around the house with it, cocked should the grouse escape the wallpapered bedroom.

He drank the dark unfamiliarly fruity tea in the shower – he knew he'd be in there a while – there was a lot to wash off, more so than yesterday and the day before that. Holding the "Number One Daddy" mug provided stability, his daughter staring back at him from the porcelain glaze. The geyser steam of the shower clouded around him and blasted the day away. Riverlets of steamy sweat poured from the corner of his eyes like tears. In an empty house, you can cry it out in any room, but a hot shower provides enough space for dignity and recovery. Your tea stays warm with herbal essences, calming in the shower. He stepped out with the tea. He'd done it again - forgotten a towel – she was right, he was "stupid." She was right to leave; it was a "stupid dream of a stupid man." Steam has nowhere to go in an unfinished bathroom. Like the steam in his heart a piston of pressure. Steam collected on the old tile like ice; with one step on it he went down backwards, faster than an Italian forward, the gun resting beside the mat went off. There was blood everywhere. Quickly the cranberry tea from the shattered tea mug mixed in with it – he was laid out naked with the handle of the mug still firm in his hands when they found him, blood seeping from behind the matted hair Michelle once cut for him, silver-black buckshot peppering the walls around the hole in the bathroom, his Nirvana tee-shirt laid out on the unmade bed.

"Call 999—get an ambulance, quick!"

Nicky, being out of his mind, grabbed him, screaming, "I should drive him!"

"55 Walton Road – a man's been shot – come quick!" Bladey had rounded up the team – they knew Wayne was on the edge.

"We can at least help him with the house!" had been their private offer.

"Agreed!" And Vasily had rounded up his traveling odd-job men, his fixers, this order of men loved order. "Let's do it now!" His empty pint punctuated the intent. He pulled out his Marlborough smokes, tapped the pack forcibly into the palm of his hand, pinched a cluster from the packet, threw them toward his beer mates as a tip. "We are ready!"

"Wayne's not gonna like vis, ya know!" Nicky trailed the group like Eeyore, worried it wouldn't end well.

Nicky had said it was nothing—"family business."

"Wayne wouldn't want the fuss. He was good to go – no worries, mate." When a joker stops joking, then there's a time to worry. When the funny man goes down, we all go down, down just a little harder perhaps. Fragments of generations died with Robin Williams.

On impact, Wayne was taken immediately to that place in the brain where dark matter resides. To the misunderstood space between consciousness and dreams, that recess between starlight and moonbeams, a universal blackness. The scent of Remington buckshot slowly dissipated over him.

Who's gonna call Michelle? thought his conscience – the brain knows when it's dying, he'd read.

CHAPTER 58

"Quiet please!" Roy couldn't hear the Cup draw.

The team gathered in his tiny office to watch the 15-inch screen. Brian and Roy pensive, they needed a big name to sustain The Club, needed the fans it would draw. Sure, it would mean higher costs – the hope being they would sell out the fixture-scarves every kid loved.

"Number 13, Chesterfield. A slight pause. "Number 58, Liverpool."

"Bloody hell, Brian! It's happening! I can feel it in me veins!" Roy looked wide-eyed at Brian like a child who'd just seen Santa leaving his presents.

They had got what they needed. Now how to manage the following, the thousands of fans that would drive over the Peak District to see the slaughter and imminent passage of their Red Army to the next round. Their thoughts weren't wrong! The back office of these mega-clubs hated these little stadiums and hated the fixture in the same vein that Brian and Roy rejoiced. Logistics for sending an EPL team to an away game were the same regardless of the venue – in most cases. Liverpool's back office had no idea and little expectation that this trip would be anything but a thorn in their side.

Brian moved quickly to Roy and gave his fragile friend a weighty hug, a kid going off to kindergarten length hug. Awkwardly long, awkwardly relieving. Proact Stadium would sell out as fast as the Elton John concert – this was Roy and Brian's concert. This new entertainment could fill out the whole stadium, but tickets would be limited to a few thousand.

Instantly Zach ran promotion after promotion in his mind – you could almost see the lift in his kilt with the news. This could re-energize their PR push – drag out old Cup players from both sides – fire up and put another blog on the fire of social media. This FA Cup game would be a test of the whole system's mettle. Plan it like it's the last hurrah! From a Liverpool standpoint, it was likely to follow a similar pattern – they would likely start a lot of their younger reserves, possibly even academy team players. Chesterfield would definitely be starting their reserves, since that was all they had. This was not a fixture that a Premier

League team gets up for even at the youth level, and absolutely not at the reserves level – there is a confidence, an arrogance when facing a much lower team. These Premier League youth and reserves were the cream – they had made it without having made the first team. The Premier League Reserves were on the ascendancy, while players from the lower leagues were naturally a notch or three behind them as peers and crossing paths with those players on their way down, their leadership ascendancy in direct correlation with their declining speed and aging skills.

Scouting Liverpool was simplified to watching them on telly every weekend – there were hours of footage. But in the FA Cup early rounds, they have seen fit to be a little more relaxed by playing their young stars. They would have a few superstars make the trip as bench warmers and insulators against humiliation as in a few years ago—2013 to be exact, when Luis Suarez came on to save the day with a classic hand-ball goal in the third round against Mansfield Town.

As lucrative as a share in a replay at Anfield might be, Town's focus would have to be on winning. This was a team of unknown qualities and speed. On their side, there would be little to no footage of their results so far. Liverpool, even as they scouted Chesterfield from League play, would be unlikely to have any FA Cup film to go on. Both teams would be coming in somewhat like a blind date. Having played three games together as a squad, this might give Chesterfield the upper hand.

Lindsey looked around the room at the hesitatingly smiling faces; the joker was missing, and her playbook for such a day was missing a vital piece – it started and ended with the twin towers at the diamond-back defense. She would have to go back to the drawing board; she would have to reinvent the team. Lindsey needed size and speed; Wayne was an impossible piece to replace. The telepathic communication between brothers melded a central fortress for opponents to challenge, like scaling the outer walls of Windsor Castle; any player coming around the outside being easily picked off. Liverpool, even in their reserves, would have the speedy talent necessary to terrorize all sides – losing fifty per cent of your field communication in battle would be devastating, not even counting whether Nicky would be in a state of mind to play.

"Let's get 'em, boys and girls!" Lindsey adjourned the meeting leading them to the practice field. *Let's see what I have left*, thought Lindsey, crushed, as a member is when they lose part of the family.

"Bladey – take a break from being in goal, will you? How fast really are you with your… prosthetic leg?"

No one ever addressed his infirmity directly. "Fairly quick, Commander!" Bladey responded respectfully as he had been trained. "Quicker than a duck, slower than a swan." Bladey's leg was missing from the knee down – he'd been so fortunate when the IED had been triggered too soon.

"Thanks for the image, swanny! Say, Robbie, come over here. You fancy your chances at being the speed demon don't ya?"

"Why yes, miss – a do!"

"Then you and Bladey line-up on the six; it's gonna be race day at the practice field! Welcome to St. Mary High School sports day!"

The Romanians gathered around and started betting their smokes – leaving them in a pile around their mud-clogged boots.

"I'll take some of that action," lauded Nicky and he threw in Wayne's smokes that he'd nabbed.

"Drivers – start your engines!" Lindsey removed her headband, and her hair shook out like a willow tree in a swirling wind. The lion-locks were untamed. She raised the familiar bright lime-green bandana above her head and strode toward the sprinters on the six. "To halfway and back – grab the bandana as you go by the finish. On your mark, get set, GO!"

The hooves of the studs pounded into the turf for traction as the coach swung her signature headband down by her side. She swung the sweaty rag hard like she was thundering down on a kettle drum in tune with fireworks. Robbie and Bladey neck and neck—Mihai, Marius, Costica, and Ionut threw down their smokes on Bladey's pile to win after a great start, but Robbie with Bladey in his sights at the halfway line touched down a close second. Bladey the veteran summoned his infantry reserve, charging hard back toward the redhead with the bandana. Disrespectfully, Robbie drew alongside him, with time to check him up and down. Lindsey, intimidated by the speed of Bladey and Robbie running full gallop at her, stepped back toward her own goal holding her lime-green bandana high for her players to see. Bladey and Robbie fought with the turf for purchase hoping to squeeze every ounce from the turf. A few schoolchildren had gathered to see the practice – young ladies from behind the bike shed, no less. A week's worth of eyeliner and make-up on each face stared over their uniform with white upturned collars, the green-grey-yellow striped tie an accessory rather than a uniform.

"Go, Robbie, Go!" they repeated the chant from over the fence and it caught his ears – he didn't know anyone at St. Mary's - how did they know his name?

"Go, Robbie, Go!" It happened again from a cluster of manicured young ladies. The dog had seen the rabbit and Robbie took off past Bladey with such rude ease. Was he famous now?

"Seventeen seconds!" The familiar headband swooped down in front of Robbie. "Bladey, well done – you're back in goal!" *And I'm back to the drawing board,* she pondered. Robbie was off to the fence of adorning fans.

"Bladey! You married?"

"No ma'am," like he was in *Gone with the Wind.*

"Would you join me for dinner tonight? Pinocchio's around 8ish?" Exocets are less direct than Lindsey.

"Yes ma'am, sounds like a plan; I can pick you up if you like!" He was excited by a chance to discuss the Liverpool match.

"Not necessary. I'll just meet y'all there!" was her riposte, and she marched off toward the Romanians who were divvying up the spoils and searching for a light, cursing the schoolgirls who had energized Robbie. She grabbed one of their cigarettes, remembered Rizzo in *Grease*, sucked hard, blew the chimney stack over her midfield, threw it to the ground, minced it with her cleats like the business end of a garbage disposal. It felt so good on so many levels.

"Robbie! Robbie! Robbie!" was the chant from the bike-shed chorus line. Girls his age had never shown much interest before. He high-fived Bladey – "Good luck with that one, Bladey!" He nodded to coach.

"Right back at yer, mate." He nodded to the St. Trinian-styled trouble at the fence.

Robbie grabbed the collar of his sopping jersey for comfort, finger and thumb rubbing that thin ring of tidy material; it was meant to calm him down as he approached his rebel fans.

"How d'you know me name?"

"Oh, we all know your name, Robbie McDonald!" came the chorus of Mo, Maggie, Mel, and Maeve. All four of them had their autograph school pens in their hands, all eagerly leaning on tiptoes at the fence, but no autograph book in hand.

"So, Red, do you always sweat like that?" Mel barely hid her sexual undertones.

Robbie, unsure of himself, half-shrugged his answer. "Well, today was a rough workout; thought Bladey was gonna beat me."

"I didn't. I knew you could beat him." Maggie slapped her arse as she fake galloped by the fence.

"Bet you're a helluva ride, eh Robbie?" joked Maeve, picking up on Maggie and Mel's lead.

There was nowhere for Robbie's embarrassment to go, and the fever flush broke the embankment of his fair, freckled face.

"You've made him blush, girls," laughed Mo, pointing with her words, not her pen. "So, are you done with training, Robbie? Can you join us at 'Pret'?"

Robbie looked Mo in the eyes, pursed a scrunched lip, checked over his shoulder, his teammates all headed off in a single direction armed with ball-bags, cones, coolers, and pinnies.

"They've taken your balls and gone home!" laughed Maeve, catching Robbie looking back.

"Do you still have your balls, eh Robbie?" Mel waved her pen like a Hogwarts faculty professor."What time?" Robbie blurted out a little too soon – a little unreserved – uncoolly hurried.

"What do you think, girls?" posed Mel.

"Well, I have a ton of biology homework…" stammered Mo.

"That's what I'm talking about, girlfriend!" Mel elevated herself as sexual leader of the posse.

"Six-fifteen! Can you remember that, jock?" Maeve checked her phone for time and appointments.

"Quarter-past six – yes, I think I can remember that!" As a top student, it shouldn't be hard as a bottom quartile dater with exactly no courting history; six-fifteen stood out in his personal history like 1066.

"Sign these before you go, pro!" Mel pushed up her "push-up" while handing Robbie the marker. "It's for me mum! Not me! I hate football." Mel had him like a bear trap, hungry with no escape. "Come on, Robbie, sign 'em, would ya? I haven't got all day!"

Robbie took the pen. Mel held her form steady, and he began to write – carefully – her pale freckled breasts, firm with youth yet soft, her pen in his hand moved over her like it was writing on a satin-draped, sand-filled, stress ball. There was no way to hide his excitement – sweat dripped on her arm as he wrote – she didn't flinch and caught a glimpse of his eyes checking her out, holding her stare as he wrote:

"To Mum with love, Robbie!" proudly Mel turned to the posse and everyone recoiled with laughter. Mel hadn't watched him to stop him – he'd been caressing her with her pen tip, it didn't matter what he wrote. This red-headed, sweat-nested, snot goblin was touching her, not them.

"You should give him your mum's phone number, Mel!" Maeve was loving it.

"She'd eat him alive!" When really that's exactly what she would do, she thought.

One date, one boy, one jealous boyfriend, four girls at six-fifteen.

CHAPTER 59

Excitedly, Zoe pointed to a large group surrounding a camera man. "Hey Dad, look over there past the souvenir stalls and pie trucks...Harry Gration is back there with the *Look North* team! Finally got back on their radar!"

"Zach an' his crew have done a brilliant job promoting this match – I think it was probably easier for Harry to say yes than muster the stamina to keep saying no! Must be something empowering in those kilts he wears! Won't take no for an answer, that kid – except when he asked me for a raise!"

"Looks like he's over by the players' tent – interviewing them, I suppose!"

"Yes, that was genius – have the players come sign autographs a couple, three hours before the match. We have had a line all morning – it's like a receiving line at a wedding!"

"Who's Harry talking to now?"

"Looks like Vasily – that should be interesting!"

"Harry Gration with *Look North* television here – pleased to meet you – I see by the photo you are holding you are Vasily?"

"Yes – vould you like autograph? I give you mine – you give me yours!"

"Actually, I don't have any photos of me, but I will happily take one of yours." The crowds gathered around both Harry and Vasily, young children held up behind Harry's shoulders so that they might appear on the news or on live telly if it was being fed live. Like dancing mushrooms, little figures appeared with their umbrellas over the shoulder and above Harry.

"You vis ze TV, eh? Ve...very important, yes?"

"Today you are a big story – any team who plays Liverpool is a big story!"

"Tomorrow ve shall be even bigger story!"

The fans crowding Harry screamed with delight, waving dripping scarves and umbrellas alike. It was a cross between *Singin' in the Rain* and the Munchkin scene from *The Wizard of Oz*.

"You sound pretty confident about a win today – that would be quite the upset!"

"Ve vill be big story tonight – you see – ve are ready – coach is ready!"

Again, the kids popped up like Whack-a-Mole, ready as pitchforks to march on the enemy!

"Liverpool is a formidable opponent – they have won this tournament seven times before. That's quite a history, you know!"

"Yes, my friend, but it is only history – this team today they are not the same players as before, or even the same players from last week. Ve are a team, ve only train together and play together, live together, eat together; ve have special reason – ve have as coach says the 'why.'"

"The why?"

"Yes – you shall see; tonight, vill be big story made up of little stories. Big team made up of big 'whys.' Now must sign autographs – ve have many fans. Here, this may be very valuable one day!" and Vasily through a hail of rain and laughter handed him his photo autographed – 'To Harry, one day you will know why, thank you Vasily."

Harry stared at the cryptic photo.

"We're still live, Mr. Gration," prompted the cameraman.

"My souvenir—ladies and gentlemen, boys and girls, and football fans around the nation." He held up the photo of Vasily; he was at the center of the team, stepped forward just slightly from the group. Each player had been given a similar photo, with each of them centered amongst their teammates, one step forward. This was a team that trained, played, autographed, and was photographed as a unit. Each had a why as they stepped forward for their photo, stepping back in the lineup for their teammate then to step forward. Over a thousand kids were able to get autographs that morning. Over a thousand kids were able to get up close and personalize their team – to see their Saturday heroes closer than they were at a throw in, to know that they were ordinary people with a workable skill. The kids could see their gratitude – a trait that isn't always perceptible from the stadium. Each player signed off with "thank you."

"Arlo White here, coming to you today from a rain-soaked Proact Stadium Chesterfield, a short drive over the Peak District for the Premier League title contenders Liverpool. This should be a stroll for the in-form Liverpool, but it's the FA Cup and you never can tell – what are your thoughts, Stevie?"

McManaman was less assured in his lilting Liverpool accent:

"Well, Arlo, it's a short trip and Liverpool is, as you say, definitely in-form, playing well and scoring a lot of goals. But they do have that Achilles heel at the back – they have been vulnerable to speed. We shall have to see how that plays out today."

"Yes, they have given up a number of goals in the regular season, but this squad of international superstars is capable of scoring many more, and one would expect that against a much lower-placed team like Chesterfield, whose league record in Division Two is rather mixed."

"You have a point there, Arlo – Chesterfield have struggled at times in their own division as their middle of the table position would indicate. But I would hope that my former team doesn't take this team too lightly. It's a cup match – an FA Cup match – it's 90 minutes, and anything can happen!"

"Spot on, Stevie; this tournament is rife with giant killers in the past – let's see if Chesterfield can put their names in the history books as we get ready for the kick-off."

"How's your dad feeling, Julia? Does he seem alright to you?" There lived a certain gravitas in Brian's cadence always, but today he seemed to report back with news that the weight of the earth above the escape tunnel from the POW camp had collapsed.

"Well enough, I suppose, but he's not left the recliner much this week. I was surprised to see that Lindsey named him to the bench again today, especially as they are gonna need all the substitutes. It's obviously a nice honor and likely the first time was a nice gesture, but it's not as if Dad can make any contribution to the match. I'm pretty certain he won't be playing today like he has in the past."

"Has he talked about the lawsuit at all?"

"Lawsuit! What lawsuit?" Julia was frazzled.

"So, I take it he hasn't?"

"What the hell are you talking about, Brian?" She reacted as if she had designed the collapsed tunnel herself—protective and defensive.

"There are issues regarding the purchase of the new stadium and the sale of Saltergate – they weren't properly disclosed at the closing, and now we are up to our necks in legal bills. These expenses were not in the original budget. These were not accounted for – your dad's funds are running out quickly. Players won't get paid, the lights will go out, even today's sell-out crowd won't make much of a difference – we should almost play for a draw – give ourselves a better payday with a match at Anfield. Cash flow is coming to an end. Julia, what I'm saying is we are only days away from flipping the off switch."

"Does Dad know this, Brian?"

"No, not all of it – he's been so sick of late and, well...." His words fell away like a declining red blood-cell count. "I don't know how much he can take, so I, well, hedge my thoughts. Then, well after a win he seems so happy... I don't want to be the one – the messenger... you know?"

"But you're his friend, Brian – you're the treasurer – it's on you to keep him up to speed!" Julia's panic was frothing into hysteria. Combining Dad's declining health and finances were too many straws for this camel. The words "ending" and "running out" gave her needle pain in her extremities, the precursor to a breakdown.

"Can you tell him, Julia? Or have your Zoe or Adam do it? I'm at a loss – your dad has done so much to save The Club, the jobs, the dreams, but it's a cash guzzler and lawyer's bills are to be paid and they're just holding off, delaying things, stalling."

Julia sank to her haunches so that the fear, the dread, could wash over her more easily so she could drown peacefully in her panic.

"Julia! Are you okay? I'm sorry. I shouldn't have said anything; forgive me." Brian crouched to meet her tear-filled, crisis pulling her close, both now on their knees; dreams of living, dreams of glory emptying with their tears. Eventually, the tears, like the coffers, would be dry.

"It's very slick out there today, Stevie! Passes flying, skipping like pebbles over players' boots. A lot of surface water. It's going to make for a very sloppy match!"

"You're right there, Arlo; neither team able to get a good footing, or able to keep passes crisp. Glad we're under cover. Any more rain, and the players are gonna need a snorkel!"

"Again, another pass slips into touch. Goodness – look at that – Chesterfield not able to get any grip on the ball to throw it in. And the ball turns back over to Liverpool."

"It's like a water-polo match, Arlo, not a football match!"

"Perhaps that goes in Chesterfield's favor, as neither team is able to really control the ball!"

"I think you might be right! If you're watching expecting a spectacle of soccer, you're gonna be disappointed – this is more like a kiddie splash pool! Let's see how the drama unfolds."

"You get the feeling that one goal could open this wide open – set-pieces are going to be critical, given that that's the one time the ball will be stationary for a second! Provided you can plant a foot without it slipping out from under you!"

"A long-range shot from the Liverpool midfield – looking for any kind of opportunity when the ball is standing still!"

"I've had better lies in the water on a golf course, Arlo! I think it's coming down even harder! No indication of lightning, so we play on."

"Yes, that shot well wide skidded into the stands for a goal kick—when the idiot fan gives it back!"

"Hey – it hit me in t' 'ead – possession is nine ten'fs of t' law!"

"Alright, son, give the ball back or its off 'ome for you, sunshine!"

"Gid 'im fuckin' ball, yer twat!" The tinnies were well down their daily quota – they'd celebrated early with a breakfast brew to top off last night's epic session, which had ended only a few hours earlier with sun-up.

"Nay, fuckem. It's fuck'n mine nar – it 'it me fuckin' 'ead! They's prob'ly gorra 'nother!"

"Sir, the ball, or I'm gonna have to ask you to leave!" The orange fluorescent security attendant's bib stretched over his donkey jacket, which stretched over a lifetime of pies. This was the idiotic exchange that frustrated him the most. Always this section – his section – these clowns were here at every match. He'd taken this job just so he could afford to watch the matches, never having enough money to pay for season tickets. He himself had trained here as a youth – this was his team – he was a player – "fastest white guy in t' north" his mates had called him. That was a lot of pie crusts and ale ago – now he was a fan of the "Two Meals for Ten Quid." Sitting by himself at the Woodside pub– he would order two meals—one for the imaginary friend the waitress looked hard at.

"Come an' gerr i', Fatty Frank!" The tinnies found their chant. It wasn't that long ago that they were all on the advertising board side of the retaining wall. Training, not wasting. "Fatty Frank! Fatty Frank!" It was neither clever nor witty from bygone friends. "Wha' yer gonna do, Frank, roll on us – yer fat bastard!" it was impossible to see the sprinter of the past in him today; it was impossible to see the sadness and joy in the tragicomedy of a pork pie friendship. Shadows of ourselves, those children of the mirror we used to be, disguised by the treatment of time and our lifestyle. You can't see the embolism running around the brain – it disguises itself from the thoughts across the mind's superhighway, popping up like a lottery ball. Frank's face blossomed like acne on a tulip – wet and angry – he charged into the stands at the tinnies his old teammates. They would pay for his misery.

"Come on then, Frank, you fat twat! Norra fuckin' winger nar are yer, mate!" The tinnies laughed as Frank stumbled over the punters in the front rows.

The tinnies turned to each other. "Fuckin' twat's lost 'is fuckn' mind!" "Fuckin' irriot!" "Yerr fuckin' mental, Frank!"

Fully flushed and breathless, like a blood clot his head strained to hold back his eyeballs. When you lose it, you lose it!

"Bit of a commotion in the stands there, Arlo – wonder what that's all about?"

"Yes, seems to be distracting a couple of the Liverpool players, who are staring right at it. Chesterfield are obviously oblivious."

"Not sure if the referee has seen it. Not sure if it's his jurisdiction to stop the game. I think I see St. John's Ambulance men – and women—running hard to the scene."

"The game is still going on – Chesterfield on the move – a rare foray into their opponent's half. Sam Gifford, making his first start, has been able to hold off a few challenges with that square physique of his."

"There's an ambulance coming in at the Kop end – lights are blinding – very distracting – I hope that it's nothing serious for the fans. Not that they're missing much in this weather."

"Gifford still on the ball, rides a late challenge from behind; he should have gone down – it would have given his team a free-kick within striking range."

"Good God, Arlo, a flare has just gone up in the Kop – bright blue smoke."

"It sounded like a gunshot – oh my! Sam Gifford after riding that horrendous challenge from behind has hit a bullet of a strike from the apex of the box. It's beaten everyone; Mignolet's outstretched hand could only waft at it. I don't know if they were distracted by the goings-on at the other end, but the whole defense seemed to pause, for a second and that's all Sam Gifford needed. Unbelievably its 1-0 Chesterfield!"

"I'm stunned, Arlo. It was a great hit, but I have to believe the flare going up and the ambulance had to have had an effect. But either way the goal counts and halfway through the first half slop, Chesterfield have broken the tie!"

"You're…?"

"Yes, I am – Mrs. Millward."

"What are you doing here?"

"I've come to watch the match – you are watching it, right?"

"No choice, I'm afraid – the nurses put it on. They thought I might be interested."

"And you're not?"

"No – I am, but—well, it's 'ard an' all…."

"I fully understand – can I sit here? None of my friends like football – can't say I do that much, but I was afraid to sit by myself in the house. By the telly – by the gin. Those that I would watch it with are there – sitting in all that rain!"

"They must be mental, Mrs. M – they're wetter than a learner surfer!"

Joan moved to the edge of his bed."Mind if I sit here? Only the chair looks very uncomfortable." They smiled a little together. He moved over, fluffing the extra pillow for her to sit up against. "Better view from up here, too."

He blushed like Beaujolais on white linen.

"It's on mute – on account of old Mr. Sotheby over there – he's nocturnal – shuffles about like a fuckin' Roomba at night."

"I'm happy with just the pictures – no need to wake Mr. Sotheby." Joan added softly, taking the young man's hand. How smooth it seemed, how young it looked, unweathered, all the veins neatly tucked inside the peachy skin.

"Thank you," he whispered back.

"You're welcome, Wayne. Come on, you Blues!" Her voice barely touched the air.

"Well it didn't last long, did it, Stevie! Liverpool have equalized with a sublime header – the ball swung from the eighteen across the six – just as they rehearsed, players unable to react, losing their footing and only two men knew where the ball was going! That's one-one – and still ten minutes – ten very soggy minutes left in the first half here at Proact Stadium."

"Took the air right out of the crowd, Arlo – damper than the inside of a frogman's speedo out there now!"

"Quite, Stevie! All to play for again – the importance of the set-piece perfectly demonstrated by Liverpool – a first-class finish. The referee has blown the restart and the ball stalls at midfield – plugged like a broken Q-Tip!"

"I think this is where you see Liverpool show their class and divisional difference; I expect them to start stringing passes together and wear this much less experienced team down."

"You might be right, but first they are going to have to get the ball out of the center circle! I believe it's raining harder now than before – players are gonna be thrilled to get into the locker room at half-time. Find a towel and wring out their skin!"

"Liverpool have paid a lot of money for this team, but I'm sure that none of them were ready to play in conditions like this. These international superstars are more comfortable playing in their Mediterranean homelands than this monsoon! I think the last time these Liverpool players were this wet was when they fell off their surfboards!"

"Mignolet has gone to his third pair of gloves, whereas Ewan Bladen – Bladey, I think, is wearing his mother's woolen mittens! Chesterfield are definitely the underdogs in this round – you could probably buy the whole town for the price of one Liverpool player."

"Zoe, have you spoken to Brian?" Julia panicked the words into her cell phone the day before the Liverpool match.

"No, why? I haven't had chance what with the kids, school, homework, and dance. Why, do we need another meeting?"

"Yes, well no, probably – there may not be time for that?"

"How do you mean?" Zoe wanted both in and out of this conversation before it started. The questioning moment when you see a family member's phone number on your phone. A required response that beckons more out of loyalty than desire and convenience. We all carry our phones so close that we might as well be telepathic.

Laundry sprinkled on every radiator beckoned to be folded and ironed; it practically implored her to be rescued from the heat and placed neatly into the daily basket. Tea had gone cold, homework just started, breakfast dishes laid for tomorrow with today's leftovers. Zoe squelched around in the kitchen looking for the floor mop, the fluorescent light a shade too bright for her mood. Rain lashed at the windows in a vain attempt to get them clean. Zoe was regretting the impulsive run in the rain – but like singing in the shower, there's a solace to running in the rain. On hearing her phone screaming at her from beneath the pile of opened envelopes, bills hurriedly pushed back in, she had scattered them and drenched them. They landed by the crayons, Legos, and a Dolly Sunshine who had been nudged enough by the tsunami of mail to jingle "Bring me sunshine, bring me...." It petered out, luckily for Dolly Sunshine. Was that an eggy soldier lying by Dolly Sunshine? *I better answer the phone.* Zoe reached behind the kitchen table, grabbed what she thought was a tea towel from the radiator, and began drying her face with her best Victoria's Secret cami.

Julia was incoherent to anyone but Zoe. Zoe continued to dry her face and neck. She heard the word Brian in the opening address – this could go either way, she thought, but likely would be the other way. Despite the crowds at the pregame and the immense popularity of the Ernie Moss bobblehead day – "Brian" had the connotation of a "Bible"—was this going to be one of those uplifting stories, or a preamble of miseries to come?"Hold on a minute, Ju." Zoe wasn't sure if she heard, wasn't sure if she was even ready, tucked the camisole into the handle of the stove and sat like a yoga instructor next to Dolly Sunshine.

"The club is broke, Zo; there's a lawsuit; all of Dad's money will be gone!"

Dolly Sunshine didn't say a word; just grinned like she'd get to eat the last eggy soldier. Zoe was happy to be on the floor. Clammy and wet, her butt cheeks adhered to the wood like the peanut butter from yesterday's lunch.

"Nothing left?" Zoe exhaled into the phone like an asthmatic. She wasn't sure if she was reacting to The Club's financial situation or making a statement of fact about herself. Zoe remained shivering in her wet running clothes – "Bring me Sunshine all the while!" *Dolly Sunshine should watch her mouth if she didn't want to be slapped across the kitchen floor,* she thought."Did you hear me, Zo?" and Zoe nodded like they were on FaceTime. Her ponytail slipped by her ear to comfort her cheek, dripping into her bra. Zoe couldn't speak through the last bites of the eggy soldier.

"Well, ladies and gentlemen – the referee's whistle brings us to half-time here at the Proact Stadium. It's still Liverpool one, Chesterfield one, an unlikely score on this monsoon-drenched afternoon – back to you in the dry warm studio, Rebecca!"

"Thanks, Arlo – we'll be back with you and Stevie McManaman for the second half; we have an ark standing by just in case, should you need it!"

"Brian said that even if they win this afternoon against Liverpool there'll barely be enough funds to get them to the next round. You going to the match?"

"Of course – nearly ready," she mumbled through the last boot of the eggy soldier.

"Good – we should tell Dad together."

"D'you think he's up to it?" Zoe knew she wasn't. Dolly Sunshine confirmed she wasn't up to it.

"Well, Lindsey listed him again as a sub for today, and he didn't decline."

"He's gonna regret that in this weather; he's mad."

"Alright, we'll have a post-game meeting"

Zoe lay back and smacked her head on the harder wood floor – ah, the ponytail – it was at the front, not the back! From here she could see the cobwebs in the space above the cabinets where they don't quite meet the ceiling. She wondered what else called that space home. The ceiling could probably use a coat of paint. A white ceiling collects the mealtime stories of a family, over the years.

"Thank you, Rebecca – myself, Arlo White, here with Stevie McManaman – sitting two by two, ready for the ark. The weather here at Proact Stadium has disintegrated further – like a fog, the rain is so thick. The lights are on already. Not sure if they are going to call this one off!"

"Referees and the FA don't like to do that though, eh Arlo? It's a tight schedule – I know as a player, I would always like to get the games in, even in conditions like today."

"Well, Stevie, the players have their wish, as Alan Ravenshead has blown for the second half, and we are off again."

"Like ducks on a pond scattering from a rock the players going in all directions. Like clowns in a circus out there – everyone sliding around. I'm not sure the lights are helping with visibility, either – seems as if there is a glare now."

"I agree, Stevie; looks as though some of the players aren't picking the ball up quite right. And with that the ball skids innocently into the Chesterfield goalmouth. You could see the run-on there, Stevie – the ball skipped on the water from that driving pass, but once it slows down, it gets plugged. Bladey, the Chesterfield goalkeeper, has no problem collecting the ball at the top of his box. He launches one. Like many keepers these days, he's got quite the leg."

"So, Joan, mind if I ask why you came?" He inched around in the sheets, slightly pinned by Joan's weight sitting on them next to him. He didn't want to complain to his visitor; he liked the company, as odd it seemed for a sort of stranger to be visiting him in hospital. He didn't want to move too much, either, in the event the scratchy sheets rubbed hard on each other and self-ignited.

"Don't you like me being here?"

"No, no—I like ya bein' 'ere very much – it's just, like well, we hardly know each uvver."

"On the contrary – I know rather a lot about you, young Wayne!"

"Wha'? Are you one of them stalker people?"

"Hardly – if I were, you'd be dead or raped by now, right?" She patted his crotch for good measure. Wayne flinched like someone had dropped a match on the bed.

"Yeh, it's not like I'm moving far with this cast on me arm!" he agreed nervously.

"I'm Michelle's aunt." She paused enough for both of them – she caught up first while Wayne stared into the half-time commercials. "Well, I'm not really her aunt, per se; I'm a friend, family friend who she calls her aunt."

"I don't remember you at the wedding – surely you would have been invited?"

"I was, but my husband was dying at the time – it's tough; and as tough as I may seem to people sometimes – it's tougher being the one left behind – rooms have so many spaces you never knew existed. There are hollows in favorite chairs that don't fit my bottom – a bespoke cavity was carved out for someone else. Like the dog whose owner has died—that's the space on the couch. It remains without them.

There are 'favorite' towels in the airing cupboard that never seem to move any more. A toothbrush whose bristles have stiffened like pillars without a building; a razor fit for a face not for a leg. Reading-glasses on a side table no one can see through. The endless piles of shoes."

"I hear you there! I thought Michelle would have taken all of them! It's her thing, you know?"

"It's all women's 'thing' you know, shoes!"

"I guess – I don't know many women. I don't even know Michelle tha' well, I reckon. I like me footy boots – that's as close as I come – I know I wouldn't leave them behind."

"You wouldn't?"

"Well if I'd forgo"en 'em I'd go back for 'em, that's for shoower."

"You would, wouldn't you." Joan hinted at something – not sure if Wayne was following; sometimes in a relationship we can be too esoteric for our own good. The Ambulance Chasers, an aptly named law firm, was rounding out their commercial – smartly dressed men and women beaming at the camera into the hospital ward, a cluster of local actors posing for the role, surrounding some sorry fool in a wheelchair.

"How come we've never met, if you say you're like Michelle's aunt? How come she never mentioned you?"

"I didn't say I was her favorite aunt, did I?"

"I suppose not – but..."

"Eric and I lived at the bottom of Michelle's garden – the other side of the fence – the dark place where footballs landed and dollies feared. Her mother and I were pregnant together – we had tea parties to celebrate and the odd cigarette. We sat for hours by our fences – peaking over – both of us too plump to walk all the way round, so we just camped in our deck chairs, taking it in turns to bring out the tea and Battenberg cake. We planned our babies' lives before they had entered our second trimesters! They would both go on to law school – become politicians, prime ministers, corporate leaders, world-beating examples of womanhood!"

"Wow, sounds like you was really close!"

"We were, are – I suppose. I was much older, as you can imagine. Michelle's mum was, in my mind, very young much like a younger sister than a friend. I would have looked like a granny next to her going to kindergarten rather than a spritely new mum, still fashionable."

"So, did your kids grow up like sisters then, too?" Wayne had missed the past tense in Joan's history. A long pause, like an honorary minute at the sports stadium, filled the patient's room; all the while, the clatter of ward-life went on in the background.

"Michelle was born; I was a few weeks behind. Michelle was the most beautiful baby you could imagine – born with hair you could almost plait and put a bow in!"

"A can imagine." He would have loved her from that moment, too.

"We dressed her together, changed her together, fed her together. We shopped endlessly for the prettiest dresses, bonnets, booties…." Another moment of silence passed, whisking the energy from Joan's voice. "She was my practice baby!" Joan let out a little chuckle.

"Did your kids match, then? Were they like twins?"

"I'd like to think they would have been."

"…. " Wayne became painfully quiet, the stranger's tears doing all her talking.

"My baby… Juliet, was still-born – beautiful, not with Michelle's hair, but she was beautiful…." Moments can become hours when our minds drift back to our departed loved ones – it seems natural to stare at the wall on the horizon, travel back in time; like a projectionist, we cast up those favorite images on the wall in front, or the horizon on a long drive. Joan's only memory of Juliet was of her death, being beautiful, but not being. Joan projected a life they would have had; then came Michelle.

"I'm so very sorry." Wayne had it right this time and listened on.

"Michelle's mum became very sick after she was born – baby blues, they called it. But it was a lot worse than that – her mum practically disappeared inside her belly button, recoiling away from life, away from Michelle."

"Tha's really sad."

"It happens more than you think – Michelle's mum was hospitalized for over a year."

"So wha' 'appened to Michelle?"

"Well – Michelle's father was very busy with his fledgling plastics business and neither one of them had family close by – so, well, I kind of stepped in for that year; Michelle lived in what would have been Juliet's room. Her dad could see her every day, stayed the night on the couch most nights when he wasn't visiting her mum. I don't think he slept in his own bed one night in that year – back and forth to Derby – or hopping over the fence and back. He'd give us updates on his wife's progress, and we would update him on Michelle. Except when she learned to walk – we let him be the first to let us know – some things are best left unshared."

"So, you are like her mum, then, not like an aunt."

"No! I'm very much like an aunt. Her mum did come home – I stayed with her oh so many nights – a one-year-old walking, talking toddler can be a lot to come home to. We ate dinner at our house most nights – Eric was gone a lot too; sometimes it was just us girls, sometimes it was all of us. Eric took out a panel from the fence, made a gate of it so we could all go back and forth; back door keys under the pot by the gate. Mi casa es su casa, as they say in Spain."

Wayne didn't know Spanish, but he got the gist of it. "So why haven't I seen you before – if you were all so close?"

"Time and well… circumstances…." One should always stop and smell the roses before saying something you might regret. So, she lingered in the garden of thought for a while. Which circumstance to go with? Which bouquet to present? "Eric was transferred to Zambia – we were given a month's notice. For me it was like losing Juliet again, being away from Michelle. Her mum was doing better; the injections kept her on track enough, at least. Seven years we were gone – didn't have much chance to come back, you see… from Zambia." And there seeped out the guilt and the heartbreak. Of course, they had been back, but seeing Michelle again and then leaving again…well, it was more than a mother could bear.

"Can you help me? Help us, Joan?" Wayne hated to ask. But the cracks in his plaster heart were coming apart. "I started on the house – started on the foyer – it's about done. I know she wanted that done. Am done in with this shoulder. Am so shtupid! Michelle was right, there shouldn't be guns in t' house – nearly killed me sen!"

"I have one – my father's service pistol from the war. Keep it locked my boy. Oh, look—Chesterfield have the ball again – bet you're glad you're not playing today!"

"Well…I'd rather be there than here – no disrespect!"

"None taken, my boy; none taken."

"Feeling up for it, Roy?" Lindsey asked in a demanding rhetorical way."What, with two minutes left? If we 'ang on, we're going back to Anfield!" Roy knew the need for cash – not the actual need but the ongoing need!

"You're soaked already – get a little mud and sweat on you as well, eh?" Lindsey stood to meet the fourth official. "Come on, Roy, it's your time – go warm up. Jog a little – it's fun in the rain – try singing!"

"Seriously, Lindsey – we've been lucky so far. Let's just leave it be, alright? Team's done well; hopefully we can just make it to t' final whistle."

"Number eight going in for number four!" Lindsey yelled through the rain to the fourth official to put the numbers in the display board.

"Are you sure?" Roy gave her a look that said "Really?"

"Yes, Roy. One more thing – have you ever played a seven, two, one formation?"

"A what?"

"I want you to be the 'one' – camp out on the top of the 18-yard box. You'll be offside, of course. I'll hazard a guess that because it's you they will leave you one on one with the keeper – do you think you can handle that? Okay, tell Nicky it's the 7-2-1 plan – have Bladey come out of goal, put Ionut in – he's big enough and has decent hands but a better leg. I'm banking on him being able to kick it far, even in this!" Lindsey paused – looked him in the eye – dead on. "Okay, Roy – attention!"

The crowd booed when they saw Roy's number appear on the substitute's display board. It made sense, Roy thought – he would have booed the decision, too.

"Well, Arlo – I expected a lot more from my boys this afternoon – I thought we'd see a goal or three here in the second half, but neither team has really been able to create chances – looks like both teams are resigned to play at Anfield, which has to be considered a win for Chesterfield!"

"Agreed, Stevie. Chesterfield have survived a few chaotic goal-mouth scrambles, with balls bouncing off shins just wide as in a couple of minutes ago. But there are some very tired legs out there—both teams have exhausted their substitutions. Oh sorry, Chesterfield have one more to make; with a couple of minutes left, I expect they'll just be happy to hold on – they have packed everyone into the penalty box – Lindsey, their coach, is screaming at them to pressure the ball, but it's a big ask at this late stage. Another deep cross in toward the Chesterfield goal, but the header goes high into the stand, landing on a few empty seats."

"Yes, the center-forward really needed to get up higher to nod the ball down but – fair-dos, it's got to be very hard to get any elevation on this heavy pitch."

"So, it's another goal kick for Chesterfield – I've just been informed Stevie that that's the seventeenth goal kick this half for Chesterfield added to the eight corners – that gives you some idea of the pressure this Chesterfield back four has been under all day."

"That must be some kind of record, Arlo?"

"I would think. Well, it does look like Chesterfield will make their final substitution. As in previous matches, they bring on their rescuer and chairman to play the last minute or so. It's a mark of great respect. Some are applauding and some are booing here at Proact Stadium as Costica is replaced."

"Probably the Liverpool fans cheering, Arlo!"

"Yes – looks like they are making field changes too. Ionut is going in goal and will take the goal kick. Bladen has moved to a central midfield role. The chairman seems a little lost and is just standing by the Liverpool 18-yard box – Mignolet is speaking to him and has him covered – the rest of the team is spread like an umbrella at the top of their own 18!"

"Very strange, this, Arlo – Liverpool happy to let the chairman go—no disrespect to Chairman Griffiths, but Liverpool may see a chance to get a late winner and end the Ark-Bowl!"

"You're right with that, Stevie – seconds ticking down – the board says only a minute of time added on – much to the relief of everyone here. Ionut lines up the goal kick – it's a bomb, like a laser headed to midfield, I'm not sure how he got it off the ground to be honest, Bladen is up high to challenge for the ball but it skips backward off the defender's head – you wouldn't believe it – the ball has landed at the chairman's feet with only Mignolet to beat – the defender's touch has played him onside – there is literally no one within thirty yards of him. The chairman can barely stand in the swamp, he slips right – loses his footing, slips left like it's something out of *It's a Knockout*. Mignolet responds, he loses his footing, they both go down, from his backside the chairman pushes out his left foot as Mignolet slips past him, he swings at the ball, he scores! It's a brilliant effort from the chairman!"

"I'll say!" McManaman is choked.

"I'm telling you, the best stories happen in real life, and it looks like Chesterfield are going to be the giant killers of the FA Cup this weekend – and there is the final whistle – the crowd is on the pitch—jumping, cheering, singing in the rain. Suddenly it's blue skies for the Blues here at Proact Stadium – Rebecca, I'm gonna hand it back to you in the studio and head to a hot bath."

"Me too, Arlo – to drown meself in! I can't believe the boys let this one get away!"

One, two, three…four down, four to go!

CHAPTER 60

"Frank! Frank! You alrate, mate? We din't mean nuffin' by it! It were just a joke, mate, 'kinnell!"

Fat Frank could hear the tinnies yelling at him to wake up. "Come on, Frank! Stop messin' abou'!"

The weighty pain in his chest brought a serenity to his mind – his left side seemed mildly high, desensitized. The rain fell on his face with odd relief, like Aloe. The voices of his "pals" became thinner in his ears, drowned out by the rush of water under the gurney. He was moving quickly but not sufficiently to unseat the smiling elephant on his chest. Even when his mattress was flung hard into the flashing red and blue lights, the Loxodonta stayed rooted to his sternum. Someone tried to smother him with a plastic bottle, similar to those he'd been beaten with as a grade-schooler. This bottle was pleasant smelling and hurried away the circus animals.

"'ere, Frank – yer can 'ave dam ball back – it were just a funny! Rate?"

"What on earth is all that commotion outside?" Joan popped sprightly to her feet, her sensible rubber soles giving her a sturdy grip. "I'll be back in a moment…." She headed for the door but was soon pushed back in by half a dozen sodden Wombles reeking of cheap beer. Their roadies had hardly been touched.

"Where's Frankie? Where's Frankie?" The tinnies spoke in the unison of the Kop.

"I can assure you he's not in here!" Joan was apoplectic with shock of the blue-and-white-scarfed louts charging around the hospital like it was a dockyard. She was starting to regret having said "Come on, you Blues"-- if this is the sort of ruffian this team attracts – and if so, how could Roy want anything to do with it? Was he like this, really?

"If 'ees no' ere, then weyer is he?"

"I'm sure I don't know and don't know who you're talking about!"

"Frankie – security ball-boy – at match – 'ee went darn 'ard – an' t' ambulance come an' took 'im away. Took im 'ere." They were incredulous that she couldn't help. Joan looked at Wayne:

"A little help here, Wayne – I have no idea what they just said – too many voices in an alien tongue!"

"Rate, Mrs. M. They are looking for a friend who is part security and ball boy for the Chesterfield team – by all accounts these characters and 'im were at t' Town match earlier." Wayne forced his best "posh" on Joan, trying to separate himself from this rabble.

"Ah, I see – couldn't they have just said that? I'm not sure Alan Turing could decode this language!"

"Eh lads – there's no Frankie 'ere!"

"Eyup duck – thar fuckin' Wayne wotsit from t' Town, aren't yer?"

"Yes, he is Wayne Wotsit from Chesterfield Football Club. And he has a very bad injury – so can you leave him in peace?"

"OOOH! Got your bodyguard, Wayne, 'ave yer, yer fuckin' puff, wid yer fuckin' cougar!"

"I'm no such thing!" protested Joan. "Though it does sound rather exciting!" Wayne slid back as fast as he could, not tempted by the offer.

"Eyup, duck, will thar sign me shir'?"

"Of course?" Joan said, bemused.

"He means me, Joan. No offense – but cougars are not star quality material yet!"

Flustered once more, she said, "Yes – how silly of me," her voice fading as the embarrassment grew.

"'Ave yer gorra a pen?" Wayne was ready to sign like a rock star.

"Are you ready to go in, Zoe?" Julia checked with her co-pilot.

"Ready as I'll ever be – is anyone ever ready for moments like this?"

"I'll lead – he's less likely to chortle on about owt if I'm first – if you go in, Zo, right away he'll be 'Mr. Bloody Social' and we'll forget why we came. If I go first, he'll realize its less of a social visit.

"Hia!"

"'eyup Ju? Y'alright?" "Yalright" goes up and down like a linguistic roller coaster!

"Hia, Dad!" Zoe jumped in over his question.

"It must be serious if you two drove together! You've not been t' oncologist, 'ave you?"

"No, Dad – nothing like that – but it is still bad news. Oh, nice goal, by the way!"

"Yeh – nice goal, Dad," Zoe added quickly.

"Well, not my best, but I did enjoy it. What's all this about?"

"Dad, you want a tea?"

"It must be bad. You sure you haven't been to the doctor?"

"No, Dad, they have rules about that – they can't call us about you. It's not the school nurse."

"Well, good."

"No, not good," Julia wanted to get on.

"Shall we wait for the tea?" Suddenly, Roy was thinking a yard of tea might be needed.

"Up to you, Dad?"

"Stop, Zo. Dad, sit down. The Club's finances are a mess – Brian took me on one side and asked me to let you know!" Julia was running the classroom now.

"Why didn't Brian tell me himself?"

"Because he feels like he's letting you down, but even yesterday's win against Liverpool only delays the inevitable."

"Inevitable? There must be something we can do? How bad is bad?"

"We can do one more payroll run – then we have to pay the lawyers, lawyers! Lawyers!! Lawyers!!! I hate them all." Julia fell off script.

"Well that's that then, eh?" Zoe almost sounded relieved; this had been such a trial – seeing her father run around pouring good money after bad into The Club; both of them were now running out of time. Out of funds, out of sand, out of the FA Cup.

"I'll mortgage the house!"

"What!!" Their combined alarm bell sounded "NO! DAD, NO! Enough is enough."

"If you're not all in, then you are not in. I can't take this house with me – we are halfway to the final!"

"Dad – see sense – it's the family home!"

"You have your own family home – you have your own world. I will take my memories with me and the funds to The Club."

"But Dad … that's like giving up on everything you've ever worked for to start repaying for it! How are you gonna make payments on a mortgage?"

"I haven't the faintest idea. Six hours—Ju, Zo – six hours, that's how close we are!"

"What are you talking about, Dad?" Zoe joined Ju's fueled frustration.

"That's four matches. The goal is in sight. I can see it! Almost touch it!"

"Then what? Then what, Dad?" Ju pestered him.

"I don't have the luxury of anymore 'then whats.' I just have this what." The soon to be mortgaged room fell silent.

"You can't go in there! These are private wards!" but the tinnies ran by her like five surgical sponges chucked out of a wound.

"I said you can't go in there!" Barely five feet tall, with a five-foot wingspan, she used the power of her uniform to not let them go deeper into the ward.

"Miss – you don't understand! Our teammate was rushed to vis hospickle – we 'ave to see 'im, we may have hurt 'im, we 'ave to see tha' 'e's alrate? We might 'ave killed 'im! We left Town match just so we could see if 'e's alrate – we didn' mean 'im no 'arm!"

"I'm afraid there are many patients on this ward who I'm sure would rather not be disturbed by you drunken layabouts – besides, visiting hours are not for another few hours." All the curtains of the ward were drawn around each bed; nurses were popping in and out administering narcotics, dressings, and other comforts that go with just being there. A full ward can be a frightening and lonely place.

"But miss!" a different tinnie tried this time, as if trying to win over his kindergarten teacher. "But miss – we have to tell Frank …" and he raised his voice – what would be his telephone voice. "We have to tell Frank that we are SORRY!" The tinnie didn't know if Frank was in the room or not – he just belted it out. But somewhere down that hallway of curtains and mini-dramas an old teammate, a rather overweight man, began to cry, one tear at a time gliding over his nose into his other eye, forming a growing wet spot on his pillow. And the elephant he was brought in with started to slide over to its side of the bed. *They left the Town match for me.* He smiled into his damp pillow, pulling it even closer to him, the way a cloud might comfort an angel.

"If you can 'ear us Frank, we're rate, rate sorry mate!"

"SORRY! SORRRY! SORRY!" the Kop of tinnies sang to Frank.

CHAPTER 61

"I'll send the appraisers out, Roy, so expect a call any day. Can they call your mobile, or would you rather they call your home phone?"

"Better off calling The Club mainline than home – that has been home for the last few months, Dean," said Roy nonchalantly.

"You've done a remarkable job, Roy – the team is in the top six and the Cup run has the whole town buzzing. Mind my asking why you need the loan?"

"No worries, Dean. If you must know, The Club is broke. I'm mortgaging the house to make payroll and expenses for the next few months. We have a great buzz, as you mentioned – there is real love for this team – but even with the bonuses from winning, it's swallowed up in debt and lawyer's fees. It's worse than I imagined when I took over! We see our lawyer bills more than we see the fan mail!"

"Well, I can't promise anything, Roy – the decision will have to go to committee before any loan can be approved. And I have to tell you, your age and illness may count against you. We're worried these days about default; we don't want to be in the home ownership business – contrary to recent beliefs!"

"Well, see what you can do – if not, I'll be forced to sell it!"

"You're not serious? You'd sell your home to make payroll and bills for Chesterfield Football Club?"

"Yes, Dean." The words came softly like cream cheese on a toasted bagel. "Have you never believed in anything that you would risk it all for?"

"I can't say have."

"Well, when you do – and I hope you do – remember this moment and ask yourself, what would you do? Think long and hard – there are only a few times in life when you can take a different direction, follow a different path to nowhere, explore the universe of dreams – do it before the path becomes too short, so short that you may never reach the end of it. And as you, as I hope you do find a path, do it with time enough to reach the end."

"Roy, I don't know what to say – I mean I … I can't promise that the bank can do anything for you."

"All you need to say, Dean, is 'Come on you Blues' in the stadium on Saturday – say it with the fans, the boys and girls who wished they could be on the green velvet stage at 3 p.m. every other Saturday. Be with the rest of us who played the game and would have given anything to be in their place." Roy turned to leave, but not before giving one last chorus of "Come on you Blues!"

"Oh, hello Joan—sorry, I didn't see you come in."

"Nice voice, Roy." Joan smiled back at him as they nearly tumbled into each other by the bank entrance. "Come here often?" She smiled further to soften the awkwardness.

"Too often!" and Roy marched on – he'd wanted to see Joan so many times in so many places – but this was neither of them.

"Ready for lunch, Joan?"

"Indeed I am, Dean – what's your fancy?" Dean kissed her and took her by the arm, like newlyweds walking side by side out into the sunshine of the day.

"Hi Lindsey – to what do I owe the honor?" There are people that unseat me in conversation and Lindsey was one of them; I maul sentences like a raccoon in a trash can when I have to talk to her.

"Enough with the proprieties, Adam – I'll never like you."

"Understood, got it, right!"

"This team is really coming together, but we're gonna need Wayne back for the coming rounds – what's the word?"

"I stopped by earlier. He should be coming home in a few days then he starts rehab of the shoulder – could be four to six weeks."

"We're gonna need him sooner than that – the stunt in the last game was just that, and with only a few minutes left, it was a hedged gamble. But Wayne has been our assist machine. I'd like to bring in one of the League guys if he can't come back. We need the height."

"I can't see Dad going for that – I'll see how long Wayne will be out and what it will take for him to come back."

"We need something, Adam – we're short and down two players – no offense to Roy, and I like that we play him; it's great PR, but we are playing a man down on the bench and on the field."

"I'll do what I can. Maybe we should all visit Wayne? Maybe you could do one of your famous training runs to the hospital?"

"Maybe I could!" Lindsey reluctantly thought that it was not a totally shit idea coming from the shit guy. "And then maybe you could take a running jump!"

On her advice, I looked back through the window of my office that I shared with Dad, Brian, and Zach. The carpark wasn't that far down – might get away with only a sprained ankle or broken leg at worst if I ran and jumped.

"You're not actually considering it?" She paused. "No wonder I hate you."

"You are the coach!"

"Seriously, you are such a jackass – in that case, I'd rather you played with trains!"

CHAPTER 62

After sitting for a while, Roy just couldn't believe how much the waiting room smelled like smoke, still. Was it embedded in the paint, the carpet, the trim, the curtains? *Bloody hell,* he thought, *did my house always smell like this?* Perhaps it was in the chairs, or more likely the fifteen or so people who sat hunched and pained waiting for the good doctor. They had all been scheduled at the 9 o'clock hour—all fifteen of them. Whoever showed up first got the winning number the rest would wait in order, for the balance of their tardiness. Regular visitors knew this and would show up early, often forming a line outside the clinic before it opened. Dad was new to the NHS game of musical chairs – it would give him time to reflect on his illness. As his eyes swept tactfully around the room, it looked to him like everyone was taking a dip in the pity pool. Some were wallowing, enjoying a magazine – *Women's Health* was a popular choice amongst the older men, it appeared. He regretted doing the crossword already, but he'd needed the break from thinking, thinking about himself and the sickness, the sickness that brought him to a clinic that smelled like his home, the way he'd always enjoyed it.

A red light went on over the doctor's door. It wasn't a bright light and everyone picked up their handbags, newspapers, plastic cups with plastic coffee and slid over one chair closer to the door. Those that were standing would move in and one patient could take the now vacant seat. The new face—elderly, not ancient; ruddy, not golden; white-haired, not brown or auburn any more; eyes sparkling with tears, not dreams; crow's feet, not tucked; layers of scarves, not pearls; a hat, not a bow; the face of the British Isle, not Greek; a face of pies, not pasta; a face of granite, not pumice.

By Dad's reckoning, he would be paddling in this pity pool for another half hour, optimistically sliding onto the next warm seat every four or five minutes. Some illnesses are easy to detect – you can see them in the very faces of the waiting room. His was--well, less so, but he hazarded a guess that he might have them beat for severity, though. A real underdog story – a coming back from the grave diagnosis – living longer than anyone previously diagnosed had ever done – being interviewed by Ross McWherter for the *Guinness Book of Records* as the longest survivor of lung cancer in history. Yes, that was a medal worth winning – worth giving up smoking for, worth losing his dignity for during chemo, worth filling buckets of puke with more masticated food than you can remember eating, worth losing his hair, losing his strength, worth winning the battle of willpower, the will to not quit every single painful exhausting ritual of a day. Yes – so many days he could sit on this preformed vinyl chair and add to the pool of pity around him. But not today; when the red light shone for him it would be routine, a schoolboy physical: "Let's check your bits, young feller – right, you're good to go, Roy; enjoy PE!" yes, that's how it will be today. Hair was growing in – the hours of vomiting had long gone – this waiting room was as close as he came to a smoke – eating well – exercising with the team just a little, at any rate – staying hydrated thanks to Lindsey's constant reminders – yes, today should be that day he could once again hear the words "everything's normal"!

"Sorry, Roy – I did the best I could – the committee just couldn't see its way to giving you a loan – I mean we could if you had any collateral – I mean if you had the funds that you poured into the team, then we could loan you the money!" Dean lowered his eyes on his friend.

"That's absurd, Dean – if I had the money I wouldn't be standing here!"

"Ah but this is a bank, Roy – you have to have the money to borrow it."

"So that's that, then? After banking here for over fifty years you're telling me I can't pull equity out of my home?"

"I'm sorry, Roy; that's the way the committee sees it. You see, you're retired—well, sort of, but since you're not paying yourself a salary, well, we have no way to gauge how much to loan you against a prospective income to back it up. Surely you must see what I mean?"

"Yes, I see right through you – looks like I'll be selling my house then!" Roy had no way of storming out. He was out of venom; he wouldn't have loaned him money, either.

Next door Wilkins and Vardy Estate Agents had a "listing coming soon" in their window fifteen minutes after leaving the bank. And late that afternoon, following his nap, he woke up to a sign in his yard: House for Sale.

"Nothing more we can do, I'm afraid, Mr. Griffiths," was what the doctor told him – he was no longer Roy but "Mr. Griffiths." Perhaps that formality made it easier on the doctor; Roy would still check over his shoulder for his father every time he heard it. There were still three minutes left of the four allocated to him. Dr. Doran had spoken softly, but instead of "nothing more we need to do," he said "nothing more we can do." Nothing more to try, no "roll up the sleeves and dig our way out" mentality. No "Escape from Colditz at all costs, whatever it takes," no Churchillian "We will never, never, never quit," no "Fight them on the beaches and in the towns," no fourth official adding extra time, no one to extinguish the burning, smoldering fuse wire, no one to crack the code at the last minute before the bomb goes off, no one to catch the existential falling tree, no one to retract the candle-snuffer above his head. The referee was checking his watch; his whistle was in his mouth. He was learning how long a piece of string is. It's not very long, and eventually the cable car reaches its end.

"We have things we can give you to ease the pain, Roy. I'll get you a prescription." Dr. Doran wrote busily on his little white pad tearing off two or three small sheets with childlike squiggles that were acceptable at the chemist, but that no kindergarten teacher would approve. Dr. Doran placed them in Roy's open hand. He hoped they were for earplugs so that he wouldn't hear the final whistle – if you don't hear it the game goes on, right?

The good doctor had a pastor's eyes, the solemnity of the last rites look about him; he could administer to the body, but the spirit was not his domain. Roy checked the pages in his hand like someone had given him the ending of a story. He tucked them deep into his jeans pocket, stuffing them far down where the lint gathers. With his other hand, he reached into his breast pocket and pulled out his silver Lambert and Butler pack of smokes, carefully flipped the lid, delicately pulled out the cigarette, and placed it in his dry lips; it was like reuniting with an old lover.

"I'm afraid you can't light that in here, Roy." Dr. Doran could only treat the body.

"I know, Doctor; I left the matches in the car." As he opened the door with two minutes remaining in his allocation, the little red light above him burst into life like a street in Amsterdam. Strangely, the room offered a gentle and growing applause – Roy thought it was quick visit, but not that quick. Or were they applauding his adolescent cigarette hanging from his mouth? Then Mavis came to him from across the room – she had sat down when he went in."Roy," and she gave him a lasting hug like a mother would. "Well done, me lad, well done – what you have brought to t' Town has been nothing short of a miracle – it's like magic – me and t' ladies are all talking about it, and we don't even like football!"

"We're having a street party! Like the Jubilee!" chirped a chip off the old granite block. "Got the bunting back out and everything!"

"After you beat Liverpool we thought that were it, Roy! Good enough, Roy… But look yer, yer in t' final now!"

"I've gorra a marquee coming – putting telly in t' back garden, I am!" whispered a lady from beneath her plastic bonnet.

"I'm 'aving t' whole family around… even t' in-laws! And believe you me ah can't stand 'em!" said Mavis' chaperone.

"Me and me college roommates are taking all the furniture out of our bedroom and putting mattresses in there instead – we have three tellies so we can doss on t' floor and see from any angle! It's gonna be a rate piss up!" added a punk with a septic nose-ring.

One person after another crowded Roy to tell him of their party plans – "like a Jubilee." Had he really created something as momentous as the Queen's Jubilee?

"We're doing a rummage sale at the Y to raise money to take buses down to London."

"I've never seen owt like it, duck! What you an' team 'ave done is rate champion, rate champion Roy! Tha's done thee sen and t' town proud."

More and more strangers came to give him a hug. Dr. Doran stood in his doorway, as no patients had come to him. He said over the din:

"We are all very proud of you, Roy for what you have done – you have put Chesterfield back on the map – now if you could do us all a big favor… go and beat Middlesborough in the final!" The good doctor had called him Roy again.

Roy hadn't noticed as he'd been waiting before, but now he could see that many in the room were wearing the signature blue and white, either scarves, hats, pins—kids were wearing team jerseys – girls with Lauren's number on the back. Then a little swell of "Come on you Blues" rippled around the room until everyone was chanting, cheering their gladiator on to battle as Roy exited the waiting room into, well –the half-painted hallway, not the cauldron of the colosseum. The cheers faded away with every step until the teabag had been squeezed of its last drop of flavor.

I met Dad at the entrance. Now outside he tried to light the cigarette, but a floodgate had opened, and it's really hard to light a cigarette when you're smiling.

"Good news then eh, Dad?"

"Sort of; can you pass me a match?" Hands quivering, he struggled to light the cigarette. A plume went up like a smoke-signal of victory. The nicotine rush hit his bloodstream like a lover's touch. "To the stadium, Ad—we have a lot of people counting on us, a lot of people!"

CHAPTER 63

Roy's house had been priced to sell. "Motivated seller," the notice had read. And it was sold in less than a week. Mission accomplished – The Club would stay open now for a couple more months just shy of May. A storage pod was at one end of the driveway and a skip dumpster at the other. Julia, Zoe, and myself all stood looking at both, then looking at Dad – what do you keep? And what do you throw away? You can't take any of it with you. "Storage is 80 quid a month, mate," the bloke had said on the phone. "Daylight robbery that!" is probably what Dad said in response – I wasn't there, but I'm pretty sure that's what he would have said. So, we stood there staring at two very different pods, two very different possibilities – what did he have that was worth 80 quid a month? 80 quid in perpetuity. Dad had held the dice to move first; it was his go."Well …" he started, "is there anything you need for your house, Ju? Zo?" Obviously I wasn't bringing anything back to the States. They pondered a while – pictured their homes – pictured what their homes, their lounges, their dining rooms, their kitchens looked like – then tried to imagine Dad's stuff in them. His oversized club chair in their lounge without him, without him in it watching telly – likely watching cricket; the dining room table – they imagined the dining room table in their dining room next to their existing dining room table, his dining room table without him poring over the quick crossword or work files. They imagined his bed – their bedrooms had beds, even the spare room was defined with a bed in it. Imagined his bed next to their bed – without him in it. The dressers, the side-table with his glasses and sipping glass of water; even the telly for God's sake! Where would they even put his telly – it was huge – they both had tellys, some begrudgingly in bedrooms; what would they do with a Cineplex version? Julia and Zoe's piano – who would take it? It could only go to one home, but it had only ever known this home – this wall. A wall that had lived in its shadow for thirty years except to get a fresh coat of paint. The indents in the carpet from its wheels are probably through to the hardwood by now. All three homes were of modest size and all were furnished, gone were the days of hand-me-downs, we had been adult children for a long time, our furniture were pieces of choice, design and spousal agreement and disagreement. Nothing was random or eclectic, unless it was specifically designed to be random or eclectic. Looking at these two pods, we couldn't help but think these are the decisions you make when your parents are passed not standing right in front of you. Roy could feel and hear the moving truck of life backing up to him.

"What do you want to bring to the house, Dad?" Julia offered. "You'll have your own place again soon enough." It was a lie that saved the air – and allowed us to breathe, filling the vacuum that had been the silence.

"We'll look into a granny flat for you, Dad!" Zoe helped out with a cheeky grin.

"Eh – less of the granny!" from the man who still denied his age.

"We should bring your chair to ours, Dad." Ju knew there was no room and the recliner club chair would dominate her minimalist family room. "Then let's put the rest in storage for now."

"Fairy-nuff!" Dad was complicit. "I'll probably bring a couple of me mugs along too."

"We can clean out the dressers in the spare room and it'll be like your own room." Ju wanted Dad with her and so did Zo; there could be no fight – Julia had the room – logical, simple enough.

But even when it's your kids' home it's not yours – you're still a guest – it's not your bed and it's not your space; its theirs and you are a guest even if you are the most welcome of guests, everything about it, every decision for décor, furniture, layout, bedding, lighting—well, it was all foreign. None of those decisions included you, there were no memories here—no marks on the wall where your kids had grown, no nail holes where the picture had been hung too low and had to be repositioned; there were no paint streaks in the ceiling that you only noticed days later when the brushes were cleaned and put away, there was no crush in the carpet where your feet had padded around for decades, there was no leaky faucet that you were going to get around to this weekend. Even the dust bunnies were someone else's pets; the familiar cracked tile in your bathroom was now someone else's linoleum; the indentation in the plaster wall from the repeated forceful and excessive opening of your bedroom door was gone, replaced by a neat little rubber stopper coordinated to match the trim. All the wall plugs were in the right places, neatly at the side of the bed where table lamps could be tidily switched on without running extension cords around the wall. Yes, you were welcome; the room told you, "guests welcome," but you were always the stranger.

The truck we rented was barely half full – mostly excess tools that Dad couldn't part with and were too valuable for the tip. The oversized chair sat majestically in the truck like the Lincoln Memorial sans Lincoln facing outward. Around it were labeled boxes, labeled "tools" – somewhat redundant, I thought.

Roy stared into the back of the truck. The roller door came down; he flipped the latch and lit the cigarette, then tapped on the back of the truck, signaling for me to take it away. He drew long and hard, as if catching up for the last ten years, like an extended hug of a long-lost friend returned from an extended stay in Zambia.

Roy looked at the house. Any day now the ceilings would be painted, the notches on the trim sanded and glossed over, the nail holes repaired and hidden with new photos of new owners; there was even a good chance the leaky faucet in the powder room might get fixed. New carpet or the modern addiction to hardwood would replace a lifetime's indentations. Rubber stoppers installed to protect the new paint. And the wall—well, it might get one of those new-fangled Clarinovas to listen to.

"Coming, Dad?" Zoe called from the car.

After a sizeable draw on the cigarette – which would have to be extinguished if he wanted a ride—he said:

"I think I'll walk."

"What, to the house? Its bloody miles, Dad. Jump in."

"I was thinking to the Highfield – I fancy a pint."

"Want me to join you?" Zoe offered. "I can give you a lift!"

" 's'alright, Zo. I need the fresh air – a walk'll do me good." He smiled at his own irony.

"See ya later then, Dad?"

"Sure."

Not only would the rooms be different, but the walks would be different too. There's no familiar gennel at the top of Julia's street, no tabby cat in the window four doors down guarding with a fiendish stare at passersby, there's no yappy shih tzu across the street that for all its cuteness looks like a gremlin when it barks, Mrs. Davis wouldn't be out "pruning her roses" while she spied on neighbors; it would be half a mile out of his way to walk down the hundred and nineteen paces of the gennel, a tight corridor that at night gave you fits of highwaymen leaping out and demanding your pocket money. The other side of it, only sixty-seven paces, was the well-lit street that was four maple trees from the pub. Worst of all, though, Joan did not live up the street from Julia and would not be taking his bus route. He couldn't tell if she was home; she was better than he at turning off all the lights. Perhaps she was home, perhaps she was with Dean, the man who said "no." Maybe he had said yes to her. Roy cupped his cigarette in his palm, hiding it as he walked by. If she did see him, he didn't want her to see his flaw and think badly of him. He missed their bus rides.

And somewhere behind the window-sheers that let the light in and the privacy out, a woman watched a man walk by.

That same woman picked up the phone. "Dean?"

"Yes – ah Joan, good to hear from you!"

Steadily she asked - "Dean – can we meet? Perhaps coffee at Joplins?"

"Name your time."

"How about, say, 11:15 tomorrow morning?"

"Perfect! See you then!" Dean couldn't contain his excitement.

CHAPTER 64

The credits rolled, the theme music played, and Harry Gration looked as calm as ever. "Among the news stories tonight – despite Chesterfield Football Club's epic run to the FA Cup Final their back room is blighted by stories and rumors that the court will order the Proact Stadium 'off-limits' until the court case can be resolved. With only a couple of games left in the regular season and of course the FA Cup around the corner, this could be devastating to their League title and FA Cup hopes."

"Is Harry right, Dad?" Ju looked across the lounge at him sitting in his maroon faux-suede recliner chair that untidily mismatched her sleek white Italian leather sectional. Roy had his feet two-thirds of the way inclined, unable to go horizontal on account of the lack of room between the wall behind and the glass coffee table adorned with chrome accent supports. He was the red grape on a vine of green. He was advised to wear support socks for circulation, an unfashionable concession to age and disease. Dad nodded, his shoulders shrugging up to meet his chin.

"Brian and I met with the attorneys, the movers, and a number of FA officials yesterday. We're also in talks with Matlock Town about using their ground to finish out our League Season – they seem willing to take our call, of course. But our two home games played there will be immensely costly, as we have more season ticket holders than they have space for!"

He wanted to recline the chair the whole way back and drown himself like an old village dunking stool – he needed to drown the witch's spell out of him. He felt the yang might not be worth the yin.

"Michelle, have you considered giving Wayne another chance? He's out of hospital now the wound is healing quickly. I think he can even do push-ups again."

"How do you know so much, Joan?" asked Michelle pointedly, turning to feed the baby, allowing Joan the time needed to squirm like an infant in her own chair.

"I like you both, Michelle; I love you, of course, like you were my own and I especially love the woman that you have become – strong, independent, loving. But you being with Wayne humbles you just a little—because, well, he is so witty, and I think you need a bit of that in your life."

"Not bad-looking either!"

"Well, that's not for me to say, but he is rather dishy even in his hospital gown!"

"You went to the hospital!" Michelle popped back around with such speed that baby food landed in Joan's eye! Banana soufflé flavor like a snot gremlin hung from her eyelashes! She flung it back to start a baby-food fight. Joan grabbed the mushed carrot tub, stuck a finger in, swilled it around, and flipped a glob of white T-shirt ruining carrot extract right at Michelle! Michelle took her index finger. swilled it in the banana mush like she was rinsing off her brush, and whipped it out like Billy the Kid, splattering Joan's sporty white zip-up top.

"Damn, that'll never come out!" Joan looked at the banana stain-maker!

"Serves you right for interfering!"

Joan slipped two fingers into the grainy carrot mush and hurled it at Michelle. The blob split apart like the Hawaiian Islands – the Big Island hitting Michelle in the forehead while Maui landed on the baby! They continued back and forth, their shirts like organic children's finger paintings! Peers would be wrestling at this provocation, but the baby was giggling, out of control, dumping food on the floor and throwing it too.

"That's a lot of food for a baby to eat!" laughed Joan as she looked at her streaked jacket.

"I don't need a man, Joan! Like Bono said – 'a woman needs a man like a fish needs a bicycle'!"

"That may be true in rock and roll – but we live in the real world where kids need their fathers, if only to see their imperfections!"

Michelle held off jumping on that one, while wiping the carrot mush off her brow.

"Leave your jacket here, Joan. I'm putting a load of wash in. I can do yours too before it stains forever."

"That would be lovely."

"My goodness, Joan! Are those new?" Michelle beamed, catching sight of Joan's new form.

"Sometimes, Michelle, an old fish needs some new gills before a country bike-ride! I was in hospital the same time as Wayne – I had all this money sitting in the bank, and these boobs sitting on my lap, so I decided to visit them both. One's a little lighter; the other's a little heavier. I feel young again when I see myself in the mirror and tie my tennis shoes. They hide the rest of me when I look down; I look pretty again when I dress them up. They have the life they once knew. You're the first person who's really seen them. Do you like them, or am I just being a silly old woman?"

"I think they look lovely, Joan." She sensed Joan's searching. "Mind my asking, did it hurt?"

"Yes, but I'm no longer invisible when I walk into the room!" Joan chuckled.

"I'll say! They are quite the statement, Joan, and you are beautiful in the before and after."

They both giggled in their bras, hair streaked with baby food like sorority sisters at a rush event.

CHAPTER 65

"Thanks for coming over, Roy – I don't know what I'd 'ave done without yer, mate."

"I like to be useful, Wayne. When you get to my age, people start to wonder 'What can he do at that age? What goes away? What stays? Should he be still driving?' This drywall gives me a chance to, for us all to see what we can do. Hand me another screw, would you?"

"Here, Roy."

"Ta – it's like most jobs around the house; it's a two-person job hanging drywall!"

"Yep – physio says I'm all rate to play an' all, burra can't do no 'eavy liftin' for another four week or so."

"Well I'm glad I stopped by, Wayne – can't tell you how many times I've done this in me life! Our Ad's useless unless it can be fixed by painting over it! Ju and Zoe are better at house projects than him! Probably my fault for not showing him better. No, actually, I did show him – he's just not a good student on these matters!"

"And I'm glad you're 'ere, Roy – its lonely 'ere. It's no' a big house but i' is when its mostly empty."

"And unfinished!" Roy checked him with a knowing grin! "Alright, that's the last of the screws. Hand me some plaster on that trowel, and I'll start running the seam. She'll be ready for painting in the morning, then that's the bathroom completed." Roy took the trowel and switched the cigarette to his other hand; the plaster smoothed over the seam and screws with the sweeping skill of a watercolor artist's skyline. "She'll be ready for sanding in a few hours. Best put t' kettle on and tek a look at t' next room to be done. This place has got great bones—it's just cosmetic stuff really. Unfortunately, the stuff you look at every day!"

"Tea I can mek, Roy. I've gorra few choccy digestives left; we can 'ave them too. Who turned out all the lights?"

"I did – it was like a Christmas tree in here – go' money to burn, 'ave yer?" Roy, chameleon-like, again drifted into an empathetic vernacular.

"No I amt, Roy. A'll pu' ke"le on."

"Be with you in a sec!" And like a rare, satisfied artist, moments later the trowel was soaking in a bucket and the lid back on the compound. The gunshot hole was repaired. *Good as new,* he thought. "This room can start over now," said Roy to the switch as he turned off the lights behind him.

Meanwhile, in a parking lot across town, chains and padlocks were being attached to the doors of a stadium on a judge's order until matters could be resolved– they hung around the building like the ghost of Jacob Marley, killing dreams, turning sleep into nightmares. In the darkness of early morning when only writers and insomniacs are awake, the chains were looped twice like the supporters' scarves and padlocked together by Dickensian bailiffs. The bailiffs pasted the orange court-order sign above their locks – they were just doing their job, and as Town fans, they were doing it reluctantly and hopefully when no one would see them. The bailiffs closed their eyes as the final lock clicked into place--the way you avoid eye contact with the vet when your family dog, sick beyond the help of modern medicine, has to be put down.

"Are you sure this is wise, Joan?"

"Well, you are standing on the doorstep in the rain with a baby in your arms, Michelle! You've come this far – just ring the bell and see if he's home."

"But there's not a light on in the house – he's probably not home!"

"If he's depressed and lonely, and he might well be, chances are the lights would be all out – trust me, I've been there!"

"What if he doesn't want to see me? This seemed a better idea an hour ago with a prosecco in me hand."

"Yes, well, an hour ago the sun was shining and you were giving me a single-mum sob story! I'm sure he'll see you – it would be a heartless man who doesn't welcome back his wife and baby as they stand on the doorstep in front of him! That doesn't sound like the man I know from the hospital. Besides, my being here might just scare him into submission anyway!" Joan reached around Michelle and pressed the bell, making up her mind for her.

"Oh, thanks, Joan!" This was punctuated with sarcasm.

"Well, we are here, aren't we? What will the neighbors think if we stand here much longer?"

"I don't care what they think! There's no lights on in any of the houses on this street any way – no one's home!"

"On the contrary, my dear – if the lights are all out, they are indeed all home, and they're staring out of the window like a neighborhood MI6!"

"Milk, no sugar, Wayne. Cheers – I'll see who's at the door."

"Ta, Roy. I'll be in t' lounge."

The foyer burst to life when Roy turned on the light, the crisp white trim bordering "Sunlight Hay" with eggshell finish. Roy knew it as "Magnolia" paint back in his day. As Roy opened the front door the guests were blindingly spotlighted by the foyer's brightness against a "Battleship Potemkin" grey day.

"ROY?" Michelle and Joan both said, perplexed. Wrong house?

"Michelle… Joan?" Roy answered, not making the connection between seeming strangers. The three of them stood catching the rain with their shoulders lit by a Gene Kelly stage light. Michelle couldn't help but think an awning of some sort would be nice over the front door. It was a thought that for now was best kept to herself.

"See, I told you someone was home!" Detective Joan knew human nature, breaking the case and the ice wide open. "Well, Roy, are you going to invite us in or not? If you hadn't noticed, there's a baby getting wet!"

"Err, yes—well, of course, come in." Roy stood aside, unsure if he was doing the right thing by letting them in. This wasn't his house for him to decide who comes in and out; it was a private matter between Wayne and Michelle. But as he had learned, Joan had a way of doing the right thing. "Wayne is getting the tea on."

"Perfect timing then, eh? Mind your step, Michelle – though it's so bright, I can see your bone structure from here." Joan was kindly steering Michelle into her own house that to her no longer resembled her old house. As she pushed Michelle forward at arm's-length, she stopped before entering the rest of the house.

"Grab your coat, Roy; we're leaving!" Joan pointed to the newly constructed wall hooks with matching shoe-bins below.

"What? In this?" The door was still open, and the grey rain looked to be in for the rest of the day.

"Yes. I think there's a couple who are going to need some alone time." She nodded to Michelle but could have been talking about herself and Roy. "You can share my umbrella, Roy. Let's go for a walk. Then I'll mix us a piña colada!"

The door closed tightly – you could see neither in nor out – the road wound up a steep corkscrew of a hill towards gentlemen farms and open tree-lined meadows, sheep nestled in the shade of the Fresians; if you kept on for a mile, or maybe it was two, there was a single hedgerow lane that cut over to the Matlock Road. Joan looped her arm, fish hooking Roy's, choosing uphill.

"Now don't get any ideas, Roy! This is a narrow pavement – I just need a little balance."

"What would Dean say if he saw us?"

She paused, looked at him carefully, and measured:

"He'd say – there's two old friends, one making sure the other one doesn't fall. So, tell me again all about this Football Club of yours."

CHAPTER 66

Roy's pocket buzzed and vibrated, and he fumbled around in the dry side of his jacket. He'd ignored it the first couple of times, wanting to just enjoy the alone time with Joan, but the interloper's buzzing was too persistent to be ignored like a Jack Russell begging to be attended to. Roy had been given the phone by Brian – "It's how we all communicate these days, Roy!" he'd said. Which made Roy a little sad, yet happy that the written word, even if butchered, was still valued when together time was not.

"Are you going to get that, Roy? It's scaring the goats!"

"Sure, sure—but we haven't come very far."

"I believe we have, Roy." Her whisper was for her own frequency, not his.

"Strewth!"

"What is it, Roy? One of the kids?"

"No – it's a message from Zach…."

"Is it about your football club?" She had given him ownership like one does a mistress.

"All the doors to the stadium have been padlocked and court-ordered closed!"

Joan pulled him under the umbrella a little closer, the steady rain getting unsteadier.

"What are you going to do, Roy?" She could feel Roy shaking, even though the buzzing had stopped. Whether it was anger, cold, or fear, she couldn't tell—but he stayed close when she pulled him near. Steady rains have a way of finally breaking the seal of your outerwear; at some point the elements, the outside world dampens your core. At the peak of the hill, and below them, they could see the spire of the town, a marker from miles around. The cows and sheep still huddled; he wanted so badly to run like a crazed child and scatter them like a bowling ball at the pins the way the text had come to him. Only change is constant, but how he longed to be a sheep in the shade of the cows, in the shade of the yews, in the shade of time.

"I'll take you back to your car, Roy."

"Actually, I walked here – needed the air."

"Then I'll drive – we should probably head to the Club, right?"

"Thanks, Joan." He was despondent, like a weather forecast of "light rain followed by heavy showers."

Team cars huddled in the car park like pregnant cows waiting to deliver their cargo. The stadium was locked tight, and the rain bounced like fireworks off the bonnets. As Joan and Roy pulled in, what drove Roy mad was seeing that he had in fact left his office light on. It was the only one.

"This doesn't look good, Roy."

"No, Joan, it doesn't – we've come so far; the Cup Final in a week."

"So that's what all the bunting is for around town – it's like the Queen's Jubilee all over again!" Joan pleaded ignorance.

"We've been inundated with requests for players to show up at fetes, street parties, office parties, new business dedications, the list goes on! We are celebrities in a very small fishbowl!"

"Literally today, it looks like! Is that the whole team crammed into those few cars?"

"Yes, we are close – when you have no money left – and when the only things left in your pockets are your friendships, you get very close."

"Like Fagin! You got to pick a pocket or two!" Joan began to sing – the keys in her voice jangled.

This was to be one of the last training days: work on set pieces, craft some new trickery. But this was the third time in a month that the club had had its gates locked. Each day of execution had sent the team of lawyers to the court, asking for a stay. The legal bills ate Roy's house. There were no funds now; Roy's light was on and there was nobody home. He'd written the last check that wouldn't bounce – the lawyers demanded payment beforehand knowing The Club's troubles. Their last home game had been played at Matlock – as Proact had been in a state of darkness on account of a Friday night lock-out by the bailiffs. It had been a season of tough pills to swallow, but on-field success had been its only reward. The first team had taken its mixed start to the season and followed the strict fitness and unique training methods of their American coach all the way to be crowned as league champions. All that was left was for the Reserves to win their 8th game in the season for the unlikeliest of "doubles" football had ever seen.

Roy walked uneasily toward the cars; his legs were starting to cramp and swell a little from walking earlier. *I probably need some of those granny-socks, compression socks, or whatever they were called,* thought Roy.

"What do you think, Lindsey?"

"Well, Roy, all the balls and the equipment are inside the stadium."

"You could take them over to Tapton Golf course for wind sprints?"

"Or we could go t' pub!" yelled Sam, who with Laurel had climbed into the back of the coach's Fiesta.

"Not a terrible idea!" agreed Zach, who had comfortably stretched out before Sam and Laurel joined him.

"You know – let's just do it!" Lindsey exclaimed like an anti-Christ to the Nike commercial.

"What, go t' pub?"

"Sort of," said Lindsey. "Zach, call the local radio stations. Chesterfield Football Club is going to do a pub crawl!"

"Are you sure, Coach?" Zach's kilt was a little troubled.

"Yes—what's that one area you always keep talking about going to on a Saturday night?"

"The Brampton Mile?" offered Zach, perplexed. "We're gonna go on a piss up a week before the final?"

"How busy are they on a Saturday before the big match? They're dry, right? Enough room for about twenty people, right?"

"Lindsey, what are you thinking?" Roy joined the confusion.

"I'm thinking we can do our stretching, our circuit training, our yoga, and sign a bunch of autographs into the bargain! We used the schools for outdoor training, and we'll use the pubs for our indoor calisthenics!"

"I'm in no matter what – I'm ready for a pint!" Sam was too eager and Laurel tempered his excitement with her fingernails in his quads. "Hey, that hurts!" Laurel gave him the look.

"Zach let the radio stations know that the Chesterfield players will be doing the Brampton Mile starting in about an hour – that'll give us time to change and the kids chance to get their autograph books! We are going to have a totally Chesterfield PR day – ending up in Queens Park. Zach, tell the stations to have the kids bring their balls for signing, and we'll need a few for practice!"

"Actually, Lindsey – I just blasted it on Facebook and Instagram on me tablet – so you'd better tell the team to get changed!"

Roy and Lindsey looked at each other, a little dated in their thinking. Roy's back was soaked from leaning into the Fiesta, and when he turned around Joan had gone. She always had somewhere to be these days. She was probably at Dean's, he thought as he stared at the empty space where she had pulled in. The parking space was empty; a little dryer than those around it but getting wetter by the minute. Soon it would look like all the other empty wet spaces.

"Can I get a lift with you, Lindsey?" Roy's face was uncomfortably close to Lindsey's; too close for comfort, as was the back seat as they headed to the Terminus pub. As he lay across the laps of his team, it reminded him of Adam's college stories – "A car is just a bus without an aisle."

"All aboard the Skylark!" yelled Sam, recalling children's telly shows of his dad's era. The innuendo was all over YouTube! A childhood could be recovered by a swipe on a tablet and shared by generations. Life was no longer recorded in folk song – it was all simply recorded and stored. What would generations of cultures think? Are we not the sum total of our songs, stories, and jokes? Are we now the sum total of internet reality?

CHAPTER 67

"The forms are ready for your signature, Joan; just let me know when you can stop by."

"Thanks, Dean!" Joan hung up her mobile phone.

"Sorry, Roger; I had to take that call. And thank you for seeing me on such short notice. Nice dressing gown, by the way. Oh, and this is your *Times* too!" The newspaper, like Roger, had been hanging half in the house and half out.

"I feel like a speed-dater on *Candid Camera*!" Roger took his paper from his older, bossy sister. "To what do I owe the pleasure?"

"It's the middle of the afternoon, Roger. How is that you are still in your dressing gown?"

"Joan – I'm retired, remember? Every day is Saturday – this is how I dress on Saturdays."

"Well – you shouldn't just let yourself go, you know, Roger...."

"I didn't think I was until just now." He stepped aside to let Joan in without asking. "Widowers become excellent tea makers! Would you like some?"

"That would do nicely, thank you." She led him to his own kitchen, looking in every room to see what else a widower might know. Roger padded behind in his slippers like a celibate Hugh Hefner.

"Not bad, Roger, I must say. Gaynor would be quite pleased – I think your mantlepiece might pass the white glove test! Tea in this caddy, is it?" Roger nodded the way you do when your big sister takes charge, with your eyes rolling like a Lilliputian avalanche. She filled the kettle. Its indicator blue light cast its brilliance like an alien landing off the ceiling of the kitchen. Roger grabbed the Union Jack mugs they both preferred.

"Rule Britannia, eh?" He clinked them together and put them on the Soapstone countertop.

"No teapot, I see." Joan looked about the counter quickly like she was anticipating a sniper shot.

"It's worse than that, Joan – no tea-strainer, either!" Roger almost said with delight. She hated the modern convenience of tea bags.

"Oh, Roger – most disappointing – most disappointing!"

"Always was, wasn't I?"

"Kettle's done!"

"What, already?" Part of the joy of brewing tea was in the patient interlude of chit-chat that a kettle afforded you; even that had given way to modern convenience. *When does one have time to talk these days?* she thought. *Everyone's in such a rush to reach the end.*

"Still take it with sugar, do you, Roger?" Joan said patronizingly. Roger pulled his robe cord a little tighter over his paunch. "You're like a child, you know."

"Too old to care, Joan my dear!" He swept his hands over his head where his hair used to be, where the Brylcreem and a comb once met. "So, to what do I owe this displeasure?"

"Ha! Very funny – where do you put the used teabags?"

"In the little silver caddy – the place smells rotten if I put them in the bin for too long."

"Ah—more clutter! Well, anyway – I need to ask a favor."

"Of course you do!" Roger imagined, his eyes rolling unintentionally, picking up more snow powder.

"Still have any of your old letterhead handy?"

"A little—why?" Roger hesitated, the way you hesitate sensing the tea is still too hot to drink. That was the way his relationship had been with Joan since childhood.

"I need you to draft something for me."

He sipped his tea, scalded his lip a little. "Ouch! Of course you do!"

"The beauty of a teapot, Roger, is that your tea has time to steep and cool," she said smilingly at his wince.

By the time the caravan of cheap, fuel-efficient cars had reached the Terminus the carpark was starting to fill. Relieved they all spilled out like marbles in Kerplunk. Kids too young to enter the pub stood by the doorway in their royal blue and white hats and scarves, markers, books, pads of foolscap, soccer balls at the ready. The Romanians led the way, signing everything as they passed, like Andy Murray exiting triumphantly from Center Court. Inside, Beryl ran from glass to tap and back again, pouring ale like she had to bail out a kayak. She was both extra staff and manager on duty today.

The players silently formed three circles to begin their warm-ups; like circus seals, the three rings of players headed, juggled, and flipped the balls for stunned pub patrons. People continued to flood in out of the rain. Beryl canceled the kitchen service; she had no time to be chef today. Sam grabbed a pint from a disgruntled onlooker, and the room burst into applause as he didn't miss a step as he juggled both beer and ball. Once Sam had finished his pint, each quaff marked with a white ring of foam in the glass, the whole team signed the random articles shoved in front of them. Nicky took great delight in autographing a Victoria's Secret 36 C-cup

As the team walked the mile, the crowd at each pub grew – more and more kids stood excitedly awaiting their arrival. It was like a swelling ticker-tape parade. Traffic on Chatsworth Road started to slow to a halt with onlookers and street parkers. As they neared the town center, the crowd funneled on to the street awaiting their arrival. Patrons emptied their pints and followed the players – one by one the pubs bulged with punters whose kids had seen the Instagrams and dragged them from their settees. "It's for the children!" that they were going to the pubs, they argued.

Sam had taken on the spirit of the Brampton Mile – he enjoyed a pint in every pub – and by the time they reached The Ship Inn, he was nearly sunk. He'd been here so many times that his "usual" was on the bar when they arrived. His ball skills improved with every pint, the way "beer-goggles" improve all of our judgment. He wouldn't remember the immense crowd at Queen's Park as Lindsey led the team out on to the cricket pitch – the Pied Piper crowd of ten thousand or more—mums, dads, children of all ages and sizes, buggies and prams traipsed behind this unlikely team of misshapen misfits. Hundreds of autographs were signed, hands shaken, hugs offered and taken, well wishes, kisses, underwear and phone numbers – a thousand or more selfies Instagrammed the nation. A Girl Guide ran out from the crowd and handed Lindsey a team flag, which she raised above her head and passed down the line of her players. The fans ringed the cricket pitch like it was an Ashes series. The players checked each other's smiles in the rain – a ball passed down by their feet not touching the ground, moving like a slinky from foot to foot, player to player, and back again, phones held high for better photos and snippets of video. As the little brown-uniformed girl in her badges and sash ran back to her family she was greeted with a chorus of "Come On You Blues!" and a sea of royal blue and white scarves. This team had taken the fans of underdogs the world over to heart – the most unlikely of teams was one win away from the greatest triumph in sporting legend. Only Middlesborough stood in their way; a team fully three divisions above them with aspirations of playing in Europe against a team with aspirations of playing in Scunthorpe.

CHAPTER 68

"John Motson here sitting in for the unfortunate Arlo White, who is at home with the flu – our best for a speedy recovery, Arlo; I know you'll be at home watching this along with the rest of the country and the world. This, a David and Goliath story for the ages! Alongside me is Lee Dixon – Lee, have you ever seen anything like this atmosphere here at Wembley today?"

"No, John – this is truly remarkable – for a team that usually plays in front of a crowd of 5,000 depending on who brings their dog that day, I'll say this is truly special! I would say that the entire town of Chesterfield is shut down today as its entire population is in Wembley Stadium, and are they ever loud!"

"The fans got here early and haven't stopped singing since they entered the building – a lot of pride for their underdogs, no matter what the result today!"

"Yes, they are gonna have their hands full today with this very experienced and mature Middlesborough side. I really can't see things going Chesterfield's way today."

"Yes, it's a Herculean task – as Middlesborough sit in fourth place in the English Premier League with a couple of aspiring England internationals in their squad. But Chesterfield have surprised many along the way with their youth and mixed formations."

"I agree, John; they keep you guessing as players move from defense to forward almost seamlessly. Whether by design or chaos, you have a team that is fluid and they have a few play makers. I know the England selectors will be looking hard at the two brothers and young Robbie McDonald."

"The Romanian national coach notably is here too, Lee."

"These five, dare I say refugees, have been embraced by everyone. Their unity has bonded the team and galvanized the town of Chesterfield. So not surprising that the Romanian coach is here – and hopefully he gets to see some of the form that has impressed in the previous rounds!"

"I believe Tesco's had to be coerced into giving them the day off to actually come here today."

"Yes—we should give a big shout out to the super-store, as they literally took these fellas in off the street and instead of sending them to jail, they put them to work!"

"Yes Lee, yet another amazing story to emerge from this most unusual of Cup runs!"

"True, John. You can't make this stuff up – it only happens in real life!"

"Too right, Lee; the best stories often happen in real life. Well, for now that's all we have for you at an electrified Wembley Stadium – Lee and I will hand it back to Gary and crew in the studio."

"Thanks, John and Lee – and we'll be back to discuss the match-ups right after this commercial break, so don't go anywhere!"

"Look, lads – it's 'Arry fuckin' Gration! O'er 'ere 'Arry! O'er 'ere!"

"Harry Gration here at Wembley Stadium with a number of the Chesterfield fans – tell me, lads, what are you feeling right now?"

"We're so fuckin' 'appy to be 'ere, 'Arry! It's a dream come true – our mate Frank 'ere. We fought he were a gonna at Liverpool match! But nar fuckin' look at us, 'Arry!" The tinnies wrapped themselves around their beers and their old teammate. Frank handed Harry a Fosters – only blue cans were allowed today.

" 'Urry up, 'Arry—come on!" The tinnies pounded their beer to the Sham 69 anthem. Frank carried his beer like it was his heart being transplanted for surgery – the tinnies just wanted him to feel the part. You can't be one for all, and all for one without your sword to raise.

"I'll put your oxygen tank behind the bench, Roy. I have it hidden in my backpack; no one should notice or suspect anything."

"Ta Lindsey, I hate to be a nuisance!" The oxygen was Roy's and Lindsey's secret. Roy had picked it up before the West Ham match. Roy hadn't scored, but going into the game his breathing was becoming more shallow as the cancer continued its journey. The oxygen Dr. Doran prescribed was more placebo than useful.

"We made it, Lindsey – you made a team out of practically nothing. You really did your homework! Thank you."

"You did it, Roy—this is your team, your club, your time, your moment!"

"We have one more game. Look at this place – you can barely hear yourself think! One more thing – I don't think I'm going to be up for going in today. I think I will enjoy this one from the bench. I appreciate you listing me; it's like being back in my schoolboy days, playing these few minutes; even just standing out on the field have been some of the most exhilarating times in my life." The needle on Roy's oxygen tank was in the green zone, but the bellows in his chest signaled that one tank might be enough.

"Dada! Dada!"

"Yes, sweetie – Daddy and Uncle Nicky are on the telly." Ringos spaghetti dripped off their baby's finger as she pointed at the telly. Michelle loved the kitchen television – it brought the outside in, a glimpse of the world from within this otherwise studio confine. There was still the hint of new paint smell. "Magnolias"- -could the paint really smell of ancient magnolias?"Five-second rule!" Michelle reached down on to her beautifully finished, mahogany-stained flooring, the spaghetti looking like a life vest in a sea of molasses. She popped the spaghetti ring into her own mouth, bringing floods of tears from the baby.

Michelle took the spoon and flipped a mini-hoop on to her fashion-forward flooring, scooped it up as before and popped it reluctantly into her baby's mouth. As much as she loved it, and she did, Wayne was right—like a black car, this floor would need constant cleaning and attention. But Wayne had installed it for her anyway. This was her favorite part of the house. The dark wood showed all of family life's daily spills and nicks, but in the end, you could always bring it back to its original sheen, scars and all. Scarring is part of life; managing to not worry about it is a human art form.

"I think I see Dad, Ju – he's talking to Lindsey on the bench. Did you bring the binoculars? Wembley is amazing – God, it's so loud in here – it nearly shook my panty-liner out!"

"I can't believe we are sitting here in the Director's Box – Zo, Dad should be here, not down on the field, the bloody idiot."

"He looks so contented; do you think he's nervous?"

"Can't tell from here, even with the binoculars."

"Nicky's been a wreck with nerves all week – actually since beating Burnley in the sixth round. All the papers keep talking about was redemption for 1997, and now here they are again with Middlesborough twenty years later."

"I'll never forget that day when Dad took us to Old Trafford – we played so well to get robbed!" Julia had said it; only the residents of the losing semi-finalist remembered that day, like only the family of the fourth-place finisher cherish the result of a race brilliantly run.

"It's mad to think here we are at Wembley – I'm so nervous for them. Lindsey looks like she hasn't slept for a week either—and that lime-green headband! Probably never washed it since she got here from America!"

"That woman is a genius – you never know from week to week who is playing what position – then when Wayne was injured she really mixed everyone up. How are he and Michelle doing, by the way?"

"She's back in the house – I think we have Joan to thank for that one. Nicky says he's never seen him so relaxed. This FA Cup final hasn't worried him one bit!"

"Me, I'm gonna run out of bog-roll at this rate!" and the two of them laughed until tears ran down their legs!

"Joan, I'm so glad you made it!"

"Wouldn't miss it for the world, Brian!"

"Who's this with you?"

"This is my brother Roger – the attorney."

"Ah, the attorney! The Club's savior!"

"Well, actually, I think that honor goes to my sister," offered Roger politely.

"I believe that honor still goes to Roy," Joan reminded them both. "He started this ball rolling over a year ago and look where we are – in the Director's Box at Wembley stadium. I have to say I'd never thought in my wildest, and there have been some wild ones, that I'd ever be sitting here!"

"I have to say, Sis, I'm a little surprised too, what with the family's history! Daddy would be turning over in his grave."

"Well, hopefully he's the right way round and can see the match!" Joan quipped.

Brian was perplexed. "Family history?"

Joan looked at Roger coolly as he began to speak. "Well, Brian – our dad and his sisters grew up very poor around the turn of the century; Dad was a bright lad and worked his way up from sweeping mill floors, to mill foreman, to shop hand, eventually buying the shop—made a lot of money in the wool business by setting up multiple shops. His first love, however, as a kid, was always football. So, as a result he championed his home team of Chesterfield Football Club--"

"Really?"

Joan jumped in.

"Daddy was one of the early investors – loved the game – made his money in the wool trade and lost it all in the 'fool trade,' Mummy used to say. She made us all promise—no, swear—that we would never have anything to do with the 'stupid' game."

"It probably hurt to hear it described as the beautiful game," said Brian.

"But Dad, like Roy, was a dreamer – always thinking big. Saw life as a place to fill with big dreams, fantastic dreams, even silly dreams at times. Even when Mummy kicked him out, his eyes saw the world like the Hubble telescope sees the universe."

"For Dad, Brian, the day was always like today a glorious swathe of bathing sunshine, a cloud, he reminded us was only there to remind us of the sun's magnificence." Roger smiled as he remembered.

"'Clouds always pass' he said over and over," added Joan. "Those could be Roy's words."

"Which is why you funded the club and brought Roger in?"

"Yes. Roy wanted to restore magic to the town – like Disney – he brought this fantasy to life – he brought in people who no one expected much of except he himself. His vision was this: those players warming up below us – half the town if not all of it awash in the warmth of the underdog, tanning themselves in the possibility that the sun shines for all of us."

"It's been a remarkable journey, Joan. I wish you could have been there with us all the way."

"I have, Brian, in a way; I'm a daddy's girl after all. But you mustn't tell Roy."

"Your secret's safe with me."

"It won't be a secret for long – I want him to know it was me. I want him to know how much I love him, love his dream, love all of this, love all of him."

"Say, Nicky, any idea who that is with Brian in the Director's Box?"

"'aven't got t' faintest Roy – Brian and Joan, nice of 'er t' come. Don' recognize uvver feller. I know a bunch of celebrities up there, Gordon Ramsey, Mia Hamm and a think tha' is Louis Tomlinson!"

"Probably a boyfriend!" Roy laughed having not heard the rest. But it was hard to see her sitting with another man. At least it wasn't Dean.

"Mark Clattenburg has blown his whistle, and the FA Cup Final between Middlesborough and Chesterfield is officially underway – a repeat of the semi-final from 1997. Both teams in their traditional colors – Middlesborough in red with the familiar white sash, and Chesterfield in their royal blue."

"Well, John, it's a perfect day for football – a little shower overnight; should keep the pitch nice and slick for a quick-paced game. It's the perfect venue and occasion for you to be reporting on your last match."

"Thanks, Lee. It has been a joy to report on all these matches over the years on a game I love; I'm going to miss this, and especially miss reporting on the magic of the FA Cup."

"Yes, John, Chesterfield and Middlesborough are divisions apart, and I expect that Chesterfield will have to come out guns blazing to have a chance today."

"Agreed. It's been a fairytale run getting here, beating West Ham in the semi-final. And for Middlesborough, too, it gives them an opportunity to play in Europe having just missed out in the Premier League. Chesterfield off to a quick start as we anticipated – Robbie McDonald racing speedily around the midfield and challenging the right back here in the first few minutes."

"Yes, that was a good little burst from the winger – trying to catch their opponents before they settle down. The defender did recover to block it out for a corner."

"A bit unusual, this – Chesterfield have brought their keeper up for the corner – he's a big lad, at six-foot six."

"Yes, John, it's a move usually reserved for last-second heroics."

"Perhaps that's what they are thinking – this match is going to require something heroic from Chesterfield. They are going to have to take advantage of any and all opportunities."

"Brad Guzan is rapidly directing his players, trying to marshal them to better match-ups – hard to organize for the three Chesterfield giants. The ball is driven hard toward the penalty spot; Bladen reaches high in the air to meet it, and it's a thundering header into the roof of the net – like a cannon. Guzan left stranded, defenders went with him, but at full leap, Bladen—or Bladey, as they like to call him—rose above everyone, including his teammates, to meet it square on, and it is, incredibly, one-nil to Chesterfield! Just minutes into the game!"

"It's exactly the start Chesterfield were looking for, John – a miracle of sorts – but that's the beauty of this competition! All Chesterfield have to do is hang on for eighty-seven minutes!"

"Lee, echoes of 'Come On You Blues' are deafening here at Wembley. These fans came here believing, and so far, Chesterfield, in a most unorthodox way, have delivered."

"I can't believe it—they've scored!"

"It's actually happening!"

"Roy's gonna do it!"

"He's gonna bring the FA Cup to Chesterfield!"

The crowd in the Highfield pub was out of its mind – barely settled in their seats from pre-match beers, tables chairs, beers, beer mats, chips, bangers, a ball pit of peas were tumbling everywhere as Bladey's header hit the back of the net.

"He almost broke t' fuckin' net, he did! Come on, you Blues! Come on, you Blues!"

The chorus ran across town from living room to living room, pub to pub; Joan and Roger had even secured Proact Stadium to be open so fans could enjoy it on the big screen. The roars and cheers buoyed a whole village.

"They'll still blow it – it's Chesterfield, remember?" and Rob's words stung with reality, like removing a windbreaker on the beach.

"Infinity switch!" Lindsey yelled out to her team as the ball rolled into touch for a goal kick. "Infinity switch!" she yelled even louder – not sure that she could be heard. The goal-kick gave a temporary reprieve, as they had been on their back foot for the half hour following the goal.

Ionut heard the instructions, checked the signals, and each player rotated like they were in a volleyball match. "We will not be predictable! We will not be understood! We will have them guessing all game, if necessary!" These were the last words uttered by Lindsey as the team marched out of the dressing room. So now each player moved over one spot, excepting Bladey – he'd already made his switch. For the next fifteen minutes, Lindsey would time the next position change; the Romanians forward for a time, moving up from midfield, then back to defense. Every sixty seconds, Lindsey would yell from a crouched and leaning position to her players: "Infinity Switch! Infinity Switch!" In the eight months leading up to this the greatest stage on earth, they had trained for this movement. They had been selected for their speed and versatility – this was why their speed and quickness drills were hammered into them every day. Strength and speed. Quickness and speed can't be coached – the rest, we practice for.

At half-time Brad Guzan was out of his mind with his defenders in the locker room."Nothing! Nothing must come through! It must be rock solid—I don't care if you have to rebuild the Berlin Wall! Nothing gets by you! Alright?"

"Brad – you've seen them – there's players coming from all angles – and these kids are fast! Even the chick!"

"Nothing, you hear? Nothing comes through you! You stop them at all costs!"

The coach let his players do his talking – Guzan's passionate demands were more than the coach himself could evoke from his players.

"And as for the other end – they have a cripple in goal. Put the ball in the net—or do I need to come and do that for you too?" The American fueled his frustrated team. "This is unacceptable! This is the FA Cup! No upsets on our watch! Got it?"

"Forty-five minutes, lady and gentlemen!" Lindsey stood on the locker room bench.

"Bit of a stretch on both accounts!" Sam threw in the humor as he watched the coach jump up on to a bench that almost brought her eye to eye with her goalkeeper.

"It was a great call, coach!" said Bladey.

"Just as we practiced – a sibling wall in front and you following in their wake. We hit them like the business end of a jackhammer. I want to keep up the infinity rotation – anyone not able to handle it?" Silence, as always, whenever Lindsey spoke. She twisted the now legendary green headband around her wrist; her wrist pulsed like a netted snapper. You always wondered if she felt the pain and whether she had garroted anyone with it back in the States.

"Okay, we stay with 'Infinity' – but we need to rotate differently. Every new change will mean that we slide over that many times – look for my signals. Roy, you got anything to add?"

"Just this." The pause lasted a while, like sitting by the door hoping for a check in the mail. "I would stand on the bench, but I'm feeling a little dizzy without it." A few chuckles patted around the room. "I would just like to say – thank you for making a dream come true – this room, this temple of legends, is the happiest place in the world for me." He had more to say; he wanted to hug and thank each one of them, but he was breathless. The heat, the disease were becoming too much for him.

Wayne saw him flagging. He reached under Roy's armpit and lifted him up with his good arm. "Let's do this – let's finish the dream! For Roy!" Nicky grabbed under Roy's other arm and led the team out – all chanting "For Roy! For Roy!"

CHAPTER 69

"Thanks, Gary, for that breakdown at half-time – indeed a fascinating time here at Wembley as we go back to the highly unlikely event of Chesterfield being ahead of their Premier League rivals."

"It certainly is, Motty! I think the rapid transition and alternating player patterns has this 'Borough' team a little unsettled."

"So right, Lee, but they've not been without their chances too and Middlesborough could so easily be ahead by a couple of scores! Mark Klattenburg has his whistle ready to go – he checks his linesmen – they are all ready, and here we go – Middlesborough with forty-five minutes left to make their mark on FA Cup history."

"Motty – look, the Chesterfield coach is up and yelling already. She had her index fingers pointing at Marius – it would appear that he is the reason for her anger. Neither teams have used any substitutions to this point, and Marius has switched wings; he's now in Coach's earshot."

"Lauren, I told you, you have to run your orders through Vasily. I know! I know! I'm not sure Marius is listening to Vasily or me. He's supposed to have switched earlier!"

"Well here's the ball – you can give it to him." Roy flipped her the ball and rather than merely giving Marius the ball for a quick throw in she dropped it as he was about to take it from her. Lindsey grabbed the back of Marius' head with both hands and kissed him passionately. He got the message and Lindsey got the yellow card.

"Well, Lee, I've done thousands of matches but that's the first one I've seen a yellow card given to a coach for kissing a player!"

"Yes, Motty – I believe the yellow is for time-wasting, but I'd beg to differ as they seemed to waste no time at all in getting to the point. The crowd loved it too – the big screen is repeatedly playing the offense!"

"Some interesting moves this Chesterfield team have been working on in practice, Lee!"

"Middlesborough as well as the rest of us have been a little caught off guard. The Chesterfield players once again switched positions during the romantic interlude. Guzan is yelling and pointing like he is out of his mind."

"Pinch me, Ju – I just don't believe it. We are still leading with only fifteen minutes left."

"I know, Zo, I'm looking at the massive clock more than the field – it's moving slower than a French lesson!"

"Sorry? What, Ju? Can't hear a thing in here!" Their words were garbled but their smiles were not as they once again stood in unison for the wave that was rapidly moving around the stadium.

"Good to stand and feel the breeze!" said Ju.

"Yes, my allergies are bad too!" said Zoe. Both nodded, having no idea what the other was saying – fourteen minutes to go – no hands to watch, just digital numbers spinning like waiting in line at the deli counter; eventually your number comes up.

"End to end stuff, Lee – players and fans are gonna be exhausted watching this one. The underdogs, Chesterfield, hanging on to the ledge of their victory for the moment, but Middlesborough continue to press hard – they have switched to a 4-3-3 formation. Both teams have used a couple of subs in this heat; it seems like a wise move – fresh legs will clearly help both sides."

"Hey, Motty, there's a bit of a commotion over by the Chesterfield bench – it would appear a couple of the St. Johns Ambulance crew are surrounding Chesterfield's third sub and chairman Roy Griffiths."

"Yes, Lee, I believe you're right – I didn't notice it right away. With the speed of this match and the cacophonous wave of the crowd it's like a festival here!"

"Looks like he might be stretchered off from the bench – the play goes on and The Boro' are pushing everyone forward – even Guzan is approaching the halfway line!"

"We certainly hope the chairman is okay—could be just the heat – the players are in direct line of the sun."

"We understand that the chairman—who usually would be in the Director's

Box, not the bench—has had some health-related problems throughout the year."

"He's been quite the good luck charm for them, Lee – but for now, that leaves Chesterfield without any substitutions available."

"Sir, sir – try to stay with me if you can – we have some questions for you...."

"I'm fine, I'm fine – just got a little overheated, that's all...." Roy fell out of consciousness.

The paramedics began to talk more loudly while wrapping a blood pressure collar on his arm and applying ice packs to his forehead. "Pulse is weak, his oxygen level is low; I'll bag him for oxygen." The room had all the modern equipment – even a defibrillator hung off the wall.

Julia, Zoe, and Joan had seen the commotion below them and made their way quickly down to the makeshift ER.

"Dad! Dad! Wake up! Wake up!" Julia and Zoe were panic yelling as soon as they saw Roy out on the gurney.

"Ladies, step back – we're going to attach an IV – he might be dehydrated; it's a long while to be sitting out in this heat. Very little air down on the field."

The three ladies didn't back off much – too anxious to not be unreasonable.

"He has lung cancer!" Julia yelled out.

Still Roy kept on sleeping. The IV was inserted and the little bag began its slow drip. Both of the girls had seen this act before with chemo.

"Gentlemen! Gentlemen! You are needed back outside, and bring the stretcher." It was the fourth official – he had left his post at the halfway line to grab the paramedics.

"You can't leave Dad like this! Not right now!" Ju's anxiety was descending into a breakdown.

"I'm afraid we need them on the pitch right now – there was a terrible collision – the young lady's leg is hurt very badly." The fourth official steered the paramedics out to the field, leaving Roy alone with his ladies. As the paramedics left, one called back:

"We'll be back—he's stable now. Not much more we can do until the fluids kick in."

It was a dismal scene of triage, Julia and Zoe holding a hand each. Joan stroked Roy's matted hair; she remembered how rich and brown it used to be.

"We should talk to him," offered Zoe. "It works, apparently, with coma victims. He can probably hear us."

"I thought you'd be at Wembley, Ad? Not out here in the car park!"

"Well, this is where it all started, right? I thought you'd be there too, Ali!"

"I gave Uncle Roger my seat. Thought it might be nice for him to sit with Mum. What about you? Isn't this, the FA Cup, everything you ever wanted?"

"Yes, but someone had to man the car park, didn't they?"

"You're an idiot—you know that, right?"

"Thanks, Ali. Every village has got one—that's the rumor, at least. You know, I just didn't feel this village could manage without me on this all-important day!"

"It should be a great match – we have a chance, don't you think?"

"They really do – I don't know a team that has trained harder! The Matlock hill sprints, for one, would undo any athlete!" Cars continued to stream by.

"Parking is free today – you can come right in! Stadium is open!" Alistair declared.

"Closer to game time we'll head into the stadium – watch it on the big screen with the fans on the Kop, like the good old days?"

"I just felt like here at Proact is where I belonged – I dunno – I felt one of the family should be here. I flew Billy and Emma over. He's on the sideline; she has my ticket but Billy wanted to be the water boy, you know, by all the action."

"Nice – he'll love it. And I think you're right, mate – when all this is over fans'll remember you were here manning the gates, welcoming them all – we don't want you getting above your station, now do we?"

Fans in full regalia of royal blue-and-white scarves, hats, rosettes, badges, replica shirts strode by them brimming with excitement and then on into the Chesterfield Football Club campus."COME ON - YOU BLUES! COME ON- YOU BLUES!"

It was a chant you could hear all the way from the back of Tesco's, the chant that probably brought some Romanian stragglers to their front door. A chant that boys and girls alike screamed with their parents as they entered the hallowed ground hand-in-hand, so the parents didn't get lost in the moment.

"Well, Lee, it's a disaster for Chesterfield – we can only hope that the young lady is okay, but you hate to see anyone stretchered off."

"Yes, John, it was a horrible challenge, and the defender's lucky to get away with a yellow on that one. On the replay you can clearly see the studs are up; not sure how the assistant referee missed it, but the game is faster these days and Laurel is one of the fastest players out there."

"It seems they've stabilized the leg. The crowd is on its feet and applauding her exit – hopefully it's not as serious as it looks – but for now Chesterfield are down to ten men, as their substitute is also in the locker room – can Chesterfield hang on for these last five minutes?"

"Yes, Motty, that's the question – you know Borough are gonna pile everyone forward."

"Yes, Lee – it should be a thrilling finish to an already captivating Final."

"Roy, my love." Joan stroked Roy's face with the back of her freshly manicured hand; his stubble scratched the back of her hand. Joan massaged his temples as Julia and Zoe looked on in fear and respect. Respect for Joan's kindness. Years had passed since —no, actually, they had never seen a stranger love their father. Roy stirred to her touch and perfume. His eyes started to clear – the IV coursed through the same veins as the chemo a few months ago. The more fluid entered his bloodstream, the clearer he could see Joan's gentle, loving smile. She was the last person he expected to see but was the first one he wanted to see.

"How are you feeling, my love?" Her whisper barely made it to his ear. He raised his IV hand and thumb.

Tears slid down the faces of everyone in the room.

"Where am I?"

"Roy, you're in the trainer's room at Wembley,"

"What happened? One minute I was watching the Romanians school the Borough defenders, and now I'm here."

"You passed out, Roy."

"Probably the heat, Dad," said Zoe as she and Julia moved to the opposite side as Joan.

"I remember it was a hot one. Oh my God, did we win?"

At that moment, four paramedics carrying a stretcher breezed into the room.

"Step aside everyone, quickly now! Quickly!" The same rescue team that had brought Roy here was now headed around the cluster of family and Roy.

"Breathe in – let us by!"

Joan shuffled in closer to Roy – she could see his eyes glistening again.

"Shit, it's Laurel!"

"Dad, her leg is in a soft cast up to her hip."

"We sedated the young lady out on the pitch—coming through!" the paramedics shouted again. They whisked through the door to an awaiting ambulance.

"The score, the score? Are we still winning?"

"Yep still 1-0 just under five minutes to go," yelled the paramedic as the door hit his backside.

"What about Dad? You can't just leave him here?"

"He'll be fine for now – she has a compound fracture, and we need to get her to a hospital immediately!"

"Time running out for The Borough – they have this free kick from about twenty-five yards out, I'd say—wouldn't you, Lee?"

"Yes, this has to be Borough's last real chance. Since blowing the whistle the half has been one of the most exciting in all of football! The fans have paid for seats, but no one has sat in them for the last forty-four minutes!"

"So, we have Brad Guzan joining his teammates around the ball – the three of them working out who is going to take this. Chesterfield trying desperately to line up the wall and figure out the remaining match-ups."

"Guzan did play a lot in the outfield for his Providence High School, so I'm not sure if he's still got the foot skills!"

"My word, he has! Brad Guzan has tied the game with an absolute rocket of a shot from outside the box. He hit it so swiftly and with such venom that Bladen couldn't react to it!"

"I think the defenders were looking for a chip, but no matter with time expiring on the pitch – the Borough have tied the game and we are headed to extra time! Goals from both goalkeepers! Whatever next?"

"What was that roar?" asked Roy.

"I'll run out," said Zoe. Her speed was halted by the big screen that read Chesterfield one, the Borough one! She fell to her knees – it wasn't supposed to happen this way. They were down to ten men – with Guzan playing sweeper as well as goal, they had the dominance to fill the space and tempo. Zoe hadn't the strength to tell her father. But he knew. Her slow return from her absence confirmed it. It was one, one.

CHAPTER 70

"Well ten-men Chesterfield have survived the onslaught of pressure throughout extra time, Lee!"

"Yes, Motty – we are headed to penalties—the crowd is on its feet applauding both teams. You'd have to be here to believe it – it's electric. Not that I would know, but it's like an earthquake in this stadium!"

"Yes, both sets of fans – calling out to their teams in verbal ping-pong – 'Come on you Blues' batted back with 'Come on you Reds!' Mark Klattenburg has visited with both teams – he's got the list of players – the first five to kick. Of course, should we go beyond that then the next five would have to kick and so on. Mark Klattenburg has flipped his coin. Middlesborough have won the toss and elected to kick first."

"I think that's wise, John, don't you? So much pressure in a situation like this!"

"I agree, Lee – I don't know how any player can get up to the mark after an enthralling two hours of play! I see a lot of Gatorade being drunk. The next five are being stretched out to try to keep legs fresh. Of course, Chesterfield are still missing their sub and chairman, who left the bench a long time ago now."

"Well for the players' sakes, I hope it doesn't go that long! As an independent observer – I want this match to last! What a day, John! What a day!"

"Borough strike first – Bladen had no chance with that low drive to the bottom left corner. He guessed wrong, but he wasn't stopping that, even if he guessed right!"

"He tried to read the hips of the shooter – maybe overthought it, and—well, it's one-nil Borough."

"I feel fine, I feel fine – I could murder a cuppa!" Roy was still hooked to the IV and there was no one qualified to remove it. The ambulance was supposed to come back, but on FA Cup Final day in London you can't move around the stadium even with sirens and lights!

"You look better, Roy – you should try to sit. There's color returning to your face again," said Joan lovingly, relieved at his progress. He looked so childlike lying there in his royal-blue jersey, white shorts and socks, with his shin guards still in place and his boots gleaming without a trace of mud on them.

"It's two nil, John – another fine strike by Borough. The Romanian five had been selected, but Marius' shot flew over the bar and handed Middlesborough the advantage, which they have just capitalized on. What a pressure cooker, John!"

"Roy, how are you doing?" Lindsey had left the sideline to come see him.

"I'm fine, Lindsey. I'll be fine." He said more slowly, "You need to get back to your team!"

"You are my team, Roy. I can't coach them anymore; we simulated penalties every day in practice, but it's like a cauldron in there! Each one of them had to do it now – do it for whatever reason they started the journey. For whatever 'why' they brought to this team – that has to be what sustains them. Besides, Vasily wanted you to have this." She handed him a Marlboro and a lighter with a scene of Bucharest at night. The whole room sucked in – oxygen was still flowing through his mask.

"We should turn this off first," offered Joan with a smile. "Let me help you, Roy. One more won't hurt." She lit it and started it herself; a trace of her crimson lipstick met his lips. The nicotine met the IV, and all was good in the world.

"Bladen and Chesterfield need a stop here Lee if they are to stop Middlesborough taking home the trophy."

"I can't take too much more – since that one miss, both teams have been flawless, giving the goal-keepers no chance."

"A stutter-step and the shot is off! And off target!"

"I think Bladen got a fingertip to it, John! Let's check the replay!"

"He did, and the royal blue end of Wembley has gone completely berserk! That was a miraculous effort from the veteran, needing all six-foot six of him to fingertip that onto the post!"

"The Borough players were jumping up, thinking it had gone in—but no, and now they lie deflated in the center circle."

"They are going to have to make way for a new five."

"I see one of the players for Chesterfield still being stretched out by the trainer. It would be Wayne, who's missed an awful lot of training in the last few weeks following the shotgun incident."

"The trainer is shaking his head, John – he's telling the referee that he will not be able to continue."

"Which means if he's a scratch, then they will have put the chairman on the list of five – we haven't seen him since he left the pitch over an hour ago."

"Well, for the chairman's sake, let's hope it doesn't come to that."

"I have to go, Roy—they're calling for a new list of five players," said Lindsey.

"We must be tied still!" added Zoe.

"You should go watch the end of it. I'm feeling a little better now—go, go and see Town win!"

"Are you shoower?"

"Yes!" At Dad's insistence, Julia and Zoe left. He needed to be alone with Joan.

"I think I have something in my eye, Joan – could you help me?" As she leaned in, he extinguished the cigarette in his hand. "See it?" As she shook her head he reached up, gently clasped it in his hands, and with the care of a butterfly, pressed his lips to hers. Joan remained, intoxicated by a little of the nicotine and a flood of love.

"Eh, you can't do that in here!" screamed the East London accent through the cheers of the crowd above.

"We're just kissing!" Joan hissed.

"No, missus, the bloody cigarette – you can't smoke in 'ere!" The paramed yelled at them like squatters. "Seriously – some people – no bloody respect! Now if you two don't mind, I'll unplug this IV and you can soon be on your way."

"Right, Officer." Joan smiled and backed away, allowing him to tend to Roy.

"You feeling better, mate? You had a funny turn there – stay out of the sun – get some water in you. Keep hydrated! I'd keep that oxygen bottle handy for the time being as well!"

"Grandad! Grandad! Come quick!"

"What is it, Billy?"

"They need you – on the pitch – right now!" Billy was in a state of near panic then shock as he saw the oxygen bottle – the tubes being inserted into his grandad's nostrils, the surgical tape on the top of his hand, and the lack of rose in his English cheeks.

"You can do this, Roy – this is not a dream any longer." Joan kissed him firmly.

"Well, Lee, the pressure has certainly got to the players, hasn't it?"

"Yes, Motty; they've been clearly overwhelmed by the emotion of the moment, but it has to be said too that Guzan and Bladen have made heroic efforts to keep their teams in with a shout!"

"We are deadlocked at four goals apiece. Chesterfield have one card to play and await their last player; he's not been seen for a while – the crowd on both sides is absolutely paralyzed by the immensity of the moment."

"Wembley wasn't this quiet when they opened the gates this morning!"

"Come on Dad! Come on Dad!" was all I could whisper to myself as I stood in the Kop at Proact Stadium. "Ali – do you think he's alright?"

"Ad, if my mother has anything to say about it, he'll be on that pitch or 'woe betide him' until she gets her hands on him!" Ali's laughter and subsequent shoulder thump were all I needed. Proact Stadium, the whole village of Chesterfield, was quiet like the day before the Romans founded it kind of quiet; just a plateaued hill of meadows above a river. I stared hard at the big screen with the rest of the faithful.

"Come on, Grandad – you can do this!"

"I'm not so sure, Billy!" He took one deep look into his eyes.

"Bags of swank, Grandad – bags of swank!" Billy checked him into the line-up.

"I see activity, John – it looks like – yes, it's the chairman himself."

"I believe you're right, Lee, and with him – it looks like, well, it must be his grandson."

"The lad is helping him carry something."

"The crowd is just seeing them on the Jumbotron – and the royal blue and white are in full voice again as Chairman Roy Griffiths makes his way to the center circle – checks in with Mark Klattenburg."

"He's moving very slowly, John – he's handing what looks to be an oxygen bottle to the lad – can you hear that, John? The Borough fans are cheering again - but I have to say I think they are cheering for the Chesterfield owner."

"Brad Guzan jumps up and down to ready himself – he's had a fantastic afternoon up to now, really shown why the United States team has confidence in him."

"As the chairman walks to the penalty spot, I wouldn't want to be either one of them; this could be the chairman's first kick, and his only kick of the match!"

"And what a match! Mark Klattenburg sets the ball on the spot, takes his position at the side of the six-yard box, he nods to Guzan, then to Mr. Griffiths. I just dropped a pin, and everyone heard it!" No one at home could hear Motty for the quiet.

"Motty, no one in the chairman's guest seats are even watching – they have their hands over their eyes. Coach Lindsey has hands on hips, twisting her famous lime-green headband – this was her call all along. I don't think that when she put him on in the Halifax match seven games ago, she thought for one minute it would come down to this!"

"So here we go, ladies and gentlemen - Guzan has settled, standing in his bright orange uniform arms wide, paws of a bear, a giant of a man in that goal. The chairman Roy Griffiths hasn't played a minute; this will be his only kick of the game. He has a single shot to take for his team and make the dream a reality, the greatest underdog story in FA Cup history – I think I can even hear him breathing, it's so quiet in the stadium. Mark Klattenburg has blown the whistle; Griffiths is on his run up."

Roy looked down at the Mickey Mouse ball below him with its fluorescent yellow, orange and green "go faster" striping. He rested his hands on his hips. Guzan looked like a brown bear protecting a Wendy House full of cubs; there was nowhere for the ball to go. He could feel the deafeningly quiet stadium half willing him on; the moist turf underfoot gave his barely used cleats a mirror-like sheen. If he looked closely enough, he would see an old and very sick man in their reflection. His odometer was near its end, with no more click to start over. He hadn't rehearsed this scene since Cromford Meadows, since Mick and Trevor's satchels were the goal posts. His honorary and cursory appearances had been just that, with no real substance or design. Like much of our lives, we react to what is around us, plan for the next minute scenario and move on, living in a world of vignettes and episodes with no central theme.

Except here, Roy had made this day his goal; the plan was near its end. The Club had stayed afloat long enough; he wasn't sure how Brian got the gates open again? This bobsled run of eighteen months had thrown him into his last curve, filled with enough chemo, painkillers, and pure oxygen to float a balloon and poison a river. The bobsledder has fractions of seconds to choose the final line, to find the perfect form, to create the fastest course; this was how the goal line appeared to Roy as he began the run up.

Life had begun as a hundred-yard race; it had been extended slightly to the hundred-meter race, but in either case, the finishing tape approached his chest at top speed, unable to brake in time, no halt in momentum, careening through.

Life is a dress rehearsal. You never live the polished show, it's always a bit raw. For all the world looking down on him now through shaded eyes, TV screens, and binoculars, Roy was alone with himself. Family and friends, Brian and Joan, this new family of players, the stage crew of kilts, plimsolls, sensible shoes, all afraid to exhale. His hand shook where the IV had been removed and the cigarette expunged. Roy was strangely conscious of the weight of his legs, which had been collecting fluid for the last few days. It was maybe only a few strides to the ball and then twelve paces to the goal line. How it all felt so close, he thought; and he was in control from within a body that was not. A body whose momentum ebbed out. Three or four good strides and it would be over, the dream would be over; one way or another it would be time to take the curtain call. Would it be the end of a tragedy or a comedy?

Roy closed his eyes. The searing sun lit up his eyelids with an orange aura; the ghosts of his Matlock childhood looked on. "You'll never amount to anything, Roy" was all the encouragement he needed.

The goal doesn't move, the ball doesn't move, gravity is a constant. Roy put his swollen legs into motion.

CHAPTER 71

"You can't make this stuff up, Ad – no one would believe you!"

"Like I said, Ali, the best stories happen in real life! Come on, Dad – bags of swank!"

"What?"

"It's an RAF saying—means do it with lots of confidence!"

"And half the stadium has erupted here at Wembley!"

"Guzan guessed right, John!"

"Yes, but it wasn't enough; the chairman, a man who barely made it onto the field, has drilled a low right-footer beyond the grasp of Guzan – it is Chesterfield's dream come true! There's a royal blue and white confetti of scarves, hats – it's all being thrown toward the field—the whole Chesterfield bench has stormed the pitch. Roy is on his knees, being helped up by the gracious Guzan. What an incredible scene here at Wembley Stadium—the most miraculous of journeys has come to an end. As the crowd chants their chairman's name all around the stadium, he is helped to the shoulders of his goal-keeper and Nicky Hatt – he looks like he's played a whole game in that one shot. This is why this is the beautiful game, this is why this is the greatest tournament in the world – and for me as my last match – one more time, ladies and gentlemen, as I leave you, I want to say thank you for all my years – what a way to end it, and now I leave you to enjoy the greatest underdog story and your newly crowned FA Cup winners, Chesterfield Football Club. Good night!"

EPILOGUE

"So, what now, Ad? You've finished your book?" Ju asked.

"Well, I need to edit it first; then I'm giving it to our Emma and my friend Jill to edit. I figured a University of Chicago English grad and a brilliant mind from Northwestern University could give me some good pointers!"

"Then what? Are you gonna publish?"

"Yes, that's the goal – sell a million or three copies – make the movie and buy Chesterfield Football Club."

"Then what, Ad?"

"Why – win the FA Cup, of course!"

CPSIA information can be obtained
at www.ICGtesting.com
Printed in the USA
BVHW031537161122
651143BV00007B/89/J

9 781977 233639